the heart of
ABSHIRE
HOUSE

TAI STITH

OWL ROOM
press

DEDICATION

For Michelle. Your insight and edits to this book and its characters truly
made it the best story it could be. Thank you.

ACKNOWLEDGMENTS

A huge, resounding THANK YOU to my editors, Mandy Rossback, Mindy Bond, Derek Stith, and Kat Wylie. You all spent so much time laboring over every small detail in the book and I truly appreciate your feedback. I am utterly in awe of your attention to detail! To Michelle Patterson, my content editor, thank you for the hours you spent reading and re-reading the various versions of the manuscript. Your honest feedback early on truly challenged me to write a stronger story. You took time to discuss the characters in ways I'd never imagined them. I loved every minute of our coffee meetings!

Much of the inspiration for the mystery in this book came from letters written by my father-in-law Gary Wallace's grandmother. They were a heartbreaking peek into life in the turn-of-the-century living in the Willamette Valley.

Thank you to Mara Pileggi and Keith Lohse at the Albany Regional Museum; your answers to my many questions helped add accuracy to the story. Also, I have a deep gratitude to the volunteers and staff at the museum who make local history accessible and interesting to anyone wishing to know about Albany's fascinating past.

Thank you to Kelly Davis for choosing the name for Ralph's Diner, and thanks to Steve Anderson for creating the name for Cascade Grove.

My thanks to John R. Bruning for answering my many questions about writing and the writing process, and for your kind encouragement about my first book. Your willingness to help is so appreciated!

Lastly, thanks again to Derek; for supporting my writing habit and also for your help in researching infectious diseases.

chapter one

Ari Cartwright rubbed her eyes as sunlight streamed into her room. She wasn't ready to get up, but a singular thought caused her to open her eyes.

I almost kissed him last night.

In a half-awake daze she recalled the night before: being high among the frothy moonlit cherry blossoms, standing on a tree branch, with Dane's arm around her. Unexpectedly, she'd reached up and almost kissed him. She started getting butterflies in her stomach as she replayed it in her head. Ari certainly hadn't planned to kiss him that night. Although she'd daydreamed about it plenty, she had never actually intended to act on it. Soon their parents could be heard calling for them through the night: dessert was ready, and they'd jogged out of the cherry orchard, past the silent earthen pool, and through the darkened oak grove back to the backyard potluck their families were having together.

Just as unexpectedly, in the warm glow of the garden lights, Dane had leaned over and whispered to her: *you're fearless and brave and I love you for that.*

His words had sent electricity and warmth through her body; she could barely believe what he had confessed. Yet the look in his eyes showed that he had meant every word.

She loved his smile, his honesty, and how trustworthy he was. He was easily one of her best friends and the person she enjoyed spending time with the most. What he had said to her seemed to suggest that he cared for her as well. Ari smiled at the thought…but now just thinking of him tied her up in nervous knots.

Ari sat up in bed. She thought she heard her seven-year old little sister Lily giggling outside her bedroom door. It wasn't unusual for Lily to jump in bed with her in the wee hours of the morning, either to snuggle or to tickle Ari. But this morning, she thought other voices were with Lily's. To her surprise, there was a quiet knock on the door before her entire family peeked into her room.

chapter two

"Happy birthday, Aribelle!" Lily was carefully holding a single cupcake, and Ari's mom and dad were carrying a small but beautifully wrapped box.

Ari smiled in total surprise. It had completely escaped her that today was her sixteenth birthday.

"Open it! Open it!" On Ari's lap, Lily placed the cupcake and a box. Ari unwrapped the box to find some nail polish, sugar scrub, and lotions.

"Lily, you're so sweet! You know just what I like," she said, squeezing her little sister hard enough to make Lily squeal. The younger Cartwright giggled and pulled on her mom's hand.

"Now *you* guys! Give her the box!"

Ari's mom handed the golden-glittered box to Ari, and she carefully untied the ribbon and opened the box. Inside was a gift card to the only spa in Rivers.

"We thought you might like to take Riley to have a spa day, you know, have some girl time," her mom said, smiling. "My first baby girl is growing up," she added quietly.

Ari blushed. "Thank you, guys—this is awesome! I'll give Riley a call and see if she can go."

"Oh, and Aribelle, we need to schedule some driving lessons," her dad reminded her. "We probably should've started that a year ago, but…"

Technically, Ari could've gotten her permit a year ago, but it was almost exactly a year prior that her family had learned they would be moving. Her dad's change in employment had uprooted them all from San Francisco, the home they had known and loved for Ari's entire life, and had brought them here: to a small rural town hundreds of miles away, and so completely opposite of everything she had ever known.

Against all odds, this place—her home, the town of Rivers, and Hadley Hill, with its history and beauty—had grown on Ari. And it was perhaps because of Dane that she had been able to make the transition in the first place.

Ari thanked her family again and reached for her phone. She had more than just a spa day to tell Riley about.

*   *   *

Ari and Riley walked their bikes along the sidewalk. The early May afternoon was sunny but had no real heat in it. Signs of spring's arrival were evident everywhere: tulip trees planted in downtown Rivers were bursting open, bright green grass was growing thin and tall, and there was a change in the air.

"Alright, hon, what's going on?" Riley pushed her glasses back up onto her nose and stared her friend down. "You said on the phone you had something crazy to tell me. Well…spill it!" Riley smiled her fantastic grin.

Ari pulled her bike over to the edge of the sidewalk and stopped. "I almost kissed him in the cherry orchard last night!" she whispered.

"Dane?" Riley whispered back. "You *almost* kissed him?"

Ari nodded.

"But what happened? Why didn't you?"

"Dad started calling for us because dessert was ready. We went back to my backyard and Dane got up and thanked my parents—and me—for helping him change his situation. Then—" Ari lowered her voice— "once the parents were having dessert and chatting with each other, he leaned over and told me that the loved me for being fearless and brave." She paused and looked at Riley.

Riley smiled. "Whoa, Ari. That's just about the best compliment I've ever heard. He's serious about how much he cares for you," she grinned madly.

"I think he was being sincere, Riley. I think he might really, actually like me as much as I like him," Ari concluded. Riley shook her head in amazement.

"Well, of course he does. You guys are attached at the hip—like best friends. I don't know him that well, but I've never seen him spend as much time with anyone as he does with you!"

Riley pushed her beach cruiser next to Ari's, and continued. "You guys have had some incredible adventures together in the last ten months. You're closer than most best friends or couples I know, but in a different way. You guys work together really well."

They'd reached the spa and parked their bikes. After checking in, they were guided to the pedicure chairs. Ari leaned back in hers and closed her eyes.

"We *do* work together well," Ari agreed. "When we had a problem to solve, or history to figure out, we got it done." She opened her eyes and turned to Riley. "I just wish I knew for sure if he likes me as much as I like him."

*   *   *

The makeover during their spa day had been Ari's favorite part. She wasn't confident in her own abilities with makeup, at least, not compared with Riley's level of skill, so any help she could get was appreciated. The stylist who had done Ari's makeup had guessed correctly that Ari was an unfussy, active girl who liked a natural look. Ari took the hand mirror and liked what she saw: her barely-there freckles were still visible, but her brown eyes had been emphasized with a hint of black eyeliner, her brows had been cleaned up, and a natural lip stain had been applied. Her long, straight brown hair had grown past her shoulders since her last haircut at the beginning of the school year, and she'd had it trimmed up, with long straight bangs added in.

"Happy birthday, by the way," Riley leaned over, looking into the mirror with Ari. "You look fantastic. Not that you don't all the time," she smiled, "but you look carefree today. This past ten months has had some

rough spots for you, and for once, you don't have anything to worry about," Riley concluded. Ari had to agree: she had no worries at the moment, and it felt fantastic.

chapter three

The afternoon was waning, and low golden sunlight was illuminating the newly-sprouted grass in the back pasture behind Ari's house. Ari had bundled herself in a scarf and a sweatshirt, and she carried a book she'd been trying to read since spring break had started. Since it was her birthday, Ari had decided to ignore the pile of homework she had at home and slip away to the underground circle to get some reading—and thinking—accomplished.

She paused at the solid stone pillars that signaled the end of the Cartwright's pasture and the beginning of their oak grove that—as she and Dane had found out—held many secrets. She ran her fingers along the bee plaque that was embedded in the stone pillar. It had a beautiful green patina with highlights of polished brass that reflected the dim sunlight.

Ari continued on to the brass circle that served as a hatch to the underground room. It was here, almost a year ago, that she'd met Dane: the boy with the haunting eyes, who had run away at the mere sight of her. The secret subterranean room had been his salvation; his hiding spot away from his abusive aunt Rhoda. Now that Rhoda was a mere memory, Ari and Dane used the underground room mostly as a place to do homework. Sometimes Ari would go there alone to read. Other times, she'd find Dane there, sitting on a large beanbag chair, his eyes closed as he listened to music in his headphones. But they always kept the hatch locked so their respective younger sisters, Lily and Molly, wouldn't be able to get in.

Ari and Dane had agreed to hang the only key on a branch, just high enough out of sight and reach that someone wouldn't be able to see it unless they knew exactly where to look. After unlocking and lifting the hatch, she felt for the recessed steps in the wall and descended carefully into the darkness. She turned on her phone screen, which had just enough light that she could locate the matches they kept in the room. Slowly she lit each candle and placed them in the evenly-spaced alcoves along the wall.

Warm light glinted off the glass tiles that lined the walls, especially the ones with gold flecks embedded in them. Ari smiled as she settled into one of the large beanbag chairs and started reading the book she'd brought with her.

Suddenly, Ari's phone vibrated, causing her to jump. She pulled the phone from her sweatshirt pocket. A text message from Riley had popped up. Ari read aloud to herself: *"Jace and a few other friends will be exploring the old Abshire homestead tomorrow at 4 p.m. You and Dane want to go?"*

Ari smiled, not minding having an excuse to see Dane. She put her phone back in her pocket and walked around the small underground room, blowing out each candle. She emerged from the hatch and headed up the path toward Dane's house. A mist was forming, floating eerily above the ground.

Ari came out of the grove and Dane's house came into view. Warm lights glowed from the windows, and she could hear music coming from somewhere inside the house.

Ari knocked and Dane's little sister Molly appeared at the front door. The scent of something warm and delicious hit Ari.

"Aribelle!" Molly exclaimed. "Are you here for dinner?" Seven-year old Molly always got excited when Ari was around. She would *only* call her Aribelle, 'because it sounds like a princess name,' Molly had once told her. Ari grinned. "Aw, not tonight. I'm just here to ask your brother a question. Is he around?"

Molly pointed up the stairs. "Yup. In his room."

Ari climbed the steep stairs. The door to Dane's room was slightly ajar. From inside, Ari could hear Ben E. King's soulful voice singing *Stand By Me*...and Dane's voice, singing along. His voice was pitch-perfect, and she couldn't believe *that* sound was coming from Dane. And yet, it was unmistakably him—just in a way she'd never heard before.

She paused outside the door and slowly pushed it open just a tiny

7

bit. Ari could just see Dane's profile as he sat at his desk.

Dane's eyes were closed and she could see that he was pouring every ounce of himself into the song. She watched his mouth, with his perfectly straight teeth and bottom lip that was just slightly fuller than his top lip.

Dane harmonized with the chorus. Goosebumps covered Ari's arms. She raised her hand to knock on the door, but she simply couldn't bring herself to do it. She smiled, closed her eyes, and leaned her head against the doorjamb. Listening to his soulful voice was so captivating that she waited until the song was completely over to knock.

"Come in," he called out.

Ari entered his room. Dane looked over and seemed surprised that Ari was standing in his room. From the look on his face, Ari guessed he'd thought he had been expecting his mom.

"Hey! What are you doing here? And, you look really nice...special occasion?"

Ari had forgotten about the makeover that had happened earlier in the day. "Ah, right," she said, blushing. "Riley and I went to the spa for my birthday."

"It's your birthday today?" Dane looked surprised. "Happy birthday, Ari."

"Thanks. But that's not what I'm here about." She smiled and pulled out her phone. "I just got a text from Riley saying that she and a couple of friends are planning to go explore the Abshire homestead tomorrow. We're invited too. So...where is this place?

Dane leaned back in his desk chair. "It's actually the closest house to our hill." He motioned to his window. "Come on out to the roof with me."

Ari hesitated. Dane saw her pause. "Don't worry, I won't let you fall."

Dane threw up the window sash and stepped out into the night. The sun had set and a blush-colored glow silhouetted a distant ridgeline. Ari carefully stepped over the windowsill and took Dane's arm. She kept herself from looking down, but even so, her heartbeat increased an uncomfortable measure. Dane turned, and keeping one arm around Ari, pointed to the southwest.

"Down there, can you see a roofline, just above the treetops?"

Ari squinted, looking down the hill. Sure enough, a rooftop could be seen above the dense foliage.

"Oh, hey, I do see it," Ari answered.

"If you go to the base of our hill and turn right, the driveway to the Abshire house is the first one you come to. I've been past it a million times, but I've never actually been inside. It's been abandoned for quite some time. I think it would be cool to finally get to check it out."

Ari pulled out her phone and texted Riley back: *We're in.*

*   *   *

The third day of spring break was slightly warmer than the previous days. Ari and Dane rode their bikes down Hadley Hill, and instead of turning left to head to town, they took a right and pedaled west along the two-lane country highway. Although the road was a main thoroughfare for farm vehicles during harvest time, at the start of spring it was nearly deserted and made for a quiet ride.

A rusty mailbox, long standing askew on a rotten post, suggested they were at the Abshire place. Ari and Dane turned north onto a once-gravel road, which was now mainly just dirt. They both wove around the potholes that threatened to swallow their bike tires. Once they rounded a corner, the ramshackle house came into view. Ari could see Riley and Jace waiting outside.

Riley spotted Ari and was waving her over. Riley was standing next to what must've been the front door; it was hard to tell with the amount of brush that was overtaking the two-story house. The sad-looking building was leaning a bit, and the whitewashed walls were showing lines of daylight through them. Swallows were streaming from a second-story window and wildly swooping at everyone below. Only a few glass windows remained; most were just gaping and dark and it made the house feel a little intimidating. She was glad she'd worn jeans and leather boots; soft green blackberry vines were intermingled with sharp, dry blackberry canes from the past season. From her gardening experience, she knew that both could be painful to walk through without the proper clothing.

Riley's crush, Jace, nodded hello. Ari had never really gotten a good look at him up close: he was about Riley's height, had olive skin, and somewhat curly dark hair. She could see why Riley thought he was attractive. He was wearing a large, professional-looking camera around his neck and was changing a lens that he'd pulled from a camera bag.

"Hey! Glad you could make it," Riley said as they parked their bikes. "Jace, this is Ari and her neighbor Dane. They live right over there on Hadley Hill," she said, motioning to the northeast.

Jace extended a hand and Ari noticed he had a strong handshake.

"I think that my friend Amara will be joining us, as well as her friends Julia and Rob. Jace likes to photograph historic and abandoned sites," Riley explained.

"This is one of the few places in Rivers that I haven't taken pictures of yet," Jace added.

"I wonder if the family who lived in this house knew Nadia and Reginald," Ari mused, turning to Dane. Just then, more bicycles came rolling around the bend in the driveway.

"Everyone's here," Riley said, and she waved to the new arrivals. Ari knew Amara; she usually sat at the same lunch table with Riley. The other friends weren't as familiar; Ari had only talked with Julia once, at the winter dance earlier in the year.

"Ari, do you remember Julia?" Riley motioned to the tall girl with curly wisps of blonde hair, "and this is Rob."

Julia nodded hello to Ari and reached out to shake Dane's hand. "I know you," she said to Dane, smiling big. "We had pre-calculus together."

"Right, that's where I recognize you from. Mr. Shane's class," he replied.

The boy next to her, Rob, was clearly a football player at Rivers Union High. He was easily over six feet tall, and Ari figured he probably spent a fair amount of time lifting weights, from the looks of his arms and shoulders. He smiled and nodded at Ari.

"I brought a few flashlights if we need them," Julia said, pulling them from her messenger bag. Ari had her backpack with her, but had only brought her cell phone and an extra sweatshirt with her. She'd never explored an abandoned house before, so she hadn't been sure of what she would need.

Jace motioned to the group. "If you guys want to go in ahead of me, I'll get some exterior shots first, before I lose any more daylight. I'll catch up with you inside, ok?"

Riley went up the ramshackle front stairs and arrived on a wraparound porch, quite similar to the ones on Ari and Dane's homes. Her steps creaked across the wood-plank floor. Riley tried the doorknob, and although it was loosely attached to the door, it was locked. "I don't want to break in, so why don't we go through the window?" She pointed to the first window to the left of the front door, which was devoid of any glass on the bottom pane.

Each person in the group filed in through the window carefully, with Amara going in first. Dusty shards of glass on the wooden floor suggested that the window had been shattered long ago. Ari was careful to avoid any unseen chunks of glass as she made her way through the window and into what appeared to be the living room. The main windows of the living room were arranged in a distinctive three-sided alcove. A once-beautiful piano with gap-toothed missing keys slumped at the side of the main windows. Ari could almost feel sad chords leaking from the piano. Who would leave such a beautiful instrument behind?

"This is probably the living room. Somebody must've loved playing this piano," Dane remarked, as if he was reading Ari's thoughts. "I wonder what the Abshire family was like."

The group moved quietly through the house. There were only a few remnants left by the previous occupants: a bare wooden chair was in the corner of a downstairs room; some tattered curtains hung from a window which Ari assumed was a kitchen window. With each step Ari could almost feel the house whispering its story.

Dane stood in a space next to the kitchen. "I'm guessing the dining room was here."

Ari walked over to the room. "What makes you say that?"

"Look at the floor," Dane pointed. Bare, unfinished wood floors showed lighter spots arranged equally in a large rectangular shape. "The floor is worn away in these spots from the chairs moving back and forth. I only know that because our floors around our dining room table look like this, too."

"I never would've noticed that," Ari said quietly. Something about the house made her feel like whispering was the only way to converse.

Soon Jace had rejoined Riley inside, and they could be heard moving through the rooms. Creaking floorboards gave away each person's location. Dane and Ari were investigating one of the bedrooms when a noise behind them caused them both to startle. Julia was peeking into the doorway, with Amara standing behind her.

"Hey guys, find anything cool?" Julia smiled and carefully leaned against the warped and splintered doorway. "This sure is an old house," she mused, looking at Dane. "Hey, Rob and I were trying to get a door open, but it seems stuck. Can you help us?" Julia asked him. Dane nodded and followed her out of the room.

Ari looked at the window. Miraculously, this particular window wasn't covered with overgrowth and it still retained its original glass pane. She ran her finger over the warped glass; it undulated like water and felt thin and fragile. Outside, the sun was skimming the horizon, and Ari felt a twinge of fear, but then dismissed it. The old house wasn't even spooky; just quiet and lonely, with nature slowly reclaiming its parts. She wondered how many families had occupied this house. Had children run across the wooden floors? How many Christmases had been celebrated here?

Voices from the group could be heard in different parts of the home: it sounded like Riley, Amara, and Jace were walking upstairs, and Rob, Julia and Dane all sounded much farther away. Ari decided to head upstairs to see the view from the second story.

The staircase was more magnificent than the rest of the house: a heavy banister with a giant round newel cap, twice the width of her hand, summoned Ari upstairs. The paint on the railing was smooth and shiny despite chips that revealed layers of paint beneath. In sharp contrast, splintered and worn indentations ran up the center of each step where people had traversed most often. It struck Ari as odd and sad that a house that had been used so much was now simply forgotten.

She arrived on the upstairs landing and, upon hearing Jace quietly chatting with Riley in one room, she decided to explore the other side of the second floor alone. Ari found an eastern-facing room that looked upon Hadley Hill. As she made her way to the window, Ari realized this room was where all the swallows had been flying in and out of. There was copious amounts of nesting material: twigs, dry grass, and hair, mixed with downy feathers. The floor was gritty with birds' disintegrated excrement, leaving only seeds behind.

From one of the windows she could just make out one corner and the entire roofline of Dane's house through the vegetation. Ari fished her phone from her backpack and started taking photos from the window. The warm glow of the sinking sun cast a beautiful hue on Hadley Hill. *Dane should see this,* she thought, and she made her way downstairs and found the previously-stuck door. Amara was coming up the staircase, which looked like it went down to a basement.

"It's a bit dark down there," Amara said, her eyes wide. "Do you have a flashlight?"

Ari looked at her phone. "I'll have to use this," she said, smiling apprehensively.

From somewhere deep inside the basement she could hear Dane, Rob, and Julia chatting. She reached the bottom of the stairs and paused. Amara was right. Ari waited for her eyes to adjust to the darkness of the basement. A chill permeated the air and the scent of stale dirt was pervasive.

The space was a single room with a crude wood-plank floor. Heavy beams held up the house above them. A stack of wooden crates were piled in one corner of the room. Shallow shelves ran along the length of one wall, which also had a tiny, narrow window near the ceiling. Rob, Dane, and Julia were standing in the far corner by the crates, talking.

"Hey," Ari called to Dane. "Come upstairs; we can see your house from one of the rooms."

Dane crossed the basement and followed Ari up to the main floor, where they turned and ascended the grand staircase that led to the second floor.

Ari was about to enter the northeastern room that faced Hadley Hill when she paused in the doorway. Something caught her eye that she'd missed the first time through the door: nearly-invisible lines had been etched on the door frame. She caught her breath. Initials had been carved next to the lines: it had served as a height chart for children who had lived in this house, so very long ago.

Ari remembered the day before she'd moved to Rivers. She'd found her mom crying in a doorway, sponge in hand. Her mom had been trying to clean similar marks off the door frame of their San Francisco apartment. A pang of sadness ran through her, although she didn't know why. Dane put a hand on her shoulder, breaking her out of her reverie.

"What were you going to show me?"

Ari shook herself out of the memory and crossed the room to the window. Pinkish sunlight was bathing the hillside in color. "There," she pointed. "You can see just the roof of your house, and we can almost see your window from here."

"I wonder how many trees were on the hill when all these houses were built. Back then, you could probably see both of our houses from this room," Dane guessed. He then pointed down to the front yard and nudged Ari.

"Hey, look down there. Is Jace her boyfriend?" Dane asked quietly, in front of the open window.

Ari followed Dane's gaze down into the yard. Jace and Riley were standing next to the old house; Jace had just kissed Riley. Ari ducked out of the window and suddenly felt embarrassed. She assumed Riley hadn't seen her watching, but she didn't want to be seen, all the same.

"I don't know," she said honestly. "I know Riley has had a crush on him for a really long time," she mused, then smiled. "This is kind of a big deal for her." She looked at Dane, who was still watching. "Geez, Dane, get out of the window! They're gonna see you!" she whisper-hissed, and pulled him out from in front of the window—which brought him uncomfortably close. She hadn't meant to do that, but suddenly he was there, inches from her. He'd stopped himself from running into her by catching her by the waist. Dane had a funny look on his face; like he was desperately trying not to start laughing. Ari's eyes got big and she shook her head *no*; the last thing she wanted was to have Riley think they were spying on her and laughing.

Dane took a deep breath and composed himself. "Sorry," he smiled, a sly smile still playing in his face. He reached up to Ari's face and brushed her long bangs from her eyes. Just as his hand was lingering at her face, a sound in the doorway caused them both to startle. Julia was once again standing in the doorway, with Rob and Amara behind her.

"Oh—uh, sorry guys, um—" she muttered.

"No, it's, um, fine," Ari and Dane both stammered, and Dane took a half-step back.

"I just wanted to tell you guys we were about to go," Julia said.

"It was nice meeting you both," Rob added.

"I'll see you at school," Julia smiled at Dane, the three of them turned and left. Ari could hear their footfalls descending the wooden staircase, which seemed to be groaning under the weight of three people. Ari was still rooted in place, but Dane leaned back to discreetly peek out the window.

"Riley and Jace aren't down there anymore. Should we go before it gets too dark?" he asked.

"Yeah, I guess." Ari sounded reluctant. Something about the house made her want to stay and explore. "I want to come back, though. I just have this feeling this house has a story to tell."

They made their way down the worn steps and back out the broken front window. Riley was getting her bike and Jace was carefully packing away his camera and equipment. Ari paused on the broken-down porch, imagining what it must've been like a century ago.

When Jace had his back turned, Ari gave Riley a thumbs-up and a big grin. Riley just smiled and raised her eyebrows in surprise. "See you guys later!" Ari called out to them.

Instead of riding back to the highway, Ari walked her beach cruiser, and Dane did the same with his bike. Ari wanted to savor the stillness of the early spring night. They crunched along the gravel driveway in comfortable silence. Although it wasn't totally dark yet, the moon was waning and bright. It felt like she had just emerged from months of rain and gray fog, and the clear sky was a welcome relief.

An overwhelming chorus of frogs were somewhere close, and the smell of cottonwood trees wafted through the air, which had suddenly gotten cooler as they rounded the bend back to the highway.

"There must be water somewhere nearby," Dane guessed. "The

cottonwood trees usually grow by a riverbank, and that sounds like a whole lot of frogs." He set his bike down in the gravel and set off through the tall grass. "Ugh," he said, and Ari could hear his steps squelching. "It's really swampy. But, check this out! There's an actual lake here. Come over and see," he said, pointing to something beyond the tall grasses.

Ari made her way into the knee-high weeds. She felt her feet sink down with each step, and hoped her boots would keep her feet dry. When she reached Dane's side, she was amazed by the lovely area that they'd neglected to see when they had passed it the first time.

A small lake, about four hundred feet wide, stretched from where they were standing to a shore that was obscured by weeping willows, cottonwoods, and conifers. To the left of them, the water curved out of sight and around the base of Hadley Hill. Newly-sprouting bunches of cattails spiked up from the lake's surface, and Ari spotted two ducks skimming around bunches of lily-pads. Blackbirds with red patches on their wings were clinging to cattails, calling out with a distinctive song.

"We've gotta come back here," Dane said, with a mischievous tone. "I know our canoe is at my house. You up for it sometime?"

"Alright," Ari said, smiling. "Sounds like an adventure. By the way, I have no canoeing experience," she chuckled.

"Don't worry, it's not too hard," he said, slapping a mosquito from his arm. "C'mon, let's go. I forgot my bug spray," Dane chuckled.

chapter four

The next night, the doorbell rang at Ari's house. Lily ran to
the door, but Ari had rushed down the stairs just as Lily peeked through
the window. Riley was on the porch, holding her pillow and sleeping bag
in one arm, and backpack in the other, ready to spend the night.

"Alright, you have to spill it," Ari looked at Riley with anticipation
as they climbed the stairs to Ari's room. "What's going on with Jace?
Dane even asked if you guys were a couple, yesterday at the Abshire
house."

Riley laughed. "That's funny that Dane asked if we were going out,
because Julia asked the same thing about you two." They had reached
Ari's room, and Ari firmly shut her door to keep their conversation
contained.

"Julia? Why would she ask? I thought Rob was her boyfriend?" Ari
wrinkled her nose.

"Rob?" Riley giggled. "They're cousins. Definitely not going out.
Can't you see the family resemblance?" she said, still laughing.

Ari thought about it. They were both model-tall, blonde, and
ridiculously good looking. Julia had the presence of a movie star, and
Rob looked like a professional bodybuilder. "Yeah, ok, I see it. But what
did you tell her?"

"I said that you guys were best friends, but that you've had a crush
on him forever," Riley said truthfully.

"*Riley!* You told her I had a crush on him! He's gonna find out!" Ari
gasped.

Riley just shook her head. "Oh no!" she laughed in mock horror.
"He'll never believe it!"

Ari rolled her eyes. "Ok, back to you and Jace…"

"Well, he kissed me at the Abshire place, and I may have ended up

18

kissing him back," she said, smiling. "After that, we chatted on the ride home. He's a really nice guy, and I'd definitely like to spend more time getting to know him. He's interesting and has a lot of good qualities."

Ari nodded, satisfied with her answer. Riley continued, "He asked me to be his date at the Last Dance, and that's a few months away, so I'm guessing he might like to get to know me better as well."

"What's the Last Dance?" Ari asked.

"Ah, it's the last formal dance of the year, only it's not quite as formal as the winter dance. They hold it outdoors in the first week of June, at the Ansley Park Garden. If you thought the winter formal was beautiful, wait until you see these gardens all lit up!" Riley looked excited just talking about it.

Ari furrowed her brow. She wasn't sure that Dane would even want to go, and she didn't want to be the one to ask.

As if reading her mind, Riley said, "Hon, he'll ask you, don't worry. Dane showed up to the winter formal, and I can guarantee he'll want to go with you," she reassured her. "And, if for some reason he doesn't want to go, you're always welcome to come with us."

Ari nodded in thanks. Riley continued, "No matter what happens, though, we need to start dress shopping. Like, this week."

*   *   *

Ari's mom sat in the passenger seat of her own car. Ari sat nervously at the wheel.

"Alright, so the first thing you need to do is adjust everything to *you*," her mom said. "Adjust your mirrors, get your seat to where you can reach both of the pedals, and move your steering wheel to where it's most comfortable for you." Her mom reached over to show Ari how to release the steering wheel so that it could move up, down, and closer or further from her.

It was Ari's first driving lesson; they were in the empty parking lot of

19

the high school. She was in her mom's car; the same car that had traveled all the way up from San Francisco when they had moved. One advantage to the move was that Ari was going to be able to take her driving test in a small town instead of urban San Francisco, which gave her great relief. There was nothing that rivaled driving up and down the insanely steep hills of the city, with the added complications of the cable cars, masses of pedestrians, speeding taxis, and tons of traffic.

Most of Ari's friends already had their permits, and Ari was a year behind. She had passed the written exam for her permit with flying colors, but studying driving and *actually* driving were two different things entirely. She felt like she had some serious catching up to do, so she wanted to try her hardest.

"Ok, got it," Ari said nervously. She moved the rearview mirror so the entire back window filled her view.

"Before you do anything," her mom stressed, "put your foot on the brake, the left pedal. As soon as you do that, you can turn the key—" she waited for Ari to start the car, "—and then put the car in gear." Again, Ari was thankful her parents only had cars with automatic transmissions. She knew she would have to learn to drive a manual at some point, but she figured that wouldn't be anytime soon. She shifted the car into reverse and slowly backed out of the parking spot.

"Good," her mom reassured her. "Now put it in drive and, well, just get a feel for the steering." Ari was a little startled when the car started moving as soon as she removed her foot from the brake. Using the accelerator, she slowly made a stop-and-start course around the small parking lot. There was a road that went behind the school, so she eventually made a few loops around the building. After forty minutes, she was feeling more comfortable with operating the car. More importantly, though, she hadn't hit anything.

"You're doing great, Ari," her mom smiled. "Do you want to try going out onto the street?"

Ari thought about it, then nodded. She was determined to get this driving thing down solidly before taking her driver's test. It bothered her that nearly everyone else her age had a year's worth of driving experience already. Ari left the parking lot and headed for the main street of Rivers.

"So, I heard you talking to Riley about the house at the base of the hill," her mom said.

"Yeah," Ari said, trying her best to have a coherent conversation while concentrating on driving. "We went down there to get photos of it. Well, her friend Jace wanted to get photos. It's a really beautiful house, mom. It would be awesome if somebody fixed it up."

"Do you know any of the history?"

Ari shook her head. "No, but it would be great to find out something about it. It has to have a story, you know? It's not just a silent old house. There's something intriguing about it."

Her mom smiled knowingly. "It whispers to you, doesn't it?"

"It *does!*" Ari exclaimed, trying not to take her hands off the wheel. "That's exactly what it's like! I don't want to tell anyone else that because they'd think I'm crazy. But you totally get it, right?"

Her mom nodded again. "There were places like that in San Francisco. Buildings you'd walk past and just feel the life and energy that had once been there. Houses with stories to tell, just waiting to be rediscovered." Her mom looked wistful.

"Do you miss it?" Ari asked. She hadn't talked about the move with her mom at all since they'd arrived in Rivers nearly a year ago. She was almost apprehensive about what her mom might say.

"Oh, honey, of course I do. But I think this little town is growing on me. And, it seems that you are beginning to like it here, and you've found friends…and Dane." Her mom snuck a sly look at Ari.

Ari rolled her eyes. "Mom, he's a *friend*."

Her mom smiled and continued. "Lily likes her school, and your

21

dad loves his job. So," her mom looked over at her, "I think it's been a good move." Suddenly, her mom pointed ahead to a building along Main Street. "Have you tried the Rivers Historic Museum? Maybe they'll have something about your Abshire house."

Ari carefully pulled into the narrow parking lot. There were only a few cars in the lot, and Ari tried pulling into one of the spots, but when she opened the driver's side door to check her parking job, she winced. She was taking up not one, but two parking spots.

She put the car in reverse and tried again. "Pull the wheel hard to the right and then straighten out," her mom suggested.

Two more tries of back-and-forth and Ari finally had succeeded in fitting the car into a single spot.

Neither Ari or her mom had ever been inside the Rivers Historic Museum. A white-haired docent named Agnes greeted them and asked if they'd like a tour. Ari and her mom nodded and followed Agnes as she shuffled to each area of the museum. Agnes explained that the building had housed many businesses over the years, but it was most notably a car dealership that had a repair shop on the second story of the building. "There was an elevator that would lift the cars to the second story. The bottom floor was the showroom," explained the small elderly lady.

Agnes then led them to the reference room. Stacks of old books, newspaper, binders, and movies lined the walls. "Members have access to all the materials here in the reference room, plus our reference computer for the photo archives. We also have catalogued boxes of artifacts that members can request to see." Agnes adjusted her bifocals. "Is there anything in particular you ladies are looking for today?" Agnes asked, pulling a small notebook from her skirt pocket. As Ari spoke, Agnes began taking notes.

"Can you tell me about the old Abshire homestead, along the west highway?" Ari asked.

Agnes smiled a small, sly grin. "Ah, you've discovered the ruins of the Abshire place," she said.

"What I have heard is that the house was built around the turn of the century. The Abshire family farmed the land surrounding the house, and I think they had several children. The mother taught piano lessons to the well-to-do children of Rivers. Unfortunately, I have no idea what happened to them or their children. I believe they were quite poor, as were many families who farmed around Rivers at the time. Perhaps you can find out more," Agnes said. "I would start by using the 1905 address directory—the oldest one we have—to find out the family members' names." She pulled out an ancient-looking hardbound book with the year prominently printed on the spine.

Ari started getting excited. Agnes excused herself and left Ari and her mom in the small, silent reference room. She scanned to the A's, and found one entry under Abshire: Joseph & Avilene, *Farmer.*

She smiled to herself and thought it was intriguing that the family's occupation would be listed. Ari found a piece of paper on a table in the room scribbled in her notebook their names and the year.

As Ari was scanning through more directories her mom stepped out of the reference room. Moments later, she returned, handing Ari a card.

"I got us a family membership," she whispered. "On the card is the access code so you can get into the photo database."

Ari smiled in surprise. "Thank you!" Ari went to the computer and logged in. Using the search browser, she entered the name "Abshire" and two thumbnail photos appeared on the screen.

Agnes shuffled back into the room and stood behind Ari. "The photos on the database are just the ones we have uploaded to the system. Upstairs, we still have many uncatalogued photos in binders. If you're interested, I'd be happy to show you where they are."

Ari thanked Agnes, then clicked on the first thumbnail. The photo was of a family standing in front of a house that looked very similar to the Abshire home, only newer and with fewer trees all around. She looked at each sepia-toned face: the handsome Mr. and Mrs. Abshire, wearing light summer whites, standing with two curly-haired children and one baby, ensconced in a blanket and giant bonnet. A scan of the back of the photo was paired with the front, and swirly writing in brown ink spelled out "Joseph Jr, Ezra, baby Aliza." There was no date on the photo. Ari clicked on the other photo, then hit "print" on both.

*   *   *

"Look at this photo here," Ari handed Dane one of the photocopied pictures she'd made at the museum the day before. On the back, swirly cursive spelled out "Christmas Day at the Abshire's." A beautiful Christmas tree, though sparsely adorned, stood proudly in the living room at the Abshire house. Two young boys, one a toddler and the other just a bit older, stood to the side of the tree.

Dane and Ari were seated on the bench swing on Ari's front porch, and from where they were at, strands of Miles Davis could be heard floating from the open window of her dad's den. The scent of pipe smoke mixed with the smell of rain in the air.

Ari watched Dane as he looked at the photograph. For a minute, he didn't say anything; he just stared at the faces of the little boys. "I wonder what kind of Christmas they had. You said the lady at the museum thought they were poor farmers?"

Ari nodded. Before she could show him her other photo, a dull pounding sound came from inside her house. Ari got up from the porch swing and walked across the deck that ran along the front of the home to the open window that spilled out slow notes of jazz. Poking her head inside, she looked to see what the noise was.

Her dad stood in the den, hammer in hand. Framed photographs were propped against the walls. He looked a little startled when Ari appeared in the window.

"Hey! Just the person I'm looking for," he said.

"Oh yeah?" Ari propped her elbows on the windowsill.

"Yep. I need a level for hanging these photos." Ari raised an eyebrow. Her dad continued. "I believe our tools are in the cellar on the side of the house. Would you mind poking your head down there and getting me the level?"

"That's the bar with the tube with the bubble in it, right?" Ari asked, and as soon as she did, she thought she heard Dane snicker behind her.

Her dad smiled and nodded. "Right." He crossed the room and handed her a flashlight. "Might need this," he said with a wink.

Ari motioned for Dane to follow her. She walked along the wraparound porch to the side of the house where she usually kept her bike. Steps led down to the yard and the doors to the cellar.

The entrance to the cellar consisted of two panel doors, side-by-side, resting on an angled concrete base. The latch was rusted in place, and after several tries by Ari, Dane motioned for her to step aside.

"Let me try," he said. Dane used a stick nearby to pry up the latch, which was designed to hold a padlock. He and Ari lifted the doors open. Stale air escaped from the opening.

"Ladies first," Dane smiled slyly, though he pointed the flashlight down the steps and held his hand out for Ari to take.

Ari peered into the vast darkness. The flashlight only showed wispy filaments of dirty cobwebs that floated along the breeze.

"Ugh, Dane. It is *so* dirty and dusty down there," Ari mused, as she descended to the fourth step down. The room had telltale signs of a place that hadn't been touched in decades: a thick layer of brown dust covered everything. Roughly-hewn shelves lined the walls in the room. Jars filled with nails and screws and random metal parts sat on the shelves. Vintage-looking yard tools were lying against the wall or propped up. Only in one corner were newer-looking tools that weren't quite as dusty. A rake, shovel, and hoe leaned up against the wall, but no level could be seen. Dirty, gauzy strands of cobwebs covered everything. Ari stood in the middle to avoid touching any of it.

"This is gross," Ari said, recoiling from a threadlike web that had drifted too close to her face.

"Yeah, nobody's been down here for ages. It looks like this has always been used as tool storage or something," Dane said. He moved around the space, poking at an object here and there. Ari still hadn't moved from the center of the room.

"Do you see anything that resembles a level?" she asked.

Dane turned and walked over to her. "Nope," he said, brushing his hands off on his jeans. Ari's eyes widened as she focused on his head. An enormous gray tangle of cobwebs had become embedded in Dane's tousled hair. Ari wanted to reach out and brush it off, but the thought of a spider, living or dead, caused her to back away.

"What? What are you looking at?" Dane's eyes followed hers and he reached up to his hair. Ari couldn't take it any longer. She waved her hands and, without touching anything, backed up the stairs and out of the cellar.

"I'm out! I just can't stand the spiderwebs!" Ari said, laughing, as she emerged from the cellar. Dane started shaking his head and the blob of cobwebs tangled in his hands.

"Oh, gross!" Dane was still shaking his hair with his fingers, and Ari started laughing so hard that she had to lean up against the house. Dane saw this and suddenly ran at her, head first. With a gasp Ari took off at top speed across the backyard gardens. She could hear Dane laughing also and he stayed right on her heels. Ari crossed the pasture, but being shorter and smaller than Dane, it was impossible to run faster than him. By the time she had sprinted through the stone pillars at the edge of the pasture, Dane had caught up with her and tackled her. Wrapping his arms around her from behind, he made a point to rub his still-cobwebby hair all over *her* hair.

"NOOO!" Ari hollered, but she dissolved into giggles and was soon just hanging in his arms. Dane was laughing so hard he'd doubled over, but still kept a firm hold on Ari. Ari tried to twist around to face him, but his grip on her was surprisingly tight. Ari was certain she had never heard him laugh so hard in the almost-year that she'd known him. His laugh reverberated right through her core and it warmed Ari like sunlight. Suddenly, though, Ari stopped laughing.

chapter five

"What?" Dane said, finally, looking down at Ari with a concerned expression. He released Ari from his grip. She was still out of breath, partly from the mad sprint across the pasture. She was bent over, facing the backside of the pillars. Ari reached out her hand and pointed at its base.

"Look…what do you suppose this is?" Ari reached out her arm and brushed her hand across the bottom of the column on the side facing the oak grove. A small, barely-visible carving was etched into the base. Ari squinted.

The carving, roughly scratched into the stone, was composed of two hearts. The top heart was oriented normally; the bottom heart was upside down. Their points touched and were circled. It was a simple, unusual icon.

"What the heck is that?" Dane said, going over the carving with his finger.

"Looks like a carving of two hearts. How have we never seen it before?"

"Have you ever really looked at the backs of the pillars?"

Ari shook her head. "No, I guess not. It's like whoever did it, didn't want it to be obvious."

Dane was leaning over her from behind, so close that she could feel his breath on the back of her neck. Suddenly her focus shifted from the carving to Dane and how incredibly close he was. She breathed in: his soap-and-laundry scent mixed with the mossy, earthen smell of the ground they were kneeling on.

He propped himself up with his arm, now leaning fully over Ari. His chin was nearly resting on her shoulder as she pulled her phone from her pocket and tried taking a picture of the carving, despite the low light.

"Do you think it has something to do with Nadia and Grekov?" Ari asked as she got down to eye-level with the carving.

"Maybe them, or anybody from the four generations of Hadley's who have lived in these two houses over the past one-hundred years."

"Have you seen this symbol anywhere else before?"

Dane shook his head. "Never."

Crouching low again, she tried to get a better photo of the symbol.

Suddenly, a sound startled them both.

"Aaariii!" Her dad's voice echoed across the pasture. "Did you find the level?"

"Oh, shoot," Ari said under her breath. "Not yet, dad!" she hollered toward the house. Dane offered her a hand up. Thanking him, she gave him a funny look.

"What?" Dane asked quietly, tilting his head.

"You've still got cobwebs in your hair," Ari said. Grimacing, she stepped toward him and reached up, brushing them away. Dane froze and seemed to be surprised that she was willing to touch his hair. "Gross," she muttered under her breath, which caused Dane to burst out laughing again.

*   *   *

It was near the end of spring break when Ari found herself standing in front of the Abshire house once more. Ari had planned ahead this time, and had brought a backpack with a flashlight and the photos she'd found at the museum. Not knowing what kind of terrain they'd be covering, Ari had donned leather boots and jeans. With those boots, she figured she'd be able to get over any broken glass or blackberry vines they might encounter.

Dane's dad had dropped him and his canoe off with the pickup truck. A cloud of dust started to settle back to the ground as the truck disappeared out of sight and Dane handed Ari a glossy wooden oar.

Ari looked up at him and took the oar. It had been awhile since she'd seen Dane's eyes in full sunlight; they were a light jade green with halos of hazel near the pupils. It was always shocking to see those incredible colors; she was quite certain she'd never seen any human with eyes like his. She abruptly realized she was wordlessly staring at him a moment far too long; he noticed it too and smiled shyly at her. She quickly turned back and looked at the house, then the canoe that was sitting in the front yard.

"If we're going into the house first, let's put the canoe out of sight; maybe stash it around the side of the house." Dane set his oar inside the wooden canoe and Ari did the same. The canoe was much heavier than Ari expected as she helped him store the boat securely out of sight.

"What are you looking for in the house?" Dane asked.

"There are a couple of pictures I want to take before we go canoeing." Ari pulled the two laser-printed photos from the museum out of her backpack. Going around the front of the house, she held out the black-and-white copy of the photo with the family. Dane stood behind her, his head bent low next to her own.

In the photo, the front door and porch were clearly visible behind the smiling family. Even with all the shrubbery that had currently overtaken the front of the house, Ari could clearly see the exterior of the house was a perfect match.

"Yep, that's definitely the same house," Dane mused quietly. Ari had Dane hold up the copied photo while she pulled out her cell phone. She tried to frame her photo to match.

They entered the house through the broken-out front window, being just as careful as before to avoid the shattered shards that littered the floor. The creaking floorboards announced once again that people had come to visit the lonely home.

Ari pulled the other photo from her bag; the one with the two boys and the Christmas tree. This photo wasn't hard to place, either. The distinctive three-sided bump-out in the corner of the living room made it easy to see that they were standing in the right place. Ari got out her phone and repeated the process, with Dane holding the original photograph while Ari snapped the picture.

"Let's go upstairs. I want to get a photo of one more thing," Ari directed.

She went up the stairs with Dane following behind. At the northeastern room, she stopped. She pulled out her phone and tried to find the best light to reveal the lines etched in the door frame.

"What are you taking pictures of the door for?" Dane squinted as he tried to see what Ari was seeing.

"Feel this right here." She took his hand and placed it on the doorframe. Dane squinted and looked closely at the lines.

"It's a height chart for the kids who lived here," Ari explained quietly. "In our apartment that I grew up in, we did the same thing. Little ruler lines for Lily and myself, all the way up the doorframe." Ari grew quiet. Dane turned and looked at her, searching her eyes. Ari paused, being held captive by his stare. Nervous flutters caught Ari's breath. There was silence for moments longer than usual.

"Do you still miss it?" Dane finally asked.

"San Francisco?"

"Yeah," Dane nodded.

Ari thought for a minute. "I'll always miss some things. But if I had the chance to move back right now, I wouldn't," she said with a slow smile.

Dane smiled back and exhaled like he'd been holding his breath. "I'm really glad you like it here, Ari." After another pause, "Is there anywhere else you wanted to photograph?"

Ari pointed downstairs. "No, I don't think so, but when you guys were in the basement, did you look through all the crates that were stacked against the wall? Might be something interesting in those."

Dane shook his head. "No, we didn't even think to look through them."

"Let's go down there before we go canoeing."

The porcelain-handled door that led to the basement was stuck shut once again, and Dane had to use a good amount of force to budge it. The door finally gave way to Dane's shoulder. He had to catch himself against the jamb to keep from flying down the steps. Before descending, Dane pulled out two flashlights from his backpack and handed one to Ari.

The basement was stale and dark. Ari and Dane crossed the room to where the crates were stacked. Going through every one, it didn't take long to realize they all were empty. Dane crossed the room and was at the base of the stairs while Ari finished stacking the last of the crates exactly as they had been.

"Wait for me! Don't you dare leave me down here alone," Ari scowled as she jogged across the room to Dane. Dane turned to face her, tilting his head to the side like he was listening.

"Ari, cross the room again, just the way you came," he instructed. Ari gave him a questioning glance, but did as she was told. Her boots made a solid sound as she walked over the wood-plank floor. She reached the crates. "Come back again, the same way," Dane instructed. Ari started to say something, but Dane held up a finger to his mouth to shush her. Ari narrowed her eyes as she stepped across the floor, but then she heard it: one step of her boot sounded completely different compared to the other footfalls. Ari backed up to the board, and stomped on it once more.

The space under the plank on which she was standing sounded undeniably different.

chapter six

Ari's mouth dropped open as she tilted her head and stared at Dane.

"It's hollow!" she gasped, incredulous.

"Sounds like it," Dane said, coming to her side. She backed off the plank and Dane knocked on the board with his knuckles. "This one," he said.

At first glance, the three-foot long plank seemed solidly nailed down. Dane tried prying at the nails, which were loose in their holes. He picked at one nail and it slipped out easily. Dane pulled out a pocketknife from his jeans and selected the longest blade. By slipping the blade between the boards, he was able lift the loose board about an inch. None of the nails had actually been holding down the board at all.

Dane removed the plank completely and set it to the side. They both leaned over the open space.

"Nothing down there," Dane sighed. He started to put the plank back in place when Ari stopped him.

"Wait a sec." Ari reached into the space under the floor. She grimaced as she imagined what kind of spiders could possibly be lurking in the darkness. Her hand felt cold dirt, the rough wooden floor joists, and then something else. Something soft, crumbling.

"Oh gosh," Ari gasped under her breath, recoiling.

"What is it?" Dane tried bending low to see what Ari had touched.

Ari took out her flashlight and angled its light to try and determine what exactly she'd laid her hand on. She then reached her hand in the open space once again. Slowly, she grabbed ahold of an object and carefully worked it free from beneath the hidden space.

In Ari's hands was a small, thin book with a leather cover that was disintegrating as she held it. Dane's eyes got wide. "Whoa," he breathed.

Dane looked over her shoulder as Ari carefully opened to the book. The pages inside were cotton-soft and tan with age. A thin, swirling script formed lines on the pages.

"Let's take this upstairs where there's more light, 'kay?" Ari said. Dane replaced the plank, but not before taking one more look to make sure there wasn't anything else under the floor.

They went up the basement stairs and went to sit in the three-sided alcove of windows in the living room. Ari leaned against the wall and Dane sat next to her. Light streamed into the silent living room. Ari opened the book once again, marveling at the elegant script inside.

On the inside of the fragile front cover was a faded name penned in ink. Ari squinted to read it.

"Ezra Abshire, 1925." Ari wrinkled her nose and turned to the first entry. "'June 3. Father decided to take a gamble and plant a new crop called ryegrass. The neighboring farmers are concerned his decision will cost us dearly if we can't sell the seed. Father assures Mother not to worry; he has faith in his decision.'" Ari had to slow down and examine each word as she read: the handwriting wasn't entirely difficult to read, but in places, some of the flourishes and swirls tangled. "'Every evening as he sits on the front porch whittling away, and Mother sits beside him knitting, I hear them discuss these things when they think Joseph Jr. and I aren't listening.'"

Ari glanced out the windows in the direction of the front porch, trying to imagine Mr. and Mrs. Abshire in their nightly routine.

Dane held out his hand, motioning for the book. Ari handed it to him. The silence in the room was occasionally punctuated by the sound of a turning page, or a birdlike noise from somewhere above them. Outside, the morning breeze swayed the brush against the house, making an audible scratching. Dust specks floated in the streams of sunlight that were moving across the room.

Dane began reading. "June 8. Aliza is ill. Mother has been caring for her day and night. It's hard to watch Aliza struggle; she is so little and we fear it is influenza. To make matters worse, Mother had to cancel teaching her piano lessons this week. Joseph and Father and I have been working from sunup to sundown to help. Our prayers are that Aliza does not succumb to her sickness.'"

"Heavy stuff," Ari said quietly.

Dane kept reading, haltingly at times, as he tried to decipher Ezra's cursive writing. "'The bright spot of the day was when Katia brought a basket of food that her mother prepared for us. I was in the field when I saw her arrive; as she left I thought about asking her if she'd like my company on the trek back, but I couldn't bring myself to approach her.'"

A small smile crossed Ari's face. "I'd say he has a crush on this Katia, what do you think?"

Dane nodded as he carefully flipped through the pages. A photograph fell to the floor.

Dane and Ari turned their heads and stared at the face that looked up at them. The photo was definitely as old as the journal, but it wasn't in black and white. Instead, it glowed with lifelike colors. The girl in the photo looked to be in her teens. She grinned back at them with one corner turned up in a mischievous grin, and a glint in her ice-blue eyes. Her hair was neatly parted on the side and bobbed at her shoulders.

"She's beautiful," Ari said, smiling back at the photo.

Dane picked up the photo and read the back: "To Ezra, with all my love, K."

"I'm guessing this girl is Katia?" Ari wondered.

Dane looked at Ari. "She looks really familiar, Ari. I've seen this face before."

Ari raised an eyebrow. "Where?"

"I don't know."

"See if he says anything more about her."

35

Dane started leafing through the journal, but the sound of a car driving past on the highway caused them both to freeze. It sped past without stopping, but Ari realized they could be caught inside the house at any moment.

"We should probably get out of here," Dane said. "I'm taking this with me, though. It's not doing any good sitting under the floor." He smiled and Ari nodded in agreement.

"Good idea."

Dane put the journal in his backpack and Ari gathered her phone and bag. They exited out the same front window and headed for the canoe they'd hidden beside the house.

"Ready for a paddle?" Dane said, smiling big.

"Ready as ever. Let's get this canoeing adventure started," Ari said, reveling in the joy of his smile.

As they approached the water, the noonday light allowed Ari to better see the layout of the lake. It looked much bigger than it had that night; she had underestimated how far across it was from one side to the other.

Dane motioned at the canoe. "Once it's in the water, you go ahead and get in the front, and I'll be in back." The knee-high weeds were making it difficult to get the canoe to the bank. Summoning all her strength, Ari helped set the boat in the water. Ari followed his direction and carefully stepped in. The canoe instantly wobbled and she gripped the sides. Dane easily sat in the back and used his oar to push off the bank.

Although Ari had never rowed anything in her life, she found it to be fairly easy—as long as she stayed balanced. Dane gave her a few pointers on steering, and she loved how easily the canoe silently glided along the green lake. Delicate damselflies landed on the side of the canoe for just seconds before flitting off again.

They were heading north to see how far the lake extended beyond the curve. Ari glanced back and noticed two things: they could no longer see the highway, and Dane had taken his shirt off. He was thin and lean, but had broad shoulders and muscles that were defined as he paddled.

She realized that once again, Dane had caught her staring at him. In her embarrassment, she quickly thought of something to say.

"That was pretty observant of you, hearing that hollow floorboard. I never would've noticed that."

Dane smiled. "I dunno, Ari, I think we make a pretty good team. I was about to put that floorboard back, but you insisted on taking a closer look."

Ari shrugged. "I'm just happy it was a journal that I grabbed, instead of a dead animal. I was really worried for a moment," she said.

Dane laughed. "It almost would've been worth it, to see the look on your face if you'd pulled out something gross."

Ari looked back at him and made a face. She switched her oar to the other side of the canoe without missing a beat.

"You're doing really well at paddling for never having done this before," Dane noticed.

"Thanks. Once you get the rhythm of it, it's not too hard."

Dane smiled. "We used to take this old canoe out on the Elgin River all the time when I was a little kid. We'd use it for fishing and exploring." He stopped a moment, thinking. "I really loved my time on the river as a kid. This is almost just as good. Maybe even better because you're here."

Ari couldn't help but smile and she felt a nervous shiver go through her.

The lake stretched out in front of them. They were now completely behind the bend, and she could finally see where the lake came to an end. There was nothing surrounding the lake but a river-rock shore and more cottonwood trees. Ari was surveying the shore when Dane got up from his seat.

The canoe wobbled and Ari grabbed for the sides, nearly dropping her oar into the lake. She rebalanced herself as Dane came up behind her. "Hey," he said, looking over her shoulder and pointing. "Do you see that over there? It looks like a path, maybe…"

Ari squinted her eyes, and sure enough, at the far end of the lake, it looked like there was a definite break in the foliage. Wide enough to be a path, she guessed. "We'll just have to go over there and see, right?" she said, digging her oar into the water. The canoe surged forward, and Dane lost his balance and rolled backward in the canoe, nearly hitting his head on the seat.

"Are you ok?" Ari looked back at him.

"Yeah," Dane nodded and sat up, and grabbing his oar.

With slow, even paddling, it only took them ten minutes to cross the lake. Ari looked down and she could see the water was getting shallower. Under the rippling surface, smooth stones were beginning to appear, and stones closer to the shore were undulating with a mossy green fuzz.

They beached the canoe on the smooth-pebble shore and heaved it halfway out of the water. The area they'd arrived at was overgrown but absolutely a defined path. "You first," Ari whispered.

She followed Dane as he stepped into the overgrowth. He tucked his shirt in the back pocket of his jeans and was methodically snapping back branches that obstructed their way. Ari had only seen Dane without his shirt on a few occasions, and for the first time, she noticed a massive jagged scar running across his spine. It looked papery and wrinkled and in stark contrast with the strong, smooth symmetry of the rest of his back. Without thinking she reached out and gently brushed the scar with her hand. Dane startled at her touch and whirled around, looking at her with surprise.

"Sorry, I—um, how did you get that scar? I've never seen it before," she asked tentatively.

He quickly turned back and shook his head. "Got it a long time ago. It's not a big deal."

His tone indicated he wasn't going to give any more details. From the looks of it, Ari couldn't imagine such an injury wasn't a big deal, but she decided it was best not to ask any more questions. They kept walking in silence for a few minutes, with Dane frequently pausing to clear the trail.

The path turned sharply and they began moving uphill in the direction of Hadley Hill. She looked back and could still make out the shimmering glint of the lake below them. Blackberry bushes were now threatening to cut off their way. Suddenly, Dane stopped and Ari stumbled into his back. "I think we've reached the end of the trail."

Ari looked around from behind; sure enough, the briars and undergrowth had finally consumed the ground in front of them. A huge tree had fallen to the side of the trail, and other smaller saplings had sprouted up from around its base. Honeysuckle vines had wound their way up the saplings, creating a fragrant screen of blossoms. Ari hopped up on the log to rest. Dane climbed on and lay back on the tree trunk, balling up his shirt to use as a pillow.

As she sat, Ari still wondered about the giant scar on his back, but she couldn't bring herself to ask him about it again. Something in his tone of voice had warned that it was a topic that he would have to bring up if he chose. Dane dropped an arm down and fished around in his backpack, eventually pulling out the crumbling journal. Without saying a word, he started reading the book to himself.

In the silence between, birds chirped and rustled the leaves and vines surrounding them. Small flying bugs hid in the closed buds of the honeysuckle blossoms, and birds were swooping in and out, actively feasting on the insects. Very little else could be heard, and it was a beautiful silence.

"Listen to this," Dane eventually said. "'Aliza is getting stronger every day. Mother was able to resume her piano lessons this week. I was supposed to be whitewashing the chicken coop this afternoon when I heard Katia playing the piano. I managed to slip underneath the window and listen to her play. Beautiful strands of Chopin filled the yard and it's hard to believe that a girl of fifteen can play with such finesse.'"

"Any idea of how old Ezra is?"

"Not yet."

"Sounds like we'll need to make some trips to the library and museum," Ari said. A moment passed and Ari realized once school ended, it would free up more than enough time to research Ezra and his family.

"Days like this make me excited that summer is almost here." Ari mentioned. "Got any big plans once school is out?"

Dane sat up on the log. "I've done quite a few driving lessons with my mom since she moved back, and I think I'll be able to take my driver's test by then, maybe even sooner. It'll be easy."

"What about a summer job?" Ari asked, brushing her bangs from her eyes. A slight breeze wove through the honeysuckle, releasing its fragrance. She was cooling down from the sweaty hike to the top of the hill, and she pulled her jacket tightly around her.

"Gosh, Ari, I haven't even thought about it yet. We have a few more months, right? What are you hoping to do?"

Ari smiled slyly. "I have an idea. It would take some doing, but it's something I really want to try."

"What's your idea?"

"I want to start a seasonal yard service. I would go around to people's houses and do yard work for them. It would be a lot like what I did last summer, only I'd be getting paid for gardening."

"Not trying to rain on your parade or anything, but how are you going to haul your equipment around?" Dane asked.

"Ah, that's just the thing. I'll use the tools people have at their homes. I won't charge nearly as much as an actual landscaping service, of course. I guess if I need to get a lawnmower somewhere, then I'll think of a way. It can't be that hard.

"I've already done my research, Dane," Ari said, almost like she was trying to convince him of her idea. "There are only two landscaping services in the area: one in Rivers and one in Allendale. I don't think I'll have much competition, so this might actually work."

Dane smiled at her once more. "That's a great idea, Ari. I bet you'll get tons of business."

Ari beamed at the compliment, then looked at her phone. Several hours had somehow passed since they'd arrived at the Abshire house. "You think we should be getting back? We've been gone awhile…"

Dane got up and stretched. "Yeah, that's probably a good idea." He put his shirt back on and Ari got up and stretched, then started down the path.

Ari reached a turn on a steeper part of the path when suddenly something in the bushes rustled and darted away. She involuntarily yelped and skittered to the side, trying to avoid whatever it was that had been hiding in the undergrowth. Without warning the side of the trail started to crumble under her foot. Ari lost her balance and she felt her ankle roll to the side just as she began to fall. The world started to pitch and turn as searing pain ripped through her leg.

chapter seven

"Ari!" Dane yelled, and she felt a strong hand catch her jacket sleeve. She had come to a rest atop a fallen log that was soft with moss and vines. Her leg still burned with pain, but at least she had stopped falling. She was about nine feet down the bank, she figured, and Dane was above her, hanging onto a thin tree for support.

"Are you ok?" he asked, just as tears started to well in Ari's eyes. She blinked them away, trying to ignore the pain in her ankle.

"I just twisted my ankle pretty good. I'll be fine though," she lied. Dane got a better grip on her arm and started pulling her up the bank. With her good leg, she was able to dig in and start her way up the hill. Any pressure on her right leg, however, brought another stinging round of tears. *Do. Not. Cry.* was all she could think.

Dane pulled her back to the stable part of the trail. Ari sat on the path, taking deep breaths to banish the tears. Dane looked at her, concerned.

"What hurts?" he asked, watching her wipe at her eyes.

"My ankle. Just give me a few minutes, and I'm sure it will feel better. When the bank gave way, I felt the top of my foot touch the ground. That's never a good thing," she breathed in deep through her nose and held it, closing her eyes. She felt her leg, down to her ankle, and noticed it was starting to bruise.

"You need to get ice on that, Ari. Let me help you get up so we can get back home, ok?" Dane sounded worried but determined. Without her help, he slung her right arm around his shoulder and lifted her to a standing position. Ari tried to hop along, leaning heavily on Dane, but the combination of the downward slope and Dane's height made it nearly impossible.

"Let's try something different, Ari. I'm going to have to carry you down the trail."

"No way, Dane. I can do this. It's already feeling better," she winced, but took another deep breath and tried to continue. Dane stopped moving.

"Ari, stop."

He turned and held her by the shoulders. "It's ok to cry," he said quietly. Hearing him say that made Ari feel like she might really burst into tears at any second, but she desperately tried to keep a straight face.

"Please just let me give you a piggyback ride down the trail and we'll be to the canoe in just a few minutes, alright? If you keep trying to walk on your ankle, you could really hurt it worse than it already is."

Dane knelt down so she could get on his back. He stood up and started back down the trail, easily packing her on his back like she wasn't even there. He was careful not to let her foot brush up against anything on the trail as he descended.

Ari hung on, her arms draped around his neck. She rested her chin on his head and tried not to feel the burning sensation coming from her right leg. They continued down the trail until they emerged onto the pebbled shore.

Dane gently set her down and helped her get seated in the back of the canoe. Once he'd pushed off into the water, Ari started paddling, thankful that it was only her ankle that she'd hurt and nothing more. It was feeling slightly better, but pain still lingered.

"Ari, my dad was planning on picking up the canoe with his truck. Let's get a ride with him back up to our houses, ok?"

"Alright..." Ari was hesitant. Dane sensed her apprehension and looked over his shoulder at her.

"What's the matter?"

"Will your dad be mad that he has to take me home? I don't want to him to be upset at me...I know I'm not his favorite person."

Dane shook his head. "Ari, you've gotta believe me, he likes you. He just doesn't show it. My dad is gruff to *everyone* all the time. It's just how he is. Please don't take it personally, ok?"

The afternoon light was waning, and masses of bugs were hovering on the water's surface. They rounded the final bend, and the Abshire home came into view. Dane hopped out of the canoe and pulled it to shore. Ari stood up, gingerly putting a slight amount of weight on the injured foot. Pain wasn't shooting up to her knee anymore, but the bruise had spread and deepened in color.

Dane saw her standing and quickly came over and lifted her out of the wobbly canoe. She was grateful for his help, but embarrassed that she'd fallen in the first place. Once he put her on the ground he didn't let go. He was still holding her, closer than arm's reach. It wasn't a hug, exactly, but Ari looked up at his eyes, closer and longer than she had ever been allowed to before. It may have been just seconds, but the way he looked at her seared into her memory: his look of concern and the color sunlight in his jade-and-chocolate eyes and details about his face that somehow, she'd never noticed before.

"I should have been the first to go down the trail," he said, quietly, ducking his head low and clenching his jaw. She noticed how his dark, curling eyelashes were catching the sweat that had beaded on his forehead. He sighed in frustration. "I'm *so* sorry you got hurt, Ari." He said it like he was blaming himself.

Ari shook her head. "Dane, I'll be fine. It's just a twisted ankle."

His eyes held hers for a split second longer. In the distance, a sound made them both turn around. Dane's dad's old truck was turning off the highway onto the dirt lane. Dane stepped back but kept supporting Ari with one arm. Ari's apprehension rose, but she took a slow breath. *Nothing to be afraid of*, she reminded herself.

The truck pulled closer and came to a stop with dust swirling about in the late afternoon sun. Dane kept his arm around Ari's waist and opened the passenger door for her. After he'd helped her up, he and his dad loaded the canoe. Dane's dad got in, smelling faintly of sawdust and grease. Dane jogged over to the side of the Abshire house and grabbed Ari's bike and put it in the truck bed as well. He then hopped into the passenger side, leaving Ari awkwardly sitting in the middle.

The last time she'd been in this truck was the night she'd marched into a bar and demanded that his dad get home to help a very sick Dane. Where that assertion and courage had come from, Ari had no clue. Since then, she just couldn't shake the feeling that Mark, Dane's dad, had a strong feeling of dislike for her. If not dislike, then a strong annoyance, at least. Ari figured she had embarrassed his dad in front of his friends and coworkers and wasn't going to live that down anytime soon.

Ari scooted as far right as she could, to be out of the way of the gearshift and as far from Mark as possible. Dane put his arm along the top of the bench seat, which made it look like he had his arm around her. Whether he meant to or not, Ari's cheeks burned and she hoped his dad wouldn't notice.

The old truck bounced and creaked along the deeply-rutted dirt road. "Thanks for getting us, Dad." Dane's voice was barely audible over the jangling of the truck. "We've gotta get ice on Ari's ankle. She had a pretty spectacular fall."

Mark just nodded. "You're welcome, son," was all he said, in a voice that matched Dane's, only much rougher. He moved his toothpick from one side of his mouth to another. Something about Mark reminded Ari of an old-west cowboy, or maybe an old-west bad guy; she wasn't sure which.

Relief washed over her as they turned up Hadley Hill. The truck pulled over at Ari's house. Dane slid off the bench seat, and Ari followed, being caught by Dane before her foot could touch the ground. Again, she felt herself blushing from her neck up, but she resolutely tried to walk as normally as possible to the front steps of her house.

Ari grimaced as she thought about the upcoming week: she'd be starting the last term of school with a new schedule of classes and a twisted ankle.

*　　　*　　　*

As Ari alternated through two days' worth of classes, she was disappointed that Dane wasn't in a single one. Rivers Union High was a small school, and Ari almost always had at least one class with him. Being a year ahead of her, though, meant Dane usually only had electives with her. *I'll survive*, she thought to herself. At least she had Riley in history class, and Rob was in her P.E. class.

Rob had remembered her and had said hello to her on the first day. He was definitely one of the more popular people in school, being a part of the football team and friends with most of the junior class. It was odd for her to have someone who was considered popular talking to her. But, she thought Rob seemed kind, and it was nice to know at least one person in P.E.

Even lunch times were staggered; Dane was nowhere to be seen during Ari's scheduled lunch period. Thankfully, Amara and Riley shared the same lunch break with Ari. They were both waiting for her in the covered outdoor courtyard during lunch the first day. Spring break's sunny weather had dissolved back into a gauzy spring rain. Ari limped over to the circular table they were sitting at.

"Tell me again where you were when you fell off a trail?" Riley squinted her eyes at Ari, a smile playing on her lips. Ari had bandaged her ankle and was thankful the rainy weather allowed her to wear jeans that hid the supportive wrap, although her gimpy gait couldn't be masked as easily.

Ari just shook her head. "Dane and I were hiking in a wooded area behind Hadley Hill," she said, truthfully.

Amara smiled shyly. She had lovely brown curly hair which softly cascaded around her dimpled face, and she often wore exotic jewelry that dangled and made melodic bell-sounds. Amara exuded peace and kindness. Ari had immediately liked Amara when she first met her. Where Riley could be bold and sassy, Amara had a gentle and quiet spirit about her that was hard to duplicate.

"Riley told me that Dane was literally the first person you met upon moving to Rivers," Amara said. "Everybody is wondering if you guys are a couple," she added quietly, so people at nearby tables wouldn't hear.

Ari just shrugged. "He's one of my best friends. I can't imagine not having him around," she said simply.

"Ari, if he asked you to be his girlfriend right now, what would you say?" Riley asked.

Immediately, Ari thought *yes, of course*. But then she hesitated. "Yes, but…I wouldn't want to change our friendship. I don't know," she shook her head. "Riley, that's a complicated question. I've never had a boyfriend, just crushes…this is way out of my area of expertise," Ari chuckled.

"What if he decided to go out with someone else, that wasn't you?" Amara asked gently, genuinely curious.

Ari felt a strange twinge in her stomach. "Nope. No way," she said, without hesitation. "Ugh, that's a terrible thought." She was so used to having Dane's complete attention. Thinking of him being with another girl made her shudder. "When you put it that way, Amara, it makes it easy to answer," Ari confessed.

"Well, there ya go," Riley smiled.

*　　　*　　　*

On Wednesday night, Ari found herself once again at the wheel of her mom's car. This time, they were starting from Ari's home. Butterflies filled her stomach as she crossed the railroad tracks and stopped at the country highway. Ari started out into the empty road. As usual, the road was quiet and lacking traffic.

As she turned onto the highway, Ari's eyes kept darting from the road to the speedometer. She was also focusing on keeping the car centered on the road. Her mom glanced over and saw her gripping the wheel.

"Honey, it's ok to relax," her mom said gently. Ari loosened her grip a little. "You're doing fantastic. Would it help if we had the radio on?" she asked. Ari nodded, thankful that her mom was sympathetic to her apprehension at the whole learning-to-drive thing. Familiar tunes came on and Ari felt herself relax a little. The sky was dark and threatening rain.

Ding. From her purse, Ari's phone indicated a text message had arrived. She ignored it, but then a succession of dings suggested she'd been a part of a group text.

"Want me to read it for you?" her mom offered.

Ari shrugged. "Sure."

Her mom fished around in Ari's bag. Bright light from the screen filled the car. "Alright," Ari's mom started reading, "Riley says, 'Jace will be photographing the old Allendale AFS on Saturday night. Does anyone want to go to explore with us? We'll be leaving at 6 p.m.' Looks like Julia and Rob have responded that they are going, but Amara can't. Want me to reply for you?"

"What's the Allendale AFS?"

"Well," Ari's mom, "I believe it's an Air Force station left over from the Cold War. It was a radar relay base during the 60's. It's been left to deteriorate and the property has been abandoned. I know the newspaper did an article about it a few months ago, how the city of Allendale wants the government to release the property to the city so they can develop it into useable space."

Ari thought for a moment. "Count me in. Also mention that I'll ask Dane if he wants to join, if that's ok."

Her mom started clicking away. "Ok, message sent. But, Ari," her mom's voice took on a typical concerned-mom tone, "aren't you worried about getting caught trespassing?"

Ari shrugged. "Not really. We're not there to vandalize. Jace is trying to take photos to preserve the history. I guess if we got caught, we'd just have to explain what we were doing."

Her mom nodded. Ari's phone dinged one more time. "Riley says, 'sounds good, hope he can come,' with a kissy-face symbol." Her mom giggled. "Is that about Dane, I'm guessing?"

Ari blushed hot and rolled her eyes. "Uhhm, I'm sure it is," she downplayed. "Everybody thinks we're a couple. But he's my best friend, *you* know that," she emphasized. Ari could see her mom nodding and a slight smile playing on her face. Still, Ari couldn't wait to get out of the car and get some fresh air.

*   *   *

The path to the underground room was dotted with crocuses. Ari hadn't noticed them before; they were peeking their heads out of the winter detritus that had formed a leafy crust over the ground. She shifted her heavy backpack to the other shoulder as she knelt down at the brass circle.

Weak candlelight greeted her as she opened the hatch. Dane was already in the small subterranean room, lying on the floor with his head propped up on a beanbag chair.

"Hey," he looked up at Ari, his eyes glinting in the wavering light. She recognized the weathered book Dane held in his hands: Ezra's journal.

"Have you learned anything new?" Ari pulled out homework from her bag and leaned up against the beanbag so she could see the journal over Dane's head. Elaborate cursive swirls filled the ivory pages.

"Well, I definitely get a sense of what life was like for Ezra: hard." Dane mused quietly. "Their dad is really sick, and they're coming right up on their busy season. Listen to this: 'Father is no better than he was last week. His neck is now disfigured and looks so different that Aliza is afraid to enter his room. Dr. Blackwell was called at once this morning and thoroughly examined Father and took notes. The doctor promised to investigate Father's symptoms, as they were unfamiliar to him.'" Dane's warm voice filled the small room. "He will get back to us as soon as he can, hopefully with answers."

Dane stopped for a moment and continued to read silently to himself, but Ari protested. "You can't stop reading there! Keep going…please."

Dane tilted his head up and looked behind him, smiling at Ari. "It's kind of fascinating, isn't it? We may be the first people to read this journal since it was written, you know?" He cleared his throat and kept going. "June 27th: The family of John Rainwater has been more than gracious in helping us during Father's illness; Louis has been swathing the ryegrass with Joseph and I, and Elmore took it upon himself to help me milk the cows and tend to the other livestock. Unfortunately, Mother has lost all of her piano students. People are afraid that Father's illness is catching.'"

"That's terrible. Even Katia?"

Dane silently read on for a few minutes. "Wait—maybe not." Moments passed as Dane scanned further ahead. "'Katia, however, still attends her weekly piano lessons. Whether or not her mother knows she is still attending, I am not sure. Katia is headstrong enough that she would probably come whether or not her mother wished it.'"

Ari raised an eyebrow. "She sounds like a rebel. I'm starting to like this girl."

Dane nodded and read: "'Katia mentioned the other day that she would rather take piano lessons than continue ballet, so it does not surprise me that she still arrives for her lessons.'"

Ari's eyes widened. "Ballet?"

Dane tilted his head up once again, making eye contact, albeit upside-down. "I wonder if she knew Nadia?"

*   *   *

The rest of the week crawled along while Ari anticipated Saturday night. She'd spent the whole week planning on what equipment to bring, and once Saturday night arrived, she'd settled on two small flashlights, her phone, a notebook, and a waterproof jacket. Ari was wearing her leather boots plus a fleece jacket and scarf. The weather had been less than appealing, with a cool, soaking drizzle continuing non-stop, but thankfully Saturday had stayed dry. Ari wondered how Jace was going to get good exterior shots if the rain continued.

Jace had planned to pick up Ari and Dane from her house. Dane met Ari on her front porch, looking ready for whatever the night might throw at them. Over his mussed hair was a knit beanie. Wearing that hat always made him look older somehow, Ari thought. It emphasized his strong nose and jaw, and paired with the olive green field jacket he was wearing, he looked nothing short of intimidating.

"Ready?" Dane said, with a glint of excitement in his voice. Something about his energy was electric, and Ari couldn't help but grin.

"You really dig this whole abandoned exploring thing, don't you?"

"Yeah, I kinda do. I like going places that have forgotten history." Dane motioned at Ari's pack. "Are you ready for tonight?"

"Ready as I'll ever be. What did you bring in your backpack?"

"Just some snacks and a sweatshirt. Is your ankle better?"

Ari nodded. "Completely fine. Well, the bruise is still healing, but it's fine to walk on."

An unfamiliar minivan rounded the corner. It was going slowly, as if the driver wasn't sure where to go. Finally, it pulled into Ari's half-circle driveway.

The sliding side door opened. Riley waved from inside, and Ari and Dane climbed in. Jace, the driver, greeted Ari and Dane, and Rob and Julia nodded hello. The seat farthest in the back was the only spot left. Ari chose the window seat behind Rob, and instead of taking the other window seat, Dane chose the middle seat, right next to Ari. She smiled as he buckled in next to her.

"I've never been up Hadley Lane," Jace commented as he turned the van around and headed back down the hill. "I've always seen the driveway for it, but never had a reason to come up. Is it just your two houses?"

Dane nodded. "Yep, just our two houses. The property used to belong to my great-great grandma and grandpa. My house was the servant's quarters, and Ari's house was the main home. Last summer Ari and I did a lot of research to piece together the history."

"That is *so* cool," Julia said, turning around and smiling at Dane. Julia's blonde hair cascaded down her back in wavy curls, and tonight, with high-heeled boots and a leather jacket, she looked more like a model than any high schooler Ari had ever seen. The whole van smelled like whatever scent Julia was wearing. For a split second, Ari wished she had a fraction of Julia's sophistication, and Ari cursed herself for not having dressed up just a little more.

"Have you ever photographed your home, Dane?" Julia asked. "If not, you totally should. It would be a great way to add to your history research by capturing what it looks like right now."

"That's probably something we should do this summer, huh, Ari? It would be a fun project." Ari nodded, and Dane wrapped his arm around her, and this time, Ari knew it was completely intentional. His tall build and broad shoulders nearly engulfed her slight frame. An excited shiver ran through Ari, and she could feel her cheeks getting warm again. Julia looked like she was going to ask Dane something else, but decided against it and looked away.

Dane lowered his voice and tilted his head so he spoke right into Ari's ear. She felt his faintly-prickled chin brush against her cheek. "After reading in the journal the other night, I was determined to find out if Katia knew the Hadleys. I went back and looked through all my family photos."

"Did you find out anything more about her?"

A look of sly satisfaction crossed Dane's face. "I sure did."

chapter eight

From his backpack, Dane pulled out a black-and-white photo that was familiar to Ari. It was of Nadia's two daughters, dated 1925. He then pulled out the hand-colored photograph that had fallen from the journal.

One of the girls had the same mischievous smile, with a slight upturn at one side. Ari grinned excitedly.

"It's *her!*" She pointed at one of the girls in the photo.

"Katia," Dane confirmed. "I knew I'd seen her face before. Turns out she didn't just know the Hadleys, she *was* a Hadley."

Ari smiled and shook her head in amazement. "That's incredible, Dane. Now we know there's a connection between your family and the Abshires! Did you read any more from Ezra's journal?"

"Just one entry. I'm saving it mostly for when you're around." A small smile crept across his face, but then disappeared. "Things have gotten worse for his dad. He's so weak he has trouble standing. Ezra's mom has to help him walk to the bathroom. The doctor called it something like 'glandular fever.' Ezra and his family are stretched to the breaking point, Ari." Dane stopped and, for the first time that Ari could remember, Dane seemed to struggle with his words and thoughts. Quietly, he looked out the van window. "There's no fallback plan if something else goes wrong."

Ari then noticed Julia glancing back at them as Dane talked. Ari hoped Julia wouldn't ask what they were so quietly conversing about.

Ari settled back under Dane's arm, looking at the passing scenery. He was completely lost in thought. She waited for him to elaborate on what he read, but Dane remained silent.

Ari suddenly realized she didn't recognize at all where they were. They had long ago left city limits and were heading toward Allendale. The highway was somewhat empty as the minivan entered the lonely twenty-five mile drive to the next town. Ari had never been to Allendale; she'd heard of it several times, but had never made the trek to actually see what was there.

On the way over, Ari listened as the others discussed photographic strategy in what would be a mostly-dark area. Jace was instructing others in the group that if they were to take photos, they would have to refrain from using a flash in any rooms with windows. "That goes for flashlights, too, guys. If someone on the outside sees any light on the inside, we're toast," he said.

Then Ari's mind replayed her mom's concerned question: *what if you get caught trespassing?* Ari shook her head. *Can't think like that,* she chided herself. *Not going to get caught.* Her mind doubled-back and suddenly she found herself starting to mull over a game plan in case they really did get caught. The feeling of warm breath and Dane's lips, only a fraction away from her ear, nearly startled her out of her seat.

"What's wrong?" he discreetly whispered in her ear so the others couldn't hear. "You look really worried." He was *so,* so close. So close that she couldn't even fully turn her head to look at him. She could still feel his breath on her face when she finally turned and whispered back.

"What if we get caught?"

Dane shrugged. "Hey Jace," he called, "What's the plan if we get caught? Have you ever had to deal with the police?"

"Yeah, once." Jace nodded. "I was at the old woolen mill in Woodward. I was getting some fantastic shots in the afternoon light, and a sheriff drove by. I explained what I was doing, showed him some of my photos, and after that he just said that I'd have to leave. As long as you're respectful and honest…" he trailed off. "I don't think it will be a problem. This is my first government facility, though. Not sure what to expect in terms of security."

Dane turned to Ari. "We'll be fine," he smiled, with excitement in his voice.

Ari took a few deep breaths and looked out the window at fields skimming by, punctuated by stands of trees. Her stomach felt acutely nervous, but she didn't know if it had to do with their adventure, or because Dane had his arm around her.

She tried displacing her fears by concentrating on scenery she'd never seen before: the countryside was beautiful in April, although she lamented the soggy weather. At least it was dry for now. High clouds indicated rain would likely hold off for their entire trip.

They arrived in Allendale, and Jace navigated through like he was familiar with Allendale. The town was much larger than Rivers, but Jace kept driving until the buildings and houses thinned to nothing. A lone road began a swooping ascent, lifting them up a hill, off the valley floor.

In the waning grayness of the clouded evening they drove through thick conifers, still winding their way up a road with no homes, driveways, or other signs of life. Near the top of the hill stood a single chain-link gate, six feet high and topped with outfacing barbed wire. A white sign with black-painted words that once suggested "No Trespassing" had faded, barely surviving the words that had been painted in red: "U.S. Government Property." Instead of stopping, Jace kept driving along the winding road.

"Where do we park?" Riley asked, and for once, Ari thought she sounded apprehensive.

"Well, I've got a pretty good idea of the layout by looking at satellite photos. There's a side road tucked in behind this stand of trees, which follows the perimeter. I've seen photos of the southeast corner of the fence and it looks like a section of chainlink has been pulled back. Let's park the van and try to get in there."

Jace pulled off the main street and onto a narrow gravel road. There was just enough of a bump-out on one side to park the van. Once stopped, everyone piled out the driver's side of the van. There was still enough daylight to see without flashlights, and the group followed the line of conifers. Ari had to walk at a brisk jog to keep up with the group: she was the shortest of them all by far, and Jace and Riley were hustling to find the entrance. Despite her mile-high heeled boots, Julia loped along with ease, and Rob had no trouble keeping up. None of them wanted to be in plain sight for long. A creeping whisper of paranoia tickled at Ari: *are we being watched?*

Dane looked over his shoulder and noticed Ari was lagging behind. He reached back and grabbed her hand, pulling her up to him. It wasn't such an unusual thing for one of them to grab hold of the other by the hand, but even so, Ari felt her whole arm tingle, and she momentarily forgot about the overwhelming feeling of eyes on them.

A gap in the tree foliage pointed them to the area where the chain link had been cut and peeled back. The opening was only about three and a half feet high, but it would have to do. Ari was suddenly thankful she was the smallest of all of them; she reluctantly let go of Dane and went first, slipping through without even getting her jeans muddy. The rest of the group had to shimmy through sideways, or, in Rob's case, peel the fence back even more. Jace gave him a hand and pulled him through.

They had come out the other side onto a large field. Surprisingly, the remnants of an old baseball diamond was directly in front of them. Across the field was a massive windowless concrete building. Several smaller normal-looking buildings dotted the area around the large, looming square.

"Guys, let's tackle the big building first. That's where the magic happened," Jace chuckled.

"Can you give us some background?" Rob asked. "I didn't look this place up before we came."

"This was a Cold War-era air defense station. Many smaller radar stations all over the coast reported to this one, and they'd process the data using a giant computer—which, at the time, was a revolutionary technology. They were watching for incoming air attacks by the Soviet Union. I'm not sure what we'll see inside, to be honest...if we even can get inside."

"Wait," Julia said. "*If* we can get inside?"

"Yeah," Jace said. "I have no idea if we can get inside. We won't know 'till we go, right?"

Ari thought she heard Julia mutter something under her breath. They were getting close to the concrete building. The closer they got, the more Ari realized just how huge the building was. Without windows, it was hard to tell, but she guessed it was at least four stories high. A subtle checkerboard pattern was etched into the concrete walls, which served as its one and only decorative feature. Ari had never seen anything like it in her life.

They crossed a cracked-pavement parking lot to a set of metal stairs. Windowless double doors greeted them. Rob tried them both. *Locked.*

Julia grunted. "Wait," Jace said. "There are still more entrances. Hundreds of people worked in these buildings. They had to have more than one entrance." He led the way and the group made a long walk around the side of the building. They paused as Jace snapped off a few photos. Dane leaned over to Ari's ear.

"This building is at least a whole city block long. It's going to take forever to check out the entire interior…"

Another worry ticked off in her mind. Ari remembered she had to be home by 11 p.m, granted they all didn't get thrown in jail for trespassing. Dane saw a shadow of concern cross over her face once again.

"You've got that look again, Ari. What's wrong?" he whispered, taking her hand once again. At that, she smiled.

"This is just totally out of my comfort zone, you know?" They had circled around to the backside of the building, where more stairs led to an identical set of doors. Riley tried the right-hand door. Locked. The left door, however, creaked open when she tried it. It must've been unusually heavy, as Riley braced herself to pull it all the way open. A ripple of excitement went through the group. They were in.

chapter nine

Everyone huddled inside the door as it slammed shut. They were plunged into an immediate, heavy darkness. A shock of panic gripped Ari. Someone else gasped. Ari hadn't been expecting such darkness…in fact, she really didn't know *what* she had been expecting. What she could smell was dank air that had hints of stale cigarette smoke. The darkness lasted for moments too long, and she found herself clutching for Dane's field jacket. Her brain registered that she *had* been holding his hand, then let go of him at the sound of the slamming door. She could feel her heartbeat ramping up to an unimaginable pace. After a terrifying moment, Ari finally found his arm, and she could tell by his scent that she'd grabbed the right person. Dane quickly put his arm around her and pulled her in. She sighed in relief, the panic subsiding. She hoped Dane didn't notice her hands starting to shake. Jace turned on his flashlight just as Julia and Riley both turned their cell phone screens on for light.

"There are no exterior windows anywhere in this building, so we're fine to use flashlights and our camera flashes," Jace said. His tone changed to a serious note as he continued: "So…we really need to stay together in here, guys," he stressed. "There are about three acres of floor space in this building. If we get separated, it might be really hard to get everyone back together. Your cell phones will *not* work in here."

"How is that possible?" Rob asked.

"The walls are super thick concrete," Dane said. "They probably built this like a bomb shelter."

Jace nodded, his face looking strange in the minimal light. "Right. So, nobody get lost, 'k?"

For the first time, Ari noticed where they were standing: a long hallway seemed to stretch out in both directions into dark nothingness, but directly in front of them, frosted wire-mesh glass windows stretched the length of the building. "What's in that room?" Ari whispered.

Jace tried the double doors. It was locked. "Shoot. I really wanted to get in here. This would've likely been where the giant computer was…or maybe still is. If you guys see any more doors to this room, let me know. The computer would've filled this entire floor."

Beams of light from phones and flashlights slowly scanned the area while the group stayed in tight proximity. Ari noticed it seemed unnaturally cold inside the concrete building. Paint chips littered the composition tile floor, and they crackled and crunched with each step. Julia's heels clacked along the ground with unsettling volume. She moved behind the group and waved her phone at the wall.

"Guys, here's an elevator. Think it works?" she smirked, about to push the "up" button.

"Julia, wait! Don't push it," Jace darted to interfere. "We don't know if there's electricity in the building or not. Don't try and turn anything on, ok?"

"*Sorry*," Julia pursed her lips and moved a few yards over. A heavy door with a small vertical window was labeled with a hand-painted sign that spelled STAIRS.

"Anybody want to try the second floor?" she asked.

The group shuffled through a fire door that led to concrete steps. Barely-visible yellow and black caution stripes had once delineated each stair, but was now worn off to the point of uselessness. Ari counted as they climbed: one, two, three flights of stairs before they arrived at the next landing. Another heavy fire door with a huge painted "2" announced their arrival at the next floor.

Dane went first, followed by Ari and the rest of the group. She was growing slightly more comfortable in the dark, but there was an eerie heaviness about the building. Once everyone was out of the stairwell, Ari realized what was bothering her: the complete and utter silence of the building was unnerving. The unimaginably thick walls, built to withstand the force of an explosion, consumed all sounds and vibrations and returned a void that was literally palpable.

The group moved as one down the hallway. There were a few doors along the main hallway, spur hallways, and rooms that had no entry doors but instead seemed like pass-through areas. They had been moving in a straight line, but Rob tried a door and found it to be unlocked. "Let's check out this room," he said, heading in without the group.

"Wait, Rob," Dane called into the darkened room that Rob had been swallowed by. "Don't go too far away from the group. One of us should hold the door so it doesn't lock behind us," he said.

"I'll do it," Ari volunteered.

"I'll stay with you," Dane offered.

The room Rob had gone into seemed vast, like it may have been nearly as wide as the building itself. Dinner plate-sized holes were punched through the floor in a methodical pattern. Riley shined her flashlight down one. "Guys, be really careful not to step in these holes," she said, inspecting it. "I don't see a bottom to these—they just go straight down. Jace, what the heck is this room for?"

Jace had been taking photos of a wall filled with electrical panels. Masses of broken-off, colored wire spewed from the wall and Jace was careful to avoid it.

"I think this room had to do with communications, and it probably had computer stations where each one of those holes are," he mused. "I believe the holes were part of the cooling system, to keep the electronics from getting too hot."

Ari could barely hear the conversation happening across the room from her. A sudden thought shivered through her. "Dane, what if someone else is in the building? What if we're not alone?"

Dane was standing in the door frame directly across from her. "What makes you think we're not alone?"

Ari trembled, partially from the bone-numbing chill inside the building. "I'm just saying, this building is so large, there could be other people in here and we'd never know."

The group was coming back to the door. "Let's keep going up," Rob said, and they headed back in the direction of the stairwell.

Once on the third floor, they noticed the layout was dramatically different from the second floor. The first door they came to opened and they spilled into a smallish room. Ari was concentrating on trying to avoid stepping in the same floor-holes they'd encountered in the other room. She was so focused on the holes, she didn't see what was right in front of her.

"Ari!! Watch out!" Rob leapt at Ari and grabbed her by the backpack, pulling her swiftly back. Ari was startled to find herself in Rob's grasp. The rest of the team ran over to them.

Ari stared agape at the sight in front of her. Her toes were inches from a vast cutoff in the floor.

"You could've fallen down there…" Rob and the rest of the group pointed flashlights at the three-sided ledge that ran nearly the length of the room. The drop over the ledge was a full story down. On the other side of the dropoff, a movie-theater style screen covered two stories of height and was flanked by giant, hand written list-boards with names of military bases on them.

"What the heck is this place?" Dane asked Jace, a tinge of irritation in his voice. "Why is there a dropoff in the middle of the room?" Julia put a hand on Dane's shoulder, as if to calm him down.

"I'll have to do some more research, but I think it was called the Blue Room," Jace said quietly. "I've read that these rooms were only lit by blue lights. It had something to do with the radar screens they used. Look at the outlines and holes on the floor." He paused to take a picture. "It looks like when this room was in use, there was a solid bank of radar screens along this edge. They must've been using the giant movie screen along with their radar stations. This is where, if an attack happened, air support would be coordinated. This room probably isn't very safe for us to explore with a dropoff like that."

At that, Dane made a soft snorting noise. Jace sounded apologetic.

"Maybe it would be better if we checked out another part of the building."

Dane shook Julia off and and strode over to Ari. He shadowed her as they left the room and turned into the dark hallway. Riley was leading the group when she paused at a door that looked unlike any door they'd come across: instead of a doorknob, it had an odd latch. Riley turned the latch and found the door slid open instead of swinging open. It disappeared into a pocket in the wall. Riley and Julia went through the doorway, and Julia's boots could be heard on a metallic surface. "Cool!" Riley's voice was barely heard from the hallway. Jace hurried to catch up, followed by Ari and Dane.

The group climbed another set of stairs, only this time, they were corrugated metal steps. The group was so close together on the steps that Ari didn't notice three stories of empty space—save more metal staircases—below them. They all arrived on a very small landing, and with their flashlights, they could see they were now on the other side of the tall list-boards, which were semi-transparent.

"So I'm guessing the lists were changed out by a person who stood here, and since the boards are kind of transparent, they either hand-wrote the information or had signs ready to put on the boards," Jace said. Ari noticed more severed wires splaying out from a hole in the wall they were next to, and shifted away from them.

"Let's keep going up," Julia suggested. Clanking up the steps, they all went one more flight until the stairs ended at a small square opening in the wall. "Where do you think this goes?" Riley asked. There wasn't nearly enough room for a person to walk through the opening, so one by one, they dropped to their knees and shimmied through. Once again Rob had the most difficulty fitting.

Second to last, Ari finally saw what was on the other side of the opening: a narrow catwalk that passed high above the Blue Room. Drop ceiling tiles were made of metal mesh that allowed air and light through, and when Jace and Rob shined their flashlights down, she could see exactly how far down one would fall if they had a misstep on the catwalk.

"Uh, guys, where does the catwalk end?" Ari called ahead.

Julia, who had already crawled to the other end of the catwalk, yelled that she was at a ladder that descended back down into the Blue Room.

Ari's breathing quickened. She could feel her hands start to tremble. This exploration trip had already taken her so far out of her comfort zone, and now she faced a three story-high catwalk. One fall would take her through the drop ceiling and down to the lowest floor of the Blue Room.

She didn't know that Dane was still behind her; she was only aware that the rest of the group was getting farther away, and she couldn't bring herself to even inch out onto the corrugated catwalk. Ari could hear Riley calling for her from down in the Blue Room; everyone had already descended the ladder. She could see their phones and flashlights moving eerily below the mesh ceiling. She was rendered motionless by acute fear.

"Hey," Dane whispered from behind, causing her heart to skip. "You don't have to do this. We can just go back down and meet them in the Blue Room."

"No, we have to stay together, that's the rule," Ari said, her voice feigning resolve. As frightened of the catwalk as she was, she was even more terrified of becoming separated and lost in the belly of the monstrous concrete building.

Ari closed her eyes and took a slow breath. More than just her hands were shaking now.

"Seriously, Ari, I don't want you to do this. It's too dangerous," Dane's voice was steel, just like it was when he used to talk about his Aunt Rhoda. Ari winced at his doubt in her.

One.

Two.

Three.

Ari started crawling out onto the catwalk, cringing in pain from the sharp corrugation on the metal surface. Three crawling steps out, she looked over the side of the catwalk. Below was the mesh drop ceiling, and below that, an open space two stories down. Her hands trembled and she paused for a moment, convincing herself that if everybody else could do it, so could she.

"Ari, don't look down. Just keep going, you're doing fine," Dane whispered from behind. Ari drew in a deep breath and focused on what was ahead. She saw the ladder getting closer with each crawling step. She felt Dane scrambling behind her, trying to keep up with her motivated pace. Her knees and hands were burning from crawling across the serrated metal, but with each crawling step, the hatch that would empty her out onto the ladder got closer and closer.

She felt a wave of relief wash over her after descending the ladder. Once her boots landed on the floor, she also felt an overwhelming sense of accomplishment. She'd pushed herself to do something that had *really* scared her.

The rest of the group waited for Dane to emerge. Once he'd descended, the group headed back into the hallway, avoiding the dropoff ledge.

Once in the hallway, Jace started adjusting his camera lens and flashlight, trying to get a shot of the Blue Room from the outside. Ari overheard Julia whispering to Dane if everything had been okay on the catwalk. Ari strained to hear their conversation, but a sudden noise down the hallway caused everyone to point their lights in the general direction of the sound.

Riley looked at Jace as if to say *did you hear that?* Julia and Dane stopped talking mid-sentence. Ari found herself silently moving closer to the group. They waited.

Another sound. This time, it was absolute. There was a dragging sound, like something being pulled along the floor. It sounded like it was no farther than two rooms down. Julia stifled a scream, Riley gasped, all as Jace whisper-yelled, "Let's *go!!*"

chapter ten

They turned and madly pointed their flashlights at walls, trying to locate the stairwell exit. Dane saw it first and motioned to the rest of the group to follow him. He took off at a jog, encircled Ari around the waist and practically dragged her to the exit before the rest of the group even had a chance to catch up. She had to clutch at his arm to keep herself from stumbling in the intermittent blackness.

Dane flung open the fire door and Ari flattened herself against the handrail as the others in the group flew past her. She was frozen in place and wildly gasping for breath. Dane saw her struggling, and once again grabbed her by the waist and propelled her down the stairs. Ari glanced back at the fire door, hoping someone wasn't following them.

Crashing down the stairs, the group of six rocketed out of the stairwell onto the ground floor, made a sharp turn, and burst through the exit door into the cold night. On the outside stairs, Riley crouched on her knees to catch her breath, but Rob pulled on her arm and urged her to keep running. "C'mon, Riley, we're almost there!" Jace insisted. The baseball field was now pitch-black dark in the starless night, but Dane and Jace pointed flashlights at the direction of the cut-out chain link hole.

Even in heels, Julia ran like a track star, taking long, flying strides, nearly matching Rob's sprint. Jace's big camera bounced on his neck and he tried to hold it still while pointing the flashlight, and Riley and Dane brought up the rear. Ari struggled to match the speed of the rest of the group. She found herself pushing beyond the fiery sideache that was slowing her down, but even so, her short legs just couldn't match up with the lightning speed of the rest of the group. Dane looked to over his shoulder and realized Ari wasn't next to him.

"Come on!" he yelled, slowing his pace so he could grab her hand. They were quickly approaching the peeled-back fence, and Dane nearly threw her through the opening. The group continued their sprint to the van. Everyone piled in, and Dane leaped to the window seat of the middle row. Ari landed in the seat right next to him without even thinking about it. She was still shaking from the adrenaline rush. Only when they were driving away down the winding forested road did Ari feel like she could breathe again.

"Oh my gosh, guys, what the heck?" Riley panted. "What was that noise?"

"It sounded like something shuffling along the floor, or being dragged…maybe it was footsteps, I dunno," Rob said, wiping sweat from his head.

"Was it a person? Or an animal?" Dane asked.

"I knew there was something in there with us," Ari said quietly.

Riley looked over her shoulder and gave Ari a wide-eyed stare.

"Guys, that was a totally awesome, crazy adventure!" Julia said, chuckling. "We've gotta find more abandoned places to explore." The rest of the group nervously chuckled, and Ari just shook her head, wishing she could be just a little bit braver..

It *had* been fun—punctuated by moments of sheer terror. A quick chill ran through her, and Dane took off his warm field jacket and wrapped it around her. Grateful, she put it on. She noticed the smell of the stale, dank air still clung to her own hair and clothes, bringing an immediate reminder of being inside the concrete building. Ari closed her eyes, exhausted from their crazy, thrilling, terrifying adventure. Somewhere between Allendale and Rivers she dozed off.

The cessation of movement caused Ari to open her eyes. She was surprised to find herself with her head on Dane's chest, his arm around her shoulders. She had sunk down into his side, enveloped by his warmth. She moved ever-so-slightly and looked up at his Dane's face. He was asleep as well, his head resting on the van's window. She stared at him for a moment before nudging him awake.

"Hey, we're home," she said quietly. Jace asked Dane if he wanted to be driven up to his house, but Dane thanked him and got out with Ari. The van disappeared down Hadley Lane, bumping along water-filled potholes. "Do you want me to walk you home?" Ari asked Dane.

Dane shook his head and chuckled. "Nah, I'll be ok." Ari started toward her front porch, but Dane reached out and caught her arm.

"Hey, wait," he said, hesitating. Ari turned to face him. "On the catwalk, I didn't mean to make it sound like I didn't believe you could make it across," he said, trying to pick his words carefully. He took a deep breath and closed his eyes for a moment. "I was trying to keep you safe, Ari. I know how much heights scare you. I didn't want you getting hurt again, like in the woods last week. Once again, you're braver than I could imagine." Dane smiled his beautiful, million-watt grin.

Ari could see he was being honest. A misty drizzle had started, coating everything in a sheer dampness. Little droplets of water glinted off his eyelashes as he stood there, eyes smiling. He started to say something else, but the porch light came on at Ari's house. Dane nodded at her and said goodnight, heading up the driveway to his home. Ari watched him walk up the road and disappear into the darkness.

*   *   *

The next day, the padlock on Ari's paint-chipped locker popped open. She was between classes; depositing her books and grabbing her freshly-washed P.E. uniform usually only took a matter of seconds. Today, however, a squarely folded piece of paper was laying on top of her uniform.

Ari was written on the top of the note, in guy's handwriting. Ari blushed, hoping it was from Dane. But…she was very familiar with Dane's neat, all-caps handwriting. This handwriting wasn't like that. She unfolded the paper. In the same handwriting was scribed two sentences:

"Ari, I'd like to get to know you better. I think you're beautiful." In place of a signature, there was just a dash, and a heart.

Ari just stood there, unsure of what to think. Who on earth would write an unsigned note to her? She shook her head, then re-read the note. When the warning bell sounded she stuffed it in her jeans pocket and rushed off to class. In passing, she saw Riley, and she sidled up to her.

"Can we go dress shopping after school?" Ari asked breathlessly. "There's something I've gotta tell you."

"He finally asked you to go to the Last Dance!" Riley smiled and gave her a little punch on the arm.

"Who? Nobody asked me to the dance," Ari answered, confused.

Riley looked utterly surprised. "Sure, I can go. Meet at our bikes after school?

Ari nodded.

*   *   *

Ari's shoes were getting soaked as she pedaled her bike alongside Riley's. The spring rain had once again coated the roads, and water fanned up from their bike tires. It didn't seem to matter that both their beach cruisers had ample fenders; Riley's jeans were soaked halfway up her calves. They were heading to a row of boutique shops along the main road in downtown Rivers.

"The Last Dance is a little more casual than the winter formal, because the dance is held at Ansley Park, in the garden courtyard. Most girls ditch the long formal gowns for something shorter and better suited for dancing outside," Riley said, as they cruised along the roadway. They hopped off their bikes and locked them up outside a shop called Elm Lane.

"Before we go in, what was it you wanted to tell me?" Riley asked, clicking her padlock. Ari dug into her jeans pocket, and handed Riley the note.

"I found this in my locker today. What do you make of it?"

After a few seconds, Riley chuckled and handed the note back.

"You have a real, honest-to-goodness secret admirer," Riley said, shaking her head. "Do you have any theories? Who would've slipped it in your locker?"

"I have no idea. I know it's definitely not Dane. That's not his handwriting at all."

"Hey, speaking of Dane," Riley asked, "he hasn't asked you to the dance yet?"

Ari shook her head *no*. "Why?"

Riley wrinkled her nose, like she was trying to decide what to say— or how to say it. "Amara told me during chemistry that Julia was upset after lunch today. I guess Julia asked Dane if he'd go to the dance with her. He said no because he had already asked someone else." Riley looked quite uncomfortable. "Sorry, Ari, I just assumed it was you."

Ari felt a weird tingle in her stomach, but it was quite the opposite of the nervous butterflies she usually got. She quickly took a deep breath and tried to look unaffected in front of Riley.

"*Julia* asked Dane? Like, Julia, Rob's cousin? The one we went to the Allendale with?"

Riley looked regretful. "Yeah, that Julia. I'm *really* sorry, Ari. I guess that's why she was asking if you guys were a couple the first time we all went out together. I didn't put two and two together at the time, but now that I look back on it, maybe I did see her flirt with him during our adventures."

Ari fought back the stinging pain in her throat. She refused to let Riley see her cry over something like this, so she quickly looked up and regrouped her thoughts. "Hey, let's go look for a dress for you." She took Riley by the arm and opened the heavy glass door by its enormous brass handles.

"Wait—" Riley stopped her. "Are you sure you're okay to do this? We really do *not* have to go dress shopping right now."

Ari smiled at Riley's thoughtfulness. "I'm fine, Riley. I want to do this," Ari insisted.

The historic shops were the most beautiful in all of Rivers; most had vintage light fixtures and flooring. Some even had the original heavy moulding around doors and windows that were adorned with carved flourishes. In Elm Lane, giant bowl lights hung down from a ceiling festooned with ornate tin tiles. Black and white checkerboard floors reached all the way back in the narrow building. Ari almost forgot her feelings of sadness and disappointment as she stepped into the shop.

Riley began browsing the racks of dresses that lined the old brick walls. The juxtaposition of stunning new clothes against the vintage details of the building made for a beautiful store. Ari couldn't help but look at dresses, though she figured she wouldn't need one. It was impossible to resist browsing through the airy chiffons and delicate laces of the formal frocks.

An armful of dresses headed with Riley to a changing room. The first gown she tried was off-the- shoulder and black. Ari shook her head. "Too formal," she said. Riley nodded in agreement and returned back to the dressing room.

While Riley was changing Ari browsed some more. A simple white lace-and-eyelet dress caught Ari's eye. She shrugged and headed to the changing room herself.

Inside, a crystal chandelier lit the room with a mirrored glow. Ari tried the dress on, and it fit like it had been made for her. It was strapless, with little white embroidered floral details around the bodice, then it flared into a lace and eyelet skirt that had just a bit of flow to it. It was short enough that it felt casual, yet elegant. She'd never felt confident in a dress before, but this time, Ari felt different. It was like she'd found something to wear that actually fit her personality.

"Ari? Where'd ya go? Need some help here," Riley called from outside the changing rooms.

Ari emerged. Riley gasped. "Oh, Ari, it's perfect," she breathed. "You found one!"

Ari shrugged. "Maybe. It might be good to have a dress just in case," she smiled. Riley agreed. "And look at you—that one is fantastic!"

Riley had stepped out in another black dress that had a gathered bodice, which created a sweetheart neckline. Two thin straps gathered at the center and tied at her neck. The skirt was full and flared. "And look—it's got pockets!" Riley exclaimed, laughing.

"It's perfect for you. Is that the one?"

"I was only on my second dress...but I love it."

They bought their dresses and the salesperson packaged them in garment bags. Ari carefully folded the bag up and fit it inside the basket on the front of her bike. Luckily, the rain had mostly stopped for their ride home, replaced with a fine mist that almost couldn't be felt.

"So," Riley began, "are you going to ask Dane who he's taking to the dance? And, are you going to show him the secret note?"

Ari shook her head. "No, I'm sure I'll find out sooner or later who he's taking to the dance," she said, a little wistfully. "And I'm definitely not telling him about the weird note. It's probably just a prank, anyway, Riley. I mean, really, who writes notes like that?"

Riley nodded. They had reached her house, which was located in the main residential part of town. "If I hear anything, I'll let you know—about either," Riley said, as she walked her bike up her front steps.

The girls waved goodbye, and Ari started home with a sad twinge back in her stomach again. She looked at the neatly folded garment bag in her basket, which now had a fine covering of mist droplets on it. *Why on earth did I buy that?* Ari thought. *I'm not ever going to need a dress like that.* She pedaled through town, turned west onto the country highway, and tried to focus on the hiss of her tires on the wet pavement, instead of the pangs of disappointment she was feeling. Ari thought about just going to the dance by herself...or perhaps waiting to see who her mystery note-maker turned out to be. Maybe *he* would go with her.

Off the country highway she turned up the gravel drive and went over the mist-slickened railroad tracks. At that point, she always got off her bike to walk it up the rest of the way. The hill became too steep at this point to continue riding. As she walked, a sudden awful thought occurred to her: what if Dane started bringing his new dance date to group outings with their friends? She shook her head. That would be more than she could bear, she thought.

The fine mist that had been hovering in the air had soaked Ari's hair and droplets of water were gathering on her nose and dripping off in a most annoying way. She regretted not wearing her hooded jacket, and then she realized she'd forgotten to return Dane's field jacket to him after their trip to Allendale. She sighed. One way or another, she would have to see him soon to return it.

The tall conifers that lined each side of the gravel road finally gave way to the clearing where her house stood. To her complete surprise, Dane was sitting on the porch swing at her house. Once he saw her, he rose to his feet. He was wearing his knit beanie, pulled low, and his black peacoat. She could barely look at him; he looked intimidating and mysterious, as always.

"Ari! I've been looking for you since school got out," he jumped off her front steps, then stopped when he saw her limply-hanging hair and droplets of rain running down her face. "You're drenched...can we talk inside?" He motioned at her house.

"Sure," Ari said, a bit surprised. "Oh, I need to give your coat back to you, too. Don't let me forget," she mentioned as she gathered her garment bag and backpack. Ari opened the heavy front door; the house was cold and quiet. Her mom, dad, and Lily would be home in an hour or so.

Ari and Dane made their way to the kitchen, which overlooked the beautiful backyard garden that Ari and her dad had worked so hard on the previous summer. Now, it was just beginning to show signs of life again. Dane seemed unusually quiet and brooding, and it made Ari nervous. She started to get butterflies as she made coffee, almost like she feared what Dane was going to say. Instead, Dane poked at the garment bag that Ari had placed on the kitchen table.

"What's this?" he asked, reaching for the zipper.

"No! Don't open it!" Ari involuntarily yelped. Dane froze. "It's just a dress. I went shopping with Riley this afternoon. She was looking for something to wear to the Last Dance. She's going with Jace," Ari explained. She desperately reached for her coffee and gulped some so she wouldn't have to say anything more for the moment. She shivered.

Dane brought over a blanket from the couch. "Here," he offered, wrapping it around her. His hands stayed on her arms, holding the blanket to her. "Are you going?" Dane asked slowly.

"I'm not sure yet," she figured.

"But you found a dress?"

"Well, yeah. I might go by myself." Ari decided, searching his eyes. An infinite moment passed. Dane seemed to be looking right through her, to her very core.

"Would you go if I asked you to go with me?" he finally said quietly.

Ari blinked. "But I heard today that you told Julia you were going with someone already," she stammered.

Dane made a soft snorting sound and shook his head. "That's why I was trying so hard to find you after school. I guess word travels even faster than I thought. I wanted to ask you to the dance during our trip to Allendale, but I never got a good chance. I had no idea Julia would ask *me* to go, so I just told her I was planning on going with someone else. You—I hoped," he explained.

Ari didn't realize she'd been holding her breath for a very long time. She exhaled in relief.

"Of course I'll go with you," she said, grinning.

*   *   *

"So Dane had meant to ask me about going to the dance when we went to Allendale. Of course, things were a little crazy that night," Ari rolled her eyes. Riley laughed. "He seemed nervous when he asked me, like he wasn't sure that I'd even say yes," Ari exclaimed. "Why would I ever say no?"

"Your secret admirer, for one," Riley joked. Ari snorted at her suggestion.

The girls were sitting on Ari's back porch, finishing homework and watching as her parents prepped for an impromptu outdoor dinner, despite the weather.

In the backyard, the scent of wet earth and barbecue smoke made for an interesting combination. Ari's dad decided to defy the never-ending spring rain and wheeled their charcoal grill off of the back porch. Soon billowing pearls of delicious-smelling smoke were escaping from the acorn-shaped grill. Ari had perched herself on one of the rocking chairs on the back porch. Leaning back, she closed her eyes and listened to the sounds of the early spring evening: some type of bird was singing a beautiful repeating call, jazz was playing from somewhere inside the house, and her dad was shuffling around on the cobblestones, tending to his cooking. Although her dad was using an umbrella as he cooked, she could hear hissing sizzles as raindrops hit the hot grill.

Ari's mom was bustling about, setting up their backyard for the late-April outdoor meal. She'd already turned on the garden lights that had been strung over the formal garden, and two picnic benches had been placed end-to-end on the cobblestones. Striped navy-and-white patio umbrellas helped keep the picnic tables dry. Spring flowers hadn't quite yet started to bloom, but the garden around them was still stunning.

"Riley, do you know what you're doing for a summer job this year?" Ari's dad asked.

"My mom knows the owner of the drive-thru coffee hut on the way to Allendale. I'm going to see if they need some help there. I've always wanted to work at a coffee place."

"Ari, how about you? We need someone to do filing in my office, if you're interested."

She shook her head at the thought of spending summer days trapped inside an incandescent office. "Actually, dad, I have an idea that I'd like to run by you and mom."

Ari's mom leaned on the porch railing, balancing a tray that held the salt and pepper shakers, utensils, and napkins. "I'd love to hear it, honey. What's your plan?"

"I would like to do yard work in town. I'd use the tools people already have at their homes, and I'd have them fill out a checklist of what they need to have done. I plan to start advertising soon, so I could begin taking appointments. There are only two other yard services in the area, and one of them is in Allendale. I figure it's worth a shot. I really enjoyed our gardening project last summer…"

Her dad nodded. "That sounds like a good idea, Ari. How about this? I'll make you a deal: you try your business idea for a month. If it's successful, then great. If you find yourself without much work, then you can come work in my office for the remaining two months. Sound good?"

Ari walked over to her dad and extended her hand. "Sounds like a deal," she said, shaking it.

Her dad chuckled. "You've got drive, kid. I like that."

She beamed. Her dad's deal made her want to succeed even more. She'd have to hustle to avoid being imprisoned in an office for two months.

*   *   *

The next day Ari buckled down and began planning her yard care business. After school she headed to Cinema Coffee, found a window booth, and pulled a notebook from her backpack.

In a long list, Ari wrote down everything she would need to accomplish to launch her business. It started with advertising and ended with scheduling, with a dozen steps between the two. Beside each item, Ari wrote a date in parenthesis. She figured if she had dates set for every task, she would be ready just in time for summer.

After another half-hour of careful planning, Ari felt she'd accomplished what was needed and decided to head home. The weather had swung from gray and cloudy in the morning to absolutely beautiful by the time Ari had left school, and now in the late afternoon, the sun was beaming through the trees as she walked her bike up the hill. A crunching sound indicated a car was coming up the hill behind her, so she moved to the far right side of the road.

Dane's dad's truck rumbled past. Through the dust Ari could see that it only held a driver but no passenger. Instead of going straight to Dane's house, it turned into Ari's half-circle driveway. Ari slowed down. Why would Dane's dad be going to *her* house?

chapter eleven

Ari did a double-take when she saw Dane get out of the driver's side. He turned and smiled at her speechless stare.

"I passed my driver's test," he said, slapping a hand on the side of the dusty old truck.

Her heart fluttered. Something was different about him now; he wasn't just the boy next door who rode bikes all over town with her. Now he was the older boy next door, standing next to the truck he'd driven to her house. It tipped the balance for Ari, and suddenly she felt terribly shy. Dane stood there in his white t-shirt and holey jeans, still looking at her, waiting for her to say something.

"Congratulations, Dane. That's great!" she said, still feeling so shy, and her cheeks burning to the tips of her ears. *This is ridiculous,* she thought. *He's the same old Dane as before…but not.* Something about the way he was standing, his shoulders thrown back, his chin up, chest out…this was the confidence that replaced Dane's default aloofness. He looked stronger and somehow more intimidating than ever.

Ari started up her front steps and Dane followed her. "Sorry I couldn't go to the coffee shop with you this afternoon. If I passed my test, I kind of wanted to surprise you," he said sheepishly.

This brought a smile to Ari's face. She was fishing around for her notebook to show him what she'd planned for her business when he plucked something from her front door. "What's this?"

A square white note with "Ari" written in pen had been wedged in the doorjamb. Dane handed it to her. Ari froze with indecision. Should she open it up in front of him? She didn't know for sure it was from her secret note-writer; it could be from Riley—but that seemed unlikely. She decided to open it. Dane sat on the porch swing and waited for her to finish reading it.

"*Dear Ari,*" she read silently, "*I know you may have thought my last note was a joke, but it's not. I really do admire you and want to get to know you better, but*

I'm just too shy. I want you to know that I think you're intelligent and I appreciate how kind you are. Best regards." Another heart was sketched simply at the bottom of the note. Ari shook her head.

"Everything okay?" Dane asked from the porch swing, motioning at the empty space next to him. She couldn't keep this secret from him. It was too personal and just a little strange. She gently sat down on the weathered, whitewashed porch swing next to Dane.

"I don't know what to make of this," she said finally as she handed him the note. "I got one last week, too. It basically said the same thing." Ari watched him as he read it. An expression that she'd never seen passed over his face. She couldn't read what it was and that unnerved her.

"You didn't tell me about the first one," he stated as he finished reading. Ari looked at him, at his hazel eyes, which glinted green with the last rays of the late afternoon sun. She was suddenly aware of how close she was sitting to him, but she didn't scoot away. She felt her cheeks burning hot once again, and she desperately hoped they weren't turning as red as they felt.

"Riley and I thought it was a joke," Ari explained.

"How are we gonna find out who it is?" He examined the note again. "Do you have any ideas? Is there anyone at school who seems to like you?" He pursed his lips—there it was again. That *look*. Ari thought she had every mannerism of Dane's cataloged, but this she couldn't place.

"Not a soul," she said, shaking her head. This time, Dane was the one to look at her without breaking his gaze. Finally, a sly smile played in his eyes.

"Well, sounds like we've got yet another mystery on our hands. Operation Secret Admirer is in effect, Aribelle Cartwright," he said, doing a mock salute. Ari couldn't help but chuckle.

"Speaking of mystery," Ari started, "have you learned anything new about Ezra?"

Dane reached for his backpack and pulled out the journal. "Nope. I've been waiting for you. It isn't any fun reading it alone."

"Good. I don't want to miss anything. Besides, your reading voice is just as good as your singing voice."

"When have you ever heard me sing?" Dane looked at her, the evening sunlight strong in his eyes. He shaded them with his arm.

Ari flushed hot again. "When I came up to see if you could go to the Abshire house the first time, you were singing in your room. *Stand By Me*, I think it was. Why don't you sing more often? You have an incredible voice, Dane."

Dane looked away and shrugged. A chill breeze caused Ari to shiver and she pulled her jacket tight. "I haven't had much of a reason to until lately," he said simply. He opened the journal and put his arm around Ari's shoulder. Ari caught her breath but settled into his side and closed her eyes as he read from the ivory pages, listening to nothing but the sound of Dane's warm voice and the occasional breeze.

"June 30th: Dr. Blackwell stopped by today to check on Father. He said that if his assumption about glandular fever is correct, Father will be weak for quite some time. We wait and pray and hope upon morning Father wakes up better than the day before. Mother has been preparing meals (which Father usually cannot eat) and Joseph and I have been doing Father's share of the farm work. Katia visits often to deliver food from her mother, which is the only bright spot during my day. Her nearness and strength of character..." Dane trailed off, silently reading to himself.

Ari opened her eyes to see why he'd stopped. She examined Dane's face: his brow was furrowed, concentrating. He cleared his throat and continued: "Her nearness and strength of character is my salvation in these days."

Ari straightened under his arm. Dane's expression hadn't changed;

his eyes were locked on the passage he'd just read. Silent moments passed.

Ari strained to see his eyes. "Are you okay?"

Dane inhaled deeply and absentmindedly moved his hand to the back of Ari's head, smoothing her hair. He was still staring at the journal. Finally he nodded. "I'm fine." Ari waited for an explanation, but he gave none.

*   *   *

"Ari, that means Mr. Mystery was at your *house*," Amara rolled her eyes. The girls were once again at lunch, and Ari had shown Riley and Amara the second note Dane had found jammed in her front door the previous afternoon. "What if you had been at home? Then you would've seen who it was."

"No, he knew she wasn't at home," Riley interjected. "That means he knew she went to the coffee shop after school."

"Oh gosh, Riley, that's creepy," Ari said, waving her off. She took a bite of her sandwich and looked across the crowded cafeteria, subconsciously looking for someone else, staring back at her.

"What if it turns out to be someone really hot and not creepy at all?" Amara shot back. "What will you do then, Ari?"

Ari laughed but shook her head and put her hand out as if to say *stop*. "I don't care who it is, guys, really. I mean, yes, I want to know who is writing the notes, but in the end it doesn't matter. Dane knows about it now, because he was actually the person to find the note on my door," she admitted.

The warning bell rang and the three girls gathered up their lunches. Ari felt slightly uncomfortable with the possibility that someone was watching her, but shrugged it off as silly paranoia.

At the end of the school day she was relieved to see Dane waiting next to her bike, as he usually did. "I'm going to the museum to try and find out everything I can about Ezra and Katia," he explained. "You want to come? Maybe some coffee and homework after?"

Ari smiled. "Heck yes, count me in." She wouldn't turn down an entire afternoon with Dane, that was for sure.

It was another beautiful early-May afternoon, and it seemed like spring had finally decided to stay. There hadn't been rain in at least a week, and the five-block ride to the museum hinted at warmer days to come. The knee-length dress Ari had chosen to wear to school—the first time she could recall wearing one since she'd moved—fluttered as she pedaled along. She was happy she'd remembered a jacket, as cottonwood-laden breezes still had some chill to them.

The museum was as quiet and still as ever. Agnes nodded hello to them both from the receptionist's desk. In the small reference room, Ari took a chair and looked over at Dane. "What are we looking for?"

Dane took off his field jacket and Ari noticed he once again looked somehow older and stronger. Since his mom had moved in, Ari thought Dane had developed something of a style in what he chose to wear. When he'd lived with Rhoda, he'd looked neglected, or maybe he just hadn't cared about what he wore. Now he seemed just a little more polished, and it showed. Dane's heather gray t-shirt was hiding his ever-present ball-chain necklace, and his dark indigo jeans showed his lean frame. His back was to her, and she could see his broad shoulders hunched over a book. His dark hair, though, was as messy as ever, and Ari hoped that was something he wouldn't change.

"Well, anything about the life of Ezra Abshire. I was hoping you had some thoughts on how to track him down," Dane said, smiling. As if on cue, Agnes came shuffling into the reference room.

"I overheard someone say the Abshire name," she said quietly. "What would you be looking for, young man?" Her stooped frame straightened slightly as she got out her notepad.

"Well, ma'am," Dane started, "we are looking to find anything about the life of Ezra Abshire, who was one of the sons that lived at the homestead off the highway. Anything you have would be appreciated."

Ari smiled. She loved Dane's ever-present politeness. When she'd first met him, she wondered if he acted that way only around her parents, but the more she got to know him, it was evident that it was inherent in his personality.

Agnes smiled. "Ah, yes, you were in here earlier about the Abshires," she said, looking at Ari. Agnes made a note. "Ezra Abshire," she repeated.

"Or, anything about Katia Hadley, as well," Ari added.

"Hadley!" Agnes stopped writing. "Now, we have quite a lot on the Hadleys; they were a founding family and they contributed much to the development of Rivers in the early days. Quite the fascinating story, if I do say so. I'm almost certain we have a small box of Hadley artifacts upstairs in our archives. Would you two like to see it?" Agnes looked over the top of her bifocals at Ari and Dane.

"Yes, ma'am," Dane said, and with that, Agnes motioned for them to follow and shuffled out of the reference room. She turned toward the staircase, and, behind her back, Ari and Dane looked at each other. Was she going to climb all those stairs?

Taking the handrail, step by slow step, Agnes pulled herself up the stairs, all the while telling what she knew of the Hadley family. "You know that Nadia was a famous ballerina, yes?" Dane nodded. "Well, she was very talented in a variety of hobbies as well. We have photos of her exquisite formal gardens and her beekeeping society. For all their wealth," Agnes said, finally reaching the top, "they were exceedingly generous people."

The top floor of the building had rows of arched windows and a high wood ceiling. Large objects surrounded the outside of the room, and were carefully labeled and covered in plastic sheeting. Metal shelving was in the middle of the room, and held stacks of boxes that were all labeled as well. Agnes made her way to the "H" section of the boxes, and pointed to a top-rack container. Dane stretched to get it down.

"Now, we may have more on the Hadleys than what is contained within this box," Agnes said. "Our archived collections are only forty-five percent cataloged at the moment. When I got here, it was only at fifteen percent. I've made a little dent in it," she said slyly.

"Who helps you catalog it?" Dane said, as he placed the box on the faded wood floor. Ari saw a sudden glint of interest run across Dane's face.

"Well, we get grants to support summer staff who are trained to sift through our repository of donated items. If you're interested, I'll give you an application before you leave. By the way, I never asked you why you're doing this research. Are you two doing a school report on them?"

Ari and Dane looked at each other with a smile. "Well," Dane said, "I'm Dane Hadley. I still live on Hadley Hill with my family." A look of utter surprise crossed Agnes's face.

"Dane lives in Nadia's first home, which became the servant's quarters after the main home was constructed," Ari added. "My family moved into the main home last summer. We've been working on piecing together her family history, and also getting the home and garden restored to what it might have looked like when Nadia lived there."

Agnes still looked dumbfounded. "Mr. Hadley," she addressed Dane, which caused him to smile, "I had absolutely no idea there were any remaining relatives to Nadia and Grekov. You are her great-great grandson, I assume?"

"That's right. Did you know they're buried on our hill?"

"So the rumor is true?" Agnes's voice turned to a raspy whisper. "I am amazed! I have heard so many stories over the years—some said they were sent back to Russia to be buried; some said they were buried somewhere on their property, and yet another story claimed there was a beautifully decorated underground tomb." Dane's eyes widened slightly as he shot a glance at Ari, who looked back at him with a raised eyebrow. "That story," she continued, "was the most-far fetched of all, but it was my favorite," she chuckled. "What does it look like, where they are buried?"

"Well," Dane said, "The two graves are fairly simple, side-by-side, and surrounded by rows of cherry trees that circle around the graves. The trees just finished blooming," he said, smiling. Ari blushed. They hadn't been back to the enclosed cherry trees since the night she'd almost kissed him. "And when they're in bloom, it's quite a sight."

"What an astounding thing," Agnes continued, shaking her head and smiling. "To think the great-great grandson of a town founder walked into our museum today, and answered one of my history mysteries. Well, please do look through these artifacts of your family's. If you'd like to check this box out, we do museum collection loans to researchers and family members. Just let me know," Agnes said. "I'll go search our catalog for anything on—" she opened her notebook and adjusted her bifocals "—on Ezra Abshire."

Ari and Dane looked at the box. Tentatively, he removed the lid. The box contained some photos, documents, and newspaper articles. Dane unfolded a yellowed pack of papers.

"Check this out. I think it's the land survey of our hill, with the Hadley's lot outlined there," Dane pointed at a large box that contained the majority of the hill. He handed the paper to Ari, then sifted through the rest of the contents. There were photos they had seen before, as well as unfamiliar prints.

The upstairs archive room was quiet, except for random sounds coming from the ground floor. Once in awhile the building would creak, sending a startled shiver through Ari. Afternoon light streamed through the southwestern windows, and dust particles could be seen floating adrift through the streams of sunlight.

"I think I'll check this box out and take it home," Dane figured. At that moment, Agnes returned with her notepad.

"I'm very sorry, Mr. Hadley. I searched our document database and we have nothing on file regarding Ezra Abshire."

Ari furrowed her brow. "Is that unusual—not to find anything on a person?"

Agnes shrugged. "No. In my experience, it usually means the person in question moved away from Rivers. But," Agnes continued, "don't give up. When you hit a dead end, you just need to find another avenue of research. Perhaps look to see if there are any Abshires still alive in the area. Try a genealogical site on the internet. If you keep searching, you *will* find what you're looking for."

*   *   *

It was nearly dinnertime when Ari and Dane sat down at Cinema Coffee. The marquis lights had just turned on and most people had abandoned the coffee shop; it was Friday night and a line was forming at the ticket booth for Alfred Hitchcock's *The Birds*. Ari had called her mom to tell her she wouldn't be home for dinner.

Earthenware cups topped with generous amounts of whipped cream were brought to Ari and Dane's table. Dane had pulled Ezra's journal out and Ari noticed a sticky note attached to one of the pages. Ari poked at it.

"What's that?"

"I read a little ahead the other night."

"Without me?" Ari stuck her lip out in a mock pout.

"Just a little," Dane smiled. "But listen to this, Ari." Dane turned to the page with the sticky note. "After Katia's piano lesson, I took it upon myself to ask her if she'd allow me to accompany her home. I was expecting her to say 'no,' but to my complete surprise, she agreed. I only hope that in the future she will allow me to walk with her. Taking the wooded trail to her house allows us a pleasant amount of time to converse." Dane stopped and looked up at Ari, expectantly.

After a half-second of thought, Ari's eyes got big. "Wait—do you think it could be the trail we were on?"

"Could be. We were headed in the direction of my house when the trail became overgrown."

Ari rolled her eyes. "I know what this means," she groaned.

"Nothing a machete can't take care of," Dane grinned. "Yeah, we'll have to see where that trail ends up, if possible. That might be something to do this summer," he mused. "Speaking of summer…" Dane pulled out the intern application for the museum as he took a sip of his coffee.

"Are you going to apply?" Ari asked.

"Yeah, I definitely am. Last summer, if you'd told me that I'd want to work at a museum, I would've looked at you like you're crazy," he looked at Ari, his hazel eyes now just nearly all brown in the low light. "I didn't know what I wanted to do with my time…I was so focused on just surviving and avoiding Rhoda that it didn't leave much room for living. Those four years were so crappy," he rasped. Unexpectedly, Dane rose from his seat across from Ari and scooted next to her in the booth, his body turned toward her. Ari felt her heartbeat ramp up as he moved close enough so that only Ari could hear him speak. She froze as he gently stared at her.

"Remember the other night, on the porch swing, when I read Ezra's quote about how Katia's strength of character was his salvation?"

Ari nodded slowly.

"What he wrote struck me because that's exactly how I feel about you. I know I've said it a million times…and I try not to think about what life would be like if you hadn't moved here."

Ari beamed. His gratitude was overwhelming and washed over her like warm sunlight. Dane was looking through her again in the way only he could. She allowed herself to stare at him moments longer than she normally would, until her attention was suddenly drawn to a tall blonde figure walking toward them. It was Julia, with several of her friends that Ari didn't know.

"Hi guys!" she came over and stood next to Dane. "Funny seeing you here! You guys watching the movie tonight?"

Dane shook his head. "Nah, we're just having coffee and talking about summer jobs," he said.

"Oh...boy, that's a good idea." Julia's wavy hair looped its way down her shoulders. "Is that an application?" She pointed at the form that was still lying on the table.

"Yeah, it's for a job at the museum," he said.

"Rivers Historic Museum? Wow, how interesting!" Julia twirled her hair and for some reason, Ari was praying Julia didn't ask her about her summer job plans.

"Ari, how 'bout you? Are you planning on working there too?"

Ari cleared her throat. "Um, no, I'm hoping to do some yard care jobs this summer. I need to start advertising soon, though." Ari quickly gulped some coffee.

"Sounds great," Julia turned her attention back to Dane. "Hey, are you guys going to the annual bonfire next Friday night? It's at Pat McCleary's farm again."

Ari started to say *maybe*, but Dane just shook his head. "I won't be going."

Julia frowned. "Too bad, it's a lot of fun!" She looked back over her shoulder, her cascade of blonde locks brushing Dane. "Time for me to get back into line. See you guys later!" With that, Julia bounded back to her friends and disappeared into the ticket line.

Ari sipped her coffee and smirked at Dane. "She likes you," Ari assessed.

Dane shifted uncomfortably. "Are you going to the bonfire?" he asked.

Her brow furrowed. "I'm not sure...if Riley or Amara are going, I probably will. Why aren't you going?"

Dane just shrugged, indifferent. "Bonfires aren't my thing. They get a million pallets and pile them twenty feet high and light it on fire. I dunno." He shrugged. "I'm just not into it."

Ari took one last sip of her now-tepid coffee. She knew him well enough now to know there was more to this story than he was letting on.

chapter twelve

The steering wheel was slick with sweat from Ari's hands. Her mom turned down the radio as the car crossed the railroad tracks at the base of their hill. Ari pulled off of Hadley Lane and headed west on the highway. The Abshire homestead flashed past as the car inched closer to fifty-five miles per hour. The road seemed so much smaller from the driver's seat of a car as opposed to riding along the shoulder on a bike.

"Ari, you're doing fantastic. Just remember to relax. There are hardly any cars on the road this evening," her mom reminded her.

It was true; this little two-lane highway was rarely used by anyone but neighbors to Hadley Hill. It wasn't really a thoroughfare to anywhere but farm fields, which made it wonderfully quiet.

"What have you found out about the Abshire place? Anything?" her mom asked.

"Well..." Ari considered whether or not she should reveal that she and Dane had taken a journal from the house. She decided to play it safe. "We've found some information on the family. It seems the dad got sick, I mean, *really* sick, and the rest of the family struggled to keep the farm running in his absence. We don't know yet what happened to the dad, but we did find out that one of the sons, Ezra, seemed to be very interested in one of Nadia's daughters, Katia."

"Wow! You guys have found out quite a bit. Makes sense that the Hadleys and Abshires would have known each other well, since they were the closest neighbors." Her mom lowered her voice. "You know there have been whispers around town that the town of Rivers is looking to expand, and the land the Abshire homestead is on may be annexed some day."

Ari shook her head. "I hope that doesn't happen."

Her mom nodded. "I know. It would be a shame. I haven't seen it up close, but I bet the home could be salvaged and restored."

"It totally could, mom. It's not that bad inside——" Ari stopped short and winced. Her mom only smiled slyly, though.

"So you've been inside?"

"Maaaaaybe," Ari said, trying to concentrate on her driving. She heard her mom snicker, and she knew it was safe to proceed. "Alright, yes. Jace wanted to get photos of the interior of the house when we were there. Mom, it's such a beautiful house, and you can almost feel the presence of the people who have passed through it. That house has a story to tell, Mom. I can feel it. I can't understand how houses like that are just left to deteriorate."

"And yet, they're all over. If you keep your eyes open, you'll see them everywhere, especially in the country."

The highway stretched in front of them, and Ari realized she'd finally relaxed a bit. Without trying, she had maintained a steady speed and was no longer squeezing the steering wheel.

"Hey," her mom said, patting her arm. "I really think you're getting the hang of this driving thing, Ari. You're going to be ready for your test in no time."

Nodding, Ari hoped she was right.

*   *   *

"Two more weeks until the Last Dance; are you excited?!" Riley looked back at Ari, who was in the backseat of Jace's van, sitting next to Amara. They were headed to the bonfire at the McCleary's farm.

"Yeah, I really am. I can't believe the school year is almost over," Ari said.

"You've almost been here a whole year," Riley mentioned.

Ari nodded and looked out the window. They'd been driving for some time now; Ari had lost track of exactly how long, but they were in a part of the country she was unfamiliar with.

"How far out from Rivers are we?"

Jace chuckled. "Well, we're about thirty minutes south of Rivers. I guess the next closest town would be Woodward. It's kind of important to have the bonfire out in the boonies," he chuckled again.

"Why's that?" Amara leaned forward.

"Things can get a little crazy. This isn't some small bonfire," he said, shaking his head. "They get a few truckloads of pallets and stack 'em as high as possible. This kind of fire would never be allowed within city limits."

Ari smiled. "Sounds exciting. It had better live up to the hype, Jace," she said, and Riley giggled.

"You won't be disappointed—" Riley started, but didn't need to finish. They'd reached the McCleary farm, and a house-sized tower of fire was already in full inferno. Ari's mouth dropped open. Jace parked, and they walked to the crowd of students that had gathered a respectable distance away. Everyone was as close as they could be, but the heat was far-reaching.

"Hol-y cow…" Amara stared up at the flames licking sky-high.

"Isn't it fabulous?" Julia's voice carried above the crackling and snapping sounds that were hissing from the fire. She walked up with a group of friends and stood with Jace and Riley. "Glad you guys could make it." Julia looked at Ari for half a second longer, as if to be doubly sure Dane wasn't by her side.

Riley and Jace made their way to a row of camping coolers that some students had brought. Most were filled with ice and drinks, some people had brought snacks, and Ari suspected some kids had brought alcohol, from the sounds coming from the opposite side of the bonfire. "That's the other reason the bonfire is held out in the middle of nowhere," Amara mused, listening to the whoops and hollers of the already-drunk seniors. "Takes forever for the cops to show up," she smirked, pushing her dark hair away from her face.

Anxiety wound its way around Ari's stomach. Maybe she *should've* asked Dane exactly why he hadn't wanted to come. She was fairly certain Riley wouldn't start drinking and getting out of control, but she really had no idea what Jace, their driver, would do. Ari tried to focus on the ever-rising heat and flames instead of the worries that were beginning deep in the pit of her stomach.

Amara seemed to be enjoying the fire, and Ari struck up easy conversation with her. They chatted for about thirty minutes when Ari realized they hadn't seen Riley or Jace or even Julia for quite some time. "Think we should be looking for Riley?" Ari offered.

"Yeah, that's a good idea. There are a lot more people here now," Amara noticed.

The crowd had swelled, but the fire had dwindled to half its size. A crew of five guys were chucking new pallets to the top of the pile. Enormous plumes of sparkling cinders spewed high into the sky with each added pallet. Amara and Ari rounded the perimeter of the pile where most of the seniors were still yelling loudly. One guy took off his shirt and whipped it into the fire. A loud roar of approval rose from the crowd, and several more guys followed, each met with more cheering. Calling for Jace and Riley would be futile, so Ari stood on her tiptoes, trying to find her friend.

Suddenly she was hoisted up into the air. "Are you looking for someone?" a senior guy yelled, throwing her onto his shoulder. At first, Ari thought he was actually trying to be helpful, but the way he unsteadily stumbled back and forth caused a swift panic to rise in Ari. He was drunk, for sure, and trying his hardest to stay upright.

"Hey, I'm good, put me down," Ari yelled, trying to be nice but firm. Amara saw what was happening, and tugged on the guy's arm.

"Ray, she's fine, put her down. You're stumbling," Amara coaxed him. Ari was relieved that he was a friend of Amara's. Maybe he'd listen.

"Oh, okay, sorry," he said, and he began to set her down, but as he grabbed her by the waist to take her off his shoulders, he stumbled and

Ari pitched forward. She hit the ground and rolled, and Amara ran over to help her up.

"Thanks," Ari said, checking herself to make sure she wasn't hurt. Ray had recovered and was stumbling away. Taunting calls and laughing could be heard nearby. Another group of senior guys were approaching, and they were pointing at Ari.

"Nice fall, little lady!" one of them whooped.

"Yeah, that was super graceful," another said, and they all laughed. Ari and Amara started walking away, but in horror, Ari realized her ankle was hurting again—the same one she'd twisted badly on her hike with Dane. *Crap*, she thought. She grabbed Amara's shoulder and started limping away, but suddenly one of the guys scooped Ari up and started walking toward the fire. "You're not leaving the bonfire yet!" he jeered at Ari. She tried to wriggle out of his arms, but he was far too strong.

"Hey, put me down!" she yelled, but the sounds all around them drowned her voice. Ari became aware of the intense heat they were approaching. She covered her face as the heat seared her skin. Another wave of panic grabbed hold of her and Ari tried twisting out of the guy's hold. Out of the corner of her eye, she saw a tall figure running at them.

It was Dane.

"Let her *GO!*" Dane's voice reverberated through the air. She'd never heard him yell like that. It was forceful, savage, all-encompassing. It was enough that the guy holding her turned around to face Dane, who was quickly approaching them.

Dane's face was stone; his jaw was clenched, and his eyes were full of anger. Sweat rolled from his wildly-tousled hair and was soaking the front of his shirt. He came at the guy with a low running tackle, effectively pushing the guy and Ari away from the fire. Dane hit him hard enough that he dropped Ari, and Dane scrambled to catch her before she fell to the ground again.

"Who do you think *YOU* are?" the guy bellowed belligerently, spewing some expletives. Dane now had Ari behind him, and he stood stock-still. She could see every muscle in Dane's body was tensed. Flickering firelight skimmed his sweat-soaked back. The guy made a lunge for Ari, and without a moment of hesitation, Dane made a swooping punch, and his fist connected with the guy's face with a smacking *whump*. The guy staggered backward and fell over.

By now, a sizable circle of silent, gawking students had gathered around the scene. Some girls gasped as the guy hit the ground. Dane took a step back and scooped Ari up. "Let's go," he said in a low growl.

Ari was still shaking from the encounter. Her breathing was shallow and she was relieved to be safe in Dane's arms, but a part of her was still scared. She glanced behind them to make sure the belligerent drunk guy wasn't following them. He wasn't, but Amara was trailing behind.

"Wait," Ari motioned for Dane to stop, and he set her down while still supporting her. She winced as her foot touched the ground. It felt as bad or worse than the first time she'd twisted it.

"Amara, do you want a ride home?" Ari called.

Amara smiled in thanks. "No, I'll let Riley and Jace know you left with Dane. Are you alright?"

"I'll be fine…but thank you so much for helping me out," Ari limped over to her and gave her a hug. "Are you sure you don't want to go home?"

"Nah, I'll be fine."

Ari waved good-bye and turned around, limping away, but in one quick swoop, Dane lifted her again and resumed carrying her across the pitch-dark field to his mom's car. Once she was in the car, Ari closed her eyes and tried to stop the trembling that had overtaken her whole body. Dane got in the car and started it without saying a word. He was still seething in anger, breathing heavily, and she noticed his hands were shaking almost as bad as hers. Was that from anger? *Or fear?* She'd never seen him that worked up, even when Rhoda was around.

Ari was fairly certain he wasn't angry at her, but she couldn't be sure. Dane started driving toward Rivers. They rode in silence for a few minutes. Dane had his window down and the fresh spring air that smelled like freshly-cut grass swirled through the car. Finally, Ari spoke.

"Thank you…" she said. "Thank you for helping me." Ari looked over at Dane. His brow was slightly furrowed, his slightly curved nose silhouetted against the sparse light from outside. It was so odd to see him driving. Without warning, he pulled over and turned the engine off. He ran his hand over his face, wiping away sweat.

"You're welcome," he said.

"Why did you decide to come?" she asked.

Dane inhaled a long, slow breath. "I went to the bonfire when I was a freshman. It has a reputation for getting totally out of control. You had no way of knowing that. I didn't want to try and talk you out of going. I really wasn't planning on coming tonight, but…" Dane shifted in his seat and inhaled deeply. Ari looked at him with a questioning expression. He looked conflicted and shifted nervously.

"Ari, the scar I have on my back…I got that four years ago. I was in a car accident with Rhoda. It was just weeks after my uncle had passed." He leaned his head back on the headrest and closed his eyes. Ari tilted her head to the side. *Why was he telling her this?* It was completely unusual for him to offer any memories that had anything to do with Rhoda. Finally, he started talking once more.

"She missed a corner and rolled the car. We weren't really hurt too badly when the car rolled, but for whatever reason, it caught on fire." Dane took a deep breath, exhaled.

"She managed to get out, but I was trapped." Ari noticed Dane clenching his fist. His arm rippled. "A bystander pulled me out through the broken passenger-side window, but my back got burned." She saw tension and fear twitch through his body, starting with his breath and moving through every muscle.

"I was looking for you at the bonfire tonight. I didn't see you at all until I heard you yelling for that guy to put you down. Ari, I was terrified. When he started stumbling toward the fire with you in his arms, it was like watching my worst nightmare unfold. I can't fathom the thought of you getting hurt like that."

He turned and looked at her.

Ari had no words to say.

Dane had faced a terrifying fear of his to help her. More than that, he'd confided in Ari about his accident. She reached over from her seat and wrapped her arms around him in an awkward hug, hindered by the center console of the car. He returned her hug, pulling her as close as he could. He was cold with sweat and she could feel a slight tremor as she held him. She turned to the side and rested her head on his chest. His heart was still racing. Dane put his hand on her head. After a moment, he continued.

"We went to the hospital and they took care of my back. Fortunately it was only a first-degree burn; I was really lucky—except the burn was high enough on my back that I needed help taking care of it, which is how the problem started. Rhoda didn't ever help me change the bandage, and it got infected and didn't heal properly. That's why I have the scar," he said with disdain.

He rested his chin on the top of Ari's head. Ari felt a wave of nervousness move through her, and she held him tighter. His scent and his warmth totally and completely grounded her. His chest rose and fell with shallow, hard breaths.

"Rhoda didn't even care enough to help a kid who'd been hurt in an accident she'd caused," he whispered.

White flashes of car headlights moved through the cab of the car. Traffic heading toward Rivers started to pick up. "The bonfire is probably over. Time to get you home," Dane said, and Ari reluctantly shifted back to her seat.

*   *   *

"OMG, Ari! I heard what happened. I'm SO SORRY! Call me!"
The text message from Riley was waiting on Ari's phone the next
morning. Ari had tenderly walked from her bed to the window seat,
where she propped up her ankle. The cool morning air emanated from
the single-pane, gothic-arch window. She pulled her bathrobe tightly
around her to keep out the chill. Despite the cold air seeping in from the
window, this seat was Ari's favorite place inside her house. From it she
could see across part of the pasture and her backyard. The tops of the
oak trees in the grove led to the roofline of Dane's house, which was just
barely visible. Given a few years' time, she sadly figured she wouldn't be
able to see his house at all.

She looked at her ankle. Once again it was shades of green and
purple. This time, though, it seemed to be more bruised than twisted,
and it hurt more to touch it than to walk on it. Ari was thankful for that,
as she had been planning to pass out posters downtown for her yard
maintenance service.

Ari's phone vibrated. On the other end was Riley.

"Ari! What happened last night?" Riley sounded concerned and
remorseful.

"Well, Amara and I were looking for you and Jace when one of
Amara's friends, Ray, picked me up. He was trying to be helpful, lifting
me up above everyone so I could find you better. But, he was super
drunk and dropped me. I hurt my ankle again when I fell. Amara was
helping me walk away when some random senior guy picked me up and
started getting closer to the fire," she recalled. "I was kinda scared, and I
was yelling at him to put me down. He and his friends had been heckling
me and Amara, and they seemed angry, and way too drunk. And then,
Dane suddenly showed up."

"That's what everybody was talking about, Ari! Dane dropped Pat
McCleary with one punch, right?"

"Oh no, Pat McCleary? The guy who lives at the farm we were

at?"

"Yeah…he tends to get really angry when he's drunk, I've heard. After you guys left, he was super-pissed that some junior kid beat him up in front of all his friends. It's really lucky you guys left when you did."

Ari winced, then, without trying to sound accusatory, she asked: "Where *were* you guys? Amara and I were looking for you for awhile…"

"We were with Julia, Rob, and a few other friends, inside Pat's house. They were playing cards and we joined in. I am so, so sorry we didn't tell you, Ari." Riley sounded genuinely apologetic.

"Nah, it's fine, Riley. Don't worry about it. I probably won't go to next year's bonfire, though," she chuckled.

"Hey, Ari," Riley said, more upbeat, "Jace, Rob, Julia and I want to help you out today. I know you were planning on passing out fliers around town, but if you've hurt your ankle again, you shouldn't be riding your bike. We'll take you around town and get it done in half the time. We all feel really bad about what happened last night with Pat. He can be a horrible jerk sometimes," she said.

Ari smiled. "I would love some help, Riley. Thank you!"

She finished her conversation with Riley and walked over to her computer. Dane's heart-wrenching revelation about his accident weighed on her heart, and she couldn't shake the sadness she felt for him. She paused before typing anything into the search engine. *Did she really want to do this?*

Finally, Ari typed a few words into the search bar. A single newspaper article, written four and a half years prior, showed up first in the results list. Ari hesitated again, then clicked on it.

The first image Ari saw was a color photo of a mangled car, blackened from the inside out and laying on its top. Windows were shattered and smoke still curled from the melted upholstery. The photograph showed the passenger side; the car's airbags hung down limply and were smeared with unbelievable amounts of blood. Ari's insides turned at the sight of it. Ari imagined Dane trapped in that seat. She could hardly stomach to read the rest of the article, but she couldn't ignore it now.

"Rollover Accident Causes Car Fire," the article headline read. "Rhoda Hadley, 42, of Rivers, was transported to a nearby hospital Thursday afternoon after her vehicle rolled off Hazelwood Drive and caught on fire. The other occupant of the car, her 12-year old nephew, was initially trapped in the passenger seat, but was quickly pulled to safety by a bystander. The boy is currently at Rivers General Hospital, being treated for minor burns. Ms. Hadley was treated for minor injuries and released. Speed was thought to be a factor in the crash and the investigation is ongoing."

Ari felt a hot, angry tear fall down her face. She wiped it away with the sleeve of her bathrobe but couldn't stop staring at the photo at the top of the article. *What if someone hadn't been there to pull him out?* she thought. Ari shook her head. She couldn't mull over the *what if's*. Dane had survived and now wore a permanent reminder of the accident. His fear of fire made perfect sense now.

She shut her laptop and went back to her window seat. Ari closed her eyes and took a deep breath, listening to the chattering and chirping of birds from the garden below.

There was a soft knock at her door. Ari was wholly surprised when Dane stepped into her room.

She suddenly felt very self-conscious. She wiped at her eyes once more and patted down her hair to make sure it wasn't flying in all directions. One corner of Dane's mouth twitched upward as he saw her preening.

"Good morning," he said.

"Hey, what are you doing here at ten in the morning?"

Dane sat on the opposite side of the window seat and looked out across to his house. "So this is what you see from up here," he said quietly. "Almost as good as the view from my roof."

"Much safer than the view from your roof, that's for sure," she chuckled.

Dane turned to look at her, his expression going from light to serious. "How are you doing?" He looked down at her ankle and winced. "I'm guessing that doesn't feel too good."

"It's actually not that bad. It's more of a surface bruise than a twist. It should be better by tomorrow, I'd guess. Is that really why you're here? To check on my ankle?" She grinned at him, but his expression remained strangely serious.

Dane shook his head. "I was wondering…what I told you about the accident, can you maybe keep that between us? It's not a secret that the accident happened, but I don't really want to explain to people my thing with fire or how it came to be…" he trailed off, trying not to sound vulnerable.

Ari leaned forward so only Dane could hear. "Of course, Dane. I wouldn't have told anyone about the accident. I know you told me that in confidence," she said honestly. Dane looked at her for an eternal moment. She felt her pulse quicken. She was face-to-face with him and she had to fight the urge to reach for his face.

"I want to thank you again for showing up last night," she looked straight into his eyes, memorizing everything about him. "Nobody has ever stood up for me like that before. I really have no idea what I would've done if you hadn't intervened." She didn't know what more to say to impress upon him her gratitude. He nodded in understanding, then got up from the window seat.

"Hey, I'll be at my dad's until tomorrow afternoon," he said. "I have an abandoned place to show you that I think you'll be interested in. If your ankle feels better, will you be up for it?"

"Yeah," she added, "as long as you don't have to beat anyone up there. Did you know that was Pat McCleary you punched last night?"

"Of course I did," Dane grinned. "That's why I did it."

*   *   *

Jace was driving and Ari was helping to direct Rob and Riley which businesses to take her posters to. They'd easily covered most of the businesses in downtown Rivers within a span of an hour. Being a small town, it wasn't hard to cover the area thoroughly in a small amount of time.

Julia had just taken a handful of fliers to a garden supply store on First Street. She jumped into the van and scooted onto the middle row next to Ari.

"Hey, you probably already know that I asked Dane to the Last Dance. I'm really sorry—I had checked with Riley and she said you guys weren't going out. I figured it would be ok," she said, pouting her lips a bit.

Ari just shrugged. "It's okay, Julia. No worries." There was a pause, then Julia smiled and took another handful of posters.

"Should these go to the restaurants on the next block?"

"Definitely. And," Ari added, "thank you for helping me today. You really didn't have to." Julia smiled back and hopped out of the van again, a handful of posters in her grip. As Julia headed down the street, Riley returned with Rob.

Riley got into the front seat with Jace. "Ari, I think after the next block, we've covered all of the places you wanted to go. Anybody hungry for lunch?"

"Starving," Ari answered.

*   *   *

The weekend turned into a crash-course in marketing for Ari. After lunch, Riley had helped Ari create a mailer that would be sent to all addresses within Rivers' city limits, plus some outlying homes. Riley's mom, a real estate agent, had talked at length with Ari about how to reach her ideal target audience, and Ari had been thankful to have professional help. Ari desperately wanted to avoid losing the agreement with her dad and end up doing office work for two-thirds of the summer.

By Sunday afternoon, Ari felt she'd done almost everything she could to prepare for her yard maintenance business. She was waiting on her front porch when Dane finally rode up on his bike, ready for their abandoned-house adventure. The temperature was unusually warm for a late May afternoon; it was the first actual hot day they'd had. Dane was just wearing cargo shorts, with a flannel shirt hanging from his back pocket.

"Whatcha gonna call your business?" Dane yelled over to her as they started riding their bikes down Hadley Hill.

"Ari's Yard Services," she called out over the crunching gravel. "I'm terrible at thinking of names. But Riley helped me make a nice logo that looks good, and her mom's a real estate agent, so she was able to help me a lot with the marketing part of it all. Her mom said a simple, direct name was fine, especially if it captured exactly what it is that I do. I hope I get enough business, Dane. I really, *really* don't want to be stuck in dad's office doing paperwork."

"You'll be fine, Ari. I promise. You'll get more business than you can handle," he said, looking back at her.

"I really hope so," she called back.

They crossed the railroad tracks at the base of their hill. The railroad ties had been baking in the hot sun and gave off a very distinct scent of tar and creosote. Tall grasses were starting to mellow from bright green to a wheaty-blonde color. The afternoon was whispering the promise of summer.

They pedaled along the highway's scorching pavement and into town. From there, they headed down the same road that had taken them toward Woodward and Pat McCleary's bonfire. However, after about two miles, Dane held his arm out and pointed that they would be turning left onto a poorly-maintained gravel road. An almost-unreadable street sign spelled "Lawton Drive."

The road was lined with tall conifers on the left side and an open field on the right, which was bordered by cottonwoods at the far edge. The road had more grass growing through it than visible gravel, but it still was fairly easy to ride on. Ari watched Dane as she rode behind him. He seemed to be looking around, and she wondered if he was trying to figure out if he was in the right place.

They followed the road as it made a long, swooping curve to the northeast. Eventually the road started going slightly downhill. Ari and Dane coasted along in silence. Ari couldn't help but glance at Dane's scar. Now that she knew how he'd gotten it, it almost hurt her to look at it.

It wasn't until they started a steeper decline that Ari finally saw the abandoned house, and beyond it, a river that couldn't be seen from the road. The home was perched two hundred feet back from the bank of the river. It was a one-story house with peeling paint and a severely sagging front porch. Its windows were mainly intact, but the chimney on one side of the house had collapsed and a pile of bricks splayed out onto the ground.

Dane stopped his bike. His shoulders stooped as he leaned over his handlebars. For the longest time, he was bent over in silence, staring.

"Are we going to go in this one? You're sure it's abandoned?" Ari looked over at him. His profile was stoic.

"Yeah, it's abandoned." There was a hint of something in his voice that set Ari on edge. She narrowed her eyes and looked again at the foreboding house.

He finally laid down his bike in the tall grass and Ari followed. Dane carefully stepped up on the porch, grabbing a railing for support. The railing broke off in his hand and splintered away. The groan of the floorboards warned them that their footing could give way at any minute. Ari tried the front door, and the knob turned in her hand, but the door itself wouldn't budge. Dane motioned for her to step aside. He lifted up on the doorknob and pushed, his arms and back rippling against the resistance. The door scraped open.

Ari followed him in. The house hadn't been abandoned for as long as she'd assumed. Unlike the Abshire home, this house still had remnants of the past family who lived there. Seeing the living room with furniture gave Ari a foreboding feeling, like they were invading someone's home.

An old TV with bunny-ear antennae stood in one corner. There was a mouse-eaten couch opposite the TV, and hunting lodge-type decor was strewn about. Broken glass littered the floor. A gaping hole was punched in a side of the wood-paneled wall. Dishes were shattered on the floor. A rotary-style phone was crushed where it hung on the wall. The place had been ransacked.

"Dane, how long has this house been abandoned? Why is all this stuff here?" Ari whispered. "I don't understand why people would just up and leave, without taking their stuff with them…"

"Trust me, it's abandoned," he said, running his finger over a dusty framed photo of fly-fishing lures. She couldn't tell if he was disinterested in the house, or what exactly. She followed him into a wood-paneled hallway. Ari didn't want to go into any of the rooms. She could still sense the presence of the people who had lived in them. There was a baby's room: all decorated in pink, but no furniture. Dane turned into one of the rooms but Ari paused in the doorway.

This room had belonged to a boy. It was also empty of furniture, save a bare mattress that lay on the floor. Sports-themed posters and car pictures sagged from the walls. Dust coated everything and dirty spiderwebs dangled in the window. Ari got out her phone and silently took a photo of a shirtless Dane, standing with his hands on his hips, darkly silhouetted in the strong sunlight coming from the window.

There was a strange energy here. Ari couldn't see Dane's face, but she could feel that something about this house affected him.

Without warning, Dane drew back his arm and punched through

the wood-paneled wall. Wood splintered and crunched and crumbled under the weight of his fist. Dust and debris exploded from the wall, making a visible cloud in the streaming sunlight. Ari gasped and stumbled backward as Dane pushed past her.

He made his way to the back of the house and threw open the French doors that led to the wraparound back porch. One of the glass panes on the French door shattered at the impact of being flung open. He stepped outside and started heading for the river.

"Dane, wait!" Ari cried. The house now had a heavy feeling that was almost suffocating. She ran to the French doors, painfully crunching over debris on the floor, but a family portrait hanging on the wall caused her to pause. The photo wasn't too old, but it was aged enough that sunlight and time had faded the image. There was a smiling boy standing with his mom, and the mom was holding a baby. The dad was standing behind them, his arms draped over the boy and the mom.

The dad.

His face.

So familiar…

Oh no, Ari breathed.

chapter thirteen

By the time Ari had caught up with Dane, he was already at the river's edge, standing next to an old wooden dock, throwing melon-sized chunks of rock into the water like they were baseballs. Dane had a defensive stance about him, and Ari hung back and waited as he took his frustration out on chunks from the river bank. Rock after rock he hurled into the water, some so large they made a *whump* as they landed in the river.

Finally Dane sat down, holding his shoulder. Ari's heart was in her throat, skipping wildly. She sat down next to him, close enough that their arms and shoulders were touching. She didn't look at him. Ari sat in silence next to him for endless minutes.

"I shouldn't have brought you here," he finally said. He closed his eyes and put his head in his hands, rubbing his face and hair and exhaling till there was no breath left.

Ari put her hand on his back, right over his scar, as if to cover it, heal him. She wished she could somehow absorb the pain that was seeping from him. She felt his warm, sweaty skin under her hand, and the papery-crinkled texture of his scar. She could feel him inhale, exhale.

Ari closed her eyes and just listened. She listened to everything that could be heard around her: the sound of the rippling Elgin River. The birds. Wind rattling the uppermost leaves in the cottonwood trees. And Dane, grasping for words.

"I shouldn't have come here," he said again. Ari opened her eyes. His jaw was clenched hard and thin glittering lines of water edged his eyes. "I didn't know most of our stuff would still be in there. It was just like stepping back into that night." He got up and stood, looking out at the river.

"Let's walk," he said in a low voice. He started walking up the pebbled shore. Ari hugged the waterline where the pebbles were smallest and walking was easiest. She looked at their surroundings: on their left, to the west, cottonwoods lined the riverbank and gave way to tall conifers.

On the opposite riverbank, it looked very much the same, only it lacked the tall conifers. What was past the cottonwood trees, she couldn't see, but she figured they were a distance from any civilization.

She could hear a loud bird making screeching cries somewhere. The rippling water danced and sparkled. The farther they walked from the house, the lighter Dane's countenance seemed. His tensed muscles relaxed, his walk became slower, and once in awhile, he'd stop to throw a stone into the river.

Ari knew not to ask any questions; this was Dane's story to tell, and he'd only start when he was ready. After a solid ten minutes of walking, Dane finally began.

"I've never told anybody about my parents. They haven't ever talked about what happened that night. When I was ten or eleven, I didn't have many friends because we lived so far away from town or anybody else." Dane picked up a stone and hucked it into the water. "It didn't matter; Dad and I spent a whole lot of time together. He didn't work full-time. He did odd jobs here and there and was always here when I came home from school. Dane looked up into the woods. "Dad and I did a ton of stuff outdoors—fishing, camping, hiking—you name it, we tried it.

"Mom was a nurse in Woodward. She'd work twelve-hour shifts and I didn't spend nearly as much time with her as I did with Dad.

"They would argue about money a lot. I remember hiding out in my room when it got really heated. Things changed for the worst when Mom got pregnant with Molly; she had to take time off after Molly was born. We had been barely scraping by, and Mom was begging Dad to get a full-time job."

They came upon the remnants of a rowboat skeleton. Somehow it had gotten lodged high on the bank and left to rot. Dane poked at it with a stick, easily crumbling it. He paused his story, not looking at Ari at all.

"There were times that if Dad and I hadn't been able to fish, we would've missed a lot of meals. We got by, but...I remember how much it hurt to be hungry.

"Maybe hunger and desperation had something to do with my parent's argument that night. I dunno," Dane said, drawing in a deep breath. He furrowed his brow, wincing at the memory. Dane walked to the water's edge and then turned, and started walking back the way they came. Ari followed.

"I don't know what it was about. They were just mad, going at it as usual, but then something changed. They were somehow angrier, more aggressive, than they had ever been before. It became violent. I went to Molly's room. I felt like I needed to keep her safe. She stayed asleep in her crib through the whole thing...."

"I heard stuff breaking in the living room. It sounded like the whole freaking house was being destroyed by a tornado. Stuff was thrown around for five or ten minutes solid. Something shattered against the living room wall. After that, there was silence." Dane stopped talking.

Ari looked at him, but he kept his gaze straight and unnervingly stoic. He was having a hard time continuing. His breathing was fast and shallow. "I stayed in Molly's room, on the floor. I was too afraid to leave the room. Frozen in fear." He was shaking his head.

"Nobody came to check on you and Molly?" Ari finally asked.

"No. I fell asleep on her floor, and woke up to her crying. She was about one at the time, I think. I finally figured I had to go into the living room to get a bottle for Molly. Only Dad was home...sitting on the couch, staring straight ahead, with a can of beer in his hand. The house was a horrible mess—well, a lot like what it looks like now. That house has been frozen in that cursed moment for almost six years, Ari."

They walked slowly, retracing their path along the riverbank. The afternoon was turning to evening. Bugs were starting to swarm and she could see insect clouds in the waning sunlight.

"I learned later that Mom had gone into town and filed for divorce that morning. That day was the end of my family as I knew it, Ari.

Everything changed so quickly I couldn't comprehend it as a kid.

"When Mom told me they were splitting up, I begged her to let me stay with Dad. She agreed, and Dad and I moved out that day. We went to my uncle and Rhoda's house and we had our own room there for awhile. Slept on the floor, went fishing as usual, but it didn't last too long. That's about the time Dad took off and left me with my uncle. Said he was going to start fresh in another state—he'd always wanted to see the southwest. So he said he was going job hunting, and he'd come back for me when he was ready. You know the rest of that story.

"That same day, Mom took Molly and drove straight to Idaho to stay with her parents. She later told me that she had only been intending to stay a week or so, but Gram had a stroke right after Mom arrived. Mom ended up staying to care for Gram, and she eventually made the decision to stay and get a job so she could care for both Molly and Gram. She'd call me every week, at first, but then calls got fewer and farther between. I think she felt guilty about everything, plus she was super busy caring for Gram and Molly. She's mentioned that it was the most difficult time she's ever gone through, and she's apologized again and again for leaving me with Rhoda. But…" Dane paused. "I've never told her about all the stuff that happened with Rhoda. She doesn't know the half of it."

An evening breeze had started to pick up, channeling through the river gully. It brought the scent of cottonwood and river water and briny sun-baked rocks. The sun was starting to disappear behind the tall conifers to the west. Dane wordlessly picked up his pace a bit and threw his flannel shirt on, leaving it unbuttoned, fluttering in the wind.

All this about his parents, about his last day as a family, was more than Dane had ever said to her at one time. Her heart hurt to think about Dane as a little boy, seeing his life divided before him. It was far worse than she could've ever imagined—Ari knew he had scars from his time with Rhoda, but didn't know they ran deeper, right into the heart of this sad shattered house.

They were approaching the final bend before the river turned and the dock could be seen. Dane stopped and finally turned to Ari. It was the first time he'd looked at her the whole evening. He met her eyes.

"So there you have it, Ari. I'm no better than my dad when it comes to anger. You saw me in there, turning the wall to dust. It runs in the family, I guess." Disgust flashed over his face.

"I thought when I brought you here today that I'd be totally fine; enough time has passed that I thought I'd be unaffected by the house and what happened here. I wanted to show you how beautiful the river is. I have so many good memories here, but they're all overshadowed by one terrifying one. I don't want to be like my dad and how he scares you. Apparently I'm still angry at everything."

Dane shook his head and sighed. "That's one of the main reasons I don't have many friends now. I avoid relationships of any kind." His eyes were sad, bitter, frustrated.

Ari stood frozen, digesting his confession. He turned and started walking toward the house. She finally un-rooted herself from the spot on the pebbled shore and jogged to catch up to him.

"Dane, wait." He kept walking, his head low.

"*Wait.*" Ari demanded.

He finally stopped. She ran around him so he didn't have a choice but to face her. He'd stopped in front of a smallish boulder, and she took the opportunity to step up on it, bringing her face level with his. This seemed to surprise him, and his defeated look started to dissipate. They were nose-to-nose and Ari took the opportunity to stare him down.

"Dane, I want to help you. Healing from something like this—" she motioned back at the house,

"—takes time. Nobody expects you to be perfect. Not your parents, *not me.*" Her voice was solid, confident.

She let the words hang there. Between them there was nothing but the sound of the running river and the wind ruffling the cottonwood leaves. They were now standing in sun-dappled shade, and the temperature had dropped dramatically. Ari shivered but held her stare. Dane sighed and moved toward her, wrapping his arms around her and holding her so tight she could barely breath, had she wanted to. She could feel his slightly-whiskered face on her neck and shoulder as he buried his head in her hair.

Her heart was fluttering as he held her there; being in his arms just felt *right*. Why couldn't he see that? He'd entrusted his secrets with her…those deep, hurtful wells of anger and raw emotion.

She was still shaking from the cold evening wind that had channeled its way through the river gully. He pulled the loose ends of his flannel shirt around her; it was large enough that she easily fit inside it. She was nearly overwhelmed by the sense of being *that close* to him. His warmth and ever-present scent overpowered her thoughts. After a minute, he stepped back and looked at her.

"It's getting late," he said reluctantly. "Come on, let's get outta here," he said, taking her hand and taking a path around the side of the house.

"Wait," Ari said. "Don't you want to get the family portrait from inside the house?"

"No."

"What if you came back here again and everything was gone? Would you wish that you would have gotten that photo?"

Dane stopped and turned and looked at her. It took him forever to answer. "I'm not going in there again," he finally said.

"Do you want me to go get it?" The thought of being in the house alone, even for a moment, unsettled her. But she also couldn't bear the thought of leaving his family portrait.

"Alright," he said, shrugging.

Light was escaping the property. Shadows from the conifers fell to the bank of the river. Ari went to the back deck and through the still-open French doors.

The photo was located on a wall above the TV. She stood on her tiptoes to try and unhinge the photo from its nail on the wall. A rattling noise made her look to the front door.

Fuzzy shadows could be seen through the thin curtains. Then, several male voices could be heard outside the door, jeering and snickering. Ari's heart started to hammer and with horror she realized someone was trying to get inside the house.

In one swift jump, Ari leapt and unhooked the photo. She did a sprinter's dash through the French doors and rounded the corner to where Dane was standing to the side of the house. He saw her wide-eyed panic.

"What's going on?" he started to say, but Ari shushed him.

"Someone's trying to get in the front door!" she hissed. Dane motioned to creep to the side of the house, staying down low. Ari adjusted the portrait in her arms so she could silently move without brushing it up against the house and making sounds.

They got to an area to the side of the house where the front deck could be seen. Dusk was quickly approaching and low light hid them well. Dane furrowed his brow as they could both see a group of three guys still trying to get in the door. Finally, the biggest one threw his shoulder into the door and it splintered into pieces.

Dane got level with her ear. "It's Pat McCleary and his idiot friends. What are *they* doing here?" he whispered. Ari saw more bikes thrown into the grass, next to hers and Dane's. How were they going to get home without being seen, Ari didn't know. Dane seemed to read her mind.

"Let's wait until they go inside and then we'll be able to get our bikes. There's no way they can see us then," he figured.

Inside the house, they could hear Pat's voice calling out. "Hey, people, we know you're here! We saw your bikes! Come on out!" His friends snickered and something smashed against a wall inside the house.

Suddenly, Ari felt Dane recoil and tense like he'd been hit. She reached out and rested her hand on Dane's back, hoping that he wouldn't react or make a sound. He was breathing hard, fast, angry.

Just then, another splitting sound: a beer bottle came shattering out of a front window, getting caught up in the curtains and dropping to the front porch among shards of glass. Dane jerked forward, but Ari caught his shoulders.

"No! We can't be seen here, Dane," she begged.

Dane nodded, taking a deep breath and stepping back. They could now hear heavy footsteps on the back deck.

"Now!" Dane hissed, and they sprinted across the front yard, silently grabbing their bikes. Ari cursed the family portrait as she tried to juggle it to fit into her bike basket. They pedaled furiously up the gravel road and Ari didn't slow down until she saw the highway approaching.

Even on the highway, they rode as quickly as they could in the dusky light. Turning up Hadley Hill, they dismounted their bikes where the road got too steep.

Ari turned to Dane. "What do you think Pat McCleary was doing there?"

"To be honest, I don't care what anyone does there," Dane said. They'd come to the clearing in front of Ari's house. Stars were starting to show up against the greenish-blue hue of the last remnants of daylight.

Dane stopped walking and exhaled, long and slow. "Going back there was like stepping right back into that nightmare. I totally didn't expect to be affected by it, Ari." Dane shook his head and started walking again. "We probably shouldn't mention to anyone that we went there."

"You have my word, I won't tell a soul that we were there...or anything you shared with me today." A look of relief crossed his face.

"You can *trust* me, Dane," she promised him.

He reached out and brushed her face with his hand. "I know," he said, smiling. Ari handed him the family portrait, and he took it and his bike and started walking up the driveway. She watched him go until he rounded the corner and vanished.

*   *   *

Ari woke the next morning with a feeling of deep sadness and uneasiness that she couldn't shake. What she'd experienced with Dane the day before had settled in her heart. Her innermost being hurt for her best friend. She wanted so badly to somehow erase the scars endured by a boy who didn't understand what had happened in his small world.

Worse yet, she knew she couldn't talk about any of this with anyone. She desperately wanted to have Riley's input on how to help Dane move past his hurts, but she'd given Dane her absolute promise of confidentiality.

At lunch, Amara noted Ari's silence. "Something has you down," Amara quietly quipped. "Want to talk?"

Ari just shook her head. "I wish I could, guys, but I'm working something out that's bothering me," was all she could confess.

"How about non-specifics then?" Riley asked.

Ari shrugged. There was no way she could say anything and not have them figure out exactly who she was talking about.

"Thanks, guys. Really. Everything is fine."

After school, Ari was thankful to see Dane waiting by her bike. Dane noticed her contemplative gaze right away. "Ari, what's up? You don't look so good today," he assessed.

"I'm fine," was her automatic response, but she then reconsidered.

"Actually, would you want to go with me to the Abshire place? I think I'd like to check out the trail that goes toward Hadley Hill. I think a hike would help clear my mind."

Dane nodded, a questioning expression on his face. "Sure, should we stop by my house so we can get some gear so we can properly explore the trail?"

Ari nodded and grabbed her bike. She noticed a folded piece of paper stuck between her bike springs again. She groaned.

Dane looked over at her as she held the square of paper.

"Another note?" he asked, amused. Ari shoved it in her pocket without opening it.

They rode back to Hadley Hill; Dane split off and went to his house to change into hiking clothes, and Ari went to hers to find boots and shorts. Twenty minutes later, they were once again standing at the bank of the pond at the Abshire house.

The afternoon was warm, with a gentle breeze, just like the day before. They didn't have the canoe this time, but instead they used a narrow footpath that skirted the pond. They headed in the direction of the path that headed up Hadley Hill. Dane threw his backpack over his shirtless back and started hiking along the narrow trail. After a minute, he looked back at Ari.

"What's up, Ari? You've barely said two words today."

She didn't know where to start. All her well-rehearsed thoughts sounded silly now that Dane was in front of her. She fiddled with the honeybee pendant around her neck, thinking of how to start.

"I can't get yesterday out of my head," she admitted finally. She looked ahead at him, watching his movements and focusing on his scar that jutted out from underneath his pack. He was following the footpath; cottonwood trees had formed a tunnel of branches over their heads.

Dane turned and looked back at her, unsure. "What do you mean?"

"The way you were hurt. I can't imagine it. I just can't shake the feeling of sadness I have for you, Dane. I saw the smiling boy in the portrait. You had no idea what was going to happen..." she trailed off. "I wish none of that had ever happened to you. That's all," she mused quietly.

Dane shrugged. "What I went through made me who I am today, for better or for worse. I have issues because of it, sure, but I'm stronger because of it too. And more grateful for life now than you could ever imagine. And *you*—you've done more for me than any one person in my life, ever. Including my parents. Don't hold them guilty for what happened, though."

His statement surprised her.

"I've forgiven them, and they're working hard to be better parents, too," he explained.

Dane then stopped walking and turned to face her. "Promise me you won't be sad about this anymore, alright?"

Ari stopped a moment, settling on his gaze. Diffuse sunlight danced through the colors in his eyes; his expression was calm, honest.

"Alright," she said finally. He smiled his beautiful grin, which caused her to smile back.

Dane turned and kept walking along the path. Moments of silence were only punctuated by the shrill song of red-winged blackbirds that were hopping from cattail to cattail.

"What do you think the chances are that the trail on the hill will lead to your house?" Ari asked.

"I have a hunch this has to either end at your house or mine, or somewhere in between," Dane guessed.

Seven minutes after they'd started walking, the wooded trail emptied them onto the farthest shore of the pond, right where they had beached the canoe the last time.

Dane took off his pack and pulled a machete from it. He unsheathed the blade and looped its leather strap around his wrist. Ari stepped back, realizing she'd have to follow at a distance to keep out of Dane's way.

"You're really serious about opening up this trail," she said, stifling a chuckle.

"I'm really curious about where it ends up," Dane admitted. "I want to be able to prove or disprove this was the trail Ezra wrote about. Only one way to do that." They started up the trail, and once in a while Dane would cut away at a blackberry vine or branch.

"Something about Ezra resonates with you, doesn't it?" Ari asked quietly.

Dane stopped walking and made a half-turn and gazed out into the trees. After a moment, he looked back at Ari, thoughtful.

"Yeah, I suppose there is. I just want to know how life turned out for him, you know?"

Dane stepped closer to Ari and turned the question back at her. "What is it about their house that interests *you*?"

Ari tilted her head to the side and took a step closer to Dane. They were now a foot apart. With anyone else, Ari knew the closeness would be considered uncomfortable, but with Dane, it never was. It was only at this distance that Ari could see every detail in his eyes.

"You'll think I'm weird if I tell you."

"I already think you're weird." Dane's eyes smiled and Ari punched him in the arm.

"Just kidding," Dane joked. "Tell me."

Ari looked out at the expanse of trees, thinking of how to capture what she felt. "There's something there—something about that house— that is really intriguing. It's the way it feels, like the energy of the Abshires and whoever else ever lived in that house is still there, in a good way. Whenever we're inside, the house whispers to me: those worn wooden floors, the door frame with the kids' heights. Even the cellar floor that was hiding the journal. It's all begging us to tell its story, Dane."

Ari looked at him apprehensively, wondering if she'd totally lost her mind by telling him.

"Well, then, we'd better get moving. We have a story to find." Dane looked at her with total seriousness. Ari's mouth dropped open a fraction in disbelief that Dane wasn't at least scoffing at her a little. With the hand that wasn't holding the machete, he reached up and brushed her hair out of her eyes. He paused there, his hand to her face, for a second longer than usual. Ari caught her breath. Her mind took a picture-perfect image of the moment: the sunlight on his face, the exact expression in his eyes. In the amount of time it took her to blink, he wordlessly turned back and started back up the trail.

They eventually came to the place where Ari had fallen off the side of the path; she could see marks in the soft dirt where her feet had dug into the hillside. Not much further past that was where the blackberry vines completely overtook the trail.

"Alright, make sure you stay back a little," Dane reminded her, as he started hacking at the new growth with sweeping cuts. His backpack swung around with every movement of his arms; eventually Dane took the pack off and handed it to Ari.

"Do you mind carrying this for me? It's getting in the way," he explained, and Ari took the bag. With the pack gone, Ari could see his scar completely. His muscles moved under it, rippling with each swing.

Ari realized she was staring at him. She had to look away quickly before Dane noticed *her* noticing *him*. But Dane wasn't looking back at her; his eyes were fixed on the trunk of a large tree to his left. He brushed at the tree with his hand and squinted.

"You've got to be kidding," he mused under his breath. "Ari, look at this."

Ari moved to his side to look at the tree trunk. At her eye level, a rough oval of bark was removed. Right in the middle of the oval was a carving of two hearts, their points encircled.

"It's the symbol we found on the pillar!" Ari gasped.

"We've got to remember where this is," Dane insisted. "Can you get some pictures?"

Ari pulled out her phone and got as many photos as she could that would identify which tree the carving was on. "Do you think this means the symbols were recently carved? If it was old, wouldn't it have grown over? Or changed somehow?"

Dane shook his head. "No, I think that carvings stay on trees unchanged for a long time. My dad told me once that Native Americans used tree carvings to convey messages, and depending on the type of tree, they can stay unchanged for a hundred years or more."

Deep in thought, Ari started walking over the newly-cut vines, careful to stay back from Dane and minding the sharp edges of cut-off blackberry canes. Dane walked on, making quick progress as he hacked away at the underbrush, and they soon began climbing further up the hill.

"Do you think it has anything to do with Ezra and Katia? Have you come across that symbol in his journal yet?"

She could see Dane shake his head. "I'm sure I haven't seen it yet, but I'll watch for it. Anything's possible."

In places, the growth wasn't covering the path at all, and they were able to take several steps before Dane had to begin hacking away again.

After about twenty minutes, Ari called up to him. "Hey, it's not fair that you get to have all the fun."

Dane looked back at her, surprised. A glint of amusement crossed his eyes. "Alright," he said, unlooping the leather strap from his wrist. He handed it to her, handle first, and slipped the strap over her hand. "Just please don't hit your own legs or body while you're swinging," he advised. He took the two backpacks from Ari and slung them over his sweat-slicked shoulders. "If I bring back a diced-up Ari, your parents will never let me go anywhere with you again. *Ever.*" Even as he said it, he smiled.

Ari took a couple of practice swings at some offending underbrush. She quickly realized there was something immensely satisfying about whacking away at the bushy salal and bright green blackberries. She took great sweeping cuts, like she'd seen Dane doing. Ari wished she'd brought something along to tie her hair back with; with each swing, her straight hair swung across her face and soon, sweaty strands of hair were sticking to her forehead. She took off the jacket she'd been wearing and threw it back to Dane.

After swinging away for ten minutes, the leafy canopy above them began to thin out. Ari could see blue sky ahead. Suddenly the trail became extremely steep. Despite the incline, Ari quickened her pace and aggressively whacked at anything that imposed on the trail they were following. The trees they were walking through became a stand of crooked-branched oaks. Ari was now mostly cutting back small oak trees, tall grass, and weedy underbrush now, and the trail had leveled out.

With a final sweep of the blade, Ari and Dane came to the end of the path. The oak trees came to an abrupt end. Even, green grass spread out in front of them. They stepped out into Dane's backyard.

chapter fourteen

"You've got to be kidding me," Dane smiled, looking at his backyard, and then back at the trail they'd just blazed. Ari, machete still looped to her hand, looked in awe at Dane.

"You were right!" she exclaimed, looking up at him. "This has to be the trail Ezra and Katia used."

"Crazy," was all Dane could say, as he wiped at sweat rolling off his forehead.

"Is your mom going to be mad that we whacked a hole in your trees?" Ari whispered.

Dane smiled. "Not when I tell her how two smitten teenagers used this trail a hundred years ago. She's a sucker for love stories."

Ari realized she was still holding the blade. "I guess you can have your machete back. Although, I have to admit, that was really fun." A smile crept across her face. "Whacking away at brush is a great stress-reliever."

"I'll have to keep that in mind," Dane mused, taking the blade from Ari. "You were like a ninja with that thing—graceful but effective. You should get one of these things for your yard-care business."

Dane walked over to his back porch and sat down on the edge of the deck. Ari followed and sat next to him, shoulder-to-shoulder. The afternoon was waning, and the cool breeze was welcoming. Dane wiped at his head with his balled-up t-shirt.

"Hey," he nudged her, "what about that note you got today? Gonna read it?"

Ari had totally forgotten about the note, but fished it from her pocket. A twinge of nervousness tickled at her as she unfolded it. Dane leaned over her shoulder. *Ari, let's meet. I want our first dance to be at the Last Dance. Will you kindly meet me in the wisteria pavilion at 10 p.m.?* A heart was drawn at the bottom. Ari snickered.

"You're gonna meet him, right?

"What?" Ari asked, shocked. "You want me to dance with this guy?"

"No. I mean if you want to, sure," Dane explained. "You should at least meet him to see who exactly is writing these notes. If you don't, we might never find out."

Ari just shook her head. "I don't know about this."

"How about this: I'll hide somewhere nearby and keep an eye on you, alright? That way, if you need backup, I'll be right there."

"Like a stakeout?" Ari started to laugh and Dane chuckled. "Alright, Dane Hadley, Operation Wisteria Pavillion Stakeout is in effect. You'd better be right there for me if things go south." She eyed him in mock seriousness, and Dane burst out laughing. She grinned from ear to ear. A sudden, stunning thought struck her as they sat there on the back porch, laughing together.

I love him.

*　　　*　　　*

It was Tuesday, three days and counting before the Last Dance. Ari had made it through another impossibly long day at school. When she arrived at her bike, she noticed Dane's bike was missing. Ari had seen him in passing between classes, so she knew he hadn't been absent. Usually Dane would tell her at some point during the day to not wait up for him if he knew he wouldn't be going home at the same time. Shrugging, she made her way across town and onto the lonely highway that would lead her home to Hadley Hill.

As she was walking up the steep stretch of the hill, her phone started to vibrate in her pocket. It was a text from Riley. "Meet me and Amara tomorrow after school—let's hang out at my house and figure out hair and makeup for Saturday." Guiding her bike with one hand, Ari was able to tap out a message: "Sounds good."

*   *   *

"So, you've seen him at school between classes, but he hasn't said anything to you, and you haven't seen him after school, either?" Riley asked, as she was struggling to braid Ari's hair. Ari had found a photo in a magazine of a twisted side-braid, but from the feel of things, Ari's hair wasn't cooperating.

"Right. We hung out after school on Monday, and really everything seemed totally normal. I can't think of any reason he'd be avoiding me."

"Oh, Ari, he's not avoiding you," Amara quipped. "Girls always go straight to the worst possible scenario. He's just got stuff to do, I'm sure. He's probably scrambling to find something to wear for Saturday."

"Speaking of something to wear, I've noticed that Dane's developed quite a style since last year," Riley mused. "In tenth grade, he looked like every other boy, with ratty jeans and a t-shirt. This year he's really stepped it up. I think he wants to look nice for someone," Riley smiled and poked Ari.

"Nah, I don't think he's doing anything because of me," Ari said honestly.

"Hey! What about your secret admirer?" Amara said, looking up from her mirror as she struggled to apply false eyelashes.

"Oh, ok, get this: he wants to meet at ten p.m. at the wisteria pavilion. Dane said I should do it, just to see who it is. Dane promised he'd be watching from a distance so if I need an 'out,' he'd be there."

Amara's eyes got big. "I can't wait to find out who it is!" she squealed.

"He's all yours," Ari joked. "So what about Jace, Riley? What's going on with you two?"

Riley blushed. "Well, we've been hanging out at the coffee shop after school, doing homework and stuff. He's really sweet. We have a lot of the same interests, which makes for some great conversation." Amara

rolled her eyes and mouthed *'boring!'* and Riley stuck out her tongue, laughing.

"Amara, who are you going with?" Ari felt bad that she didn't know yet.

"I'm going with a guy in my calculus class. His name is Aaron. We're just friends— heck, I don't even really know him that well, but he asked me, so I figured, why not?"

Riley had finally given up on Ari's hair. "I think we're going to have to do something else other than a braid or a twist," she admitted. "Can I try something?"

Ari shrugged. "Go for it. I haven't a clue what to do with my hair. Or anything else for that matter."

Amara pulled a book off of Riley's desk and flipped to a vintage photo of Audrey Hepburn. "Ari, you've always reminded me of Audrey. Look, you have the same strong brows and big brown eyes," she said, pointing at the photo.

"Yeah," Riley chimed in. "Let's try an updo with side-swept bangs that emphasizes Ari's eyes. Ari, you're always wearing your hair down, so let's change it up a little," Riley sounded excited about trying something new. By the end of the night, they'd settled on final hairstyles and taken photos of how they were planning their makeup. Ari felt as ready as she ever would.

*   *   *

It was Friday evening. Dane had been at school, but once again, he was a no-show for riding home. Ari figured she'd need to at least check with him to see when they would be leaving for Saturday's dance. She was feeling uneasy as she made her way into the oak grove. He hadn't said more than a few words to her since Monday evening.

Ari checked the circle first. The path through the grove had become slightly overgrown with new spring growth; neither she nor Dane had been coming to the underground room as much since the weather had improved. Ari reached up for the tree branch that they always hung the key on. The key was there, as usual. She unlocked the door with a clink and peeked down into the underground room. It was dark: no Dane.

She put the key back on its high branch and walked the rest of the way through the oak grove, coming out on the other side at Dane's driveway. She went up the old porch steps and rang the doorbell. Molly came to the door.

"Hey, Molly!" Ari smiled. Molly had Dane's eyes—but full of joy and lightness all the time.

"Hey, Aribelle!"

"Is your brother here?" Ari asked, looking around. Molly started to say something, but Mrs. Hadley came to the door and welcomed Ari in.

"Hello, Ari. Dane thought you might be by. He wanted me to give you this," she said, handing her a note. 'Ari' was scribed in Dane's familiar handwriting.

Ari thanked Mrs. Hadley and stepped back onto the front porch. She unfolded the note. *Ari, I'm sorry I haven't been around this week. I'm at my dad's. I'll pick you up at your house at 6.30 on Saturday. See you then. Love, Dane.*

The note made Ari smile. Her uneasiness melted away and made her way back home through the oak grove.

*   *   *

"Alright, girls, we have four hours until our dates will be here. Nails first, then hair and makeup, then dresses," Riley said as she hauled a professionally-sized makeup case up the stairs to Ari's room. Ari's house had been the chosen location for pre-dance preparation, and the only thing Ari wished for at the moment was that her house had air conditioning.

"Whew, it's hot up here," Amara said, reaching Ari's room. She was right. The unusually warm early June day had baked its way up to the top floor. "But, this is the absolute best place for hair and makeup because of the incredible natural light."

"I've got fans! Fans coming through!" Ari called, her arms full of three different fans collected from around the house. She arranged them about the room as Riley and Amara unpacked their hair accessories and makeup at Ari's vanity.

Ari had opened the gothic arch window in her room. A gentle breeze wafted through the space, ruffling the white chiffon curtains that hung floor-to-ceiling. On the back of her door hung three garment bags that held their dresses.

Butterflies were already filling Ari's insides. She tried to concentrate on doing her nails, but it wasn't long until she noticed her hands were shaking ever-so-slightly. Riley looked over from painting her toes.

"Excited about tonight?" she smiled, revealing gummy-looking tooth whitening strips. Ari snickered. "What?" Riley managed to say, through her clenched teeth. "I drink a lot of coffee. Need white teeth," she started to laugh.

"I *am* nervous. I don't know what I'm more nervous about, to be honest: finding out who the note-writer is, or being there with Dane."

"Why on earth would you be nervous about going with Dane?" Amara asked, looking up from her nails, which she was drying in front of one of the fans. "You spend nearly every waking minute with him."

"Just because I really don't know if he's going to enjoy it," she said. "Aren't you nervous about going with Aaron?"

"Nope." Amara smiled a fabulous dimpled grin. "I have no expectations," she laughed.

Hours later, Ari found herself standing in front of the antique full-length mirror in her bedroom. Riley had expertly done her makeup: Ari's full brows had been shaped, and she'd drawn subtle cat-eye liner, with shimmering brown and gold eye shadow. Barely-there lipstick completed the look.

Amara had smoothed Ari's straight brown hair into side-swept bangs, then twisted her hair into the most delicate high bun. Riley had attacked Ari's head with enough hairspray to permanently freeze it in place.

Ari had Riley zip up her dress. The strapless white eyelet and lace A-line was perfectly casual but elegant. Ari felt the dress looked like her; she felt confident in it. Most importantly, it was comfortable.
Riley looked equally as stunning in her black dress. "Check out the pockets!" she exclaimed, showing Amara the favorite feature of the gown. Amara had chosen an off-white chiffon dress that flowed like water as she moved. Ari thought it looked just perfect on her.

There was a knock on the door and Ari's mom poked her head in.

"Are you girls ready for photos? Can we get some on the stairs and front porch before you go?"

Ari's mom glanced at her daughter. She walked over and stood next to Ari at the mirror. "Look at you, Aribelle," she sighed. "My little girl is growing up…you look absolutely stunning." Her mom reached over and side-hugged her, being careful to not disturb her hair.

Ari beamed. "Thanks, mom."

The girls headed first to the staircase, where Ari's mom took some photos. On the front porch, the early evening sunlight was still strong, so Ari's mom suggested they try the back yard.

The formal garden was starting to bloom with the first round of late spring plants. Pansies were everywhere, and a wisteria vine was dangling fragrant clusters of lavender blooms across the back porch. Ari's mom gestured at the porch, where she began taking photos.

Aaron was the first date to arrive. Ari hadn't met him before. He had sandy blonde hair and freckles, and he seemed more nervous than even Ari felt. She liked him immediately. He'd brought a delicate pink rose corsage for Amara and was cautiously putting it on her wrist. Ari could tell that Amara was taken with his sweetness; Ari guessed Aaron had been admiring Amara for some time.

Ari remembered that she'd left Dane's boutonniere in the refrigerator. She excused herself and went to fetch it; her dad was fixing dinner for Lily. Jazz flowed from the countertop radio by the sink, and she swore she could already smell a pipe smoldering somewhere. Her dad did a double-take when Ari walked into the room.

"Oh, Ari," he said, taking a break from stirring whatever was on the stovetop. "You look beautiful. Your mom is getting photos of all of you, right?"

Ari nodded, and Lily squealed in delight as Ari pulled the boutonniere from the fridge. It was carefully housed in a brown paper box.

At the florists', Ari hadn't been able to find an arrangement that looked like anything she thought Dane would ever wear. She simply couldn't picture him sporting a flower on his suit. Instead, she'd asked if one could be made using forest greenery: a perfect green oak leaf, a salal leaf, and a tiny fern curl.

"Ari," Lily asked, "are you going to wear earrings? Got any sparkly ones?"

"Oh my gosh," Ari exclaimed, "good catch, Lily. Gotta go get those."

She bounded out of the kitchen and rounded the newel cap on the staircase when the sound of a vehicle crunching on the driveway caused her to look out the front windows. It was a truck she didn't recognize: a classic old Chevy, light blue and white, shined to a high polish. She waited to see who would get out of the truck, figuring it had to be Jace.

But when the driver got out of the truck, her heart skipped wildly. It was Dane.

chapter fifteen

Ari couldn't take her eyes off the person coming toward the front door. It was Dane, to be sure, but she could hardly reconcile the sight of him to the person she knew.

Dane was wearing a gray sport coat over a crisp white shirt with the top button undone. The coat was expertly tailored and emphasized his broad shoulders. He looked taller than ever somehow. Dark, fitted slacks with a brown belt and brown oxfords finished the look. His once-shaggy hair had been tamed and cut shorter than she'd ever seen it. Hands in pockets, he walked with confident strides toward the front porch. Ari opened the door before he could ring the bell.

Dane Hadley stood there, gazing at Ari, completely speechless.

The faint scent of Dane's aqua-scented cologne floated in on a warm breeze. Ari suddenly felt so shy, she could barely look at him—but she couldn't look away, either. Her eyes settled on his. This was the boy next door who she'd solved mysteries and shared adventures with. But standing here in front of her, looking at her with an intensity she had never felt before…this was a version of Dane that she had not yet seen.

Ari moved one step closer to him. A slow smile spread across Dane's face, and he tilted his head to one side. Just as he was about to say something, Riley, Amara, and Aaron came through the house, looking for Ari.

"Hey! Dane's here!" Riley exclaimed, and Dane nodded hello. Ari noticed Riley did a double-take at the sight of Dane as well.

"Dane, you look fantastic!" Riley exclaimed. Dane smiled shyly. "We're just waiting for Jace to get here before we finish up taking pictures," Riley continued, giving Ari a big thumbs-up.

On cue, Jace pulled up in not the minivan, but his mom's BMW.

"Oh, shoot, Riley, looks like you missed out on the van," Amara joked, and Riley rolled her eyes.

Jace hurried to join the group, and Ari's mom hurried to get photos finished before it was time to leave. For the first photo, her mom had the girls stand in front, with their dates behind them. Next, she had each couple stand together. Dane wrapped his arm around her waist and Ari felt herself blushing. For the final pose, Ari's mom photographed each couple alone by the hydrangea bush in their front yard. Ari stood facing Dane, and he wrapped his arms around her in nearly a full hug. Something about the awkwardness of the pose made Ari laugh, which in turn, made Dane start to chuckle as well. The lightness of the moment made some of her nervousness fade away.

As each couple went to their cars, Ari suddenly remembered Dane's boutonniere was still inside her house. She ran inside to get it, as well as the pair of earrings she'd forgotten. By the time she got back outside, the other two couples had already left.

Dane was standing by the truck, talking with Ari's dad. Ari nervously hung back; it looked like they were having some sort of serious conversation. Her dad's arms were crossed, and Dane was shaking his head and saying something. She cautiously approached.

"It's a '64 Chevy C-10 stepside," Dane was saying. "It was a birthday present to myself," he continued. "It wasn't in bad shape when I bought it, but Dad and I worked on it all this week to clean it up a bit."

Ari's dad smiled when he saw Ari approaching. "Have fun, you two," he said, giving Ari a big hug. He waved good-bye as he retreated into the house, and Ari thought he had an air of sadness about him. She could hear faint strands of jazz floating from the house as she took out Dane's boutonniere.

"A *birthday* present?" she said, looking at Dane as he leaned up against his truck. "I missed your birthday?"

Dane smile an ear-to-ear grin. "I have this great new truck, and all you're concerned with is the fact you missed my birthday?" he teased her, then in seriousness, he admitted, "Yes, I turned seventeen on Wednesday. But, I was gone all week because I bought the truck on Tuesday and Dad spent the rest of the week helping me fix it up for tonight." Dane looked at his watch—the first time Ari had ever seen him wear one—and mentioned that they'd better leave soon.

"Hey, I need to pin this on you before we go," she said, carefully taking the boutonniere out of its case. Dane smiled and held Ari's waist to steady her as she wobbled on her tiptoes to reach the lapel of his sport coat. When she was done, he pulled a box from the truck and opened it. Inside was a corsage made of four huge gardenia blossoms.

"This one was made to be pinned on, or it has a clip so you can wear it in your hair. Which would you like?" His confident demeanor had faltered a little bit; Ari could tell he'd never dealt with this type of thing before and was way out of his comfort zone.

"Hair. Definitely," Ari grinned, and turned her head so that Dane could clip the heady, fragrant blossoms onto her head. He ever-so-carefully secured it, and flowers cascaded around her upswept hair.

"Wow," he breathed. "Ari…you look absolutely stunning," he admitted. He looked right at her, not a hint of shyness in his eyes. Ari blushed and followed him as he went to the passenger side door and opened it for her. She gathered her eyelet-and-lace skirt and pulled herself onto the bench seat of the truck.

The old truck was expertly restored inside. It already had Dane's soap-and-laundry scent, plus whatever new cool-smelling cologne he was wearing. He got in and started it. It roared to life with the throaty purr of a refurbished engine.

"How did you find the truck? Impulse buy?" Ari teased.

"Nah, I've had my eye on it for some time now. A guy that works at the coffee shop owned it but put a sign on it about a month ago. I couldn't pass it up. I figured if I get the museum internship, it might be helpful to have a car to get there with. And," he smiled at her, "we won't have to ride bikes to school in the rain anymore." Ari grinned, liking the thought of driving to school with Dane.

She snuck a look at him as he drove along. He wasn't the boy next door anymore, she realized. He was relaxed back into the bench seat, steering with one hand draped over the wheel and shifting with the other. Even his profile looked older to her—he was no longer the kid who had shaggy, wild hair. His closer-cut hair revealed a refined jawline. He saw her looking at him and smiled. "What?" he asked, looking shy.

"You look fantastic," she finally managed. "And this truck suits you. It's exactly something I would picture you driving."

At that, Dane grinned broadly. "Thanks, Ari."

"Did you have a good birthday?" Ari asked. "I feel terrible for missing it."

"Well, there's no way you could've know about it, so you're off the hook," he smiled again. "My birthday was amazing. Ari, it was the best birthday that I can remember since I was about seven years old. Think about it," he stated, looking straight at her. "Last year at this time I was practically living in the underground room, just trying to stay out of Rhoda's way. I had no clue about where either of my parents were, and I was just…surviving." He stopped talking for a moment, reflecting. "Yeah, this year was awesome."

They had passed through Rivers and were now heading out of town. Fields with knee-high crops of grass lined each side of the road as they continued through the valley to the southeast. Ari draped her arm over the side of the open window and closed her eyes for just a moment. The highway-whipped wind smelled of fresh hay and sun-baked fields.

Ansley Park Garden was located up in the hills above Rivers. Dane turned off the highway onto a smaller curved road. "I've only been to the gardens once, a long time ago," Dane mused. "It was before my parents split, so I really don't remember what the gardens look like at all. Haven't had a reason to be back. Now," he said, looking gratefully at Ari, "I have a reason. A good one," he said, his eyes smiling.

They were climbing a twisting road that lifted them away from the floor of the valley. Dane downshifted as the road inched upwards. Ari twisted in the passenger seat so she could see what was behind them.

Endless valley and hills beyond were becoming visible. She could even see the top of a snowy mountain, bathed pink in the evening light.

"Whoa…Dane, this is incredible!"

Dane looked at Ari and beamed.

They rounded several more corners before arriving at the entrance gates for the gardens. Tall stone pillars presented a brass plaque announcing *Ansley Park Garden*. They drove through the gates directly into a massive tunnel dripping with wisteria. Ari gasped as she looked up. The sweet smell of the wisteria drifted through the truck's open windows. At the end of the tunnel, massive ceramic urns, half the height of the truck, held sculpted topiaries.

The lane curved down and around the main garden house, which was a two-story stone building with an observation deck at the top. The parking lot was nearly full when she and Dane got out of the truck.

"I think we just made it in time for the dance lessons," Dane remarked, checking his watch again.

"The what?"

"Dance lessons. They have a dance instructor do forty-five minutes of basic dance lessons for anyone who wants to join in. Did you want to try it?"

Ari smiled, thinking it was almost ridiculous that Dane wanted to do dance lessons with her. Six months ago he had barely made it to the Winter Formal. Now he was holding his arm out, waiting for her to take it.

"Of course I'll do dance lessons with you," she grinned.

A stone staircase led from the parking lot up to the main dance area. The evening light had turned pinkish, and globe lights were strung across the cobblestone circle that made the dance floor. Ari was silently thankful she was wearing ballet flats instead of heels.

A circle of students surrounded the instructor, who was wearing a headpiece microphone. He was beginning to describe the basic steps for a swing dance. Ari looked across the circle and saw Riley and Jace, who waved at her. Amara and Aaron were sitting at one of the wrought-iron cafe tables that lined the dance area. Ari saw the back of Julia's head; she was dancing with a tall boy that Ari wasn't familiar with. Rob was paired with his date, a senior that Ari knew was on the volleyball team.

Dane put his hand behind her back, and took her other hand as the instructor described. It was easy enough to follow along with the basic steps, and within a few minutes, they had both picked up the rhythm. Ari beamed at Dane. He was doing a perfect job of following the instructor's movements, and he held Ari lightly and guided her well.

"Alright, folks, looking good," the instructor praised. "Now, let's rotate partners. Men, you move clockwise to your next partner." Dane raised his eyebrows in surprise. Ari grimaced. She wouldn't see Dane again until he had rotated around the whole circle.

The next partner that came to Ari was a guy she knew from history class. "Dylan, right?" she asked. He nodded.

"Yep. You're Aribelle?" He smiled. He was not as tall as Dane; Ari was almost at eye-level with him. Somehow being nearly the same height made dancing a little easier and they worked through the new steps easily. Dylan seemed to have some prior dancing skill.

"Yeah. You can call me Ari." The instructor talked them all through the next step: a basic underarm turn. Dylan turned Ari into a spin and she smiled.

The next few partners came and went in near silence, until a well-muscled guy named Sven made his way to Ari. He smiled as he took her in his arms and the instructor informed them they were moving on to the waltz.

"Hi Ari, I'm Sven. We have P.E. together," he smiled. Ari nodded. *Of course.* Sven was familiar, but she couldn't remember where she knew him from. As they began the basic box step, Ari looked over to see where

Dane was. He had rotated around to Julia, and she could see Julia beaming as she swayed with Dane. They were both the same height, and together they looked quite intimidating, like a model couple out of an ad. She could hear Julia laughing at something Dane had said.

"You're Dane Hadley's girlfriend, right?" Sven asked. Ari winced.

"He's my best friend," she said awkwardly. Sven apologized. Ari just shrugged.

"I just see you guys riding home all the time and made an assumption. Well, then, if I may say so—you look amazing tonight, Ari," Sven smiled. "I've always thought you were lovely, but tonight you look exquisite." Ari blushed. She nodded and thanked him, and a sudden thought struck her: could Sven be her note-writer? He seemed much more familiar with her than she was with him. Before she had time to think on it more, the instructor indicated another rotation, and Ari looked across the circle just in time to see Julia kiss Dane on the cheek as he moved to his next partner. A hot twinge ran through Ari.

Sven bid farewell, and Rob rotated to Ari. She smiled, thankful she was back with someone she knew slightly. The new step to practice was a spin turn, and Rob guided her through it with ease. "Having a good time tonight?" Rob asked, as they moved together into the turn.

"So far so good," Ari said. "I haven't stepped on anyone yet, and I haven't fallen, so I'm doing better than expected," she joked, and Rob laughed. Dancing with him was easy, and they moved onto a more complicated step.

"Are you having a good time? Who is your date?" Ari asked.

"Jen McNary. I've known her since we were kids. Neither of us had dates, so we decided to come together," he explained.

"That's sweet," Ari said, and they continued to practice their turns together.

Three more partners later, Dane was back to Ari. Dane smiled broadly as he took her back in his arms. "Miss me?" he joked.

"More than you'll ever know," Ari's eyes brightened. "Hey!" She pulled him closer to her and hissed in his ear, "I might know who the secret note-writer is!" She covertly glance over her shoulder. "Sven. Do you know him? Blonde, muscular, over there," she discreetly twitched her head to the left.

"What makes you think it's him?" Dane whispered back, clearly enjoying the mystery.

"He said something about seeing us ride home together all the time. And he asked if you were my boyfriend."

Dane looked at her seriously. "Wha'd you say?"

"I said you weren't, but that you're my best friend," Ari said honestly. Dane furrowed his brow. Before he could say anything else, the instructor indicated the lesson was over, and thanked the group.

Dane held out his arm and Ari took it. Riley and Jace jogged over to meet them.

"Glad you didn't wear heels, aren't you?" Riley joked with Ari.

"No kidding. I'm also really glad I didn't end up tripping on that cobblestone dance floor. That would've been ugly," she laughed.

Riley pointed to the stately building that served as the event center. "Let's go check out the inside."

Stairs led to the entrance of the garden house. More topiaries guarded each side of the staircase. The entrance had heavy, massive carved doors. Riley suggested they go to the observation deck. Music started up on the dance floor and echoed through the entryway of the building.

Inside the house, candlelit sconces hung on the walls. The interior space was set up with round tables with white tablecloths, a candle on each table. A coat attendant was taking jackets behind a closeted door, and Dane handed her his sport coat. Ari looked at Dane in his crisp white shirt: he cut an intimidating silhouette and looked so much older than seventeen.

A buffet table lined one wall. Students were lining up with plates to load up on hors d'ourves and drinks. Riley pulled Ari past the buffet and ran up the spiral staircase, her dress swishing with each step. Dane and Jace followed behind. As they rounded the top of the staircase, Ari drew in her breath as the scene in front of her unfolded: a vast observation deck spread out the length of the second story.

From up here, it felt like they were literally on top of the world. Ari could see the valley floor stretch in all directions, gently hugged by low hills on all sides. Ari got to the middle of the observation deck before she stopped. Riley and the rest of her friends were standing at the railing, looking down on the couples below that had already started dancing. Dane looked back at Ari with a questioning glance.

Ari couldn't make her feet move. Although she knew it wasn't, the deck felt like it was swaying, and Ari wanted to grab for anything that was closest to her. Dane saw her look of panic and moved to her side and put his arm around her waist.

"You ok?" he whispered in her ear. Ari nodded.

"It just feels like we're really high up," she said quietly.

"Well…we kinda are," he whispered.

That didn't exactly help Ari, but she continued to focus on the incredible view.

"If I'm right next to you, will you come to the railing?" he asked. She nodded. He kept his arm tightly around her waist as they approached the side of the deck. Once she was holding onto the railing, her fear almost lessened. She still didn't want to look straight down, but from this vantage point, Ari could see the full layout of the garden: paths wound in and out of an expanse of blooming plants and trees. Candlelit outdoor chandeliers glowed in the dusky light. There was a formal English garden with a large fountain in one corner, and a pond with lily pads in another area.

Dane's face brushed against hers as he leaned over. "Hey, there's the wisteria pavilion," he whispered, pointing out across the garden. In the far southeast corner of the property, a tiny trail led to a far-off domed pavilion that was covered in blooming wisteria.

Ari eyed the layout of the garden. "We should figure out where you're going to need to stand so you can have a clear view of the pavilion," she mused. "Come on," she said, looping her arm around his waist. "We need to do some recon." At this, Dane laughed, and Ari's heart melted at the sound.

They rounded the spiral staircase down to the main floor, Ari's dress billowing out as she descended. They went around the cobblestone dance floor and into the formal English garden. A grid of square raised planters held flourishing lavender bushes. Several couples were making their way through the English garden. Dane and Ari followed the straight path to a giant fountain that was in the very center of the garden. Ari watched a couple toss pennies into the tile-lined fountain.

They continued down the center path, and Ari looped her hand around Dane's bicep. He smiled and placed his hand on top of hers. Walking along the garden like this, Ari felt like a better version of herself: she walked a little taller and wished this exact moment could last forever. She snuck a glance at Dane and still was having a hard time believing that he was here with her.

Beyond the fountain, they followed the path to an exit gate, which transitioned into a Japanese garden. Ari could still hear the music faintly once they were inside the Zen landscape. A tranquil pool with lily pads was surrounded by a meandering gravel path. Tiny brass lamps in the shape of downturned blossoms drew little circles of warm light on the pathway. At the pond's midpoint, there was a small square landing composed of four concrete squares, where the path split into two directions.

"Which way is the pavilion?" Ari stood with her hand on her hips.

The garden was nearly silent, save for a few solitary cricket chirps, the bubbling of pond water, and wisps of music floating on the breeze.

Without warning, Ari felt Dane's hand on her waist as he slowly pulled her to him. Ari was unsure of what was happening at first.

Dane looked down at her with an expression she'd never seen before; something between awestruck and timidity. Her heart raced and she could hardly breathe. He was looking straight through her, with a clarity and honesty that she recognized. Dane reached to her face to bring her closer. Ari caught her breath in anticipation as he leaned down, his lips an inch from hers.

Suddenly a crashing noise startled them both. Ari skittered sideways as two big bodies stumbled past them: Pat McCleary and one of his friends that Ari recognized from Dane's old house. They were laughing and snickering, shoving one another, and Pat nearly teetered into the pond.

"Whoooo! It's *you* two," Pat slurred, obviously drunk. The other guy wolf-whistled. Dane clenched his jaw.

"Let's go," Dane grunted and wrapped his arm around Ari's waist, guiding her toward the path to the left.

"Hey Hadley!" Pat shouted. "Nice house you had over there on Lawton!"

Dane stopped and swiveled around to face Pat. "What'd you say?"

Ari looked at Pat, stunned. How did *he* know about the house?

"Me an' my buddy here found an abandoned place down by the river the other day! And guess what we found inside? A whole photo album of little Dane. I remember what you looked like in third grade, boy." Pat coughed and belched.

"What'd you do with it?" Ari demanded. She saw Dane look over at her in surprise.

"Whoo, little lady. What do you care?" Pat staggered toward her, but Dane placed himself between Ari and Pat. Pat narrowed his eyes and closed the distance between himself and Dane. "How about a dance with the girl, Hadley? She dances with me and I'll let you know where your precious photo album is," Pat slurred.

"Not a chance," Dane growled.

"Y'know, Hadley, you owe me one from the bonfire. Comin' to my house and thinking you can punch me in front of my friends? Who do you think you are?" Pat hissed, slurring the last words.

"If you touch her, I'll drop you again." Dane's voice was dangerous. The air between him and Pat pulsed with angry tension. Ari was frozen in place, nearly concealed completely by Dane, who was standing in front of her. She saw Dane's hands close into hard fists. Even through his starched dress shirt, she saw the muscles in his back tense and contract. Ari knew she had to act fast: suddenly she ducked out from behind Dane.

"Pat, let's go to the courtyard. I'd be happy to dance," she said, in a cordial tone. Pat and Dane both looked at her in complete surprise.

"No! Ari—," Dane protested, but Ari had already taken Pat's arm and was leading him back through the English garden. Ari looked back at Dane with a knowing glance, as if to assure him that she had everything under control. Dane looked halfway between confused and angry, but he and Pat's friend followed them back to the dance floor.

They arrived at the courtyard, where a slow dance had just started. It was a waltz, and Pat took Ari by the hand and tried his drunken best to follow the beat. She gritted her teeth as he stumbled into her at least a half-dozen times. Pat grinned and gave a thumbs-up to his friend, who was standing next to Dane, watching. Dane stood with a wide stance and arms crossed, with a seething look on his face. The song seemed to go on forever. At long last, when the music ended, Ari leaned over to Pat's ear.

"Alright, Pat, what did you do with the photo album? A deal's a deal."

Pat made a snorting sound and started laughing. "Little lady, we threw it into the woods. Good luck finding it!" He turned to leave the floor, but Ari grabbed him by the shirt. Pat swiveled back around, startled.

"*Where* did you throw it?" Ari insisted. She wouldn't let go of his shirt.

"I dunno! Somewhere near the brick pile." He jerked away, swearing, and rejoined his friend, who was jeering from the side of the dance floor.

Dane was at Ari's side almost immediately. "Ari, what were you thinking?" He looked at her intensely, shaking his head. "Why did you grab him like that? He could've hurt you!"

Ari just shrugged. "Well, he didn't, and I found out where your album went. It was worth it."

Dane closed his eyes in frustration and sighed. "I promised your dad tonight that above all else, I would keep you *safe*," he insisted.

"What?" Ari crinkled her brow.

"Before we left, when you were in the house and I was out at the truck, he told me to take care of his little girl," Dane explained. "I gave him my word that I'd protect you no matter what. You have to let me try, Ari."

Ari was speechless. Before she could say another word, Riley and Amara rushed up to Ari and grabbed her, one friend on each arm.

"Hey! Dane, we're gonna borrow Ari for a minute, ok?" Riley shouted over the music. Dane watched as Ari's friends literally pulled her across the dance floor as a fast song started.

"Ari! We just saw you dancing with a drunk Pat McCleary and Dane looks super unhappy," Amara tried to be heard over the music without shouting. "Is everything ok?"

Ari took a deep breath and shrugged. "Yeah, everything is ok. Tonight is just going a little differently than I hoped it would," she admitted. A garden clock, suspended on a wrought iron post, declared the time to be three minutes to ten.

"Guys! I have to go. It's almost ten," Ari realized.

"Good luck! We want to hear who Mr. Mystery is," Amara said, giggling.

Dane met Ari on the edge of the dance floor. They walked through the English garden and back around the pond in the Japanese garden. At the square landing where Dane had almost kissed her, she paused once again. "Dane, I'm sorry about dancing with Pat. I was so worried you were guys were going to fight, I had to do something to stop it," she confessed.

"You don't have to apologize, Ari. I appreciate what you did." He looked at her with kind eyes. Ari smiled.

"Which way?" she asked. Dane pointed left.

They walked down a tiny path made of hazelnut shells which crunched and shifted under their feet. Bushy plants with fragrant, trumpet-shaped white blossoms lined the pathway. After a short distance, the wisteria pavilion came into view: it was solidly draped in pinkish-lavendar blossoms which hung down from the domed roof. White lights wound around the pavilion frame, making the blossoms glow from the inside. The pavilion was empty.

"Remember, I'm counting on you to have my back," a sly look crossed Ari's face, getting back into the spirit of the stakeout, and how silly this whole situation was. "Where are you going to stand so you can see me?" she asked Dane. He smiled back and played along.

"I'll go back to the Japanese garden. There's only one way to the pavilion, so I'll definitely be able to see if anyone goes down this path. I'll trail him at a distance and watch from this spot, ok?"

Ari nodded. The plan sounded good. She walked to the wisteria pavilion and entered the cloud of sweet-smelling flowers that hung down like clusters of grapes. She turned and saw Dane looking at her. For a second longer he just stood there, gazing at her, with a serious look on his face. He then slowly turned and disappeared down the path.

chapter sixteen

It wasn't long before Ari heard the crunch of footsteps
approaching on the hazelnut path. A shiver of nervousness went through
her. She turned to look, and saw a couple heading her way. When they
noticed the pavilion wasn't empty, they started to giggle and turned back.
She could hear their retreating footsteps.

After that, she heard nothing. Minutes passed, and Ari finally pulled
out her phone. It was 10:15 p.m. She shook her head, realizing her secret
note-writer had stood her up. In frustration, she went back to the
Japanese garden to meet Dane.

She looked all around. Dane wasn't anywhere in sight. She
continued on through the English garden, looking carefully at each
person she passed, but none matched the tall, broad-shouldered boy she
was searching for. Disappointed, she headed back to the courtyard,
where the dance floor was packed with couples dancing to a slow song.
There, in the middle of the crowd, she picked out Dane. He was dancing
with Julia, their tall figures standing out amongst the rest of the dancers.

Her stomach sank. He was supposed to be watching out for her, but
instead, he was holding onto Julia, and she looked contented to rest her
head on his shoulder. Ari turned and found a cafe table to sit at. She
hadn't even gotten to dance with Dane yet, and the night was nearly
over. Disappointment clouded her emotions.

A figure approached the table. She looked up to see Rob holding
out his hand to her.

"Wanna dance?" Rob wore a sympathetic smile.

Ari took his hand and nodded. "I'd love to," she said.

Rob took her on his arm and guided her to the floor. They made
their way into the swaying crowd of dancers. She looked at him in
thanks, and he grinned back at her.

"So how's your night going? Are you having fun?" Rob asked,

genuinely interested.

"It's certainly been an interesting night, that's for sure," Ari said, rolling her eyes. "How about you? How's Jen?"

Rob shrugged and smiled. "She's fine. I think she is more interested in someone else, though. It's alright, I'm having a good time anyway." He looked across the crowd. "Where's Dane? That's who you came with tonight, right?"

Ari nodded. "He's with your cousin right now," she tried to say in a neutral voice, but something must've given away her disdain.

"I'm sorry," Rob said. "I wouldn't worry about Julia, though. I know how much Dane cares for you," Rob commented, and Ari raised her eyebrow. The song soon ended and Rob thanked Ari for dancing with him. Ari looked up at him and gave him a grateful smile. Just then she felt a hand on her back. Dane had returned from his dance with Julia.

"Ari, I am *so* sorry," Dane pleaded. He had an almost-panicked look on his face. "I was in the Japanese garden, and Julia found me. She insisted we dance together. I didn't want to be rude, so…" he trailed off. "Was Rob the note-writer?" Dane asked.

"What?" Ari said, shaking her head. "No, why?"

"I saw you dancing with him. I assumed he met you at the pavilion?"

Ari snorted and laughed. "Gosh no. He just asked me to dance because I was waiting alone on the edge of the dance floor. Nobody showed up at the pavilion. I got stood up by my secret note-writer." Ari made a face.

Dane looked sorry, but before he could say anything else, the garden lights extinguished, leaving only the tiny dots of glowing candlelight to illuminate the garden. A collective gasp rose from the dancers on the floor. The effect was stunning. With the lights off, Ari could clearly see the stars above them. She hung her head back as far as she could without falling over and did a slow turn. It was like the heavens were close enough to touch.

Couples started to pair off for another slow dance. Dane took Ari's hand. "Ari, will you dance with me?" he asked, perhaps with a tinge of timidity.

"It's about time," Ari joked, and even in the darkness she could see a smile making its way across Dane's eyes. He put his right hand on her back and held her other hand. A slow waltz started to play. They started the basic step and Dane led Ari around the dance floor. The effect was like floating when she danced with him. He led her in an underarm turn and her skirt billowed out in a circle. She couldn't help but smile from ear to ear. After a few turns around the cobblestone dance floor, Dane stopped dancing. He put her hand to his shoulder and wrapped both his arms around her waist.

Ari smiled and closed her eyes, resting her head on his chest. He held onto her like he didn't want to let go, ever. She breathed in the scent of Dane and his cologne and the mix of fragrant flowers that surrounded them entirely. Once again she lifted her head to the sky to see the swath of stars that pulsed above them. All too soon, the music ended and the garden lights were turned on again. The last dance of the night had ended, and couples began to disperse.

A brisk breeze blew through the garden, tousling the leaves of a nearby aspen tree. For the first time, Ari felt a chill wash over her. It was nearly eleven o'clock.

"Hey, let's grab my coat and go," Dane said. "I told your dad we'd be back by eleven-thirty."

They entered the garden house and Dane checked his sport coat from the attendant. As they left the house he slipped it over her shoulders. They made their way down the stone steps to his truck. Dane opened the passenger door for her and let her in. As she sat on the upholstered seat, she noticed a square of paper had been tossed to the center of the bench seat.

"Oh my gosh," she muttered. Dane had just gotten into the driver's seat. Ari unfolded the paper and started reading.

"What's that?" he asked, looking over.

"It's another note. It says, "*Dear Ari, this is my last note to you. I'm sorry I didn't meet you tonight. Perhaps someday in the future our paths will cross.*" The same small heart was drawn at the bottom.

Dane shook his head. "So he has time to write you one last note, but not to meet you...?" Dane sounded annoyed as the truck roared to life.

"Yeah, worst secret admirer *ever*," Ari scoffed, and they both started laughing. She snuck a peek at Dane as he drove out the garden exit. She loved the lingering smile on his face. For the first time that night, he actually looked relaxed...or relieved. As the truck turned and left the gates, the expanse of the valley could be seen below. Tiny lights from homes and cars below dotted the landscape and Ari reveled in the beauty of the vista.

"Did you have a good time tonight?" Ari asked, but almost immediately regretted asking. It almost seemed like a silly question, when she thought about the events that had unfolded.

"It was interesting, that's for sure," he said, chuckling. But suddenly his expression got more serious. "I enjoyed every minute with you, Ari. I'm sorry that we only got to dance once."

Ari smiled. "Well, perhaps someday in the future our paths will cross again," Ari quoted and made a face, and Dane started laughing again as he steered the truck down the twisting lane.

They descended to the valley floor, where the road met up with the highway. Upon reaching Hadley Hill, Ari was surprised when he drove to his own driveway and parked. He then went around the truck and opened the door for her, holding out a hand as she gathered up her skirt and jumped down. "I'll walk you home," he said simply, but when he took her hand, he interlaced his fingers with hers. *That* was different— he'd never held her hand that way before. Her heart skipped at the change, and she felt a warm heat rising in her cheeks, burning against the cold night. They walked in silence, and Ari noticed Dane looking up at the brilliant swath of stars above the treetops.

At Ari's house, the porch light was on. Ari took off Dane's coat and he threw it over his shoulder. Ari mounted the first porch step and turned around. At this height, she stood almost eye-to-eye with Dane.

"Goodnight, Dane Hadley," Ari said, her heart in her throat. She kissed him on his cheek so quickly that he hardly even had time to look surprised before she breathlessly darted away up the porch stairs. Ari fought the urge to look behind her.

chapter seventeen

Ari sat up in bed. Morning light was inching its way through the windows. Ari's brain did a double-take as she recalled the night before. Her hand went to her forehead as she recalled kissing Dane on the cheek. Part of her was incredulous that she'd done it; the rest of her chided herself for not looking back to see his reaction, good or bad. She didn't have much time to mull it over before her phone started vibrating across her vanity. Ari checked it and didn't recognize the number.

The person on the other end was inquiring about Ari's yard service. Inwardly, she was beyond excited. There was only one week of school left, and this was the third appointment she'd scheduled for her business. She grabbed her monthly planner from her vanity and penciled in a time slot for the first week of summer.

One week of school left. Ari smiled at the thought of being finished with classes and homework. Summer was her sweet spot; her favorite season by far. Nothing could compare with three months of sunshine, no school, and the beautiful countryside that mellowed out around her in the heat of summer.

Ari sat in her window seat and looked out across the treetops to Dane's house. Her phone rang again with an unfamiliar number. It was another inquiry about a yard care, which Ari penciled in once again on her calendar. She was absolutely ecstatic when she burst down the stairs to where her parents and Lily were having breakfast.

"Guys! I just got two more calls for yard care!" she said, waving her calendar at them. Her mom and dad looked up from their breakfast and greeted Ari.

"Sit down," her mom smiled and patted the spot next to her. "That's great! Do you know the customers? Are they friends of ours?"

Ari shook her head. "Not at all. Two people saw the fliers at businesses, and the others all said they got the mailer."

Ari's dad grimaced. "I might have to look for another office assistant after all."

The melodious sound of the doorbell interrupted their conversation. Ari went to the door.

She opened it to see Dane standing on the front porch. His short hair was a little wet and disheveled and he smelled like he'd just gotten out of the shower: soap and shampoo and the same aqua-scented cologne from the night before. He looked wide-eyed and a little panicked. At first, Ari was worried.

"Hey! I need your help with something…what are you doing today?"

"Well, nothing, I don't think. Come in, we're eating breakfast. Want to join us? Is everything okay?"

Dane smiled and followed Ari through the house and into the dining room. "Everything's fine, but last week while I was at my dad's, the museum left a message with my mom. They want me to come in Monday after school to interview for the internship. I need your help figuring out what I should wear, plus I want to try and finish reading Ezra's journal with you. They may ask me what experience I have with history-related research. That would be a great story to tell, if we're able to piece together the rest of the Abshire story." Dane ran his hand through his hair, looking a little overwhelmed.

Ari beamed. "I'd love to help," she said. Dane paused before they reached Ari's kitchen.

"Thanks, Ari." Dane looked genuinely relieved.

Mrs. Cartwright looked up. "Well, hello, Dane. Nice to see you. How was the dance last night?"

Ari held her breath, wondering what exactly Dane would say. However, he just grinned. "It was really good. Ansley Park Garden was beautiful. Have you and Mr. Cartwright been there before?"

"We never have. We should go sometime, Jess," her dad said,

between bites of scrambled egg. "Dane, you're welcome to grab some breakfast. Eggs are on the stove and you can fix yourself some toast and orange juice if you like. We would love to hear more about the dance, and Ari mentioned you have a job you're looking at."

"Thank you," Dane said, sitting at the table. "That's actually what I'm here about. I have an interview on Monday and I need Ari's help. I want to be able to have some examples of research experience for the interview. If I can tell the story of what we've discovered about the Abshires, maybe it will give me an advantage over other applicants."

"That's a really good idea, Dane," Ari's mom said. "I'm sure you'll do great."

Ari smiled as her parents conversed with Dane. He seemed totally at ease as he chatted with Ari's mom and dad. As she listened to them discuss the museum job, Ari noted that the veil of aloofness that she'd become so accustomed to was absent when he spoke with them. It fascinated her to see him at ease with her parents.

Ari realized she was once again staring at Dane. She picked at her scrambled eggs and finished her toast as Dane grabbed some orange juice.

"Hey, I've got some news too, you know," Ari joked when there was a lull in the conversation. "See my June schedule? I have four yard care appointments on the books already," she said, pushing the calendar towards Dane.

"Really?" Dane said, reading over her calendar. "Ari, that's amazing. You'll have a full schedule in no time, I bet." He looked at her with a lingering smile, and she found herself smiling back, but just as quickly, blushed and looked away.

They finished breakfast and walked through the oak grove to Dane's house. Ari hadn't made many morning trips through the grove, and she noticed how beautiful it was when the early sun filtered through the oak leaves. Even more new spring growth had started to obscure the beaten-dirt trail between their homes. It took longer than usual to traverse because Dane had to stop every few feet to snap back overgrown brush.

They arrived on the other side of the path Dane's new old truck was parked where his mom's car usually was. The house was quiet when they started up the stairs to his room.

"Where's your mom and Molly?" Ari asked.

"They went grocery shopping. Why?"

"Just wondering," she shrugged.

When they stepped inside Dane's room, Ari was taken aback.

She hadn't been in his room for a few weeks, and it looked completely different from the last time she'd visited: the walls had been painted a warm gray color, with white trim around the windows and black trim around the floor. A modern-looking corner desk had replaced the beat-up student's desk he used to have. A new laptop was centered on the desk. Notebooks and local history books lined a bookshelf to the side of his office chair. His bed was still along the wall, but his bedding and curtains were all new and were actually part of a matching set. Old posters had been removed, and framed photos hung in their place: a photo of Molly and his mom, taken on the front porch. A few black-and-white photos of Nadia and Grekov hung in a collage. The old photo of him and his dad sat on his desk. And, on his nightstand, housed in a black-matted frame, was a photo that Ari had never seen before.

She crossed the room and picked up the frame. It held a nearly colorless photo that had been taken inside the concrete building at the Air Force station: Dane was standing on one side of a doorway, and Ari was on the other side. The photo was perfectly silhouetted: someone's flashlight had backlit their profiles, but there was just enough detail that you could see they both were smiling at each other.

"Jace gave that to me," Dane explained. "He printed all his photos from that night, and he said that particular photo was one of the best ones that turned out."

Ari turned and smiled at Dane, who was leaning up against his door. *Of all his photos, the one of us is on his nightstand,* she thought.

Putting it back, she confessed, "I'd forgotten that he was even taking photos that night. I was too focused on all the spookiness, and not falling to my death." Ari quipped. "By the way, what made you decide to change your room? It looks really nice…and grown-up."

Dane crossed his arms and leaned against the door frame. "Well, Ari, this is *my* home now. I'm not just a squatter in Rhoda's house anymore, which is basically what it was like before. So I changed it to the way I've always wanted it. Plus, I didn't want to be embarrassed every time you came into my room," he said, and Ari thought she detected the faintest hint of color blushing across his face. "Now, I think it looks pretty presentable."

"You did a great job," she agreed. "So, what did you want me to help you with first?"

Dane opened his closet. Inside was a nearly-full wardrobe of new clothes, some that Ari had never seen before.

"First, I need to figure out what to wear to the interview. Can you help me decide?"

Ari nodded, and started sifting through the clothes hanging in the closet. There were polo shirts and dress shirts, all in dark or neutral colors, plus blazers and his leather jacket. She pulled out a solid gray dress shirt and navy tie.

"Do you have any jeans without holes?" she chuckled.

"Yeah, here," he said, pulling a dark indigo pair that had been folded in a drawer.

"Let's start with this," she said, handing him the clothing. "I really don't have any idea what I'm doing, Dane," she admitted with a chuckle. "I've never dressed a guy."

"Gotta start somewhere, right?"

Ari shut the door to his room and walked down the hallway. The door to Nadia's former ballet studio was slightly open. This room was the largest on the second floor; perhaps it was even larger than the living room downstairs. She slowly pushed the door fully open.

The space had been turned into a study and bookshelves lined the walls. Sunlight streamed through the windows and caused the room to glow. A large Oriental rug covered most of the wood floor. Photo albums and boxes with Nadia's artifacts had been sorted and labeled. Large wingback chairs were placed in each corner. A large framed photo of Nadia dancing in one of her performances hung above a mahogany desk. Ari couldn't believe how regal the room looked; it was like she'd stepped back an entire century. Ari immediately went to one of the wingback chairs and sunk into its padded comfort.

It wasn't long before Dane came down the hallway. He stepped into the study and smiled at Ari. "I thought I'd find you in here," he said. "How does this look?"

Just like the night before, Ari was stunned by how he was transformed, only this time he looked even more professional with the addition of a tie. But, Ari wrinkled her nose—something was off.

Dane frowned. "What's wrong?"

"I think it's the jeans. They seem too casual. Did I see a pinstriped dress shirt hanging in your closet?" Ari asked, trying to remember. "Try that with some navy pants, and your oxfords from last night."

Dane nodded, and came back a few minutes later. This ensemble was just the right combination: professional without looking like he was trying too hard. Whether he realized it or not, Ari noticed that when he wore his dress clothes, he stood taller, with his chest out, and had a confidence in his walk.

At the sight of him, Ari suddenly felt shy again, and realized why: Dane's confidence was intimidating, even to her. He was shedding the fear that he'd lived under for four years.

She beamed. "Much better. That will land you the job." Dane nodded and sighed in relief.

"Alright, that's done then. Let me get out of this and then we can continue reading the journal. Be right back." Dane left the room and returned, once again wearing his regular t-shirt and jeans, and brought with him Ezra's journal and a notebook. He sat down in a wingback chair and Ari sat on the armrest, leaning on the back of the tall chair.

Ari's phone dinged. She grunted after looking at the screen.

"What's up?" Dane asked.

"Riley wants to know all the details about why on earth I was dancing with Pat McCleary," Ari muttered. She turned her phone face-down and looked at Dane.

"Dane, what's up with you and Pat, anyway?"

Dane narrowed his eyes. "McCleary and I go waaay back," he grumbled, running a thumb along the spine of Ezra's journal. "It all started one day in about second grade, when he decided to throw my lunch out the bus window one morning. Back then, he lived closer to town. It pretty much snowballed from that day on." Dane stopped talking and looked at Ari. In the hazy morning sunlight, his eyes were a shocking light jade, rimmed with dark brown. Ari couldn't look away as he continued to talk.

"I've actually done a pretty good job of ignoring his idiot behavior all these years, until last night. I draw the line when it comes to you. He's not going to get away with harassing *you* because of *me*." He shook his head. "You were pretty ballsy, grabbing his shirt like that. I saw the look in your eyes when you were talking to him."

A glint of amusement crossed Dane's face, but then he suddenly got serious. "How do you do it, Ari? Your sudden steel-willed moments of courage—like when you went into the bar to get my dad, or back at the Lawton house. I know you didn't want to go inside again. That house scared you. Yet you did it anyway…"

Ari took in a deep breath. She was starting to get nervous butterflies again. It was the way he was looking at her again: unabashedly honest with a soul-rendering stare.

"I only do that kind of stuff when it's for you, I guess…" Ari trailed off. A million things that she could say, that would describe her feelings better, came flooding into her mind. But she could only verbalize one thing:

"You make me brave, Dane Hadley."

A look of pleasant surprise passed over Dane's face. He leaned closer to her, not taking his eyes from hers. She held his gaze. It was the most honest thing that she could say to him that wouldn't cause her to spill forth the million other things she felt about him. He opened his mouth to say something, but Ari's phone rang, breaking the silence between them.

Ari looked at her screen. "Sorry, Dane, I should take this. It's Riley." She excused herself from the room and took the call in the hallway. On the other end, Riley's voice was ecstatic.

"Ari! Guess what? Jace asked me to be his girlfriend last night. It's official! I wanted you to be the first to know!" Ari smiled at the news, happy for her friend.

"Riley, that's awesome! I'm sorry we didn't see you before we left last night. How did he ask you?"

"Well, we were on the observation deck, and there weren't many other people around. It was during the last dance, when they turned all the lights off. He just said, 'Riley, I really like you. Would you allow me to call you my girlfriend?' That was it. Well, and then he kissed me. Great view from up there, by the way." At that, Ari laughed, and she congratulated Riley.

Riley's tone became serious. "Hey, you have to tell me about what happened with Pat. Things didn't look like they were going very well for you last night. Is everything ok?"

Ari glanced back at the door of the study. It was open, so she made her way to Dane's room and partially shut the door. "Well, Pat and Dane nearly got into a fight, so I intervened and ended up dancing with Pat. In the end, everything turned out ok."

"Why would Dane try and get into a fight at a dance, of all places?" Riley said, a scowl carrying over in her voice.

Ari sat on Dane's bed, shaking her head. "No, Dane was trying to defend me. Pat was being obnoxious again," she said quietly, hoping Dane wouldn't overhear.

"What about Mr. Mystery?" Riley said, clearly excited.

Ari snorted. "He stood me up! I went to the pavilion and waited like an idiot, but nobody showed up. Later, we found a note in Dane's truck, after the dance was over. It said he wouldn't be writing anymore notes." Ari said. "Most ridiculous secret note writer ever, right?" She rolled her eyes and Riley laughed on the other end. "I'll tell you more later when I see you next, alright? I have to help Dane with a project. But, congrats again on Jace." The two hung up, and Ari headed back toward the study.

The room was quiet and the sun had moved into position through the eastward-facing windows, filling the study entirely with light. Dane was still sitting in the giant wingback chair at the far end of the room. Ezra's journal was open in his hands. She entered the study and returned to her spot on the armrest of the chair.

Dane looked up from the journal. "What's up with Riley? Do you have to go or can you still stay and help?"

"Oh, I'm not leaving. Don't worry. She just called to tell me that Jace asked her to be his girlfriend. And she wanted to know about the secret note-writer."

Dane nodded in approval. "Jace seems like a really nice guy." He scooted over in his chair and patted the narrow space next to him. "Better get comfortable," he said. "We've got some reading to do."

Ari slid down into the chair next to Dane. It was a tight fit, and she found it was more comfortable if she turned and sat sideways facing Dane. Sitting this way, it was really only possible to read over Dane's shoulder if she rested her head against his arm. Ari suddenly felt shy and was almost certain she was beginning to blush, right to the tips of her ears, and she hoped he wouldn't scoot away from her. Instead, Dane seemed to relax into the chair.

Ari glanced at the book and saw it was opened to the halfway point.

"You really think we can finish the journal today?"

"I think so." With that, Dane started reading aloud. "'July 4th. Not wanting us to miss the parade, Mother stayed home with Father. She offered to borrow a wheelchair from the McClellan's so that Father could attend today's fair, but he refused and insisted that he would not be seen as he is now: thin and gaunt and unable to walk far under his own power. Thus, Joseph Jr. and I were put in charge of Aliza and sent to town. Joseph drove the buggy. We watched the parade and Aliza was thrilled with the decorated carriages.'"

Ari closed her eyes and got lost in the story and the sound of Dane's voice.

"'All the while I kept a lookout for Katia and her family. Halfway through the day, I spotted Katia and Eva at a fair booth. I told Katia that we were planning to watch the fireworks by the crooked tree on the bank of the river, in hopes that she would join us.

"'To my delight Katia stole away from her family long enough to watch the last half of the fireworks show with us. We dropped back behind Joseph and Aliza and while everyone else was mesmerized by the colorful explosions, I dared to kiss Katia on the cheek.'"

Ari's eyes snapped open. "Go, Ezra!" she chuckled. Sheepishly she realized she'd pulled the same move on Dane the night before.

"Wait, wait," Dane held up a hand. "'I feared I'd made a misstep when Katia froze in place for seconds. My fears vanished when she kissed me back, this time *not* on the cheek."

Ari gasped and smiled.

"Well, I guess there's no doubt that she likes him too," Dane chuckled, then continued. "Shoot, the next entry isn't until July 15th: 'I haven't written in weeks because of Father's dire condition. Shortly after Independence Day, Father took a turn for the worst and became bedridden. Dr. Blackwell assumes enlargement of the spleen. He insists that Father must rest as much as possible, which is all Father is able to do presently anyway.

"Dr. Blackwell took Mother aside privately. Joseph and I hid ourselves in the kitchen to hear the conversation. In as gentle a way as possible, he encouraged Mother to have the family's affairs in order, should Father pass."

Dane stopped reading. Ari straightened in the chair. She could tell Dane was skimming now; speed-reading—as much as the elegant cursive would allow. Ari didn't prompt him to read aloud anymore. Her mind wandered to the Abshire house and she wondered what room had Ezra's father been bedridden in. Ari watched as Dane turned page after page. Ari wanted to stop him and ask to paraphrase what he was reading, but she refrained.

"Do you want me to read for awhile?" Ari finally asked, after a few minutes of silence passed.

"Sorry," Dane apologized. "He starts talking about every single step his mom goes through to both care for his dad and prepare for his possible death. There's mostly stuff about how his mom is trying to learn everything she can about how to run a farm by herself."

Ari shook her head. "Wow. I can't imagine…"

"Yeah, it's pretty intense. It sounds like Ezra and Joseph know a lot about farming, but Ezra admits he doesn't know anything about the business part of it, and with the gamble they took with the new ryegrass crop, it's all foreign territory."

"Is there anything more about Katia?"

"On July 30th, he says his house has been 'silent and devoid of the beautiful strands of music Katia would play during her lessons.' But, he has mentioned several times that Katia has delivered food to them, though Ezra can no longer spare the time to walk her home." Moments of silence passed again as Dane skimmed more pages.

"On August 13th, he says the Hadleys have 'taken Aliza under their wing to care for her while Mother spends her days and night tending to Father's needs. Aliza shares a room with Eva. Aliza comes home on the weekends, taking the wooded trail back. She misses home, she tells us."

Dane continued to read silently for several more minutes, until he breathed in sharply. Ari leaned over his shoulder and strained to see what he was reading. "Wait, what happened? Did his dad die?"

Dane shook his head and read: "'Mother has become aware of my affections for Katia. It seems my feelings toward her have not gone unnoticed. Mother gently informed me that the son of a poor farmer has no business courting a wealthy debutante, no matter how great my love for her is."

Ari sighed. "Oh…*ouch*."

Dane turned more pages, scanning. "August 29th. It is no longer feasible for our family to continue to support ourselves as we are. Our debts are great. Tomorrow I am moving. Katia convinced her family to put a good word in for me with a family friend in Woodward who owns a mercantile. I will begin work there as soon as possible, so that I can begin sending money home to Mother. Joseph will stay here to run the farm in its entirety. My heart cannot comprehend days without Katia, and yet it must and it will."

Dane turned the page, but instead of walnut-colored words in swirly ink, blank ivory pages stared back at them.

"No!" Ari exclaimed. Dane flipped through the last quarter of the book: not a single word appeared on any following pages. "We have to find out what happened!"

"It just...ends." Dane shut the book and looked at Ari. "What do we do now?"

"Is the museum open today?

"No, it's closed on weekends."

Ari furrowed her brow. "We're going to need more help from Agnes."

chapter eighteen

One week to go before school is out, Ari thought. *One week until homework will be a thing of the past for three glorious months.* Ari grabbed her bike after school ended and rode to the coffee shop in downtown Rivers. Cinema Coffee was the only sit-down shop in the entire town, and some days it was so full that it was difficult to find a seat.

This day, however, the unusually perfect June weather had beckoned people outside, and only a few patrons sat scattered around the shop. Ari smiled as she settled in with a hot cup of coffee and her homework. She realized that the silence and solitude was just what she needed, but she couldn't help but wonder how Dane was doing at his interview.

Ari popped in her headphones and found music on her phone. She'd started listening to jazz while doing her math one night, and she found there was something just perfect about the sound of it and the way her brain worked while figuring out a math problem. She smiled inwardly as strands of John Coltrane wound through her headphones.

Thirty minutes later, math was finished, and Ari took one last sip of coffee from the heavy ceramic mug. She pulled out her calendar and glanced with concern at the first week of summer. She had the four appointments that had been made for yard work, but hadn't received any more calls after that. Ari started making a list of possible ways to spread the word about her business when she glanced out the window. A familiar old truck rumbled slowly down the street. She saw Dane park his truck along the curb.

Her heart ramped up a notch as he got out of the driver's side. Even though she had helped him choose his interview outfit, something about the way he looked at that moment took her breath away. He couldn't see her looking at him through the coffee shop window, but it was as if he was moving in slow motion toward the door of the shop. He'd taken his tie off and unbuttoned the top button of his dress shirt, and his hair was disheveled, as usual.

He entered the cafe and scanned the booths, obviously looking for someone. When his eyes settled on Ari, she noticed his intense but calm demeanor. She couldn't immediately read whether he was happy or not. He strode over to her booth and sat across from her, leaning in. She searched his eyes to try and determine how the interview had gone. So far, he wasn't revealing anything.

"I saw your bike parked outside and thought I'd stop in and see if you wanted a ride home," Dane said quietly.

"How did your interview go?" Ari asked, leaning in and meeting his gaze. Her heart was still fluttering from the sight of him.

"Well," Dane looked out the window a moment, "it went well. They asked about my family research, and I told them the story of how we discovered Nadia, Reginald, and Grekov, and I followed that with our current research project on Ezra. It was an easy interview because I basically just recounted the last year of my life. Agnes and the director of the museum interviewed me."

Ari smiled. "When will they let you know if you got it?"

"Well," Dane smiled, "they offered me the position on the spot." Ari memorized his exact expression at this moment: his eyes were smiling, and a look of pride spread over his countenance. "It's a minimum twenty hours a week, and I can come in any time they are open. I just need to make sure I get twenty hours in. I start the first week after school ends."

Ari was ecstatic for him. "Dane! That is awesome! I'm so happy for you," she exclaimed. "Were you able to do any more research on Ezra?"

"I looked through the binders of un-archived photos. They have them arranged by year, roughly, but many of the photos weren't labeled. In the 1925 binder, I didn't see any photos of houses or people that looked familiar. Agnes showed me how to use their online newspaper database. I did a search for Ezra Abshire for the two newspapers that existed in Rivers at the time."

Ari raised her eyebrows. "And?"

"Nothing." Dane shook his head and looked disappointed. "Unfortunately, not all newspapers in the state are archived on this online database. I told Agnes that we thought Ezra moved to Woodward at one point, but no newspapers from Woodward are listed on the database."

"Where do we look now? It sounds like a dead end."

"Agnes suggested to start looking at genealogy sites; looking for family members who might still be around. Maybe talk to some of the older residents of Rivers who might know what happened to the family."

Ari groaned. "That sounds like some advanced searching."

Dane shrugged. "Maybe it won't be so hard. Doing that type of research might even be something I learn to do during the internship," he figured. "By the way, did you get any more yard appointments since yesterday?" Dane looked at her expectantly.

She just shook her head. "No. I'm starting to worry this won't work."

Dane looked at her right in the eye and leaned in, almost nose-to-nose. He took her head in his hand and brushed her hair from her cheek. "Ari, if anyone can do this, it's you. I believe in your success."

There was a pause as Ari absorbed what Dane had just said. It reverberated in her heart as she looked at him and smiled.

"Thank you for believing in my idea," Ari said quietly.

*   *   *

"Campfire at Jace's Saturday night! Let's celebrate the END OF SCHOOL!" The group text had caused a succession of vibrations that had woken Ari. Rolling over to her nightstand, Ari rubbed her eyes and looked at her phone. Riley's initial text had set off a string of excited responses.

Even in her half-asleep haze, Ari wondered if Dane would agree to attend with her. She considered declining the invitation out of consideration for Dane, but then realized that a campfire at Jace's house wouldn't likely be crazy like Pat McCleary's bonfire. Maybe Dane would agree to go; she made a mental note to remember to ask him.

"I'm in," Ari wrote, then rolled over and buried her head into her pillow. What she really wanted to do was fall back asleep again, but a sudden realization caused her eyes to snap open: today was the first official day of summer break. School had ended the day before, on a Thursday. The possibilities of a completely unscheduled Friday rolled around in Ari's mind.

She shuffled downstairs and saw her parents hurrying along in their normal routine; Lily was finishing breakfast and Ari's mom was gathering Lily's backpack.

"Looks like someone has a day off," Ari's dad wrinkled his nose. "I'm jealous."

Ari's mom slipped the backpack on Lily. "I'd leave Lily with you today, but her summer day camp has their first field trip of the summer and she really doesn't want to miss it. You're on your own, Miss Aribelle." Her mom leaned over and kissed Ari's forehead. "Please text me if you go anywhere, okay?"

Ari nodded in agreement. "Will do."

The house emptied out and, for the first time in ages, Ari didn't have a clue what to do. The silence of the morning was broken only by the sound of birds singing in the garden.

Ari drained the last cup of coffee from the pot and headed out to the back porch. A wooden rocking chair had been warmed in the new rays of the morning sun. She pulled a blanket around her and closed her eyes. The quiet of the morning was serene. Ari's mind drifted to thoughts of Dane, as usual. She wondered what he was doing; if he was at home or if he had stayed at his dad's house the night before.

Ari's thoughts then jumped to Ezra and the Abshires. She'd been dying to find out more, but her brain was wrapped around the dead ends she and Dane had encountered.

On a whim, Ari went upstairs and fetched her laptop and notebook and brought them back out to the porch. She started methodically typing in Ezra's last name into online phone directories, trying to determine if any Abshires lived in Rivers, Allendale, or Woodward. She was surprised and disappointed when no matches appeared. In her notepad, she wrote down every search she completed, with the results scribbled on the side. Ari was so intent on her work that she didn't notice the figure standing nearly in front of her until he spoke.

"Hey, there," Dane said, and Ari startled so badly she nearly dumped her computer on the ground.

"Whoa!" Dane's lightning-fast reflexes caught the laptop just before it hit the deck. Ari moved to catch it at the exact same moment, and their heads unceremoniously thumped together.

"Ow!" Ari reached for her head.

"Sorry!" Dane winced, as he simultaneously placed Ari's computer on her lap, and his hand rested on her head where they'd collided. "Are you okay?"

"Yeah…" Ari looked up at him. Dane's shorter hair looked slightly damp, and he was wearing a hoodie and jeans. "You just startled me. I was searching to see if any Abshires still lived in the area." She rubbed her head again.

"Any luck?" Dane settled in the rocking chair next to hers.

"No, and honestly I'm kind of surprised. You'd think with three kids in the Abshire family, there would be someone who stayed in the area." Ari looked down at her laptop, and then over at Dane. "Why can't we find anything? It's like they disappeared into thin air, Dane."

Dane looked at Ari. Once again, she realized how different he looked—in a good way—with his hair shorter. "Maybe his dad died after the journal ended, and the family had to move? Maybe they joined family in another state?"

Ari considered this. "Maybe. It would be great if the house would give us more clues."

"Well, it just so happens that we now have a handy shortcut to get to the Abshire place anytime we want to go there." A slow smile crossed Dane's face.

"Give me five minutes to get dressed," Ari said, bolting out of the rocking chair.

*　　*　　*

The trail heading from Dane's backyard to the Abshire place was an easy ten-minute downhill trek. Ari loved how the mid-morning sun filtered gently through the canopy of overhead trees. It wasn't long until shimmering reflections from the pond could be seen through gaps in the foliage. Ari paused when they passed the tree with the heart carving. Silently she touched the hearts with her hand, pressing her hand over them.

"We've got to figure out what this means," Ari said softly.

"We will, Ari. We've just got to keep digging."

They reached the lake and used the path that skirted the shore.

"It's so much easier going down the path than coming back up," Dane observed. "It probably didn't take Katia all that long to get to the Abshires. Ezra probably wanted to escort her home just so he could have more time to chat with her."

"Can you imagine making that climb after doing a hard day of farm work, though?" Ari shook her head.

"I have a feeling that no matter how tired or sore he was, Ezra would've walked a million miles with Katia," Dane mused. "When you love someone, you'll go to any lengths." A shiver went through Ari; she wanted to know how Dane could be quite so sure of something.

They walked in silence until they came to a break in the cottonwood trees. The shoreline trail ended and Ari and Dane crossed the marshy strip until they stopped, once again, in front of the broken-down front porch of the Abshire place. Ari walked slowly in front of the house, picking her way around arcing blackberry vines. Sunlight filtered through the eastern windows of the house and a diffuse glow illuminated the interior of the house.

"Did you bring the journal?" Ari asked quietly as she stepped up onto the porch. Something about being at the house urged silence whenever they approached.

"Got it right here." Dane's voice was equally quiet. "You want it?"

Ari nodded and took it from his hands. She carefully lifted her leg over the broken-out front window and stepped into the house. She passed the three-sided alcove of windows and stood, quiet and still, in the main living room.

Specks of dust floated through the air like lazy snowflakes. Only a few things could be heard: muffled bird noises and sounds caused by light breezes outside. The house was as still and peaceful as before. Ari found herself trying hard to imagine every detail of the home they had read about.

"Do you think the bedroom Ezra's dad was in was upstairs or downstairs?" She started thumbing through the pages.

Dane thought for a moment. "I remember in the journal Ezra mentioned his dad stayed on the main floor after he was too weak to use the stairs. So, maybe in the room to the side of the living room here?" Dane walked past the staircase, toward the basement door. There was only one small room on the left side. Two windows, one per wall, were both fully darkened by tangles of blackberry vines that were pressed against the glass. Ari noticed how dark and cold the room was compared to the rest of the house.

"You think he stayed in this room?" Ari asked.

"It would make sense. It's awfully small though. Room enough just for a cot."

"We've gotta find out what happened to them, Dane." Ari paused, pressing her hand up against the door frame. "There *has* to be at least one family member who still is alive, at least, if not nearby—"

A soft crunching sound could just barely be heard and Ari stopped talking. She knew that sound by heart now: car tires on a gravel road. The same sound as when cars crunched past her own house.

"Someone's here," Dane whispered. They both crouched low and walked toward the closest window that looked out onto the driveway.

"Crap! It's a sheriff's car!" she exclaimed in a whisper. Dane reached for her hand as they ran toward the basement door, both of them jogging in a crouch so they couldn't be seen through the windows. He tried opening the basement door but ended up running into it. The door was solidly stuck again. Ari looked furtively over her shoulder—the crunching had stopped.

"He's parked, hurry!"

Dane took hold of the porcelain doorknob and threw his weight against the door. A tremendous noise reverberated through the bones of the house as the door flung open and smacked into the wall. Ari gasped in fear that the noise was heard all the way up Hadley Hill. Dane caught himself against the handrail and reached back for Ari at the same time. Stumbling down the steps, Ari landed hard on the wood planks but recovered just in time to see Dane pointing at the crates.

"Behind those!" Dane whispered.

"Wait! I have to shut the door!" Ari bolted up the stairs and tried closing the door silently. It came to a stop and wouldn't latch, but at least it was no longer fully open.

Ari heard heavy footsteps on the front porch. She crossed the basement floor as silently as she could, but her boots made it difficult to be completely stealthy. Dane madly motioned at her from behind the stack of crates. He pulled Ari down behind them just as an ominous creak, then footsteps, could be heard inside the house above them.

Very little light came through the small window that was near the ceiling of the basement. Ari's eyes slowly adjusted to the dimness. Dane had one hand on Ari's shoulder, and he'd frozen, stock-still, as his eyes followed the sound of the footsteps. Ari hardly dared to breathe. The succinct sound of footsteps got nearer. Ari felt Dane's hand grip her as if to pull her closer to the ground.

Ari tilted her head toward Dane. In the barest whisper, she asked, "do you think he's looking for us?"

She felt Dane's hair brush her ear as he shook his head 'no.' "I really doubt it. There's nobody around for miles. Who would've seen us?"

The footsteps stopped at the basement door. Ari could hear her heartbeat in her ears. She took a jagged deep breath. The darkness of the room seemed to press closer. The basement door opened with a creak. Through gaps in the crates, Ari could see a flashlight beam dance around.

chapter nineteen

Ari felt Dane inhale sharply and hold his breath. Both of them crouched as low as they possibly could. Ari closed her eyes and fervently hoped the officer wouldn't come down the steps. The top step to the basement suddenly creaked under the weight of the officer. Ari felt her hands start to shake slightly. The flashlight beam illuminated the area all around them

Everything paused. Ari willed herself to not move or breathe. After an eternal moment, the officer stepped back up and tried to shut the basement door. It resisted his attempt. The door suddenly slammed shut with such force that the walls shook. Ari felt Dane exhale next to her. Heavy footsteps traversed the house and sounded like they were getting further away.

"That was close," he whispered. Ari narrowed her eyes.

"You don't think we're stuck down here, do you?"

Dane gave her a questioning look.

"The door…it's not stuck shut, right?"

Dane looked at her, nearly nose-to-nose. He still had his hand on her shoulder. A fraction of a playful glint crossed his eyes. "Probably not," he whispered. He then looked up at the ceiling, listening for footsteps. Something else slammed up above. Then Ari heard a staccato set of noises she couldn't identify. More footsteps. Ari counted them, crunching away. Next, the muffled sound of a car engine starting, then tires on gravel, slowly fading.

Ari and Dane stayed huddled behind the crates until moments of undisturbed silence returned to the house. Ari allowed herself to breathe again and Dane let out a huge sigh, and Ari felt him relax. His hand moved down her back. With that one movement, the atmosphere changed.

Reflexively Ari turned to him. The darkness prevented her from seeing his expression but she knew he was looking intently at her. In the barely-there light Ari wished they were upstairs so she could really see every detail in his face, his eyes. Dane's other hand went to her face and Ari felt herself move ever closer to him.

Suddenly, a *thwack!* from above startled them both. Ari gasped and Dane tightened his grip on Ari.

"What was *that?*" Ari uttered.

Dane looked up toward the ceiling and shook his head. "C'mon, let's go."

Apprehensively Ari stood. Her legs were cramped and stiff from being hunched over behind the crates, and adrenaline was causing her arms to shake. Dane moved toward the stairs but Ari grabbed his hand, if only to steady herself. He stopped and looked at her and entwined his fingers with hers. She felt a shock of heat run through her arm as they ascended the stairs together.

At the top of the stairs, the bright light of the house seared their dark-adjusted eyes. Dane pointed at the front door.

"That's what made the noise," he said. The front door had blown open and was slowly oscillating in the gentle breeze. A gust sent it knocking into the house's siding.

"The sheriff came in through the front door?" Ari was puzzled. They'd tried the door the first time they'd visited the house and it had been locked.

"He must've. Maybe he had a key."

Ari stepped through the door and Dane followed. She turned and faced the house; her eyes widened. The unidentified noises she had heard had been the sound of a staple gun piercing the siding of the house. Shouting in red letters was a sign that read POSTED, NO TRESPASSING. Ari's heart sank.

Dane looked over at Ari. "Somebody must've seen us here at some point."

"Maybe. We're going to have to be careful if we come back."

Dane nodded. "It's strange, though. Somebody would've had to see us from the highway, passing by. There just aren't any houses anywhere nearby...except for ours. Think we should get out of here? In case someone's watching the house?"

Ari was disappointed, but she agreed. They made their way, single-file, along the shoreline trail. Following Dane, she could get whiffs of his soap-and-laundry scent. She watched every movement he made. Every ounce of her heart wished he would turn around, stop, and just tell her how he felt about her. But ten minutes passed in silence until they reached the steepest ascent of the trail.

"Hey, you hungry?" Dane asked, looking back at her, then up through the canopy of trees. "I'm guessing it's getting close to lunch time."

Ari nodded, and they appeared out of the trail, much to the surprise of Molly, who had been playing in the backyard. Dane's mom was stepping out onto the back porch with a kid-sized sandwich on a plate when she did a startled double-take.

"Well, it looks like you guys have been on another adventure. Let me guess, the Abshire place?" Mrs. Hadley had a sly look on her face as she handed Molly her plate. "Do you guys want me to make some lunch for you?"

Breathless, Dane and Ari both nodded and sat on the back deck.

"That was quite a hike back up. How often did Katia take things to the Abshires?" Ari asked as she wiped sweat from her brow.

"After Ezra's dad became bedridden, it was several times a week, I think. She took them eggs, bread, even whole meals. As I was reading it, I got the feeling Ezra was almost...embarrassed, maybe? Embarrassed to be in need and to have so much help from the family that he was trying to impress? I sure wish I could've found pictures of Ezra with the old photos of Nadia's family. I'm worried that he and Katia never ended up together, since we haven't found any photos."

Mrs. Hadley appeared with lunches for both of them, then retreated back into the house.

After a few moments of eating in silence, Ari turned to Dane. Quietly, she leaned in and said, "Speaking of photos, we should probably go back to your house on Lawton Creek and find that photo album. If Pat found it that day he was there, then it's been outside awhile." She looked at him, worried he would say no, but he just shrugged and finished his sandwich.

"You sure you want to go there again?"

"Not really, but I think we need to get that album. We'll just find it and leave." Ari figured.

"Alright. Let's drive this time."

*   *   *

Dane turned the truck from the highway onto Lawton Drive. The early afternoon was starting to gain some heat. Ari had the window down and her brown hair was swirling in the wind. She was still getting used to seeing Dane in the driver's seat; it still sent nervous butterflies through her every time she looked at him.

The lonely gravel road looked just as it had the day they were here last—overgrown and becoming reclaimed by the surrounding grass fields. Dane went slowly, looking at the fields and trees, just like he had the first time they'd visited.

"Hey, what are you looking for?" Ari finally asked. Dane ticked his head to the side.

"There was a treehouse in one of these trees somewhere," he said, "but I can't remember exactly where. I feel like it was actually closer to the house maybe…" They had just turned toward the river and started descending toward the driveway of the house. The roofline came into view, then all of the house in its broken-down state appeared.

Dane parked the truck in the driveway. Ari felt twinges of apprehension. The house just looked so foreboding, despite the sunny early-afternoon light. The image of Dane punching through the wall replayed in her head. She looked over at him. He had turned the truck off, but hadn't moved from his seat. He was leaning back against the upholstered bench, one hand resting on his face, staring at the spiderwebbed shatter-hole in the front window, courtesy of Pat McCleary and his beer bottle.

Ari took a deep breath and let herself out of the truck. She started heading toward the collapsed chimney, where Pat had told her he'd thrown the photo album. She heard the truck door slam shut; Dane was jogging to catch up with her. Ari started climbing over the stack of bricks to make sure the album hadn't landed on top and fallen into the sideways-lain chimney hollow. Dane reached out and grabbed her arm.

"Ari, be really careful of your ankle. Any of these bricks could crumble—they're super old."

Ari nodded in thanks and kept balancing on the pile. She didn't see the album anywhere. Dane helped her down and they started off into the woods, where ferns and the undergrowth were thick.

"Dane, if you were Pat, where would you be standing when you threw the album?"

Dane snorted. It looked like he had something acrid to say, but he kept it to himself. He pointed at the front porch, which was closest to the chimney pile. "I would guess he came out of the house, stood on the porch, and threw it this way—" he pointed to the right of the chimney pile. Ari picked her way over ferns. "Watch for poison oak," Dane warned. "Looks like a tiny oak tree, but with leaves in groups of three."

Ari and Dane combed the area, walking slowly back and forth. Ari was approaching the base of a thick oak tree when she spotted something orangish-red amongst the ferns.

"Hey…look! Dane! I think I found it!" Ari reached down into the lush undergrowth and pulled out a vinyl book with gold-foil letters that said "PHOTOS." The gold foil had long since faded and almost rubbed away. A few pages were dangling from being flung so far from the house, but it seemed otherwise intact. She desperately wanted to look through it, but instead held it out for Dane to take. He gingerly opened it to the first page. Ari watched his eyes as he went over the photos in front of him.

He started walking toward the river, all while flipping through the pages of the album. They both stepped into the sun, coming out from under the shadow of the tall conifers. The heat of the day was starting to bake the rocks on the shore of the river.

Dane stepped up onto the old wooden dock and carefully made his way to the end. The dock gently rocked with each step he took; the moorings clanked against the pilings that held it in place. Coming to the end of the dock he removed his shoes and sat, dangling his legs in the water. Ari sat cross-legged next to him, not looking at the photos, but at his face.

She couldn't get a read on his expression. It was stoic, blank. If he felt anything as he gazed at the plastic-sleeve pages with photos underneath he certainly didn't let it show. Finally, he wordlessly handed the entire book to Ari. He took his shirt off and balled it into a knot, lying back on the dock and placing the shirt under his head as a pillow.

Ari opened the photo album. She had to shield her eyes from the glinting reflections that came off the water. The photos inside started with yellowed photos from his parents' wedding. His mom, smiling, looked quite a bit younger, with long, dark flowing hair and a simple wedding dress. His dad, clean-shaven, looked nearly exactly like Dane. Ari looked from the photo to Dane, lying on the dock with his eyes closed. *So* similar it scared her.

More photos followed: a chubby baby Dane, held by his mom while she sat in a rocking chair. His dad, holding his boy while sitting on what looked to be the same dock they were currently sitting on. His parents looked happy in every single photo. The Lawton house, while still old, looked cared for and beautiful in every photo. Ari couldn't reconcile the bereft house behind her as being the same home in the photos. The photos continued until Dane looked to be about eight or so.

"Your parents looked happy on their wedding day," Ari finally commented, looking at Dane, wondering if he had fallen asleep. He'd been still and silent for fifteen minutes.

"Sure," he finally said. "And five months later, I came along."

"Oh..."Ari realized she was now treading precariously on deeply-buried family secrets.

"Mom was nineteen. Dad was thirty," he huffed. "Think about it, Ari. Can you imagine being in my mom's shoes... she was just a few years older than we are now and having a baby and a shotgun wedding."

Ari just shook her head. "Do you think your parents would've gotten married if they hadn't been expecting you?"

Dane sat up, almost visibly recoiling at the question. She had accidentally, unknowingly stumbled upon the crux of every childhood hurt.

Ari was frightened to see the glimmer of anger boiling in his eyes. "No," he growled. "And that's just the thing, Ari." He narrowed his eyes and she could see his shoulders tensing.

Ari moved back from Dane slightly. He took a deep breath and closed his eyes, trying to bleed off the tension that had momentarily struck him.

"At least once during every argument they had, it would come up that if it hadn't been for me, they wouldn't have gotten married so soon, if at all." Dane looked out at the water, the sunlit reflections wavering on his face.

Ari didn't know what to say. That same feeling of despair started to overwhelm her: sadness for her friend, regret that she even asked the question, and the fear of his anger.

"I know everyone always asks if you and I are a couple," Dane then said quietly. He wouldn't make eye contact with Ari; wavering reflections bounced off the water as Dane looked out onto the river. "If there's a reason I haven't asked you to be my girlfriend yet, it's because I'm determined not to make the same mistakes my parents did. I feel like I owe you an explanation, and this is it."

Ari felt like all the breath in her lungs had been sucked out. All her hopes of finally knowing that Dane mirrored her affection slipped away. Searing disappointment filled her heart.

Part of Ari wanted him to stop speaking in fear of what he might say next.

"I know it's difficult to understand and I'm sorry. I've gone my whole life being told that I was the reason for a failed marriage, Ari. I still haven't gotten past that. I've sworn to myself that I won't follow in their footsteps and wreck someone else's life because of my messed-up past."

Ari stood to her feet, feeling dizzy with the sway of the dock under her weight. Dane stood as well, picking up the album and his shirt.

"I don't think you would make the same mistakes, Dane," she finally said, her voice catching. Dane looked at her, making eye contact for the first time. A pained expression crossed her face. Just as he raised a hand to brush hair from her face, Ari turned and headed for the truck, her heart in her throat. She could feel her cheeks burning hot in the fear that she might start crying and she wasn't even sure why. All she knew was that she wanted to get away from this place as fast as possible.

Without even looking behind her, she got in Dane's truck and shut the door. Dane finally caught up with her and got in the driver's seat. She could see that he looked angry again, even though he was trying not to. His jaw was clenched; his arms were tensed. Finally he started the truck and headed back to the highway.

The hurt in Ari's heart burned deep. Dane turned back toward Hadley Hill. Ari closed her eyes and leaned her head on the door, letting her hair whip and blow as the truck gained speed.

*   *   *

Ari texted Riley as soon as Dane had dropped Ari off at her house. Ari assumed Riley would probably be with Jace, but to her surprise, Riley told her to come over that evening—and to bring her sleeping bag.

The plush window seat in the second-story room of the old Victorian house was one of Ari's favorite places at Riley's. From this window she could see most of Rivers. Ari sunk into the softness of the purple-hued cushions and blankets as twilight fell across the landscape. The bedroom was almost dark, though the soft white Christmas lights that were strung around the top of her room reflected off Riley's purple-hued walls, casting an ethereal lavender glow all around. Outside, lights were twinkling on all across Rivers and the outlying valley. The Elgin river glinted in the last reflections of daylight.

"Are you sleeping up there?" Riley said, smiling. "I mean, you certainly can if you want to."

Ari turned to Riley and smiled. "Done deal," she said. Riley noticed a sad lilt in Ari's voice, belying her smile.

"Alright, hon, what's going on with Dane? Spill it," she said, pulling her sleeping bag right up to the window seat.

Ari shook her head and couldn't form the right words at first. "That's just the thing—I don't know what's going on with him, Riley. I'm just…disappointed. We had a great morning together, but then we ended up going out to the house on Lawton Creek. Being there changes him."

"Wait, back up," Riley stopped her. "Why did you go out to Lawton Creek? That house is friggin' spooky."

"*You've* been there?"

"Yeah, last year some friends and I went down Lawton Drive just to see if there was a good swimming hole. Turns out it just had a dock right on the Elgin, but no really good places to swim. We poked around the house inside a bit. It looked like it had been abandoned for awhile, but it

180

definitely had a bad vibe."

Ari sighed, knowing that by telling Riley why she was there, it would break part of her confidence with Dane. But she desperately needed Riley's wisdom, so she told her as much as she dared.

"That house is the one Dane grew up in," Ari explained. Riley's eyes got big. "We were there today to find a photo album of his. He told me a lot about his family and growing up, and he's trying to get past a lot of the hurtful things that have happened since his parent's divorce. Today he tells me that he doesn't want to repeat his parent's mistakes, and that's why he hasn't asked me to be his girlfriend," Ari stopped, catching her breath.

"What mistakes?" Riley wrinkled her nose in confusion. "The divorce?"

Ari paused. "Riley, you can't tell a soul about what I'm going to tell you. His mom was nineteen and pregnant when she married his dad. Dane grew up being told that it was because of him that their marriage failed."

Riley looked sad. "That's terrible," she said quietly, then Riley wrinkled her nose. "You don't think Dane likes Julia, do you?"

Ari shrugged. "I don't know…but I *really* hope not, Riley."

Riley nodded. "So he was probably telling the truth. I don't think it has anything to do with *you*, Ari. You should just give him some space for awhile. It sounds like he's trying to work out a ton of stuff. I bet going back to the place where all the hurt happened brings out the worst in him still.

"In any case, be gentle with him," she concluded, and Ari nodded. *That* she could do.

chapter twenty

Ari woke the next morning curled in the comfort of Riley's window seat. She had to scrunch her knees up to fit, but it had worked out just fine. She noticed Riley had moved her own sleeping bag from the floor to her bed and was sprawled out, still deeply asleep. A chill air was seeping from the thinly paned glass, and Ari turned away from it and closed her eyes. She drifted off and an hour later awoke to Riley gently nudging her.

"Hey, you want to go on a hike today?" Riley whispered to her. Ari sat up and rubbed her eyes.

"Yeah, let me call my parents, make sure it's ok," Ari mumbled.

Ari dialed and talked with her mom. "Where are we going?" Ari asked Riley, who was looking through her closet for hiking shoes.

"Cline Ridge. It's on the way to Woodward. Jace is driving."

Ari relayed the details. She had never heard of Cline Ridge, but she was ready for an adventure that would hopefully clear her head of the day before.

She put her phone in her backpack and looked at her clothes. She hadn't planned on hiking, so she asked Riley if Jace would stop by her house so she could get the right gear.

"I don't have hiking boots. I mean, I have my leather boots, but I don't think they'll be great for hiking a long distance. What's the next best kind of shoe?" Ari asked, making a mental list of the things she would need to gather.

"Running shoes, probably," Riley said. She donned a pair of khaki shorts and a tank top. "It could be pretty cool up there, since it's at a little bit of an altitude. I'd bring a sweatshirt," Riley commented.

"Have you done this before?"

"Yeah, last summer. It's technically not a difficult hike, just lots of uphill. The view is entirely worth it though," Riley said, putting her long curly hair up into a tight bun.

Not long after, Jace pulled up in the minivan, and Julia, Rob, and Amara were already packed into the middle row of the van. Riley hopped up front. Rob gave Ari a nod hello and a big grin. Ari made her way back to the rear seat. She had noticed that Rob and Amara were dressed properly for hiking: they both were wearing actual hiking boots and backpacks. Julia, as usual, was more fashionable than the rest of them. She had black leggings, a white tank top, and tan hiking boots that had wedge heels. Ari hadn't ever seen boots with heels like that, but somehow, she wasn't at all surprised in the least that Julia was wearing them.

Jace headed toward Hadley Hill. A nagging thought started to bother Ari: would Dane feel left out since she hadn't invited him? She shook her head. He'd made it pretty clear yesterday that he was fine on his own. She thought Riley's advice about giving him some space was a good idea anyway. Ari relaxed into the minivan seat and watched the scenery go by, closing off any thoughts about Dane.

Jace pulled up to her driveway and Ari let everyone know she'd be back quickly. She dashed up the stairs to her room and changed into the only clothes she had that would be appropriate for hiking: shorts, a t-shirt, and running shoes. She jogged into the kitchen, refilled her water bottle, and stopped in the entryway to pull her long brown hair into a ponytail.

She got back into the van and did a double-take. Dane, wearing a heather-gray sleeveless shirt, jeans, and his black beanie, was sitting in the spot Ari had vacated, looking out the window. Riley looked at Ari, her eyes wide. With a knowing look, Riley explained to Ari, "Jace thought ahead and invited Dane too, since you were with me."

Ari made her way to the back row. She felt Dane look at her, but she couldn't bring herself to return his glance. A huge pit was forming in her stomach and she felt slightly claustrophobic as she put her seatbelt on. Panicked thoughts crossed her mind: what if Dane didn't talk to her at all during the whole trip? What if he ignored her completely? In a split second, Ari decided to ask Jace to not leave yet—she would say she had forgotten something inside her house. Before the words could leave her mouth, she felt a hand slip behind her neck. Dane had leaned across the backseat and pulled her close. His mouth was at her ear, his head against hers.

"Ari?" he said. The way he said her name was halting and lacking confidence. Ari looked at the passenger seat and saw Riley looking at her through the visor mirror. As if on cue, Riley turned up the music in the van just loud enough to cover their conversation. Jace was already pulling out of Ari's driveway; Ari's avoidance plan wouldn't work now.

"Ari, yesterday at the house…I made a mistake. I didn't mean to hurt or confuse you with what I said. I don't regret telling you about my family—" Dane took a jagged breath in and sat there for a moment, just holding her head against his. She could feel his breath on her cheek. Ari's heart fluttered. "I wasn't upset at you. I never meant to make you feel disappointed or sad. I went over to your house last night to apologize, but you were already gone. Ari, I'm sorry…"

Ari turned to face him. He backed away just enough so that she could clearly focus on him, but his hand still lingered behind her head. For the first time ever, Ari saw a vulnerable fear in his eyes. Through every hurt and tumult she had seen Dane experience, he had never shown a shred of anxiety. Something was different.

Riley's advice echoed in her mind: *Be gentle with him.*

In the passing sunlight, she memorized every detail of him: the way he had his beanie pulled low over his eyebrows; how the filtered sun pronounced every fleck of color in his eyes. She reached out and put her hand against the side of his cheek. At her touch, he closed his eyes and leaned into her hand. A flutter ripped through Ari. Dane had never seemed vulnerable to her. *Ever.*

Ari suddenly became aware that conversation in the van had abruptly stopped. She didn't want to look to see if others in the van were watching their wordless exchange, but both she and Dane straightened up in their seats.

The van had just passed Lawton Drive. They continued on toward the town of Woodward. Conversation in the van resumed, but Ari couldn't bring herself to do anything but be silent and watch the scenery as they followed the narrow country highway. It was eleven in the morning, and the sun had begun to burn off the cool morning air.

Twenty minutes into the drive, the scenery began to change from rural farmland to conifer forests. Signs of human habitation began to recede from the landscape.

Amara looked back at Ari. "Hey you back there, have you ever been to Cline Ridge?"

Ari shook her head. "Never even heard of it." Ari looked to Dane. "You?"

"Nah, but I've heard stories about it," he said, a glint in his eye.

Ari's brow furrowed. "Stories? About a hiking trail?"

Riley craned her neck back from the passenger seat, smiling. "It's got some history behind it," she hinted, but wouldn't say more.

As with all roads that went away from the valley floor, Ari noticed they had started to climb upwards on a twisting road. A forested hill was on her side, and she leaned over across Dane to see his view: a breathtakingly steep draw fell away from the pavement. The tops of fir trees rose up above the edge of the road. They hadn't been climbing for long when Jace pulled the van over at a small bump-out next to an unmarked metal gate that blocked off a paved road.

The van doors slid open and the group piled out. Ari got out, but hesitated next to the van.

"Wait, guys, is this the hiking trail?"

Ari had envisioned an actual parking lot with a map of the trail system. This wasn't a wayside of any kind—just a metal gate barring a narrow road that disappeared into the trees.

Jace smiled, pulling out his camera. "Well, it's a trail that you can hike, but no, it's not really a hiking destination for most people. This was the location of the Cline Air Force Station radome."

At the words 'Air Force Station,' Ari froze. She wasn't sure she was up for another adventure in a concrete behemoth.

Riley saw her tense up. "It's ok, hon, it's not like the direction center. It's just a structure that housed radar. Plus, it's a really great view from the top," she smiled, patting Ari on the back.

Everyone started grabbing their packs and water bottles. Dane strapped on his bag and took his beanie off. His hair, though shorter, was almost as messy as ever. Ari watched as Riley and Jace easily climbed over the metal gate. Amara and Julia went through the sideways-V shaped bars, and Rob just stepped over the lowest point. Dane stayed behind Ari as she climbed over, which proved to be more awkward than everyone else made it look.

"Are we supposed to be here, or is this private property?" Ari asked Jace as they began their upward climb. The road was paved, but seemed unmaintained and a network of cracks looked like grassy veins below her feet.

"I think it's fine," Jace reassured her. "I know people who have gone to the top, but I've never heard of anyone getting in trouble or anything. I'm sure it's ok."

"Don't worry so much, Ari. Just try and relax and have fun!" Julia said, looking back at Ari.

Ari knew Julia was right, but it stung a little that her apprehension was so obvious to others.

Dane leaned over to Ari's ear. "Ten bucks says she can't make it to the top wearing those boots," he whispered.

Ari snuck a sly smile at him and nodded. "Alright, you're on." She stuck out her hand and he shook it. "You're going to lose," she declared. Dane snickered quietly. Ahead of them Jace, Julia, and Riley were discussing the history of the station, while Rob and Amara were talking about the Last Dance. Ari inwardly groaned, hoping her dance with Pat McCleary wouldn't come up. In fact, Ari thought, there was a whole bundle of topics she hoped wouldn't be discussed. She and Dane walked in silence for long stretches of time.

The road was plagued with soft, bright green blackberry vines that snagged and tore at their clothes. Ari wished she'd worn jeans instead of shorts and made a mental note for next time they went hiking. The group was forced to condense down to a single-file line in some areas. Rob pointed out places where poison oak grew to the edge of the road, and everyone made wide arcs around the patches.

They climbed through thick forest for twenty minutes. It was beautifully quiet when occasional lulls in conversation occurred. Sometimes the only sound was the wind weaving through the treetops, making a sound that was similar to rushing water. Once in awhile, a raven's brazen *caw CAW* would echo out.

Several times Ari thought the trees would clear away to reveal some sort of view, but it wasn't until they rounded a tight turn and came to another metal gate that she could see the forest thin away. They all made their way over the barricade. The chain holding the gate to the post was locked but hanging loosely, and with each person that went over, a terrible loud clank rang out through the forest.

"Well, if we're trying to be sneaky, I think we've just been outed," Rob joked. His comment made Ari wonder if they would encounter any other hikers at the top.

Once past the barrier, hints of structures came into view. Far on the other side was a round, eerie white dome. As they rounded the curve to the top of the hill, the conifers fell away and wind-whipped grassland covered the top. The paved road continued to curve around, lifting them ever higher above the tree line. Ari spun around and looked behind them. Ridge lines drifted in and out of valley haze, just peeking from behind the rows of conifers at the edge of the grassland. She walked faster, eager to arrive at the summit. Dane jogged to catch up.

As the group exited the protection of the trees, a strong wind began to buffet them. Ari got her sweatshirt out of her backpack and pulled her hair into a tight ponytail. Dane fished his beanie from his pack and put it back on, pulling it low. The wind wasn't chill, but forceful enough that it brought the temperature down noticeably.

The first building they went past was an old tin shed with barely-attached hangar doors. The doors were gaping open and sagging on their tracks. Fractured patches of pavement suggested that a driveway once approached the building. Amara and Riley walked through the structure while Jace photographed the exterior. The rest of the group continued along the main road. Ari started to smile as more of the surrounding view began to present itself. They were much, much higher above the valley floor than Ari had perceived as they had been hiking in cover of the conifers.

The road beneath them was becoming nonexistent: Ari had to watch for large cracks and deep potholes. Whole sections of the road were falling away, and in some places, nature had reclaimed the asphalt completely. Ari was elated as they rounded the final turn to the summit of Cline Ridge. The road—or what was left of it—ran directly between two groups of buildings, one on the east, and one on the west.

Ari paused to take in the scenery: small, concrete block buildings with peeling paint stood on either side. More than a dozen power poles, transmission towers, and all different sorts of antennae rose from the buildings and grounds. Ari marveled at the variety of instrumentation that was still standing.

"Wow…" Ari breathed, then hustled to catch up with the rest of the group. Jace was lagging behind everyone, taking photos of every single building. He seemed surprised that the buildings they'd encountered, so far, were unfenced.

Dane pointed at the stark white dome, which was now coming into view on their right side. "Hey, Jace, what's the deal with that thing?" he asked, gesturing at the golfball-looking structure that was propped on a stout cylindrical base.

"That's the radome," Jace explained. "The ball is just a protective cover to keep the important stuff out of the weather."

"What was the 'important stuff'? Amara asked.

"The radar dish," Jace said.

"Makes sense," Dane mused. They were now directly between groups of buildings and at the exact summit of Cline Ridge. Barbwire-lined fencing enclosed everything on their right and left, and although part of the panoramic view was obscured by those buildings, Ari moved around in a small circle and took in the beauty of the view.

Wind rushed between the buildings and made eerie whistling sounds around the antennae. A change in wind direction would alter the chorus of whistles. Another sound came to Ari's ears: a rattling chain link fence. Startled, she turned around.

Jace had handed Riley his camera and was trying to scale the fence enclosing the radome side.

"Dude, what are you doing?" Rob said, incredulous.

"I really want to get in to see that radome up close," Jace explained. He'd picked a spot where the fence met a gate and there seemed to be enough of a gap between the barbed wire where it looked like he might actually get through.

"Someone hand me a jacket?" Jace strained as he reached the top of the fence. He was so close to being able to turn sideways through the gap in the barbed wire. Rob handed him a sweatshirt, which Jace threw over the top of the barbed wire to his side. Jace carefully supported himself with his arms before throwing his legs over to the other side. His jeans snagged on a bit of barbed wire and tore, but he smiled as his boots hit the ground.

Without hesitation Julia anchored the toe of her boot in a the fence and gracefully swung herself over. Riley went next, struggling with the barbed wire. Suddenly Ari felt herself tensing. She didn't relish the thought of scaling a barbwire fence that housed electrical and radio equipment. All the while, Dane was helping to hoist Amara up, then Dane followed her over. Rob knelt down so Ari could step on his knee, but she backed away.

"Thanks, Rob. You guys go ahead. I'm gonna stay out here and enjoy the view." As soon as she said it, Ari felt the searing pang of disappointment. She really *did* want to join the rest of the group, but an overwhelming unnamed fear made her stay outside the fence.

"Ari, there's nothing to worry about," Jace assured her, hanging onto the fence. "It's all abandoned. Nothing up here is in use anymore. I'm sure there isn't any sort of security whatsoever."

Ari smiled in appreciation, but inside she felt a crushing disappointment in herself for not being brave. "Go ahead, guys," she said simply. Dane looked at her with an eyebrow raised in surprise. Julia put her hand on Dane's back as the group walked away.

"Her loss," Julia said under her breath to Dane. Ari's mouth dropped open in disbelief in what she heard and cheeks burned hot with embarrassment. But no matter how hard she tried, she couldn't make herself scale that fence. This was a different fear from her aversion to heights. This was a gut feeling. She watched as the group made their way to the base of the radome.

Ari walked the perimeter of the fence, seething in embarrassment. Various concrete buildings obscured her view of the radome base and she could no longer see or hear her friends. Ari stopped walking and tried to distract herself from her disparaging thoughts by appreciating the expansive view, which was magnificent. They were far above the rest of the rolling, forested hills. Sunlight and an almost cloudless light blue sky made for perfect visibility. The wind was still strong; Ari guessed that the blustery breezes rarely stopped at this unprotected elevation.

A sound met Ari's senses: a palpable hum; almost inaudible. She really rather felt it in the back of her throat than actually heard it with her ears. She continued walking, following the fence line. Within the barbed wire fence, there was another cluster of transmission towers; these had hazard signs on them. *'Don't touch! RF burn hazard!'* the signs warned. These signs looked new. The buzzing feeling was intensifying; rather quickly Ari realized that those radio towers were neither old nor abandoned. She suddenly hoped that there wasn't other live equipment where her friends were exploring. Ironically, a corner of fencing had been peeled away closest to the radio towers. Ari thought about pulling her phone out to message Riley but then stopped.

A startling sound came along on the wind: a familiar, faraway clanking noise. It certainly hadn't come from inside the fenced area. Ari started walking quickly along the perimeter, suddenly wishing that she wasn't alone. That noise…it had to be the last, loose gate they'd climbed over before reaching the summit. Ari suddenly realized someone had just passed over or through that gate.

chapter twenty-one

Ari strained to look down the road. So far, she didn't see anyone. She pulled out her phone and frantically dialed Riley.

"You guys gotta get out of there," Ari said breathlessly. "Someone is coming, Riley. I heard the gate…" On the other end, Riley was having trouble hearing past the gusting wind on Ari's phone. Just then, to Ari's shock, she spied a white truck making its way up the barely-there pavement. Ari moved to the south side of the complex, hoping the group of buildings would hide her, at least for awhile.

"Riley, it's someone in a truck. They got past the gate somehow. You guys need to get out of there!" She paused as Riley desperately relayed the message to her friends.

"If you come out of the building, there's a hole in the fence due west of the radome," Ari yelled. The white truck had almost made its way to the apex of the hill, and it was at the farthest point from Ari. "Guys, go *now*!"

Ari noticed the truck was heading her way. Her heart started pounding. She ended her call to Riley and started taking photos of the view. She did her best to look purposeful, like she was just a lone girl on a hike, taking in the fantastic vista.

She could hear the tires of the truck slowly approaching. In her mind, a story was forming. Though she desperately wanted to, Ari avoided looking behind her to see if the whole group had made it out of the compound. Ari was standing right next to the locked gate where Jace had jumped the fence. She could hear the truck idling to a stop. Finally, she turned around and looked behind her.

To her horror, she saw the door at the base of the building just starting to open. Julia peeked out, and the whole group emerged from the open door. From Ari's vantage point, it looked like they were headed toward the hole in the fence, but she couldn't be sure.

She looked at the truck. A guy wearing a bright yellow hardhat and safety vest had just gotten out. He looked at her and nodded *hello* as he procured a key to open the gate. She caught his attention right away and casually walked up to him before he could look at the gate behind him. Over his shoulder, Ari saw the group frantically looking for the hole in the fence.

"Afternoon," Ari nodded, smiling. She gathered every single bit of nerve she had and strode up to the worker. "Hey, I came up here to get some photographs of the view, but these buildings are kind of interesting. Do you know the history of this place?" She spoke too fast, but smiled and tried to act casual. She had to distract him long enough that the group could at least make it out of the hole.

The worker shrugged. He looked youngish, maybe in his twenties, and he seemed surprised to see a small girl all alone at the top of a big ridge. His embroidered name badge said 'Phillip.' Phillip smiled a little.

"Well, all I know is this was some sort of Cold War radar place. I think it has something to do with the military station in Allendale. At any rate, they were lookin' for planes or something. Don't really know more than that," he smiled apologetically.

Ari allowed herself a single glance to the side. She could just see Amara's backside disappearing through the hole in the fence. Ari kept talking.

"So if this is left over from the Cold War, what are *you* here working on?" Ari tried to sound interested yet casual. It worked. Phillip kept talking.

"Oh, my company has several transmission towers up here. Other companies have radio antennae, cell towers, and I think even the military has an array up here still. I'm checking to make sure one of the radio towers is working properly. Been having wonky signal issues with KR-41," he said, pointing to a red-and-white striped antenna. "That's the one, right there."

Ari nodded and thanked him. "I'll let you get back to your work then. Hope you figure out your signal problem."

Phillip nodded and let himself into the gate, then closed it behind him. Ari slowly started around the road that followed the perimeter and started descending the hill. She let out a huge breath as her heart was finally starting to return to a normal, slower beat. She smiled, relieved that she had been able to distract Phillip the radio guy just long enough for her group to escape.

She tried to enjoy the view as she neared the first tin building off to the left of the road. *Where was everyone?* She dialed Riley again, but there was no answer. Ari furrowed her brow and continued down the road. Apprehension and a tick of annoyance filled her. The last thing she wanted to do was hike down the entire wooded road alone. As she passed the tin building, footsteps behind her caused her heart to ramp up and she whirled around.

She quickly realized it was Dane. She let out a huge breath in relief and Dane smiled wide.

"Oh my gosh, you're trying to kill me, Dane. What were you doing in there?" Ari asked, putting her hand over her heart.

"I told them to go on ahead and I would wait for you. What happened with the guy in the truck? It looked like he was trying to get into the gate."

"Yeah, he was," Ari emphasized. "There are still live transmission towers up there, Dane. You guys could've gotten fried. The towers closest to the hole in the fence? Those are all functional; Jace was wrong. This place isn't abandoned. Well, the buildings may be, but some of the towers are still in use." They had now reached the first gate. Ari turned around, looking at where they had been.

"I hadn't noticed it when we came up here, but look," Ari pointed at the grouping of tallest towers, now just barely visible from their vantage point. "They all have blinking red lights on top."

Dane turned back, too. "Oh. Shoot, you're right. How did you distract him while we got out of the fence?"

Ari made a face. "I pretended to be photographing the view. I mean, I *did* take photos. But I got his attention as soon as he got out of the truck and started asking him about the history of the site. He didn't really know much, so then I had to ask him what he was doing up there, getting into the gate."

Dane smirked. "He must've been delighted that someone was interested in his work."

Ari rolled her eyes. "At any rate, it bought you guys just enough time to get yourselves out of the complex and through the hole in the fence. What did it look like inside the radome?"

They had now started the steepest part of the road's descent. The truck had pushed through much of the overgrowth and had widened the path considerably. A chipped-out chunk of pavement tripped Ari up, but Dane grabbed Ari's arm and steadied her. She smiled in thanks, and took his arm as they continued down the road.

"Well, inside was a conical-shaped base that the radar used to be mounted on. The radar dish was gone, but just being inside a nearly circular dome was really cool. Riley took lots of pictures, and Jace did too."

"Was it dark inside?"

"No, that's the thing. It was darker than outside, sure, but the material that made up the dome was thin enough that it let some light in. It was spooky and kind of cool all at the same time." Dane slowed as he walked. "Ari, why didn't you want to come with the rest of us? Was it the height of the fence? I would've helped you."

Ari shook her head. "No, not at all," she insisted. "It was something else. Like, a gut feeling. Do you ever get those? When you just know something isn't quite right?"

Dane shrugged. "Maybe. Once or twice."

"Well, it was that. I just couldn't make myself go over that fence. I felt horrible about it too. I wanted to be with you guys more than anything, especially after what Julia said under her breath."

Dane shook his head and stopped Ari as she walked. "Don't listen to Julia, Ari. She's just jealous of you, and..." Dane trailed off.

"And what, Dane?" Ari tried to remain totally composed and even-toned, but it was difficult. Yesterday's conversation on the dock gave her reason to be cautious. *Be gentle*, she reminded herself. "She has no reason to be jealous of me. I'm nothing to her." Ari dropped her hand from Dane's arm and shoved her hands in her pockets. Dane was looking uncomfortable again; his jaw was set hard and he put his hat back on, pulling it low over his eyebrows.

Ari took a deep breath and plunged ahead, barely speaking. "I understand that you don't want me as your girlfriend," she managed. Her voice faltered. "If you like Julia, I understand." Ari turned to walk away, satisfied that she'd settled that topic, but her heart burned in pain at what she'd just said.

Dane's hand on her arm pulled her back to him before she could even take a step. She swiveled into place, inches from him. Dane raised a hand to her cheek and rested his other hand on her shoulder, holding her in place with the lightest touch.
Ari looked straight at Dane, trying hard to read into his soul. The stippled sunlight coming through the forest canopy illuminated every variation of color in his eyes.
"I'm not interested in Julia at all, Ari. You have to know that," Dane emphasized, shaking his head.

She looked at Dane: he wasn't waiting for a reply or any sort of reaction. He brushed a strand of hair from her eyes as a whisper-soft breeze moved the air, and then followed the line of her jaw with his finger, stopping under her chin. A shiver rippled through Ari as she stared at him.

Before she could say a word, a faint and distant crunching sound caused both of them to look up the road. Phillip's truck was slowly coming down the road. Ari and Dane climbed up onto the dirt bank, allowing just enough room for the truck to get past. Once gone, Ari and Dane hopped back down to the gravel road.

"I wonder if he's confused about where I appeared from?" Dane smirked. They were almost at the gate; dust from Phillip's truck was starting to settle back down as they made the final turn on the old road.

When they reached the gate, they could see a barefoot Riley sprawled out on the middle seat of the van, her shoes resting on the ground. Amara and Jace were chatting, and Rob and Julia were sitting on a boulder.

Ari went to the van and sat next to Riley. Riley reached over and gave Ari a pat on the back. "Ari, hon, that was epic. You have some mad skills, distracting that guy so we could get out. What on earth would've happened if you hadn't stayed outside the fence?"

Ari smiled at Riley, but Julia cut in. "Maybe we should leave Ari outside on all our adventures. You know, like a lookout or something." She laughed and tossed her blonde curls.

"Julia, Ari literally saved our butts today," Rob cut in.

Dane chimed in. "Yeah, Julia, did you know those transmission towers were live? The ones we got within feet of as you came through the hole in the fence?"

"Wait, what?" Jace looked up from his camera.

"The guy in the white truck—Phillip—he was up there to fix a faulty tower," Ari explained. "He said there are all sorts of live towers up there: radio, cell, even the military still has working equipment." Ari looked right at Julia. "The live towers were the ones you guys ran closest to on your way to the hole in the fence."

Everyone was quiet for a moment. Finally, Amara quietly chimed in. "You knew the towers were live? That's why you didn't go in?"

Ari shook her head and stood up. "No, not at all. I just had a weird gut feeling, guys. Sorry. I don't know how else to explain it." Julia made a soft snorting sound, like she didn't believe what Ari was saying.

Rob came over and gave Ari an unexpected hug. She hugged him back, appreciating that he had defended her. "Let's get home. I think we've had enough adventure for one day," Rob commented, giving Ari another pat on the back. Leaning close to Ari, he smiled. "Thanks for having our backs, Ari. I'd go on an adventure with you any day." Ari suddenly felt super self-conscious and blushed to the top of her cheeks, but she couldn't help but smile.

The others in the group had gathered their gear and were piling into the minivan. Ari climbed into her normal spot in the farthest back before anyone else had a chance to sit. Ari closed her eyes and tilted her head back, trying to relax against the headrest.

Ari felt someone settle in next to her in the middle seat. She was surprised to see Riley there, and Amara on the other side of Riley. Riley leaned close to Ari. "Hey, what did you think of Cline Ridge?" She then lowered her voice even more. "Sorry Julia was so rude."

Ari turned to Riley. Amara was leaning in almost as close as Riley. Ari just shook her head. "Whatever. I wish I was braver. She's totally right about me being chicken."

"You're not chicken, Ari," Amara remarked. "You're just cautious. And that played out in our favor today; don't forget that."

The van pulled out and Jace started to head back to Rivers. Ari glanced to the front seat. Dane had called shotgun, and Rob and Julia were in the middle row.

Ari straightened up and looked over at Amara. "Hey, next time we go hiking, you should invite Aaron to go with us. Do you think he would?"

Amara smiled. "I actually asked him this morning if he wanted to come with us. He had relatives who were visiting from out of town, but he said it sounded fun."

Ari leaned closer to Amara. "So...do you like him?"

The question brought another smile to Amara's face, confirming Ari's suspicions. "He's nice. We had an awesome time at the dance, so I really would like to get to know him better."

Riley grimaced. "You didn't answer Ari!" Riley chuckled and nudged Amara.

"Yes, ok, I do! Now, if you two can keep quiet about it..."

"Of course, Amara. We won't say a word. But we expect Aaron to join us on our next adventure. Maybe he'll be as chicken as I am. We can be on the lookout together," Ari joked. Being able to make fun of herself released some pressure. She had appreciated Dane and Rob backing her up against Julia, but it was only when Ari started to forgive herself for not going over the fence that she started to feel better.

Ari glanced up at the front seat. Jace and Dane were talking in low voices, and she could see Jace's eyes in the rearview mirror. Whatever they were discussing seemed serious.

Somewhere along the way, Ari leaned her head back and drifted off. The sound of music, the road noise, and conversation had lulled her into a quick and deep sleep.

Sometime later, Ari blinked, waking from the heavy slumber. The sunlight suggested early evening was settling across the landscape. She looked around; nobody was in the van but herself. The side door had been left partially open.

The van was parked in a gravel driveway in front of an exquisite, turn-of-the-century farm home. It was even more ornate and stately than Ari's house. A green, neatly trimmed lawn was enclosed by a whitewashed picket fence. Hanging baskets filled with tiny, newly-planted pansies hung along the covered front porch. A familiar BMW was parked next to the van.

Ari got out of the van and slowly turned around. The house was in the middle of miles of fields; only distant hills broke the horizon. The fields to the west emanated a beautiful light green glow as sunlight filtered through strands of tall grass. Ari thought she heard the sound of voices being carried on the slight, cool breeze.

A cobblestone footpath led Ari from the driveway, through the front gate, and around the house. Finally, Ari could see where the voices were coming from. Amara, Riley, and Jace were a distance away from the house, sitting around a large stone fire circle. A mighty bonfire was roaring in the center of the circle. Dane had been walking toward the house when he looked up and saw Ari.

"Hey, you're awake," Dane said. His confident demeanor was missing, but he seemed delighted to see her.

"You were asleep for quite some time. I was actually coming to check on you and bring you this blanket," he explained. Ari noticed a fleece throw draped over his arm. Dane had his hat on again; his eyes nearly hidden by it.

"Where are Julia and Rob?" she asked, glancing over Dane's shoulder. "And, where *are* we?"

A huge smile spread over Dane's face as he started to chuckle. Ari's heart melted at the sound of his laugh and at the sight of his big grin.

"Ok, first, Rob had to be somewhere tonight, and Julia said she needed to get home, so we dropped them both off before we came here. Aaron called Amara to see if she could hang out tonight, and he got here a little while ago. This—" Dane motioned to the house behind them, "—is Jace's house. We went ahead and brought you to the bonfire to celebrate the beginning of summer."

Dane unfurled the fleece blanket and wrapped it around Ari's shoulders, smiling again. "Riley already called your parents to let them know you were here," Dane said, hesitant. He was still holding the blanket that hung around her.

Ari thanked him for the blanket. They both startled at *whooping* sound and looked over to see Jace throwing something into the fire, causing it to explode into a quick flash of crackling flames. It would've been unnoticed by anyone else, but Ari saw Dane tense at the sight of the sudden inferno.

"Are you going to be ok with this?" Ari asked quietly.

Dane looked back at her. "I figure part of moving past the crap I've been through is facing my fears. This one is by far the easiest fear to deal with," Dane said in a low voice. He put his arm around Ari's blanketed shoulder and started walking toward the fire with her. Amara and Aaron were sitting shoulder-to-shoulder on the grass, and Riley waved to Ari from her Adirondack chair. Jace was breaking off leafy branches from a shrub that was on the border of the backyard. He balled the branches into a wad, then tossed them into the fire. Another crackling *whoosh* of flames went up. Dane paused until the flames died down again.

"Forsythia branches. They really burn quick, even when they're green," Jace hollered, obviously enjoying throwing his plant-based pyrotechnics.

Ari stayed by Dane's side. If this was his easiest fear to face, she hated to think what his other fears might be. He hadn't moved from his spot; he was solidly anchored in place. The look on his face was blank, distant. She looped her arm around his waist and Dane suddenly looked down at her with a different expression: a mix of surprise and gratitude. He moved forward with her and they sat in the grass just close enough to the bonfire that Ari could feel its heat on her cheeks.

The sun had just set and dusk had fallen. A warm light lingered by the horizon. Riley and Amara were talking about their first trip to the Abshire house. Ari was surprised when Dane spoke up.

"Ari and I went back there not too long after Jace took his photos. We found a journal under the floorboards in the basement," Dane confessed. Everyone in the group quieted down and started listening.

Ari watched as he began to describe what Ezra had written in his journal. Firelight flicked across his face, showing the strength in his profile. In that moment Ari realized just how much she'd come to love the sound of his voice as he told his story.

"He's just a kid, but Ezra has huge responsibilities," Dane explained. "He works the fields with his mom when she isn't teaching piano. His dad is sick and Ezra is afraid that he'll die. Ezra feels the pain of hunger, but he skips meals so his sister has enough to eat."

It hit Ari like a flood of ice water; she almost audibly gasped. *Hunger. Fear. Pain.* This is why Dane related to Ezra, and why Dane's voice wavered with compassion and conviction when he recited the story he was uncovering. It was personal: deeply, painfully, relatable. Ari felt a deep sadness well up in her, nearly so powerful that she could barely keep tears from forming. She put her hand on Dane's back and took a deep breath. At her touch, Dane looked over at her.

"Dane, what an amazing find. You have someone's history in your possession. That's really, really cool." Jace had finally stopped throwing his flammable wads of shrubbery into the fire.

"Ari and I also found a carving; one on the base of a stone pillar, and the same one along a trail that connects my house to the Abshire place."

"Have you figured out if the carving relates to Ezra? Or anybody?" Amara asked.

"Not yet."

The fire had died down to a shell of quietly crackling embers. With the firelight low, and the dusk exchanging for inky night, stars were starting to become more bright and visible than Ari had ever seen them.

Ari laid back onto the soft grass and pulled her blanket tightly around her. "Jace, where exactly are we? I mean, I know this is your house, but where is Rivers?"

"Ah, right, you have no idea where we are," Jace chuckled. "I forgot about that. Well, we're out in the middle of absolutely nowhere." For that, he was right: Ari hadn't been on such a long stretch of flat ground anywhere near Rivers. "We're about half an hour from Rivers, to the east."

As Ari lay in the grass, she could hear slow cricket chirps somewhere out in the fields. The sky was dark enough now that a thick swath of stars was becoming visible, running from northeast to southwest.

Ari smiled to herself. A year ago the stillness and silence of this landscape was one of her hardest adjustments. The week she'd moved into her house, she had longed for the sights and sounds of the city she loved, and imagined she'd never adjust to the rural countryside. And yet, here she was, drinking in the solitude of the stars above her.

She closed her eyes and just listened: the night breeze was rustling grass in the fields surrounding Jace's house. Crickets, the low voices of her friends talking, distant noises from the farm home, and the last pops and crackles of the low, glowing embers were all she could hear.

"Are you asleep again?" Dane whispered in her ear, startling her. Her eyes snapped open. Dane was lying down beside her in the grass, his head propped up on an elbow. He was as close as he could've possibly been. His fresh laundry-and-cologne scent surrounded her as she made eye contact in the near-dark.

"Yeah," Ari said. "I definitely am."

Dane snorted and started to laugh, and Ari had to smile back. "By the way, you owe me ten bucks," Ari said in her most serious tone.

"What? Why?" Dane said quietly.

"Because Julia made it to the top wearing those boots."

chapter twenty-two

Ari stood looking at her calendar. The address she'd scrawled on the page matched the address of the house in front of her. Ari had ridden her bike into town to meet her first yard care customer. It was four days after school had finished, and Ari reveled in the fact that summer had finally arrived.

Ari made her way to the front door of the neatly-kept Craftsman-style home. In her hand was a clipboard which held an organized checklist. Butterflies filled Ari's stomach. She took one deep breath before pressing the ivory-colored doorbell.

An elderly lady, her hair neatly arranged in short curls, answered the door. She introduced herself as Eleanor. Eleanor stepped aside and gestured for Ari to enter. "Won't you come inside for a moment, dear?"

Ari nodded in thanks and entered. It was overly warm and slightly stuffy inside; a rush of memories flooded Ari's heart. Something about Eleanor's home reminded Ari of her own grandmother's house: a macramé plant hanger held a gangly plant by the front window, and Ari could see well-worn paths in the carpet.

Eleanor motioned for Ari to sit on the afghan-covered sofa by the front window. Eleanor slowly lowered herself into a reclining chair. Books were stacked on the side table next to the recliner's armrest, and a teacup balanced precariously on the top of the stack.

"Well, my dear, tell me about yourself. We will be seeing each other once a week, so I'd like to get to know my new gardener a bit." Eleanor's voice was soft and smooth and kind, and Ari liked her at once.

"I moved here at the beginning of last summer," Ari started. "I'm from San Francisco. My dad changed jobs and we spent most of last summer working on the garden at our house. I decided I liked doing that enough that I would try and make some money at it this summer."

Eleanor nodded thoughtfully. "Where in town do you live? You must have quite the garden if it took all summer."

"We live on Hadley Hill." Ari saw one of Eleanor's eyebrows tick upwards.

"Oh, my. You don't say? The Hadleys were quite the family, I've heard. I actually grew up in Woodward, but when my husband and I got married, we moved here and built this house. Gerald passed years ago, but when he was alive, he was the one to mow the lawns and care for the roses. I tried to keep it up for as long as I could, but I'm slowing down, dear. I swallowed my pride and realized I can no longer care for Gerald's gardens on my own."

Ari detected a hint of sadness in Eleanor's voice. For a moment, her eyes drifted past Ari and focused on something far away. As quick as it happened, Eleanor refocused on Ari and motioned to the front door.

"Let's go get your equipment, dear. Here, I'll show you where to find everything you'll need."

Eleanor slowly made her way out the front door and down the steps of her porch, and led Ari around to an old shed which contained a myriad of neatly organized tools.

"What I've been needing to do for ages is get the rhododendrons trimmed up, but getting on a ladder is no longer a good idea for me," Eleanor explained. She pointed to a simple wooden ladder in the shed. "Use that one to trim the rhodies. And don't be afraid to trim them back hard, Aribelle."

Ari made a note on her checklist. *Trim rhodies back far.* One by one, Eleanor went through all the tasks that would need to be done in her yard: mowing, edging, roses trimmed, and baby blackberry bushes eliminated.

"Do you have leather gloves with you, Aribelle?" Eleanor adjusted her glasses as she looked at Ari.

"No, ma'am. But I can get some if I need to," Ari assured her.

Eleanor shook her head. "No, no, take these." She handed a pair of tan leather gloves to Ari. They were too large on her, but Ari figured she could make it work. "These were Gerald's. Whenever you work on roses or the blackberries, use these. The thorns can't get through." Ari took the gloves and thanked her.

"I have you for two hours, is that correct?" Eleanor smiled at Ari, who nodded. "Alright then, get done whatever you can in that time and I'll be back outside at noon to check on you."

Ari checked her list and ordered the tasks in the best way she could figure: do shrub trimming, roses, and blackberry removal before edging the lawn. She figured mowing would be the last logical task. With the morning sun already heating the day, Ari put on her sunhat that she'd bought last summer, plus Gerald's gloves, and began working.

*　　*　　*

One thing Ari hadn't counted on was how much energy she would expend as she did yard work. She had felt alright the night after doing Eleanor's yard, but after her second appointment, Ari found herself laying out on a blanket in the pasture behind her house, barely able to stay awake at five o'clock in the afternoon. The last customer was a middle-aged man who had a half-acre yard that was in the process of being replanted. He'd had Ari dig out an area for landscaping, and on top of being dead-tired, Ari had developed blisters all across her hands from shoveling.

She had just closed her eyes when she heard footsteps crunching through the oak grove. Ari turned to see Dane walking up to her. He was dressed as if he'd just come from work; he was still wearing a dress shirt and slacks. Ari blushed at the sight of him.

"Hey," Dane said, stretching out on the blanket next to Ari. He propped his head up on an elbow. "How has your job been going? You look tired."

Ari smiled and nodded. "Yeah, it's a lot of work. I mean, I'll just need to adjust to it, assuming I get more jobs. But I love being outside, so it's all good." Ari propped her head up as well, looking straight at him. "How is everything at the museum? Is the job what you expected it to be?"

Dane smiled. "It's interesting. There's just so much information that has to be sorted. Agnes has been training us so we know how to properly catalog everything."

"We? There's more than just you?"

"Yeah, there are two other interns. One is a guy who is a sophomore at school, and the other is Julia."

A ripple of something unpleasant washed over Ari. "Julia, Rob's cousin?"

"Yeah, that one." Dane's tone was neutral. "But all of us come in on our own schedules, so it's unlikely that any of us will be there at the same time once our training is over." Ari sighed in relief.

A mischievous look came over Dane's face. "Hey, you know what today is, right?"

Ari looked at him with a funny look. "Tuesday?"

A knowing grin spread across Dane's face. "You really don't know?"

Ari sat up on the blanket, perplexed. "No…?"

"A year ago today, I accidentally scared the life out of a small, brown-haired girl who was snooping around my underground room."

"You remember the exact date?" Ari was beyond surprised.

"Well, yeah. It was really memorable," Dane said with a chuckle. "Had I known that you'd eventually turn my world upside down in the best possible way, I wouldn't have run away from you that night."

It was Ari's turn to laugh. "Why did you run away? Was I really that terrifying?"

Dane paused a moment. "That night Rhoda had come home from

work and immediately started yelling at me. I can't even remember what she'd been mad about. I took off into the woods, heading for the circle, and to suddenly see this lovely girl standing there…it was surreal. I just froze. I was so caught off-guard that I couldn't think of a thing to say." His voice was raw, honest.

A smile started to tug at Ari's face. *This* was the real Dane. Unashamed, unafraid, not spilling everything to her, but allowing Ari glimpses of his heart.

Ari laid on her stomach next to Dane and they stayed there in comfortable silence for a moment. Dane relaxed next to her, stretching out on the blanket. They were facing west; the sun was just skimming the roofline of Ari's house and a great shadow was falling on the pasture.

"Have you had dinner yet?" Dane asked her, after several minutes of silence had passed between them.

"No. You?"

"Nah, I just got home. Would you like to go somewhere to eat?"

Ari rolled to her side and looked at Dane. For some reason, she was caught completely off-guard by his question. Ari glanced at her dirt-streaked legs and the amount of grime that was under her fingernails.

"Sure. But I need to get cleaned up first. Can you wait fifteen minutes?"

*   *   *

"Hey! I'll be back before ten!" Ari called to her mom as Ari descended the staircase.

Ari's mom rounded the corner from the kitchen and noticed the summer dress that Ari was wearing. "Ari, you look nice! Where are you going?"

"Dane asked me to go to dinner. Not sure where yet," Ari explained.

"Is it a date?" her mom winked.

Ari shifted uncomfortably. "I...I don't really know," she stammered.

Her mom grinned. "Have fun, honey."

Ari grabbed her bag just as Dane's truck pulled into the circular driveway. When she got in, she noticed Dane had changed into jeans and rolled up the sleeves on his dress shirt, leaving the top two buttons undone. He looked perfectly comfortable sitting there with one arm draped over the large steering wheel. He did a double-take and smiled as she gathered her skirt around her and sat on the upholstered bench seat.

"You look beautiful," he said, as he pulled out of the driveway.

Ari beamed. "You don't look so bad yourself," she said, chuckling. Something in her heart beseeched her to say more, but she didn't even know where to start. She must've looked at him a second too long, and he sensed her gaze. He glanced at her as he turned east onto the highway.

"Where are we going?" Ari finally asked.

"I have a place in mind," Dane said. "It's in Woodward, so it's a bit of a drive to get there, but I think you'll like it."

At the mention of Woodward, Ari's conversation with Eleanor suddenly came to mind. "Hey! My first customer today was from Woodward. She's an elderly lady whose husband passed a few years back. She said she grew up there, but moved to Rivers after they married."

"Will you be going back to her house again?"

"Yeah, next week."

"Can you ask her if she knows anything about Ezra? If he moved there, maybe she would've known about him and his family. How old do you think Eleanor is?"

Ari shrugged. "Maybe eighty-five or so?"

"It's worth a try."

Ari draped her arm over the side of the truck door, window down and air whirling through the cab of the truck. The warm evening air smelled of dry grasses; fields were turning from green to golden in the warm, late June air. She smiled to think that going on a drive with Dane was quickly becoming one of her favorite things to do. It still caused her heart to flutter every time she looked at him.

"I've never been to Woodward, but I've heard a lot about it. What's it like?"

"It's quite a bit larger than Rivers and Allendale combined. It's actually the largest town for about two hours in any direction. There aren't any huge buildings like you'd see in San Francisco or anything, but it's not as rural as our town."

Dane seemed to shift nervously. "Will you stay here after high school? Or go back to California?"

The question was both thrilling and a little scary to Ari, but she tried to answer as best she could.

"I honestly have no idea, Dane. When we first moved here, I was sure that I'd be moving back sooner than later. But now…this place has really grown on me. I guess I need to decide what degree I'm going for before I look into where I'm going to go after graduation."

Dane nodded. It seemed like there was more he wanted to say or ask, but he stayed quiet.

A few minutes later, he reached over and turned on the radio. Reception was sparse where they were, but after scanning the entire band, Dane finally settled on an oldies station. "Unchained Melody" by the Righteous Brothers was halfway through playing, and Dane started singing along. Ari couldn't help but smile and listen to him in absolute disbelief, once again, at the stunning sound of his voice. He held every note perfectly, knew every lyric without hesitation. And the way he looked when he sang…it was the closest thing to pure joy she'd ever seen on his face.

The song came to a staticky end. "I could listen to you all day, Dane," she smiled. "Don't ever stop singing. Your voice is your soul," she said, in all seriousness. Dane looked over at her and took her hand, interlacing his fingers with hers and squeezing her hand. Warmth ran up her arm, and she felt her heart quicken. The look on Dane's face as he glanced at her was one of contemplation, and Ari wished for nothing more than to know what he was thinking at that exact moment.

The drive to Woodward passed quicker than she'd hoped; before she knew it, signs of civilization were coming into view. Dane turned south onto a road that skirted Woodward. In the midst of a wide, flat field, Ari could see lines of bright lights dotting a paved runway. A small airplane was taking off in the early evening light. Ari was more curious than ever to see what an airport had to do with having dinner.

She didn't have to wait long; as Dane turned into the airport parking lot, a 50's-style sign announced the *Swept Wing Restaurant*. A small restaurant was built into the side of a berm overlooking the runway.

"How do you know about this place?" Ari asked as they got out of the truck and began walking up the ramp-like sidewalk to the entrance.

"I think my dad brought me here as a kid once. We were maybe coming to pick my mom up at work or something like that," he explained. "This building was built during World War II. I think this runway was used by the military during that time. I think it's been a restaurant since right after the war." As they entered the building, Ari could definitely see signs of age in the little restaurant, but there was something quaint and friendly about it.

The entire front exposure was composed of floor-to-ceiling windows, and though the restaurant was busy, Ari and Dane were led to a table next to the windows. She glanced at the menu and realized how incredibly hungry she was. After figuring out what she wanted to eat, she looked over at Dane. It dawned on her, in one quick moment, that this time next year, Dane would be finished with high school. Dane saw her looking at her with a strange expression.

"Everything ok?" he asked quietly.

She tilted her head to the side. Color from the western sun was a deep red, filling the restaurant with a unearthly glow. Dane's hazel eyes were shocking in the light.

"What are you going to do after high school? I just realized that in a year you'll be done."

"Yeah," Dane nodded. "Here's the thing: when I was living with Rhoda, I never gave much thought to my future. My basic goal was to get away from her. I figured that the day I turned eighteen, I was outta here. I didn't know where or how. But now everything's changed. I have a world of possibilities in front of me, and I guess my goal for the next year is to figure out what's most important." He smiled at Ari. "I have some ideas of what I'd like to do, but it's going to take some time to sort them all out."

Ari hesitated. "Are you planning on leaving? For college?" She knew the closest state college was two hours away. A tiny fear crept into her heart. She couldn't think about him not being next door; not being around to share whatever crazy adventure was next.

Dane shrugged. "I don't know yet," he said honestly.

Ari turned to the window. Another small aircraft was landing on the runway. Her brow furrowed as she tried not to think again about him leaving. Dane leaned forward, impossibly close. It was like her apprehension about him leaving was written across her face. "Don't worry about that stuff now, Ari," he stated. The confidence in his voice reassured her.

A waitress, dressed in a classic apron-covered shirtdress, arrived at their table with food. Dane dug in and Ari suddenly remembered a question she'd wanted to ask him.

"Hey, when we were at Jace's bonfire a few weeks ago, you said that facing your fear of fire was one of the easiest of your anxieties to deal with. What did you mean by that?"

Dane chewed on his food for awhile, thinking. He was careful when he answered. "You already know some of it, Ari: every time we go to my old house on Lawton Drive. My anger. Becoming like my dad. Making the wrong choices. Screwing up the best thing I've ever had." He stopped short. He looked away, out the window. She saw his jaw clench and Ari worried she'd crossed a line in asking. But then, quick as he turned away, he looked back at her, his countenance relaxed. He ran a hand through his hair and smiled.

"Thank you for coming to dinner with me," he said.

"I wouldn't have said no," Ari said, taking a drink of water. She watched as the small airplane taxied to a slow stop at a parking spot below the window.

After finishing dinner, Dane held out his arm for Ari as they made their way out the restaurant. She looped her hand around his bicep. The sun was skimming the horizon and cast long, stick-thin shadows on the sidewalk as they walked to the truck. Ari drank in every minute of being next to Dane; the thought of him being around for only one more year lurked in the back of her mind.

The drive back to Hadley Hill was beautiful as they chased the dusky sun to the horizon. The western sky glowed with shades of green and blue as they pulled into Dane's driveway. To Ari's surprise, Dane's dad's truck was parked in the driveway.

"Did you expect your dad to be here?" Ari asked nervously.

"Well, I knew he was dropping Molly off today. They've worked something out where he has her during certain days of the week, I think. I'm not sure why he's still here, though," Dane mused, checking his watch. "I'll walk you home."

They started heading down Hadley Lane toward Ari's house when the sound of the slamming front door caused them both to turn around. Dane's dad was walking to his truck with a book in his hand, but when he saw Dane, his dad stopped. Ari noticed Dane's mom nervously standing near the front door.

"Dane," Mark called out to his son, his voice gravelly. Dane turned toward his dad.

"Mark, let's all talk about this some other time, it's late," Dane's mom pleaded.

The hairs on Ari's neck started to prickle. She sensed animosity in the air. Mark held up the book in his hand, which Ari couldn't quite make out in the darkness.

Mark strode toward his son. "Where did you get this album, Dane?"

Ari felt Dane tense. There was a long silence.

"Mark," his mom begged again, "let Dane walk Ari home and we can talk about this inside."

Ari wanted nothing more than to leave the scene but she stayed next to Dane.

Dane finally spoke. "I got it from our old house on Lawton Drive." His defensive tone edged with anger.

Dane's dad strode toward them. "The Lawton house? You went there?" His voice was sharp, rising in volume.

"Mark! Leave him *alone!*" Dane's mom didn't withhold her emotion. Dane's dad whipped around and was about to shout something at Dane's mom when Ari suddenly stepped forward and inserted herself into the family tempest.

"*I* did it, Mr. Hadley. I'm the one who found out about the album and I'm the one who got it from the Lawton house," Ari said, her voice firm. Inside, she could feel her breath shortening and her hands shaking at her sides. But a fire was starting to well up inside, and Ari could feel her voice getting stronger. "This doesn't have anything to do with Dane.

Leave him out of it." Inwardly Ari gasped at what she'd just said.

A look of surprise, followed by hostility, crossed Mark's face. Dane's dad paced closer toward them both, and Dane tried to move himself between Ari and his dad, but Ari stepped forward. She could feel her legs trembling, but she stood firm.

"You mean *you've* been inside the Lawton house?" his dad sounded angry and incredulous all at the same time.

"The album was outside," Ari said simply.

Dane stepped up to his dad, meeting him face-to-face and pushing Ari behind himself. "I'm taking Ari home now," Dane said, nearly growling. Ari could tell he was struggling to keep his temper in check. His jaw was clenched and even the veins in his neck were starting to show. Dane took Ari by the hand and started walking briskly down the lane. Ari nearly had to jog at his side to keep up. They rounded the first corner and Ari could still hear Dane's parents arguing outside.

Ari looked over at Dane: he looked angry and embarrassed. He slowed to a stop when they were halfway between their houses. Even in the darkness, Ari could sense tension rolling off him.

"Ari, why did you do that? You had no business getting in the middle of that," he said forcefully, but his tone was more worried than scolding.

She looked at him squarely. "Everything I said was the truth."

Dane put his hands on Ari's shoulders and shook his head. Sweat was beading on his forehead. Ari could see the stress of the encounter with his parents had pushed him to his limit. His hands trembled as they rested on her.

"I'm so sorry you had to be in the middle of that," Dane said, hanging his head. His breath was jagged. "I have no idea why my dad was flipping out about a stupid photo album," he breathed. "We're all broken, Ari. My whole family. I don't want you to have to deal with this…with me, my family…the anger I have…"

Ari stepped closer, resolute. She put a hand on Dane's cheek.

"Dane…" she started, shaking her head. The words were unstoppable and came tumbling out without reservation. "I don't care what your family is like; I just care about who you are right *now*, and who you're becoming. I love seeing every new facet of *you*: the person that was hidden beneath the fear you lived under when Rhoda was here. You have always been beautiful to me, Dane, no matter your circumstance." Ari was shocked at the words that came spilling forth. They'd been held in for so long that she no longer had the power to contain them.

Dane froze in place. He was motionless for an endless moment, completely speechless and stunned. Her confession caught him completely off-guard. He put a hand to her neck and pulled her face as close as he could while still keeping eye contact. In the barely-there dusky light, Dane looked at her in the same way he always had: with an electric intensity that made words completely unnecessary. Ari felt her heart start to pound in her core and her hands continued to tremble, but this time, for a completely different reason.

Dane gently drew her face closer and put his lips on hers. Ari felt the softness of his touch: slow, hesitant. In the instant that his skin touched hers, Ari realized that anything Dane hadn't said with words was instead being conveyed with his gentle contact. He kissed her once, then backed away, looking at her with the same searching intensity. He brushed strands of her hair to the side of her face. Ari moved toward him again, and he kissed her a second time, longer. Ari could hardly breathe as he stayed within inches of her face. Dane put his forehead against hers and stayed like that for seconds before kissing her once more.

He wrapped his arms around her, holding her so tightly to him that Ari could barely inhale. She could feel his breath on her neck as he buried his chin in her shoulder, and faint prickles of his unshaven face scratched her skin. Another wave of butterflies rippled through her entire being. Ari closed her eyes and put her arms around his waist. She breathed in Dane's scent and reveled in the warmth of being held by him. Wordlessly they stood there in middle of the forested gravel road that spanned the distance between their houses.

Minutes passed before Dane pulled back and looked at his watch. "Hey, I've got to get you home; it's close to ten," he whispered. He took Ari by the hand and walked with her to her front door. As she reached for the doorknob, Dane turned her head toward him once more and kissed her on the forehead. A smile broadened across Ari's face, and Dane looked back at her with the most caring expression she'd ever seen. Ari watched him as he turned and walked back toward his house, up the lane and out of sight.

chapter twenty-three

The next day, Ari had a difficult time concentrating on her last new yard care appointment. She was riding her bike on the outskirts of town, looking for an address along the highway to Woodward, but her mind kept drifting to the previous night. It was almost unreal; Ari had a hard time believing that Dane had actually kissed her. It replayed in her head over and over as she pedaled along the lonely road. Every time she thought about it, nervousness and disbelief overcame her.

After she'd gotten home, Ari had immediately wanted to message Riley about Dane, but something had caused her to hesitate. In fact, the more she thought about it that night, the more she wanted to hold onto the memory of the evening without sharing it with the world yet.

Ari struggled to refocus as she squinted at the address she had written on her calendar. The call had been from an Arthur Bellamy, her notes stated. The numbers on the mailboxes along the empty highway indicated that she had to be getting close.

Finally, Ari came to a rusty, tilted mailbox that was overtaken by tall dry grasses. The address on the box matched the one Mr. Bellamy had recited to her over the phone. Ari saw no house in sight, but decided that the dusty gravel road before her must be the driveway to Mr. Bellamy's home.

Ari pedaled her bike down the pothole-ridden lane. It went straight for quite awhile, then made a gentle turn to the left. A large stand of tall, dense trees had obscured a massive house and Ari then understood why it couldn't be seen from the highway. As she rode around the front of the house, a chill overtook her. Something about the three-story, Italianate-style house felt absolutely frightening.

The house had once been painted dark brown, but years of weather and wear left strips of paint dangling from the exterior. Paned windows were missing squares of glass. Old, tattered lace curtains covered the windows on the first floor. A very unique, half-round stained-glass window adorned the space above the front door, resembling a glass spiderweb. A "No Trespassing" sign was tacked to the front porch. The front door itself was crooked and the frame splintered. And yet, there was a note stuck in the doorjamb, resting on the brass doorknob. Ari apprehensively approached the creaking front steps and unfolded the note.

"*Ari,*" the note began, "*I won't be available during your appointment. Please use the tools in the shed behind the house to do the following: mow the yard with the push mower, trim the hedges, and use the clippers to cut back the roses in the front of the house. Here is payment for two hours of work. Thank you, Arthur.*"

Ari wasn't sure if she was relieved that the owner of the derelict house wasn't there, or if she was terrified that she'd have to be working around the perimeter of the house all alone. The house seemed to have an aura about it; Ari had the distinct feeling that she was being watched. The windows of the house were all dark, and there seemed to be no movement inside, but it took a few seconds for Ari to convince herself to go around the house to find the tools she'd need.

A once-splendid arbor held the gate that appeared to lead to the backyard. Ari opened the gate and one hinge splintered off its frame, causing the gate to droop. Ari bit her lip, thinking she'd have to track down a screwdriver to fix the hinge. Vines tangled all around and Ari had to bat at them as they sprung back and forth, snagging in her hair. A narrow path led between the house and the thick stand of tall trees that hid the house from the road. Ari brushed away spiderwebs and tall grass that had completely overgrown the path to the backyard. Sunlight was hidden from this side of the house, and Ari was relieved when she finally made it to the backyard, where at least the sun was illuminating the yard, or what was left of it.

The building that she assumed to be the shed was a precariously-leaning structure made of planks of wood. Ari opened the door, and there, placed on the floor, were hedge trimmers, clippers, and an ancient-looking push mower. Other various tools were shoved into the back of the shed, all rusted in place and covered in layers of dust. Only the tools on the floor looked like they'd been used in the last century. Ari shrugged and pulled the push mower out of the shed. The grass was sparse and not terribly tall; though Ari figured it had likely been spring since it was last mowed. Since then, the grass had died and flattened out in the dry heat.

She started with the backyard. It wasn't a difficult job at first; the backyard was rather small and surrounded by shrubbery on all sides. The dry grass disintegrated as she pushed the mower along, creating a dusty cloud behind it. Ari glanced up at the back of the house as she walked the mower in neat lines up and down the yard.

Usually Ari loved mowing; she enjoyed making even, straight lines in the grass...but the dry remnants of what used to be grass didn't create the nice, tidy patterns she liked seeing. Ari frowned, as one could barely even tell that she'd mowed. The only real evidence was the fine coat of wheat-colored dust on her legs, socks, and shoes.

Empty windows glared down at her. The back of the house looked even more forlorn than the front. The back covered porch was broken down and a bottom step was missing. She looked away from the house, feeling like eyes were on her again.

Ari thought back to the night before to keep her mind off the spooky house that loomed near her. It wasn't hard for her to slip back into the memory of Dane's kiss; she revisited the memory again as she made her way to the front yard with the push mower.

The front yard was much larger, but thankfully flat. Ari was starting to sweat as she pushed the mower over dry holes and ruts that covered the expanse of yard.

After placing the mower back in the shed, Ari got the clippers and hedge trimmers. Ari could see that it had been ages since the hedge had been trimmed back; she tried to figure the best amount to clip it and wished that Mr. Bellamy had been there to instruct her on the way to do it properly. Soon, a large trail of hedge clippings laid piled along the ground. Ari wondered what she should do with all of them. No yard waste container could be found anywhere around the house. The best solution Ari could figure was to gather the clippings up and pile them in a vacant, grassless corner of the backyard.

After trimming the gangly reddish-pink wild roses that bloomed with abandon, Ari put those on top of the debris pile as well. It had been tricky because she had to use the rake to grab the thorny vines, as she had forgotten to bring the leather gloves with her. By the time she had finally finished, it was noon, and Ari's two hours were up.

She grabbed the note from Mr. Bellamy out of her backpack and fetched a pen. She flipped it over and began writing: *"Dear Mr. Bellamy, I wasn't sure where to put the yard debris. It's piled in the corner of the yard. Please give me a call and I'll finish putting them wherever you would like."* She included her phone number and folded the paper neatly.

Ari rounded the corner to the front of the house. She walked up the creaking front steps and carefully placed the note where it had been found, tucked into the doorjamb and resting on the knob. Just as she turned to leave, a deep *whump* emanated from somewhere inside the house.

Ari froze.

Her first instinct was to bolt and run as fast as she could to her bike, but she took a deep breath and calmly walked to it. Once she started down the lane she shook off the eerie feeling that had settled over her the whole time she had been on the property. Just getting away from the house was a relief.

Pedaling into town, she wondered when Dane would be finished at the museum. Ari knew he usually started working when the museum opened, so she figured he would still be there. Upon reaching the parking lot, Ari saw Dane's truck and smiled.

She parked her bike and realized how sweaty and dirty she was: her gray t-shirt was streaked with sweat and her legs were coated in dry grass flecks, which had also made their way into her socks and shoes and were itching like mad. She took a moment and tried to brush off as much dirt and grass as she could before entering the museum.

Inside, the building was cold and quiet; a welcome relief from the hot summer day. Agnes was hunched over at the front desk and smiled when Ari approached.

"Well, hello, dear. Is there anything I can help you find today? Looking for more information on the Abshires?" Agnes procured her ever-present notepad and was poised to start writing. Ari found it quite impressive that after only meeting her twice, Agnes was able to remember exactly what Ari had been researching.

"Actually, I just finished my work for the day, and I was coming by to see when Dane would be done," Ari smiled.

"And what kind of work do you do, dear?" Agnes looked over her glasses at Ari, her brown eyes sparkling.

"Well, I've been trying to do yard care for people in town," Ari explained, looking down at her dirty clothes. "I have my customers tell me what they need to have done, and I use the tools they have to do the job. Because I don't bring my own equipment, I charge a lot less than the other yard maintenance business in town. I just finished up working on a house off the highway to Woodward—that's why I'm so dirty," Ari said with a chuckle.

Agnes nodded. "Do you have any business cards? I might have some neighbors who would appreciate your services," she asked.

Ari dug into her backpack, thankful that she still had a dozen fliers left over. She handed them all to Agnes. "Thank you, dear. Dane is upstairs in the main storage area. Go up the staircase; the archive room is on the right. I imagine he's almost finished for the day."

Ari thanked her and headed up the two flights of stairs. She could hear a faintly muffled voice which sounded vaguely familiar. Rounding the top of the stairs, she turned right through a giant double doorway to the large upper room that contained the stacks of archival boxes. Light streamed through the windows and her eyes settled on two figures: Dane was sitting at one of the computers, and next to him was Julia. Julia was leaning over her chair, her blonde hair cascading over Dane. She was holding Dane by the shoulders, eyes closed, kissing him.

chapter twenty-four

White-hot heat ran through Ari's body like a shock of lightning. Her heart started hammering in the middle of her chest so hard that she could feel her whole torso moving. Her arms started shaking down to her hands. Through her core she could feel herself trembling. Silently Ari backed out the doorway and ran down the stairs. She slowed just a tiny bit as she moved past the reception desk; she was sure she heard Agnes call her name, but Ari was already out the door and running toward her bike.

She didn't think that Dane or Julia had seen or heard her, yet she had the overwhelming need to flee. Ari got on her bike and pedaled furiously to the closest place she could figure: the coffee shop. The heat of the day didn't deter her as she sped the four blocks to Cinema Coffee.

Inside the shop, she realized her hands were shaking so badly that it was hard for her to pay for her coffee. She dropped two dimes on the floor and had difficulty picking them up again. She could hear impatient customers behind her, which just made things acutely more nerve-wracking.

Ari looked around the seats in the shop; the darker corner spots were already filled, much to her dismay. Ari just wanted to hide away where nobody could see her. Unfortunately, the only seat open was a window booth. Ari took her ceramic mug and sat at the booth, gripping the mug with both hands until she knew she could drink it without spilling.

Ari replayed what she'd seen, analyzing what had happened. She had heard Julia's voice seconds before reaching the top of the stairs. They must've just kissed right before Ari had walked into the room. Scenes, like from a movie, flashed in front of her: Julia's hands on his shoulders. Her blonde curls, cascading over his arms. His eyes, closed. Nothing made sense anymore.

Ari felt tears threaten to overflow, but she inhaled deeply and used a napkin to dry the corners of her eyes. For a moment she just sat, eyes closed, as she concentrated on all the sounds around her. Coffee mugs clanked on the tables. A cloud of quiet conversation. The occasional car passing by. A voice, close by, asking if anyone was sitting at the seat across from her.

Ari opened her eyes and looked up. Rob was standing at her booth, looking down at her with a sympathetic expression. "Anybody sitting here?"

She shook her head. "It's all yours."

Rob sat down and nodded in thanks. "Hey. I saw you over here and you look...well, you look tired. Done with work for the day?"

"How could you tell?" Ari said dryly, wiping away dried dirt from her shirt. "Yeah, I just finished with a house out in the country. What are you doing here?"

Rob just shrugged. "I'm working for my uncle's construction company this summer. He wanted me to get some coffee for the guys, and this was the closest place. Actually, I'm glad I caught you here, though." Rob paused. Ari looked at him with a curious expression. Rob lowered his voice and leaned forward. "I have something I need to get off my chest, Ari."

Ari raised an eyebrow. Rob, the six-foot-something football player had something to confess to *her*?

"I wrote all those notes to you, Ari." His eyes were apologetic.

Ari's jaw dropped open.

"*You* were the note-writer?" she asked, incredulous.

"I have to explain," Rob said, leaning back in the seat. "It was actually Julia's idea." At hearing Julia's name, Rob saw Ari's revulsion. "I know, Ari, it was totally wrong of me to go along with her stupid plan. This was before I really had a chance to hang out with you and get to know you. I never meant to hurt you."

Rob paused, looking to see if Ari was willing to hear him out. Ari leaned forward. "Why on earth would Julia have you write notes to me? Riley and I just thought it was a prank, anyway…mostly."

Rob looked relieved. "I'm glad you saw through it. Julia wanted to draw you away from Dane. She's had a thing for him for awhile now, and she just saw you as a distraction. Since you weren't his girlfriend, Julia figured he was fair game. So, she wanted to do something that would get your attention focused on someone else. She figured it would be a harmless way to do that."

Ari rolled her eyes and took a sip of coffee. "Well, I just came from the museum. I was going to see when Dane would be finished with work today, but I walked in on them kissing upstairs." Ari tried not to choke on her words. "Julia got what she wanted," Ari said quietly, and looked out the window instead of at Rob.

"Hey, I am so, *so* sorry." Rob put his hand on Ari's arm. "Listen, I've known Julia my whole life. She is tenacious and almost always gets what she wants. When we were in fifth grade, she desperately wanted to win the spelling bee for some reason. I don't know how she got away with it, but Julia bribed a friend—one who could spell better than her—to switch tests. Julia just wrote her name on the friend's test and turned it in as her own." Ari raised her eyebrows in surprise. "What Julia didn't know was the district spelling bee was an oral test. Julia was out on the first word.

"She's always done stupid crap like this, Ari." Rob shook his head. "I wouldn't be surprised if this is all her own doing—she's got such a thing for Dane, she'd probably kiss him whether he'd want her to or not."

Ari stared at Rob, right through his pale, ice-blue eyes. She didn't really know him well enough to judge his honesty, but the look on his face suggested he was being truthful.

"Thanks for letting me know about the notes, Rob. To think I've been telling everyone that I had the worst secret admirer ever…." Ari chuckled ruefully and Rob shook his head.

"That's the truth; I'll be the first to admit it," he said, looking apologetic. Rob got up from his seat, motioning toward the counter. "Hey, I've gotta get some coffee ordered for the guys." He leaned over so only Ari could hear him. "I hope everything works out with you and Dane." Rob gave a her a pat on the shoulder and left.

Once again, Ari closed her eyes and inhaled deeply. She needed time to think.

*   *   *

The backpack of chemicals on her back sloshed around as Ari squirted streams of weed killer on the dandelions that had sprouted up in the immense rock hardscape. The day after she had handed Agnes her fliers, phone calls had started rolling in for yard care help. Ari figured most of the ladies who had called were friends or neighbors of Agnes: all retired, living on a fixed income, but with beautiful old homes and gardens to match.

It had been two days since Ari had been at the museum; two days since she'd seen Julia and Dane kissing. She wasn't trying to avoid him, but she also hadn't heard or seen Dane's truck roll by her house. Ari wondered if he was staying at his dad's house…or if Dane was actually avoiding *her*.

Ari had wanted desperately to tell Riley everything that happened. Ari had even picked up her phone three times, intending to message her or call her. Each time, though, tremendous waves of sadness stopped her. Every time Ari replayed the scene in her head, tears welled up. She couldn't imagine speaking of it out loud. As much as she wanted Riley's advice, Ari couldn't speak of what she'd witnessed.

Ari tried to block out any thoughts of Dane as she went around the elderly Mrs. Byerley's Zen garden, squirting each leggy dandelion with a healthy dose of poison. Mrs. Byerley explained that she'd just had back surgery and toting around a backpack full of heavy liquid was no longer an option.

Mrs. Byerley had tightly curled white hair with a faint purple hue.

She'd patiently explained all the work that needed to be done: besides weed killing, there were weeds that had to be pulled by hand in the rose gardens. Additionally, Mrs. Byerley mentioned that the roses would need to have finished buds trimmed off. She'd hired Ari for three hours. With only three tasks, Ari was dubious that it would actually take all that time to complete them.

After Ari was sure she'd doused every weed in the rock garden, she headed to the meticulously-kept rose beds. At least, they had been well-kept once, but now slender blades of tall green grasses stuck out among the sharp, halved hazelnut shells that were in the rose beds. Mrs. Byerley had explained to Ari that she'd surrounded her rosebushes with hazelnut shells "to keep the cats away." Indeed, as Ari poked around the shells, she understood why cats wouldn't want to use the rose beds as a litter box. This time, though, Ari had remembered her gloves, and she started digging away at the strands of grass.

After working for twenty minutes, Ari had found a rhythm to digging out the grass. She actually found it somewhat cathartic, and as she pulled at the green blades with long white noodle-like roots, she found her mind drifting back to Dane and Julia. She tried not to think of them, but her heart hurt from simply missing Dane. *It's only been two days since I've seen him*, she scolded herself. A panicked thought came to mind: *What if he's chosen Julia? What if he's been with her these past two days?* She shook her head. The photo-clear memory of Dane and Julia kissing was seared in her mind.

Three hours passed, and Ari was shocked to find that she hadn't had time to trim the roses. She rang the doorbell to Mrs. Byerley's house, and apologized for not finishing.

Mrs. Byerley adjusted her reading glasses, which were adorned with gobs of glittering rhinestones. Looking over the glasses, she smiled at Ari. "No worries, dear, can we make an appointment for next week?" Ari beamed, overjoyed that her calendar was actually beginning to fill up. With each appointment, she saw the possibility of getting stuck in a dreaded office job was fading away.

It was three in the afternoon when Ari left Mrs. Byerley's house. The late June day was scalding hot, and Ari felt a nasty sunburn beginning to form on her neck. She shook her head in disappointment that she'd remembered to bring her gloves but had completely forgotten about her sun hat. Of all days, this was the day the hat would've been most helpful. She had also forgotten to pack a lunch; her stomach was aching with hunger by the time she began her ride home. Ari made a mental note to set out her supplies so she wouldn't forget the essentials again.

The empty rural highway that Ari took home was blistering in the heat; the asphalt was turning to liquid waves in front of her. Despite the heat, Ari decided to pass the turnoff to Hadley Lane. She continued riding her bike along the desolate road, right to the driveway of the Abshire house. Something compelled her to visit the homestead. The gravel driveway beckoned her to follow it. Whispers from the past floated on the wind, right to Ari.

She walked her bike to the front of the lonely whitewashed house and set it down in the grass to the side. The ache in Ari's heart moved her to the front porch. The ugly *No Trespassing* sign still shouted its warning but Ari put her hand on the front door. It opened easily. Without hesitation she entered.

Ari didn't know what she was looking for inside the house. Perhaps the forsaken building resonated with her. Maybe she was just hiding in its reverent silence; shying away from the world, just for a moment, to sort out her thoughts.

Room to room Ari went, looking at every abandoned detail. The floorboards creaked as she stepped across them, welcoming her into its space.

Upstairs, she went to the room that had the window that looked upon the top portion of Dane's house. She could almost make out the window of Dane's room and the space on the roof where she'd sat with him. She closed her eyes, squeezing away sudden tears that came on without invitation. Ari turned away from the window and went to the first floor, pivoting her hand on the smooth, giant round newel cap at the base of the stairs.

The small dark room in the back of the house called to her. She walked down the narrow hallway and stepped into the tiny space with the vine-covered windows. Ari closed her eyes, trying to clear her mind, but visions of Dane and Julia came rushing back. Her stomach twisted.

Brushing away detritus, Ari took a seat in the middle of the room, facing the windows. In the space and stillness of finally being completely alone, Ari allowed two days' worth of tears to seep out. They came slowly at first. Once they started, though, they couldn't be stopped. An uncontrollable stream of tears landed on the dry wood floor, peppering it with dozens of dark spots. Ari had no concept of how much time had passed when a creaking sound somewhere in the house caused her to hold her breath in silence.

She couldn't tell if the sound was inside or outside the house. Silent minutes passed and Ari used her shirt collar to wipe at her eyes. She stood up and brushed off her jeans, wiped her nose with her arm.

"Ari?"

Gasping, Ari whirled around.

chapter twenty-five

Dane stood in the doorway, a look of confusion clouding his face.

"Ari, what's going on? Are you ok?" He crossed the room in two strides and reached for Ari, but she backed away a step. Dane froze in place.

Ari shook her head. "I'm fine."

Dane furrowed his brow. "You're sitting alone in a dark room in an abandoned house that we're technically not even supposed to be in...and it looks like you've been crying for hours." Dane reached up again to try and touch Ari's cheek, but she stepped away once more. Her back was a foot away from the window and didn't have any more space to avoid him.

"Ari, what's going on?"

Ari drew in a jagged breath.

"You and Julia, I saw you. At the museum." Ari squeezed her eyes shut, trying to get through the next sentence without fresh tears. "I saw you kissing her the other day."

Dane shook his head and a look of disgust crossed his face. He exhaled forcefully.

"Ari... Julia kissed *me*. I was sitting at the computer doing my work when she said my name. I turned to her and had no warning about what she was going to do next. I'm guessing that's when you came in the room. When I told you before that I'm not interested in her, I was being truthful. I don't know what else to say about it."

His explanation hung there in the silence of the room. He wasn't pleading or making excuses. Ari understood that she could believe and accept his explanation or leave it. Her head was spinning with hunger and thirst and fatigue and the stuffy feeling that happens after sobbing for a long time. She couldn't bring herself to say anything at all.

Dane took one step closer. In the monochrome dimness of the room, Ari was near enough that she could just see the faintest rim of jade around his pupils. He locked eyes with her.

"Listen," he said, barely above a whisper. "You know me better than any person on this earth, Ari. You know about my life with Rhoda. You know about the accident. Geez, you even know about the Lawton house and that horrible night. You're the only person I've ever allowed in, Ari. *Ever.*"

Dane dared to touch her, holding the side of her face and brushing her cheek with his thumb. This time, Ari didn't recoil. She stared at him so hard it was almost like she was willing his thoughts to become her own so she wouldn't have to guess what he was thinking any longer.

"Please trust me, Ari."

She straightened up. "I do." Minutes of silence were punctuated only by the occasional sound of a car flying past on the highway, or vines scratching on the windows every now and then. In a proximity that would've otherwise been uncomfortable with anyone else, Ari stood staring at Dane. Her mind couldn't comprehend the million thoughts she had for him, save one.

"I don't want to lose you as a friend."

In one quick motion, Dane stooped over and scooped Ari into his arms. She felt him exhale hard. He was gripping her shoulders with his arms and his head was next to hers. In her ear, he spoke. "Why would that ever happen?"

"When I didn't see you for two days, I wasn't sure what to think...if you wanted to hang out with me still...or...I just didn't know."

Dane held her at arms' length, one hand still on her face, and shook his head. "After work that day, I went to my dad's to confront him about the photo album and his fight with mom the other night. I wanted to know what caused him to be so upset. Turns out it wasn't the album he was angry about."

Dane reached back and pulled a folded piece of paper from his back jeans pocket. She could see his hand was shaking slightly as he handed to her. "He didn't want me to see what was *inside* the album."

Ari unfolded the page; it appeared to be a legal form of some sort. It was too dark inside the small room see the typewritten words.

"Let's go into the living room," Ari said. Once there, her eyes adjusted to the relative brightness of the wide-open space. She looked at the paper again and read quietly: "Confidential Certificate of Adoption." Reading down the form, she saw a printed name below one line: William Marcus Hadley. Dane's dad's hastily-written signature was scrawled above. The blank above Olivia Harrison's printed name was empty.

"I don't understand, what is this?" Ari looked up at Dane. His face was stoic.

"When mom found out she was pregnant, they decided to give me up for adoption, Ari. My dad had already signed off on it. Look at the bottom of the form. They had parents lined up for me already." Sure enough, the printed names of two people had matching signatures above them: Dane's future adoptive parents.

Ari stood there in stunned silence for seconds, her mouth agape. "I…I don't know what to say, Dane. Why did your dad tell you about this?"

"Because I straight-up asked him why he was pissed off the other night. He went over to the album and pulled this out of the back. He said if I was old enough to snoop around, then I'd be old enough to handle the truth."

"And…how do you feel about finding out about this?" Ari chose her question carefully and frankly didn't know what else to ask. She could see that although he was trying to hide it, anger—or maybe disappointment—edged his voice.

"I've spent the last two days trying to process everything. I don't know if I don't care, or if I'm angry they didn't go through with it—"

"Wait, what?" Ari looked at him, surprised.

"Well, I was one signature away from making some family really happy, Ari, instead of going home to a dad who spent the next eleven years reminding me I was the reason *they* were unhappy. Think about it."

Ari's heart twisted. It seemed like ever since their first visit to Dane's old house, his past had started to unceremoniously unravel in front of her—but she hadn't been expecting something like this.

"Dad said that when the time came to finalize the adoption, mom couldn't bring herself to sign the papers. So they somehow figured the next logical option was to get married."

Ari nodded. Dane ran his hand across his forehead and through his hair. He strode out the front door and Ari followed. She didn't see his truck outside.

"Did you walk here?"

"Yeah, I've been looking for you since I got off work. I went to the circle, then to the pool, then I used the path to come here. I wasn't surprised to see your bike by the house. But...aren't you worried what will happen if the sheriff comes back?"

"No."

Ari picked up her bike and they walked along the pond path. The narrow trail made it difficult to walk with her bike, but she did the best she could. Dane slowly walked ahead of her.

When they came to the giant fallen log by the honeysuckle vines, Dane sat. The afternoon was blistering hot even in the shade. Ari sat with him, close enough their arms touched, and though a million questions circled in her mind, she waited for Dane to talk—if he chose to.

Small birds fluttered and hid in the honeysuckle vines that rose up above them. Ari watched as sunlight caused ferns to glow. Occasionally a cool breeze would temper the shimmering heat; otherwise, Ari wiped sweat from her brow as they sat.

"I'm not going to tell my mom that I know," he finally said.

Ari nodded in agreement. "Good idea." She put her hand on Dane's back. Tension bled off him with every movement he made.

"Dane, I feel like ever since we went to your old house for the first time, you've had to deal with so much emotional stuff, it's been like a roller coaster ride for you. I'm sorry you had to find out about the adoption thing. I shouldn't have suggested we go back for the photo album. Your family stuff…it's not my business." She looked at him apologetically.

He looked at her for endless seconds before putting his arm around her back. He leaned over and rested his forehead against hers. Even that slight touch made her shiver despite the heat.

Finally, he spoke. "None of this is your fault, Ari. This is all just stuff I just have to work through." He sighed and Ari closed her eyes, just feeling the closeness of Dane's presence.

"If you had been adopted, you wouldn't be here right now," Ari figured, her eyes still closed.

She felt Dane's hand brush her jaw. "You're absolutely right. And I honestly believe this is *exactly* where I'm supposed to be at this very moment in time."

Ari backed away and looked straight at Dane. His eyes were catching every glint of sunlight. He looked strong and determined. Ari smiled at him, once again a singular thought rushed at her: *I love him.*

*   *   *

Molly and Lily were chasing each other around the picnic table that had been set with candles and dishes of food. Ari's mom was balancing a tray filled with slices of watermelon when Mrs. Hadley appeared with Dane from the oak grove trail.

"That's the first time I've ever been through the grove," Mrs. Hadley admitted. "Now I see why you kids use it all the time. It's much faster to cut through the woods than to take the road. Handy when you have an armful of food."

July Fourth had arrived with much anticipation: the Hadleys and Cartwrights had planned a potluck during the late afternoon. It was the first time they'd all gathered together for a meal since the beginning of spring break. Ari realized she also hadn't been back to Nadia and Grekov's graves and the surrounding cherry trees since that night.

Molly tugged on the skirt of Ari's dress. "Aribelle, play with us? Tag!" She looked up at Ari with her big hazel eyes. Lily circled around Ari and declared Ari 'it', then took off at top speed across the yard.

"You're lucky I'm wearing sandals, Molly!" Ari called as she took a swipe at one of the girls. They all ran giggling toward the pasture, and Molly passed in front of her brother, though not quick enough. Dane scooped Molly up and held her so Ari could tag her. Molly dissolved into a fit of little-girl giggles, and Ari watched, smiling, as Dane played with his sister.

Ari's phone rang. Seeing it was Riley, Ari walked through the stone pillars at the edge of the pasture and answered the phone.

"Hey, what's up?" Riley said on the other end. "Are you going to the fireworks tonight?

Ari shook her head as she walked along the path. "I don't know anything about them. Are you?

Riley sounded excited. "The whole town of Rivers shows up for the fireworks. The whole crew is meeting me and Jace tonight. We wanted to know if you and Dane wanted to join us."

Ari paused. "Will Julia be there?"

"Think so, why?"

"No reason. Can I text you back soon?"

Riley agreed and said good-bye and Ari walked out of the oak grove.

From her vantage point, Ari could see the picnic tables set beautifully, with candles and white lights strung above striped umbrellas. The formal gardens were finally in full bloom. Ari noticed how everything she and her dad had done the previous summer had come back bigger and better than she ever could've imagined: the roses were full of color, daisies and irises were standing tall in borders around the lawn, and her mom had added hanging baskets filled to the brim with geraniums all across the back porch. She stopped and took it all in as she stood with one hand on a stone pillar at the edge of the pasture.

She watched the table full of smiling adults who were passing dishes of food to one another. Her eye was drawn to the end of the table, where Dane's dad sat; Ari figured he must've shown up while she had been on the phone. He wasn't smiling, but he didn't look as gruff as usual. Ari looked at Dane's expression, and Dane seemed relaxed.

Something in Ari's heart paused in absolute astonishment at the scene. She stood stock-still as she saw two families: families not without their flaws, not without their struggles...but at this moment, the two families were *together*, sharing a meal.

Sunlight illuminated the scene: blades of golden grass and tall backlit crowns of Queen Anne's lace glowed in the pasture. Bugs hummed and buzzed. Molly and Lily started giggling at a shared secret. Ari's mom passed a dish to Dane's dad, who nodded in thanks.

Ari's hand absentmindedly went to her honeybee necklace. She touched it and made a silent prayer that Dane's mom and dad would get along for the day, and that Dane would be able to be at peace with his past. She was lost in her wish when she realized Dane was staring at her from his spot at the picnic table. He gave her a puzzled look and gestured at the spot next to him on the bench.

She crossed the pasture, sending small flying bugs into a frenzy. She sat next to Dane and Lily immediately handed her a platter of watermelon slices. Dane leaned over and whispered in her ear. "Everything ok?"

Ari smiled at him. "Yeah, totally fine."

Ari's dad piped up. "Hey, how is the research on the Abshires going? Anything new?"

"Did you guys know about the trail that Ari and Dane found?" Mrs. Hadley had a sly look on her face. Ari and Dane looked at each other.

"Trail? We didn't hear anything about a trail," Ari's mom said.

"Well, um," Dane started, "we may have hacked a hole in Mom's backyard," he said, chuckling. "To be fair, it was Ari who did it—"

"Hey!" Ari cut in.

"—but yes, we found a trail that connected my backyard to the Abshire homestead. In the journal we've been reading, Ezra writes that Katia Hadley would use a wooded trail to take food to the Abshires. Ezra wrote that his dad got very sick with something called glandular fever. Life got really difficult for the Abshires, so the Hadleys helped them out as much as possible. Toward the end of the journal, they even took in Ezra's sister, Aliza. Sounds like she lived with the Hadleys for awhile."

Ari listened as Dane recalled the story. His whole countenance changed as he described the events they'd read about: his eyes sparkled and his voice was confident. Ari found herself smiling and getting excited about their discoveries as she watched him recount the facts.

"What happened? Did the father survive?" Ari's mom leaned in to hear the rest of the story.

"That's the thing, mom," Ari piped up. "In the last entry in the journal, Ezra said that Katia knew a mercantile owner in Woodward. It sounds like she used her family's connections to possibly get him a job there. He was brokenhearted to leave Katia, but he needed to be able to send money home to his family."

"That's quite a story," Dane's dad commented, and Ari almost startled at the sound of his deep voice.

"And then it just ends," Dane finished. "We have no idea what happens."

"My customer Eleanor was born in Woodward," Ari added, "and I'm working at her house again next week. I'm going to ask her if she knew anyone named Ezra Abshire when she was a kid."

Ari felt her phone vibrate. She saw a group text from Riley saying they'd meet everyone at the park gazebo for the fireworks.

Ari turned to everyone at the table. "Is anyone planning on going to the city fireworks tonight?"

"Didn't know there were any," Ari's dad mused. "Jess? Were you planning on going?"

"I hadn't thought of it. Are you kids going?"

Ari turned to Dane. "Riley called a minute ago. Everyone is meeting there. She wanted to know if we wanted to join up."

"Sounds good to me," Dane agreed. "I haven't gone since I was a kid."

*　　　*　　　*

It was a carnival-like atmosphere when Dane and Ari arrived in town. Families were streaming toward the riverfront park, hauling folding chairs and wagons with toddlers and armloads of blankets. Kids waved around sparklers and people milled about in the roads as cars tried to slowly navigate through the crowd.

Ari couldn't help but compare it to San Francisco's celebration, which was over-the-top in only the way a big city could do it. She had a lifetime of memories spent watching jaw-dropping pyrotechnic displays from Fisherman's Wharf with her family. Although it was the same holiday, Independence Day in Rivers had an entirely different flavor: it felt small and down-to-earth, although by the time Ari and Dane had reached the waterfront, she could see that nearly the entire town really had shown up.

Dane found Ari's hand and they wove through the crowd. "Where did Riley say to meet everyone?" Dane asked, his voice straining over the noise of kids hollering, whistling fireworks, and barking dogs.

"She said they'd be by the gazebo in the park." Ari pointed over the top of the crowd: a medium-sized gazebo was built onto the upper bank, above the river's waterline.

They wove through more crowds of people, trying not to step on picnic blankets that were saving people's spots on the ground. It was still half an hour until the fireworks were scheduled to start, but crowds were already sitting in place along the sandy bank.

"I see Jace," Dane said. An ear-shattering firework went off somewhere close to Ari, causing her to startle. Dane stopped walking for a moment and leaned down close to Ari's ear.

"Hey...does Riley know about...the thing with Julia?" Ari could see him shift nervously.

"No," Ari looked at him. He seemed surprised.

"I didn't tell her about what I saw," she explained. "And I figured that if you and Julia ended up together, then everyone would know about it soon enough anyway."

Dane looked down and pursed his lips. Ari wanted to ask why he wanted to know, but a familiar voice drew their attention to the gazebo.

"Hey guys!" Riley jumped up and down on the side of the gazebo, trying to be seen over the mass of people. Beside her were Rob, Julia, Amara, and Aaron. Ari smiled as she saw Aaron standing next to Amara, his arm over her shoulder. Amara was beaming.

"Sorry to be the last ones here," Ari apologized. A strange feeling started to grow in her stomach as she saw Julia trying to make eye contact with Dane. He, however, wasn't looking in her direction.

"Where's the best place to watch the fireworks?" Amara asked.

Riley had a mischievous glint in her eyes. "Guys, I have a secret spot that I'll only show you if you *promise* not to reveal it to anyone else.

Ever." Ari raised an eyebrow and smiled.

Riley started walking away from the gazebo and the group followed. "This is my family's most closely guarded fourth of July secret," Riley continued, only-half joking. She led them away from the throng of people, across a footbridge that crossed a stream, to the other side of the river's edge. There were just as many people on this side of the park, but Riley stopped at the edge of some thick shrubbery that clung to the hard, sandy bank.

Dusk was falling, and it was getting difficult to see distinct features of anything—people or landscape included—so everyone stuck close to Riley. She looked over her shoulder, scanned the area, then seemed to disappear right into the foliage. The group followed in a single-file line through some woody underbrush that scraped at their skin. Ari hung in the back and she noticed Dane stuck close to her. A trail opened up that skirted the high-water line of the river. Nobody was on the trail.

"Riley, you weren't kidding," Rob remarked in amazement. "How is it that we're the only people on this part of the bank?"

"When I was a kid, this is where we'd put our blanket down," Riley said quietly as she came to a stop. "Over the years, the path has become overgrown and forgotten. We just make sure nobody sees us when we duck into the bushes."

Around them, there was a bare patch of earth about twelve feet long. Below them was the sloping bank of the river. The water wasn't at its lowest point, but close to it, Ari figured. To their backs was a thick swath of foliage, cottonwoods, and a large crooked tree that had a sturdy limb that jutted out over the bank. Ari could see more than a few swings had been tied to the limb; frayed segments of rope moved in the breeze.

Jace was already climbing the limb when Riley looked up at him. "I fell off that limb when I was seven. Broke my arm in two places." She didn't hesitate to grab Jace's hand and shimmy up to where he was perched. Riley held her hand out for Ari. "There's plenty of room!"

Ari stepped back and shook her head. "Thanks, Riley. I'll stay down here." Disappointment panged at her heart once again. The limb was so high, made more so by the depth perception-skewing darkness. Julia pushed past Ari and, once again wearing her heeled boots, swung herself up to the limb. Amara and Aaron had sat on the sandy ledge, and Rob was leaning up against the tree.

"I really think we have the better view up here," Julia said with a flip of her hair. "C'mon, Dane. There's room for ya."

"I'm good, thanks," Dane said casually.

"Dane. Seriously." Even in the darkness, Ari could see Julia patting the spot next to her. Ari held her breath. Dane just turned his gaze to the sky, waiting for the show to begin. Ari exhaled in relief. He'd succeeded in ignoring her.

"You'll sit next to me every day at work but you won't tonight?" Julia jutted out her lip in a mock pout. "I thought that fabulous kiss of ours would mean you'd at least acknowledge me in public now, right?" Ari heard everyone around her gasp, followed immediately by a core-pounding *whump* from the first cannon launch. Fireworks exploded in the sky, followed by sizzling embers that floated back to earth.

chapter twenty-six

Ari stood, her mouth hanging open. Immediately she realized her group of friends were staring back at her with equally horrified looks, save Julia and Rob. Rob was glaring angrily at Julia, and Julia was staring at Ari with a proud, pursed pout. Ari suddenly felt her stomach drop and twist in a sickening way. She then noticed Dane was no longer standing next to her.

"Dane?" Ari said, her voice shaking. She turned in a circle and looked everywhere. Riley pointed at the trail, indicating he'd left the way they had come.

"Looks like he had somewhere more important to be," Julia mused.

Ari turned and jogged down the path, her legs wobbly.

The last thing she heard was Rob yelling: "That's *enough*, Julia! Why can't you just be *nice?*"

Exiting the shrubby path, Ari looked around in a panic. Crowds of people were looking up at the sky, *oohing* and *ahhing* at the fireworks behind her. Her lack of height prevented her from seeing over anyone's head, so she cut through the mass of people, constantly scanning for a tall guy wearing a heather-gray sleeveless muscle shirt. Bumping through the crowd, she finally reached a clearing. She saw a figure striding toward the parking lot.

Amid the crackling flashes, Ari broke into a jog. The field had been converted into a giant parking lot for the occasion, and the lot full of cars showed no signs of life, save one.

Dane had reached his truck. He braced himself on the tailgate, then suddenly brought his hand down hard on it, sending a cloud of dust into the air. Ari heard him swear under his breath and he hung his head, shaking it in anger.

Ari hung back, standing in the field, twenty feet behind him. She waited. He remained with his back to her, leaned over behind his truck.

She could see his back was tensed; his arms were flexed against the tailgate. "What is her *problem?*" Ari heard him hiss to himself.

"She likes you." Ari said simply.

He whipped around, startled. He clearly hadn't known anyone was behind him. His eyes were fire; his jaw clenched and his posture was ready to fight. Ari knew Dane wasn't angry at her, but it still caused her to back up a step.

"This is why I don't have close friends, Ari. They just end up getting hurt because of me. Now everyone thinks I'm a big jerk who doesn't give a damn about you." Dane's voice rasped under the strain of his anger, but there was something else in there: sadness, although he was desperately trying to hold himself in check.

Ari shook her head. Her heart was still thumping at a dizzying pace from the scene Julia had made. When she'd finally caught her breath, she started walking toward him.

"Not everyone. Rob knows you're not a jerk."

Dane gave her a hard, questioning look.

"After that day at the museum, I saw Rob at the coffee shop. He confessed to me that he was the note-writer."

Dane's expression changed to confusion. "*Rob* likes you?"

Ari held up her hands. "No. Julia had him write the notes to distract me…away from you. He realized it was stupid and decided to stop on the night of the dance. He told me that Julia will do almost anything to get her way. I did tell him about the kiss, but he told me he was almost certain that Julia was the one to initiate it. He has your back, Dane."

Dane stood there, his eyes fixed on Ari, his face intermittently illuminated by flashes of light. A stunningly large boom caused them both to focus on the show: a great golden explosion filled the sky and transformed into glittering embers that sparkled as they dissolved into darkness.

"You're not embarrassed by what just happened? Because I sure am." Anger still tinged his voice.

"Yeah, I'm embarrassed too." Ari looked away, kicking at the dry grass under her foot. "But...I'm not going to let Julia ruin tonight, you know?"

Minutes passed and they turned back to the dazzling display of explosions. Ari leaned back against the tailgate next to Dane. She breathed in the night air which had lost all its heat. The faint scents of sulfur and briny river and dry grass surrounded them.

"You're right," Dane said quietly. "But I think I'm going to watch the rest of the show here."

"Do you need some space? I understand if you want to be alone." Ari started to step away. She wasn't sure where she was headed; though she knew she didn't want to go back to her friends—not if Julia was still there.

"No." Dane reached for her arm. "Please. Stay...if you want to."

She stopped walking and looked back at him. Whistling fireworks corkscrewed up into the sky and burst into brilliant shades of copper that reflected off Dane's features. Long before now she'd memorized the exact gentle curve of his nose and even how his dark eyelashes had the faintest curl to them. She could still hear the emotion in his voice, but his expression was no longer one of anger. He took her other arm and pulled her in front of him.

"I am *so* sorry for what happened with Julia, Ari. Both for what you saw at the museum and for what happened tonight." He put his hand on the side of her face and brought her closer. "You don't deserve all the crappy things that happen to *you* because of *me*."

"It's not about deserving, Dane. When you care for someone, you stick by them." She looked at him with an unwavering stare.

Another round of concussive explosions echoed through the surrounding air, and fireworks sizzled above in them in hues of magenta and candy-green. Dane slowly bent low and placed his lips on Ari's, kissing her slowly. She closed her eyes, felt his hand move against her face. Everything happened in slow motion; his lips hovered near hers for a moment before he kissed her again. Ari thought she could hear her own racing heartbeat. Every movement of his was cautious and deliberate, maybe even unsure. As Dane touched her, everything around Ari disappeared. She no longer heard the fireworks or felt the cool air. She only felt his breath on her lips as he backed away. He ran his hand through her hair and stayed bent low, looking at her.

"Thank you for sticking by me, Ari." His voice was low, rough.

"That's what friends do." Even as she said it, the word *friends* felt strange now. A salvo of stunning, never-ending fireworks suddenly drew their attention to the sky. Those fireworks were followed by groups of sky-swallowing bursts in red, white, and blue. Cheers and whistles and whoops erupted from the waterfront crowd. Ari felt her phone vibrate in her pocket, but she ignored it.

Dane lifted himself over the tailgate of the truck and held out his hand for Ari. She climbed over and they sat with their backs against the rear window of the cab. People were now streaming toward their cars; engines and headlights were coming on all around.

The half-moon was high and bright in the cloudless sky. Ari pulled her knees to her chest and shivered. Dane hopped out of the truck bed and rummaged around in the cab. He tossed two blankets into the back of the truck; Ari took one. The blankets were awash in Dane's familiar scent, and Ari pulled the soft fleece around as tightly as possible. She couldn't help but smile as she sat shoulder-to-shoulder with Dane. He had also wrapped himself snugly in a blanket, his head was tilted up to the sky.

Cars were vacating the parking lot. There were a few people still lingering and voices echoed across the open space. Ari felt her phone vibrate. She peeked at her screen and saw several messages from Riley.

Ari! Where are you? Is everything OK? read one message. Another: *Ari, Julia left. You and Dane should come back.* The last message: *We're leaving. Can you do a sleepover tonight?*

Ari quickly texted back a message: *I'm with Dane, everything is fine, sleepover tomorrow be ok?* She put her phone back in her pocket. She didn't want to be anywhere else than exactly where she was.

Dane tilted his head towards Ari's. "How many jobs do you have next week?"

"Eleanor, Mrs. Byerly, a new client named, uhm, Albert Winsor, and the weird Bellamy house. I've got something every day but Tuesday."

"What's the weird Bellamy house?"

"Oh…the day I went to the museum to see you, I had been out to a house on the way to Woodward. It's way off the highway with a long driveway, and the house is hidden behind a row of trees. Honestly, the house looks vacant, but after I was finished working, I heard a noise inside. The windows were all dark but the whole time I was there, I felt like I was being watched. It made the hair on my arms stand up—it was *so* weird, Dane."

"What was the customer like?"

"That's the thing; I never saw him, he just left a note on the door. When he made the second appointment, he called my parent's landline."

"When do you go?

Ari leaned her head back, trying to remember. "I think my appointment is from three to four on Friday. Why?"

"Do you want me to go with you? I could work early that day."

"Would you?" Ari looked at him appreciatively. "I mean, it's not like I'm scared or anything," she rolled her eyes, and Dane chuckled. "But I'd love the company. The house definitely had a weird feel about it."

"I'll be there."

Ari felt a sense of appreciation and relief wash over her. She slipped her arms around Dane's waist and gave him a sitting side-hug. He unfurled the blanket and pulled it over them both as Ari rested her head on him. For minutes they sat there, and Ari closed her eyes. As she did, though, the night's events replayed in her mind.

Ari swallowed hard and opened her eyes. She decided to take a risk with the next question. "What are you going to do about Julia at work? She is obviously really into you."

Dane huffed and shook his head. "I don't know. She's so unpredictable. After she kissed me, I told her that I wasn't interested in a relationship. I think she thought I was joking, because she just flipped her hair and laughed it off."

By now, Dane's truck was one of the few cars left in the entire field. With the exception of a few slow crickets, silence surrounded them.

"What time do you need to be home?" Dane asked.

"Midnight. It's my all-time latest curfew ever. What time is it now?"

"Ten thirty-five." Dane paused, then out of the blue: "What do your parents think of me, Ari?"

Ari hadn't been expecting *that* question. "Um, I don't know, Dane. My mom jokes about you being my boyfriend all the time, but they've never said anything specific about you to me." Ari shook her head. Her answer wasn't sounding right. "Dane, when you're at my house, they treat you just like any other person. I can tell they are interested in you and they care about you, because *I* care about you. They see how much you mean to me. Does that answer your question?"

Dane shrugged. "Yeah. I mean, they don't disapprove of you spending time with me, right?"

"If they did, I wouldn't be here right now."

He nodded. "Good point."

Ari looked over at him, but could only barely make out his profile in the low light. "Why?"

Dane tilted his head toward Ari again. "I want them to trust me. You and I spend a whole lot of time together. It would make it really difficult for you if they didn't approve of me, right?"

Ari had to agree. "I have never gotten the sense that they dislike you in any way, Dane. Do you want me to ask them—"

"No!" Dane emphatically shook his head. Ari tried to hide her smile.

"Hey, your parents seemed to get along tonight at dinner. Even your dad seemed...happy?" Ari thought.

"Yeah, when dad showed up, I was a little worried," Dane admitted. "This week wasn't the greatest and I was hoping he wouldn't say anything about the adoption papers. But tonight, everything was chill. It gives me hope that they could be like that all the time...civil, you know? Not letting crap from the past ruin the present."

Ari nodded. The stars were stunning and bright. "Have you decided anything about college?" she asked.

"Yeah, actually, I have. I want to check out the state college and maybe go in the direction of getting a history degree. I've talked with Agnes and a few of the other employees at the museum, and they either have a degree in public history or general history. I really enjoy the work I do there, Ari. It's so strange that it's something that I like, but I totally do." Ari could hear the smile in his voice as he talked about it, and it made her heart happy. "How about you?"

Ari shook her head, which was now ensconced in her blanket in order to keep her ears warm. "I just know I don't want to work at a desk, Dane. I love being outdoors. Beyond that, I have no idea what I want to do."

"Well, you have more time to figure things out," he said quietly.

"Yeah."

A sudden streak of light, burning white-hot and blue, arced across the sky. The shooting star left a ghostly trail behind it. Ari gasped just as Dane exclaimed,"Whoa!" They watched as the faint trail faded away. Sounds of the night filled the space: frogs and crickets somewhere near the water, far-off voices in the distance, and the occasional barking dog.

"Just think of it: a year from now, you could be getting ready to move to college," Ari mused.

Dane exhaled and rubbed Ari's back in small circles.

"Don't worry about that right now, okay? If I've learned anything over the past year, it's that anything is possible."

Ari smiled and only wished she could put away her concerns about the future that easily.

*   *   *

Besides her own room, Ari figured, there wasn't anywhere else that she felt quite at home at like when she was at Riley's house. Ari was once again in the plush window seat, looking down on the multicolored lights of a nighttime Rivers. She had barely just sat down when Riley looked at her incredulously.

"Ok, let me get this straight. Dane kissed both you *and* Julia in less than a 24-hour period? And this happened almost a week ago? Hon, how on earth did I miss all this?" Riley threw up her hands and leaned back in her enormous beanbag chair. In the dim purple-ish hue cast by the lights strung around the ceiling, Ari could see Riley was a bit exasperated.

"Honestly, I just didn't want to talk about what I saw at the museum. Every time I thought about it, I could hardly hold myself together. I kind of figured he was through with me; I'd lost my best friend. Even after what Rob told me, I wasn't sure."

"What Rob told you?"

"That he was the note-writer and Julia put him up to it."

Riley's eyes went big and her mouth dropped open. "What?!"

"Yeah, Julia asked him to write the notes to distract me away from Dane. I let him know that you and I basically thought it was a prank anyway, and that he sucked as a secret admirer."

Riley belly-laughed at this. "Julia is crazier than I even imagined. Wow, Ari. Just...*wow*."

"What happened after I left last night? The last thing I heard was Rob yelling at Julia."

"Ahh, yeah," Riley said. "Rob got really upset at her. He said something like, 'Dane has never been into you, and you just don't know when to stop, do you?' And then she left without saying anything else. Poor Aaron; he had no idea what the heck was going on. Rob eventually told us some of the story so we weren't totally confused. I really wish you'd told me everything because Rob isn't very good at explaining things." Riley chuckled, but Ari felt bad. "Something tells me," Riley continued, "that Julia won't be joining us anymore when we do stuff as a group."

"Oh darn," Ari said dryly, and Riley laughed again.

"So what happened with Dane last night? Where did you find him? Was he embarrassed by what Julia said?"

"He was at his truck," Ari said, looking out the window at the quiet town. "He was really angry, actually. He has trust issues, and that's one reason he says he doesn't make friends easily. I mean, he trusts you guys, I think—just not Julia now. After he calmed down, though, we had a really good night. We ended up watching the stars and talking for quite awhile, which is unusual, for Dane."

"Aaaand...did he kiss you again?"

Ari felt her face turn warm. In the darkness, she smiled. Riley didn't need an answer.

"So, that's what, twice then? Can I finally please just start calling him your boyfriend?"

Ari rolled her eyes. "You know what I don't understand, Riley? Why do other girls have such a problem with me? Last year it was Jenelle. Now it's Julia. I don't get it."

Riley nodded as she lay back in the beanbag. "He does seem to attract a certain type," Riley admitted. "I know it might be hard for you to imagine, but before you moved here, Dane had sort of a bad-boy thing going on."

Ari tilted her head and squinted at Riley in the low light. "What do you mean?"

"You know, always getting into trouble, not caring about school. I worked in the office as an assistant year before last, and he was constantly getting detention. A couple of times he got into fights. I was a little bit afraid of him, actually."

"Really?"

"Well, yeah. He was on the verge of either being expelled from school or being kicked out because of bad grades at the end of sophomore year, I think. That was the rumor, anyway. I never talked to him enough to know the truth. He always had a mysterious aura about him…quiet, brooding, with haunted eyes."

Ari knew those eyes. "I can imagine that, I guess. I remember exactly what he was like the first day we met: guarded, and almost reluctant to interact with me."

"Not anymore," Riley laughed.

Ari shrugged. "Actually…he still can be. He has a really hard time trusting, Riley. I get this feeling that there's a part of him that he never reveals to me or anyone."

*   *   *

The brass knocker on Eleanor's door made a resounding *thump thump*. Ari took a step back to the edge of the concrete porch and waited for the door to open. She could picture Eleanor slowly making her way to the living room. Ari had learned that it usually took her older customers awhile to come to the door.

Eleanor's house was located in an older neighborhood that was built around a marshy area that ran through the center of Rivers. Red-wing blackbirds called back and forth through the marsh as Ari waited on the front porch. After several minutes, Ari heard the lock click open. A smiling Eleanor appeared.

"Aribelle, nice to see you again. Won't you come in?"

Ari smiled and stepped inside the too-warm home. The same scents and typical neat-as-a-pin grandma décor surrounded her.

Eleanor motioned at the sofa. "How are you, Aribelle?"

"I'm fine, thanks, Eleanor."

"I have just a few things for you this time. I wrote them out on this paper. Why don't you take a look and let me know if you have questions."

Ari took the sheet. *Wash windows, trim roses, deadhead geraniums, mow lawn.* She nodded, thinking today would be easy.

"Now, I wasn't sure about the windows, Aribelle. I know it's not yard care, but…"

Ari waved her off. "I'd be happy to, Eleanor. I'll do anything outside, really."

Eleanor smiled. "Wonderful, thank you, dear. Would you like some tea before you begin?"

Ari nodded. "That sounds great," she agreed. Eleanor motioned for her to follow to the kitchen. More hanging plants in macramé holders hung from each corner of the kitchen. As Eleanor set the teapot on the stove, Ari took the opportunity to ask about Ezra Abshire.

"Eleanor, you mentioned you grew up in Woodward, right?"

A sparkle crossed Eleanor's eyes. "Why, yes I did."

"Did you ever know Ezra Abshire? He may have worked at a merchantile in town."

A look of recognition came over the elderly lady's face. "Ab? Of course I knew old Ab. Everybody did, dear."

"Ab?"

"Yes, yes, that's what everybody called him after he started his store. It started as a hardware shop and he called it Ab's Hardware." Eleanor reached for some delicate-looking china cups with ornate floral patterns. "As a little girl, there was nothing more uninteresting than going to the hardware store with my father. *However*," Eleanor stressed, "the lovely jar of peppermints he always kept on the counter was the prize at the end of the trip. Ab would give me a wink and slip me a piece of candy when Father wasn't looking. How on earth do you know about Ab?"

"My neighbor who works at the museum has a journal written by Ezra. Unfortunately, it ends right before he moves to Woodward. We're trying to figure out the rest of his story. Our houses are right above the Abshire homestead."

Eleanor tilted her head. "Ahh, that's right, Ab grew up here, didn't he? I'd forgotten that. Let's see…Aribelle, all I can seem to remember is that Ab ran his hardware store until he was elderly. Unfortunately, I stopped keeping up with the goings-on in Woodward after Gerald passed."

"Do you happen to know who Ezra—er, Ab—married? Did he have a family? Any kids?"

Eleanor nodded. "I do know for sure he had a child. Unfortunately, I don't remember who he was married to. Ab would've been probably twenty years older than myself, I'm guessing. As a youngster I didn't really take note of those things. I just remember him being a family man."

Eleanor handed Ari a teacup. "Dane—my neighbor—and I have figured out that Ezra was smitten with one of the daughters of Dane's great-great grandma. I guess I'm trying to figure out what happened with them after he moved."

A look of sympathy came over Eleanor's face. "Oh, that would be an interesting story to figure out. Aribelle, you two really should go to Woodward. Go to the hardware store, if it still exists. Someone must know something. I'm sure he still has family around."

"That's the thing, Eleanor. I've checked online and I can't find any Abshires in our area. It's like they vanished. We know Ezra had an older brother and a younger sister. I just can't find any of their relatives."

"Keep looking, dear. Ab was a very important part of the Woodward community at the time. He and his family couldn't have just vanished."

Ari nodded and thanked Eleanor for the tea. Taking her list, she gathered the supplies needed for her day's work. Eleanor handed her a stack of old newspapers and a bottle of window cleaner. Ari looked at the newspapers with a questioning glance. "The newspapers are for the window. Much better than rags," Eleanor explained.

In the late-morning sunlight, Ari first started on the windows. As Ari found her rhythm, first spraying the cleaner, then wiping with newspapers, she realized it was more exercise than she'd expected. Thirty minutes into it, Ari was streaked with sweat and her face smudged with ink.

Moving on to mowing, Ari realized she should've probably done that first, as her arms were so tired from window cleaning that she could barely start the mower. Eleanor's lawn was one of Ari's favorites to mow; the thick, lush green grass made crisp lines as she mowed on the diagonal. Ari smiled with satisfaction when she was finished.

As the sun rose higher in the sky, Ari went to her bike and pulled her sunhat from the handlebars. She was thankful that for once, she had finally remembered everything she needed for work: her water bottle, sunhat, and Gerald's leather gloves, which would be necessary for trimming the roses.

Ari worked along, trimming the spent blossoms on the roses and nipping off dead buds on Eleanor's large geranium bed. All the while, Ari mulled over what few details Eleanor had told her about Ezra. She didn't want to forget a single detail before she was able to relay the new information to Dane. For once, Ari was slightly annoyed that Dane still refused to get a cell phone.

*   *   *

There were no cars at Dane's house when Ari walked out of the oak grove trail. She wasn't surprised. Ari pulled a piece of paper out of her bag and scribbled, "Found out info on Ezra. Come see me ASAP! Love," Ari smirked and signed, "your secret admirer."

Ari wedged the folded piece of paper in the doorjamb and turned back to her house, returning along the path. Late afternoon sunlight was streaming through the crooked branches of the oak trees, and Ari couldn't help but walk slower than usual. When she came to the brass circle, she bent low and brushed debris off the top. It had been ages since she had actually gone inside. It seemed like summer had come with a whirlwind of adventure and jobs and everything except just going to the underground room like she and Dane used to. She ran her hand over the delicate floral-and-heart design that encircled the lid, thinking back to that very first day when she'd encountered the hesitant, guarded boy.

She continued on to her house. Nobody had arrived home yet either; Ari went up the back deck, through the back door, and to the kitchen. Hunger nagged at her and Ari decided to start making dinner. She figured if she started now, it would probably be ready by the time her family came home.

Ari turned on the radio in the kitchen. Her dad had set the station to local public radio; blues were playing. Ari smiled and started searching for recipes. Within fifteen minutes, Ari had the cutting board out and was chopping away at onions and garlic. Nina Simone's *Feeling Good* was playing while Ari scraped the diced vegetables into the pan. Something about the song resonated with the warm summer evening; soon Ari was singing along to the lyrics while using a wooden spoon as a makeshift microphone.

Suddenly another voice joined hers and Ari startled so badly that she dropped the wooden spoon and whirled around.

Standing framed in the back door was Dane, singing. "*It's a new dawn, it's a new day, it's a new life, and I'm feeling good…*" His voice reverberated through the room, and Ari stopped still.

He walked toward her, smiling and singing. As the song ended, Ari motioned to one of the bar stools at the counter. "Feel free to stay here and sing to me while I cook," she said, turning back to the sizzling pan on the stove. "I will *never* get tired of hearing your voice."

Dane approached her from behind and brushed her long brown hair to the side and put a hand on her shoulder, looked over at the pan. A shiver ran down her back as he spoke next to her ear. "What are you cooking?"

"Making pizza sauce. We've got some crusts in the pantry; I thought I'd make something before everyone gets home."

"There are no onions in pizza sauce," Dane said, wrinkling his nose.

"Well, there are in this recipe," Ari pointed to the recipe card with her wooden spoon.

"Hmph," Dane snorted. "Hey, I got some weird note from a 'secret admirer.' You wouldn't happen to know anything about that, would you?"

Ari smiled. From the other room, the sounds of Lily's voice could be heard. Dane backed up to the bar stool and took a seat.

Mrs. Cartwright came into the kitchen and was surprised to see Ari at the stove. "Why, Aribelle, you're making dinner! Hey, Dane," she said, nodding in his direction. "How was work for both of you today?"

"I was just going to tell Dane what I found out about Ezra. I was at Eleanor's house again this morning, and she definitely did remember Ezra."

Dane looked surprised. Ari's mom put down a bag of groceries. "Well?" she asked. "Did you find out the rest of his story? What happened with Katia?"

Ari stirred the sauce on the stove. "Eleanor was a little girl and she didn't know much about Ezra, except that he owned a hardware store called Ab's Hardware. Ab was his nickname, and she said he worked at his store 'till late in his life. Her suggestion to us—," she looked at Dane, "—was to go to Woodward and see if the store still exists. She said he was such a notable person in the community that someone must remember him, or he may have family still around."

"So he did have kids?" Ari's mom concluded.

Ari nodded. "Eleanor knew for sure he at least had one, but she can't remember who his wife was."

"What are you doing tomorrow afternoon?" Dane asked, a sly smile on his face.

Ari returned his grin. "Finding clues in Woodward. How about you?"

chapter twenty-seven

Ari snuck a peek in the side mirror of Dane's truck. She'd spent some time putting on a little makeup, and had tried doing her hair in a different way. She wanted something more professional than a ponytail, but it turned out to be harder to do than she'd imagined. With the summer heat, her straight hair had resisted all attempts at curling, and it now hung down in loose waves.

"I like it," Dane said.

Ari looked at him. "What?"

"Your hair. And your outfit. Everything," he said quietly.

Ari thanked him. She had struggled to find something to wear that wasn't cutoff shorts and a t-shirt, which was her standard summer outfit. She'd finally found a sleeveless dress that was just right. Absentmindedly she tugged at her ever-present honeybee necklace and took a sideways glance at Dane.

Dane had dressed nicely, too. They'd agreed beforehand that if they'd dressed up a little, people might take them more seriously than if they looked like high schoolers doing a school report. He had chosen a white button-down shirt with khakis. As usual, he was wearing his black Converse. Ari noticed his hair was shorter again; she figured he'd gotten it cut for the first time since the dance.

They were approaching Woodward. They passed the small airport with the restaurant. A few roadside houses sat back from the highway. They all looked to be postwar single-story houses, with square patches of lawn that faded into pasture all around. A wooden sign announced "Welcome to Woodward, Home of the Pioneer Spirit."

"We should probably head to the hardware store. It's four o'clock right now, so that will give us some time to do exploring. What was the address again?" Dane slowed down as they entered the downtown area. Old-timey buildings with tall facades edged a wooden walkway that ran up and down the entire length of the main street.

Ari looked at her phone. "Looks like the hardware store is on Church Street. Go one more block and turn right."

Dane found Church Street and parked the truck in an angled spot. The hardware store was across the street. A vintage-looking sign declared it was indeed Ab's Hardware. Dane held the heavy wood-and-glass paned door open for Ari.

The interior of the store was unlike any place Ari had ever been in before. Heavy gray wood planks made up the floor, and she could tell the interior was genuinely old. Attempts at modernizing parts of the store stuck out like a sore thumb: modern metal shelves looked out of place against the rough-hewn wall timbers. An old shop counter with wainscoting supported the modern cash register. The whole building was a clash of old and new.

A younger man, maybe in his early twenties, looked up from his magazine from behind the counter. "Can I help you two with anything?"

Ari nodded. "Do you happen to know anything about the history of this shop?"

The man looked puzzled. "Um, I sure don't. I've only been here a year."

Ari bit her lip. "My friend and I are doing a research project. It has to do with someone who lived here in Woodward some time ago. We knew he owned this store at some point in time. His name was Ezra Abshire. Do you know anyone who might know something?"

The man pulled a notepad from behind the register. "Well, I can give you the phone number of the shop's current owner. He's pretty old and might know something." He started writing, then handed Ari the number.

Severin Gray, the note said, followed by a phone number.

"Thanks," Ari said, getting excited.

"Good luck getting ahold of him," the guy said. He had an ominous tone. "In the entire year I've worked here, I've never seen him. Not totally convinced he really exists," he sniffed. Ari glanced at Dane, who looked concerned.

Outside the hardware shop, Ari motioned to a bench that was bolted to the wooden sidewalk. She started searching on her phone for Severin Gray's address. Dane looked over her, resting his chin on her shoulder.

"Are you ever planning on getting a cell phone?" Ari asked as she scrolled through the online directory.

"Nope."

"Why?"

"Because when I have something to say, I like to do it in person. I want to look people in the eye when I speak to them."

Ari nodded, not expecting any different answer from him.

"There are two Grays listed in Woodward. One is an S. Gray, and the phone number matches the one here," she said as she held out the paper. "But there's no address listed."

"So he must live in Woodward," Dane concluded

"Looks like it. Should I call the number?"

"I'll do it," Dane offered.

She handed him her phone. After he entered in the numbers, there was a long pause. When Dane finally started speaking, Ari figured he was leaving a message. "Hi, um, my name is Dane, and I got your number from an employee at the hardware store in Woodward. A friend and I are doing a research project on Ezra Abshire, and we were told you might know some history on him. If you could give me a call back, my number is—" Dane looked at Ari, and she hastily scribbled her cell number on the piece of paper. Dane repeated it on the message and hung up.

"What now?" Ari asked.

"We wait, I guess. Maybe explore Woodward a little?"

Ari looked at him. The evening light pierced through the green in his eyes. Dane noticed her looking at him just a moment too long. He looked at her back and brushed a wavy strand of hair from her face.

"What do we do if he doesn't call back?" Ari asked.

"Like, tonight?"

"No, ever."

Dane exhaled. "I don't know. Maybe check the museum here. If Ezra stayed here and had a family, I'm sure we could dig up something there."

Ari searched on her phone. "Shoot, the museum here closed at four. We'll have to come back."

"Do you want to walk around for awhile?" Dane held out his hand for Ari. She took it, and Dane immediately interlaced his fingers with hers. It was like a shock of electricity ran through her arm; the connection was somehow more powerful than Ari could understand. Anyone on the street would just see two teenagers holding hands; yet somehow it was a bond between them; a communication. The slightest brush of Dane's thumb on Ari's hand sent a shiver through her despite the July heat.

"So when—*if*—Severin Gray calls us back, do you know exactly what you're going to ask him?" Ari questioned.

Dane thought a minute. "I'll ask if he knew Ezra, and if he did, then I'll see if he can answer the big questions: who Ezra married, if his dad survived, that kind of stuff. I feel like this Severin guy is a long shot, though, Ari." His voice was dubious. "I have a feeling he's probably just an investor and has no real knowledge of the history of the shop. I mean, if an employee hasn't seen him in a year, I'm not getting my hopes up that he has any real connection to the business's history."

"I hope you're wrong about this one, Dane. Ezra is becoming a real challenge to track down, isn't he?"

"Yeah. I feel like we're chasing a ghost."

After walking in silence up one side of the main street, they approached a two-lane bridge that connected to a road which made a ninety-degree turn out of sight. "You said Woodward was much bigger than Rivers. Where's the rest of the town?" Ari asked.

"This is just the historic district," Dane explained. "The rest of the city is over the bridge."

They turned back the way they came, passing a little park off the side of the street that consisted of nothing more than a footbridge and a few benches. Ari leaned over the side of the bridge and watched the creek pass underneath. Dane put one hand on the railing and his other hand on Ari's lower back.

"Ari?" Dane started. The tone of his voice was hesitant and immediately Ari's heart picked up a notch.

"Yeah?"

Dane cleared his throat. "Are you hungry? Maybe we should grab some dinner?"

Ari exhaled. She was convinced that wasn't what he had intended to ask her. "Yeah. I'm starving, actually."

Dane looked relieved. "There's a place east of Woodward that I think you might like—if it's still around. It's been a long time since I was there. Wanna try and find it?"

"Sounds like an adventure. Let's go," Ari smiled at him, and he took her hand again. They made their way back to his truck, passing shops that had already closed for the day, a restaurant, then a bar. Bass beats from the bar reverberated on the wooden sidewalk; three burly leather-clad bikers exited the bar and cigarette smoke wafted from the doorway.

They reached the truck and then drove over the bridge and through the more modern part of Woodward. Dane was right; the city was surprisingly large. In stark contrast to the historic district, the bulk of Woodward was bursting at the seams with strip malls and gas stations and architecture like any midsized American city. This went on for miles. Finally the buildings and shops started thinning out and older, fifties-style ranch homes started appearing here and there, set far back from the main road, which had now turned back into the highway. Eventually, only wide-open valley and a thin two-lane highway spread out in front of them.

"I don't remember exactly where this place was. Keep your eye out for a diner."

"When were you here last?"

"Right before my uncle passed away he brought me out here while he was looking for parts for his '68 Ford. There was a wrecking yard out here in the middle of nowhere, and we stopped at this old diner. I remember having the best hamburger I've ever had there. I mean, I just could've been really hungry, and any food was better than what Rhoda ever made, but I have never forgotten that meal."

Ari watched Dane carefully as he reminisced. One hand was in his hair, the other on the steering wheel. Dane's white collared shirt whipped in the wind as they drove along. The summer sun was still blazing strong in the western sky, and sweet-smelling sunbaked air permeated everything.

In the distance, Ari could see two semi-trucks parked side-by-side. Above, an overly-tall neon sign blinked *Ralph's Diner*. The parking lot was dusty, with only a suggestion of pavement. More than a few cars were lined up in front of the building.

"Hey, it's still here!" Dane exclaimed as he parked the truck. Upon getting out, Ari looked at Dane and the truck against the backdrop of the vintage eatery.

"Looks like you and your truck belong here," Ari smiled. "All you're missing is a white t-shirt with sleeves rolled up and greased-back hair," she joked.

"I don't even have enough hair to slick back anymore," Dane jested as he smoothed his hands over the top of his head. "I keep cutting it back to look all professional." Dane held open the door for Ari and a small brass bell clanked against the glass.

Inside, the diner was frozen in time: Ari guessed by the décor that the restaurant had opened in the late 40's or early 50's and had simply remained untouched while the world around it changed and grew. Booths lined the long front window, and a lengthy bar counter with red vinyl stools bordered the kitchen. The restaurant was packed, mostly with elderly folks at the booths and truckers at the bar.

A waitress in a mustard-yellow dress and white apron seated them at a window booth.

"When I met you, your hair almost covered your ears," Ari remembered.

"Long or short, then?"

"Your hair?" Ari looked at him, thinking it funny that he was even asking her such a question.

Ari reached across the table and ran her hand through his hair. He stopped moving and wouldn't take his eyes off her as she touched him.

"I like it just as it is now. I like being able to see your ears," she laughed. "But seriously, you look so much older than the boy next door that I met just a year ago."

The waitress came and took their orders. Dane leaned forward and took both her hands in his. "I feel older. In a good way. A lot has changed."

"Hey, when I was talking to Riley the other day she said you had a bit of a bad-boy thing going on before I moved here," Ari said casually, hoping he wouldn't take offense.

He just smirked, one corner of his mouth twitching upward. "Yeah, I think my anger at Rhoda didn't stop when I got to school. I didn't want to make friends and I didn't trust a soul. I honestly didn't care about anything. After Dad left, I really thought he was going to come back to get me soon. It was after a year passed that it hit me that he might not return." Dane stopped for a minute. "That's when I went adrift, Ari. There wasn't anything left to anchor me."

"It's almost hard to imagine, Dane. I mean, look at you now."

"I found my anchor." He looked at her straight on, unwavering. Ari caught her breath. Before he could say anything more, a ponytailed waitress came over with a coffee pot.

"You two lovelies want some coffee?"

Ari turned over her cup on its paper doily, and Dane followed. Ari sipped hers and coughed as the coffee burned its bitter way down her throat.

"*Ohmygosh,*" Ari wheezed. "That is *strong* coffee."

Dane laughed at her, a gleam in his eyes. Without even blinking, he gulped down the contents of his mug.

Another waitress set down a burger in front of Ari and Dane. Ari watched as Dane took a bite.

"Well? Is it as good as you remember?"

Dane had closed his eyes. "Absolutely. Turns out it really *was* a good burger. Try it."

Ari bit into hers, and she had to agree. Something was just perfect about the burger—it was simple but utterly delicious. They sat chewing in silence.

"Hey, how was work today?" Ari asked.

"It was fine. I started cataloging unlabeled photos in the archive today. I'm afraid I'm slower than I should be because I'm looking

265

carefully at each one, checking for the familiar faces of people we've researched. Really I should just be checking the backs of the photos for any written description and entering it into the online database."

"How's Julia?"

Dane rolled his eyes. "Well, I tried asking her a question about the filing system, and she glared at me and walked away. I am guessing that she's given up on chasing me, which is a welcome change."

Ari took several more bites and then pulled her phone out to check for calls, even though she was fairly positive nobody had tried to reach her. Sure enough, no calls had come through. Ari sighed.

"With or without Severin, we'll figure out Ezra. Don't worry," Dane said between bites. "Are you going to be disappointed if we find out Ezra and Katia didn't get married?"

Ari thought a minute. "Well, yeah," she finally said. "Do you realize that if they *did* end up getting married and had kids, then you might have relatives somewhere that you didn't know about?"

Dane nodded. "That crossed my mind. They'd be kind of distant relatives, but family all the same, I guess."

The two finished their meal. The diner was emptying out by the time they pulled away from Ralph's; the sun was lowering on the horizon when Ari and Dane headed west, back towards Rivers.

The long stretch of straight road left much room for conversation, but Ari turned up the radio. She started scanning through the FM band.

"What kind of music are you looking for?" Dane asked.

"I'll know it when I hear it."

Out in the middle of the valley, few radio stations came through strongly. Eventually Ari flipped over to the AM band. Staticky talk shows were mixed with crackling honky-tonk country, all of it having the distinct low-quality sound of AM radio. After cycling through the half-dozen stations, an oldies station came across the airwaves. Sure enough, two songs in, Dane started singing along. Ari couldn't stop smiling. The sound of his voice, the scents of grass and mint fields and the hum of the road, the hazy dusk sky; she took a mental photo of everything, because at that moment, it was all pitch-perfect.

When they arrived at Hadley Hill, Dane parked at his house. The sun made dark silhouettes against the oak trees that ran along the road down to Ari's house. The gravel road was quiet, shadowy. Noises were muffled by the trees that bordered both sides of the road. Approaching her house, she could clearly hear Lily laughing in the backyard, mingled with her parent's voices.

Ari ascended one stair and suddenly turned around. She was at eye level with Dane. "Hey, what were you going to ask me when we were at the park in Woodward? I know it wasn't about dinner."

Dane's eyebrow twitched upward and a wicked, mischievous glint sparkled in his darkened hazel eyes. Without hesitation, he put his hand around the back of Ari's head and lowered his face to hers. For an endless second he hovered right there, an inch in front of her. Footfalls could be heard coming through Ari's house; Lily was running somewhere nearby. Dane looked down and stepped back. He still had a glint in his eye; but instead of answering Ari's question, he wordlessly turned toward the road.

Ari's heart twisted at his silence as she watched him disappear.

*   *   *

The next week was Ari's most scheduled of the summer thus far. She had seen two customers and Monday and Wednesday, and a new one, Mr. Winsor, on Thursday. By Friday, Ari was tired and sore and completely thankful that Dane still not only wanted to help her at the Bellamy house, but he insisted on driving her there.

"I really appreciate that you changed your work schedule to come with me today," Ari mentioned as she got in the truck. She noticed Dane was wearing something just slightly different than she'd ever seen before: torn up jeans, a thin white tank top, and work boots. If she hadn't known better, she would've mistaken him for a construction worker.

"I wouldn't miss a creepy house for the world," he said with a sly smile. "Hey, you haven't heard from Severin Gray, have you?"

Ari shook her head. "I haven't missed a single number. Every call has been a customer or Riley."

Dane shrugged. "I never expected him to call back, anyway."

When they reached the driveway, Dane turned the truck and went down the long gravel lane. The giant, house-hiding row of cypress trees eventually revealed the large, brown Italianate house behind them.

"I've been past this driveway a million times, Ari. I honestly had no idea there was a house back here."

Dane parked the truck and they got out. Like before, there were no cars parked or any other signs of life. Ari tilted her head back and stared up at the house. Dark windows, tattered lace curtains, same *No Trespassing* sign. And a white note shoved in the doorjamb, just as before.

Ari felt a shiver claw through her. It didn't matter that Dane was with her; the house was no less foreboding than it was the first time. She inhaled and moved to the front porch, being careful on the uneven planks that were sagging and buckling. Dane moved behind her to read the note over her shoulder:

"Ari, please remove the dead rosebush from the southern rose bed. Also, tear the ivy off the house on the north side. Please water the plants that are still alive. Yard refuse can be piled in the same place as last time. Thank you, A. Bellamy"

"So is Mr. Bellamy home right now?" Dane asked quietly.

"I really don't think so. There are no cars here and I doubt he would leave a note if he was home." Ari looked around. "I'm not sure where the ivy is that he's talking about. Let's go around to the side."

Ari made her way to the small wooden gate and the dark, overgrown north side that was shaded by the tall cypress trees. Dane had to duck under the arcs of wild roses that made a tunnel between the house and cypress trees. Ari looked up the side of the house.

She shaded her eyes and frowned in dismay.

"Oh my," Ari sighed.

Sure enough, vines of English ivy climbed all the way to the second-story windows. The shadowy side of the tall house had been nearly consumed by dark green leaves.

"Where are the tools at? Is there a ladder anywhere?" Dane asked.

Ari showed him the decrepit tool shed. She saw all the things they'd need for the day's jobs except for a tall ladder. Only a rickety painting ladder was propped up in a dark corner of the shed.

"How about I go home really quick and get a taller ladder?" Dane asked. "Are you going to be ok here?"

Ari rolled her eyes, but inwardly she didn't relish the idea of Dane leaving. "I'll be fine. I'll start on digging out the dead rose bush out while you're gone."

Dane patted her on the back and headed for his truck. "Be back in ten," he yelled. Ari put on her leather gloves and pulled a shovel out of the shed. The dead rosebush wasn't hard to find: right in the middle of five beautiful rosebushes was a thorny mass of dead leaves and brown stems.

Ari dragged a garden hose over to the bed and soaked the area around the bush. After a few minutes had passed, water started to seep out of the bed and onto the old sidewalk that Ari was standing on. She plunged the shovel into the mud and started working her way around the dead plant. She tried to use the shovel as a lever to pop the bush free, but the dead stems tangled with the living bushes on either side.

Ari sighed. She went to the shed and found bypass pruners. Thankful that she'd remembered her leather gloves, Ari cut and cleared the blackened stems. At the base of the bush, the main canes crumbled, revealing a rotten core.

She worked the shovel around the root ball once again, even

standing on the shovel to pop free the remaining roots that still firmly held the bush. With a satisfying snap, the last root broke and the root ball rolled onto the sidewalk.

Ari leaned on her shovel, catching her breath. She smiled in satisfaction that she hadn't even been there half an hour and already had the first task completed. Suddenly a *whump* came from inside the house, followed by a scraping sound. Ari gasped, stumbled, and backed away from the house. More sounds followed; muffled, indistinct. Ari briskly walked to the front of the house and stood by the driveway.

She hadn't been standing there for long when Dane showed up. A long aluminum ladder was sticking out from the truck's bed. Dane gave her a funny look.

"You ok?" he asked as he hopped out of the truck.

"Yeah…just waiting for you to get back," Ari lied.

Dane narrowed his eyes at her. "What happened?" He walked up to her and stood nose-to-nose. "You're not telling me something."

"How do you know that?"

Dane stood silent, waiting for her to talk.

She rolled her eyes. "There were more noises coming from inside the house," she admitted.

Dane strolled up the front steps and walked to the front door.

"What are you doing?" Ari asked, dubious.

"Mr. Bellamy must be home," Dane concluded as he rang the doorbell. He stood and waited. Ari held her breath. Moments passed but nobody came to the door, and no sounds came from the house.

"Or not…" Dane shrugged. He walked to his truck and Ari helped him pull the ladder from the bed. The two hauled it to the north side of the house, being careful not to hit it on anything along the narrow pathway. Dane lifted the ladder and leaned the top between two second-story windows.

Ari shaded her eyes and tilted her head back. She noticed how high up she would have to climb to reach the highest ivy vines. Her heartrate started to increase just a tick.

"Do you want me to do the stuff on the ladder?" Dane asked.

Ari wanted to say *yes*. The thought of working on a high ladder wasn't appealing. But she swallowed hard and shook her head.

"No, I can do it." She pulled her hair into a ponytail.

"You sure?"

"Yes." Ari was determined. She put her hands on the first rung and took a single step up. She then felt Dane's hand on her back.

"Ari, you don't have to do this. I'd be happy to pull the ivy from the top of the house if you want to stay on the ground and cut the vines with the hedge trimmers."

She turned her head to the side. Dane was standing next to her at eye level. Ari looked at him appreciatively.

"No, it's ok. I can do this. Really."

She continued up the ladder, looking straight ahead, only focusing on her hands as they grasped each new rung. The ivy vines were beginning to thin out. She started carefully pulling the vines away from the house and was pleasantly surprised that they were easy to remove.

"Hey, this isn't too hard." Ari turned around to see how Dane was doing—and immediately regretted it. As she looked down, she suddenly realized exactly how high off the ground she was. A small gasp escaped from her mouth and she dropped all the ivy vines and returned both hands to the sides of the ladder.

"Ari, are you doing ok up there?"

"I'm fine."

Ari refocused on what was straight in front of her. She continued gripping the sides with one hand while she tried to tear at the vines to her right. She could hear nothing below; Dane had stopped cutting away at the ivy. Ari felt him watching her so she tried her hardest to act normal. But every time she leaned over she was overcome with dizziness. Her vision started to fade around the edges and she leaned her forehead against the ladder.

Ari thought she felt the ladder moving. A fresh wave of panic hit. She wanted to step down, but her muscles were tensed and frozen in place. She felt someone standing behind her. Dane's head was next to hers; he'd climbed up behind her and was standing one rung below. He placed his hands next to hers on the sides of the ladder. Having his arms around her allowed her to relax; at least she knew she couldn't fall off now.

"Hey, let's trade places, ok?" He tried to sound casual about it.

Ari nodded but disappointment filled her. Dane stayed behind her as she climbed down one slow step at a time. When she reached the ground, she realized that anger and embarrassment were edging her senses. She hated being seen as weak and her face started to burn. Dane put his hand on her shoulder, but Ari shrugged it off.

"I want to be able to do this, Dane." Her voice was strained. "I want to beat this fear." She looked at him with a fierce determination and put her hand on the ladder again. "Let me move the ladder closer to the window. That way I can at least have the window frame to grab onto while I'm up there. Hold the ladder steady, ok?"

Though her hands were shaking, Ari ascended the ladder once again. This time, she made sure not to look down. Reaching the top, she grabbed the sill. Momentarily she was distracted from her fears as she peeked into the curtain-less window.

The glass on the window was wavy with age. Inside, the bedroom was small and dark and bare. Sections of ceiling plaster were missing, revealing slats of wood underneath. Cracks ran along the walls and the floor was covered in debris. A bare bulb hung from a wire suspended from the ceiling. Through the doorway, Ari could see a hallway.

Ari could hear Dane had resumed hacking away at vines below.

"Dane, I don't think anyone lives here," she called out, being certain this time to not look down at him.

"What makes you say that?"

"It's empty inside and it looks to be in even worse shape than the Abshire house." Ari clawed at vines that grew around the window frame. She could still feel her hands trembling, but as long as she kept a steady pace of pulling at vines, her fears lessened. Soon she'd cleared the whole window area and descended.

Dane had nearly severed all the ivy vines at the base of the house. Ari moved the ladder to the next window and repeated the same process. Every time she stepped up the ladder, she felt slightly less bothered by the height—as long as she didn't look down. As she tore away at more ivy, Ari could see this room was much the same as the other one, although brown-stained water damage streaked from the ceiling to the floor. The dusty wood floors had been badly damaged; planks were missing and shoe tracks were visible in the dust. Through the doorway and across the hall was another bedroom; sunlight streamed through the opposite room and reflected off the wood floors.

Strands of ivy were falling away from the house as Dane started pulling them from below. Ari watched as vines to her right were coming off the siding with satisfying pops as they fell away. Dane had collected the ivy in a heap and was starting to haul it all to the debris pile. Ari was just lowering herself down a rung when something inside the window caught her eye. A definite shadow had moved through the hallway, disrupting the stream of sunlight across the floor. Ari gasped.

chapter twenty-eight

"Everything ok? Dane had his arms full of ivy, and Ari had climbed down the ladder as fast as she could.

"There's someone in there," Ari hissed. "Let's get this cleaned up and go."

"What did you see?" Dane tried to keep up with her as she grabbed an armful of vines and briskly crossed the yard.

"Someone was walking in the hallway on the second floor!" Ari tried to keep her voice down.

"Was it a man?"

"I don't know, I just saw a shadow, and movement," she shook her head.

After cleaning up the ivy completely, Ari remembered she had to water the plants. She grabbed the old hose and made a circle around the backyard, dousing whatever living plant was surviving the summer heat. Dane had loaded the ladder and was waiting for her at the truck when she was finished.

Ari took one last look at the house. Its dark windows stared down at her. She brushed off her shorts before getting into the cab.

"Let's go home, yeah?" Ari asked.

"I take it that wasn't a usual day at work for you," Dane chuckled. Ari shook her head and wiped sweat from her forehead, smoothing back her hair as she pulled out her ponytail. She exhaled deeply and closed her eyes, tilting her head back in the seat. With her eyes still closed, she felt Dane take her hand. She looked at him and smiled back, feeling his warmth and the undeniable sense of connection she had when he held onto her.

"Hey…you got back up there, Ari. Once again you faced your fears." His eyes reflected something different and stunning: pride. *In her.*

Warmth filled her core. She took another mental recording of that exact moment and burned it in her heart.

*   *   *

Riley reached for a slice of pizza from the center island in Jace's kitchen. Amara and Aaron were shoveling salad and breadsticks onto their plates, and Dane had settled down at the bar counter with his piece of pepperoni pizza. Ari poured herself some soda and picked up her plate of food. She sat with Riley at the long farmhouse-style dinner table.

"Is Julia coming tonight?" Amara asked from her seat at the table.

"Uhh, definitely not," Jace said, covering his mouth full of food. "For the sake of everyone here, I decided not to invite her."

"What about Rob?" Ari asked.

"He said he'd stop by after he was done with work. He won't mind that Julia isn't here, that's for sure." Jace sniffed.

It was a Friday night, a week after July 4th. Jace had invited everyone to his house for a spontaneous summer evening get-together. Jace's parents swooped in at one point to grab some pizza, introduce themselves, and then had disappeared into the entertainment room in the basement.

Rob eventually burst in, covered in sweat and sawdust. "Hey guys," he said, guzzling a huge glass of water before doing anything else. He grabbed four slices of pizza and sat down next to Dane. Before long, Rob started conversing in low tones with Dane.

Ari asked Riley how her job at the drive-thru coffee was going, but over Riley's voice, she strained to hear what Rob was talking about with Dane. She caught phrases here and there: Rob said something about being sorry about Julia. Ari snuck a look out the side of her eye: Dane nodding once, saying something in response. Rob smiled in return.

"How's your job going?" Riley's voice snapped Ari's attention back.

"It's going well," Ari said. "I've been getting steady calls, and I've had my schedule filled with one appointment almost every day. It's exhausting sometimes, though. At one house, the owner wasn't there, and I had to figure out how to do a lot of stuff on my own. Dane came and helped me with that one last week, though. The house was super creepy, guys."

Jace came back over to the bar and refilled his soda cup. "Which house was creepy?"

"It's on the way to Woodward; it's the Bellamy house. You can barely see it from the highway, though, because there's a row of tall trees that hides it almost completely."

Jace stopped pouring his soda and smirked a little. "You did yard work for Arthur Bellamy?"

"Yeah. He left me a note on the door about what I needed to do."

Jace shook his head. "That's not possible. Arthur Bellamy died about a year ago."

The kitchen fell silent. Ari's mouth dropped open and she looked over at Dane, wide-eyed. "What...?"

"The house is an old one, at the end of a long lane? Weird spiderweb-looking window on the front of the house?" Jace asked.

Ari nodded, her eyes getting big. "That would be the one..."

Jace took a sip of his soda. "I'm pretty sure that's the guy who passed away. He was a hermit, and his family hired my dad to settle his estate. You said you talked to him?" Jace leaned forward, clearly interested. Dane came over and joined Ari at the table.

"The first time he made an appointment, he called me and I took down his information. Then, when I got to the house, there was a note at the door and payment for the day. When he called to schedule my last appointment, he actually called my parent's landline and my mom took down the message."

"What did he sound like on the phone? Old?" Rob asked from the bar.

"Gosh, I honestly can't remember. It was awhile ago. Sorry."

"Something is weird about this," Dane mused, his brow furrowed. Ari had an idea and reached for her phone. Only clicks could be heard in the silent kitchen as she typed something.

"Yeah, here's his obituary," Ari handed her phone to Dane.

"Arthur Bellamy passed March 29th in his home…" Dane trailed off.

"It's haunted!" Amara gasped, and Rob and Jace started laughing. Ari just sat there, wide-eyed and stunned.

"Has he called back to make another appointment?" Riley asked.

"Not yet," Ari said.

"If he does, are you going to go back?" Jace asked.

A funny look crossed Ari's face. "Well, as long as he keeps paying me, then yes…"

Everyone laughed at that, but Dane put his arm around Ari, pulling her head close. "If he calls back, I'm going with you again," he said quietly, amid the laughter in the room. Ari furrowed her brow at his serious tone.

Jace had finished his pizza and grabbed a basketball that had been tucked under the dinner table. "Who's up for some basketball?"

Rob made a whooping sound, and Aaron nodded. Jace looked at Dane. "We need you to play so we have even teams. You in?"

"Yeah, I'm down."

The boys fled out the back door to the expansive driveway behind Jace's home. A hoop was set up on one end. The girls found a spot on the lawn to sit. The summer evening was warm and still; the sun was skimming a far ridge and waning in light. Ripples of heat rose up from the fields all around the house. All that could be heard was crickets starting to chirp, the sounds of the basketball, shoes on the pavement, and the boys hollering at each other as they played.

"Watching guys play basketball on a summer night and eating pizza…is there anything better?" Riley chuckled.

"Can't say that there is," Amara smiled, watching Aaron.

"Hey, how are things with Aaron?" Riley asked Amara.

Amara smiled coyly. "I like him. I mean, *really* like him." Her gaze went over to where the guys were playing. Dane and Jace had taken off their shirts; Aaron and Rob had kept theirs on.

Ari had never seen Dane play any kind of sport before. She watched in fascination at the intensity that he played with. He was quick, nimble. Rob towered over him and Jace could shoot better than anyone, but Dane played with such ferocity that nothing threatened to break his focus. While the other guys would sneak a peek in the direction of the girls once in awhile, Dane was entirely, one hundred percent fixated on the game.

"Hon, how's Dane doing?" Riley touched Ari's arm and brought her out of her reverie.

"He's good…I think things are going better with his parents lately. How's Jace?"

Riley smiled. "He's fine. He's super busy with work so we haven't seen as much of each other since summer started."

Ari wrinkled her nose. "Riley, how do you feel about him? Would you say you love him?"

Both Riley and Amara backed up a bit. "Whoa. That's a big question, Ari. He hasn't thrown out the 'L' word yet. I definitely really like him, that's for sure. I dunno. It's just too early to say how this is gonna go."

Ari nodded in understanding.

"Why?" Riley suddenly gasped. "Did Dane say he l—"

Ari waved her off. "No! No, not at all." She shrugged, and went back to watching the guys play. Sweat was streaking off Dane's forehead and down his back, which was tensed like he was ready to pounce at any moment. She saw the scar on his back and winced, thinking of his accident. Jace passed him the ball; Dane made a quick catch, spun away from Rob's attempt to swipe the ball, and jumped up for a lay-in.

"You love him." Riley's words startled Ari. It wasn't a question. Riley lowered her voice gently. "I see it

in how you look at him."

All Ari could do was shrug. "Even if I never find out how Dane feels about me, I will never forget what I feel for him. *Never.*"

*   *   *

The bright morning light that streamed through the windows had roused Ari from a deep sleep. Upon waking, it dawned on Ari that she had nothing planned for the day.

She buried her head in her pillow once again. In the hazy place between awake and asleep, Ari's mind started working through images her mind had taken over the past month: thoughts of Dane, of going to Woodward, watching him play basketball the night before. A knock on her door suddenly disrupted the stream of images.

Ari's dad peeked his head in the door. "Hey, you awake?"

Ari mumbled a muffled *yes*.

"We need to do some work on our garden today. Are you up for helping me? Maybe start before it gets too hot?"

Ari wrinkled her nose, thinking of all the aches she had at the moment, but she didn't want to pass up a day of working in her most favorite garden of all. She had, after all, noticed that the geraniums were in desperate need of deadheading, and the wisteria vines had started to overtake some of the garden trellises.

"Yeah," Ari said, turning her head out of her pillow. "Give me a second to get dressed. Got anything good for breakfast?"

Her dad smiled. "Come down and see."

After putting on her work clothes, Ari descended to the kitchen, where fabulous smells hit her. Her mom was cooking up hash browns on the oven, but when she saw what Lily had chosen for breakfast, Ari made a beeline for the counter.

"Donuts!" Ari said, swooping down on the bakery box.

"Hey! Don't eat them all!" Lily cried from the table, but Ari looked over and saw Lily had two large donuts already. Picking a maple bar and an old-fashioned donut, Ari joined her sister at the table.

"So, Dad, what do we need to do today?" Ari stuffed a donut in mouth. She'd already dressed for the too-hot Saturday morning by wearing a tank top and shorts with her work shoes.

"Well, the wisteria and hydrangeas are getting out of hand, and every single flowerbed needs to be weeded. Now, I know you're probably sick of doing yard work, but I figure if we all work together, maybe we can be done in two or three hours."

After breakfast, Lily went to the greenhouse to play with dolls that she'd brought outside, while Ari and her parents worked away at the formal gardens. Ari realized just how little time she'd spent in her own garden over the summer—it felt like between work and being with her friends, she hadn't appreciated the incredible beauty that was in her own backyard.

Ari worked first on hacking away at the severely overgrown wisteria vines. Her arms were tired from holding the hedge trimmers above her head, but it didn't take too long to trim back the top-heavy bush that had consumed an arbor.

Her mom and dad were kneeling over a flowerbed that contained giant purple bearded irises. Ari eventually joined them, bending down and tearing away at the creeping weeds that had tangled themselves around the bases of the bulbs.

"So, Ari, have you found out anything new about the Abshires?" her mom asked. "Did you have any luck when you went to Woodward?"

Ari shook her head. "We've hit another dead end, mom. The person we were told to contact never called us back. At some point, we might just have to go there again when the Woodward museum is open. I guess that's our next step."

"You guys are really having to work at this one," her dad commented. "Why do you think it's so hard to find the information you're looking for?"

Ari straightened up and pushed her sunhat back a little. "I don't know, Dad. It's like his family disappeared and Ezra is just a ghost we're chasing."

"I probably should call Severin Gray back," someone said from behind them. Ari smiled, knowing that voice by heart.

Dane stepped to the flowerbed and nodded hello to Mr. and Mrs. Cartwright.

"Well, hello, Dane," Ari's mom said. "Ari was just filling us in on your mystery."

"I wish we had more to report. Ari, can I borrow your phone? Before I forget, I think I'll call back Mr. Gray and see if I can catch him at home."

Ari led Dane to the back porch where her phone was sitting. She pointed at it, not wanting to touch it with her dirty hands.

Dane scrolled through her past calls and found Severin Gray's phone number. Ari sat on the rocker in the shade, appreciating the much-needed break. She closed her eyes as she heard Dane leave another message:

"Hi, this is Dane Hadley, calling about information on Ezra Abshire. A friend and I were hoping you'd have some information on his life. Please give me a call back," he said, then repeated Ari's number.

He hung up, looking frustrated. "Maybe we should hit up the museum in Woodward today."

"It's Saturday, are they open?"

Dane rolled his eyes. "No, forgot about that."

Ari motioned toward the garden. "Hey, I need to finish helping fix up the garden. Can you hang out afterwards?"

Dane smiled. "Can I help? Might make things go faster."

Before he finished speaking, Ari handed him the hedge trimmers and some gloves. "Hydrangeas need trimming," she said, and they both started chuckling.

It was another hour before the garden work was finished. Ari stepped up onto the back deck and surveyed the garden in front of her. Everything looked cleaner and tidier. Crisp lines were mown in the upper lawn, and Ari crossed her arms in satisfaction. Dane had finished trimming every unruly plant in sight, and Ari's dad clapped him on his back.

"You're hired, Mr. Hadley." Ari's dad joked. Dane smiled with a single nod. "But honestly, Dane, thanks for your help. You didn't have to do anything but we sure appreciate it."

Dane and Ari rested on the rocking chairs on the back porch while Ari's parents went inside to fix lunch.

"Look at you," Dane pointed at Ari. "You're a mess."

"You're not looking so hot yourself," Ari joked back.

"Actually, I'm burning up out here. Who turned up the heat?"

Ari nodded in agreement. The noonday sun felt like it was searing the very air around them. Ari looked at her phone.

"Ninety-five degrees at the moment."

"Any missed calls?"

Ari frowned. "No. Sorry, Dane."

Dane suddenly leaned forward and a had a mischievous glint in his eyes. "You know where we haven't gone since last summer?"

Ari's interest was piqued. "Where?"

"The pool."

"Like, our pool? The freezing cold hole-in-the-ground?"

Dane got up from his seat and bounded off the porch, heading toward the oak grove. "See you at the pool in five!"

Ari shook her head. "I never said yes!" she hollered, but Dane had already disappeared.

Five minutes later, Ari headed into the oak grove herself, towel in hand. It was such a hot day that even in her swimsuit, she could feel sweat beading on her forehead and the sun scorching her back. The grove was just slightly cooler; the lush oak trees with vein-like branches created shaded tunnels on the way to the pool. Ari forked right instead of heading toward the circle.

It had been months since Ari had been to the perfectly round pool. Making her way along the path, the shady overhead tunnel opened up into a bright, open area. Sunlight filtered through the circular gap in the foliage and pierced through the emerald-green water. Dragonflies hovered above. Wide slate stones encircled the pool, with ferns and horsetails bordering those.

Ari had arrived there before Dane. In the silence of the moment she was able to take in the beauty of the one of the most unusual features of their hill. The earthen pool seemed to be fed by an underground source and was always freezing cold. Ari walked to the slate rim and immediately had to back away, as the stones were searing hot from baking in the sun.

Suddenly, running footsteps pounded behind her. Before she could react, strong arms grabbed her from behind. Dane took a running leap with Ari in his grasp, and jumped. Ari yelped and laughed before they both plunged into the stunningly cold water.

Ari came gasping to the surface. The water had shocked her lungs into unresponsiveness for several seconds. She clamored for the slate rim, still chuckling with chattering teeth. Dane was laughing but gasping as well. Ari climbed out of the pool and welcomed the sun-warmed slate. It no longer felt too hot on her skin. Grabbing her towel, she wrapped it around her and watched as Dane tread water in the middle of the circle.

"Well, I'm no longer too warm," Ari smirked as her teeth chattered.

"You didn't stay in long enough to get cleaned off, though. Might have to give it a second chance."

Ari looked at her hands, which were still streaked with dirt and grime. Even the tops of her feet still had imprints of dirt, where soil had worked its way into her socks while she was gardening. She scooted to the edge of the pool and dangled her legs over the side. She washed the dirt off her hands and feet, keeping an eye on Dane as he slowly swam closer. Her first thought was that he was going to pull her in by her feet, so she swiveled to the side and put her feet on the slate stones.

Instead, Dane stopped at the edge and got out as well. He took his towel and wiped his face and hair dry.

"Hey…do you think Julia has anything to do with the Bellamy house?"

Ari gave him a funny look. "What makes you say that?"

"I've just been thinking about what Jace told us about Arthur Bellamy being dead. Something isn't adding up, Ari." He sat next to Ari on the sun-scorched slate stones, dangling his legs off the side.

"Do you really think Julia is that cunning? And that she would keep paying me to come to an abandoned house, just to get a little spooked?"

Dane cocked his head to the side in thought. "Well…when you say it that way, it doesn't sound quite right. I dunno, Ari. Whatever happens, let me know if you have to go back to the Bellamy house. I don't want you going there alone."

Ari shrugged but smiled in agreement. "I don't mind the company. I suppose I'll allow it," she joked.

Dane chuckled and looked at her right then. Where he was sitting, the reflected light from the pool illuminated the dance of green and brown in his eyes in a way that she'd never seen before. His short but damply-spiked hair was sticking out in all directions, and Dane was still smiling. Ari realized she wanted nothing more than to get a photo of Dane as he sat there, just as he was. She quickly got up and grabbed her towel.

"Where are you g—"

Ari cut him off, waving her hands to stop him from following. "Don't move a muscle," she said. "I'll be right back."

Dane gave her a questioning look but just shrugged. Ari dashed off, weaving through the oak grove, until she reached the pasture. She found her phone on the back deck where she'd left it. When she returned to Dane, she was happy to see that the light hadn't changed and he had stayed put.

"I just wanted to get a photo of you. The light here is unbelievable," she said. Dane just chuckled again, and at that moment she snapped the photo.

"Perfect," she said, smiling. Suddenly her phone rang. The number that showed up on her screen was unfamiliar.

"Dane, did Severin Gray's number start with five-oh-three?"

Dane's eyes went wide. "Yes!" He quickly dried his hands on his towel and reached for the phone.

"Hello?" he asked. There was a pause. "It is." Another pause, this one longer. "Yes, same one."

Ari watched every tiny change in Dane's expression as he listened for several moments more. Finally, he spoke: "I can be there. A.M., you said?" Dane then nodded. "Please thank Mr. Gray for agreeing to meet me."

Dane hung up and gave the phone to Ari. "Write this down, ok? 15230 Kendall Heights Drive. Six-thirty a.m. on August first."

Ari paused as she was entering the information into her phone. "August *first*? That's so long from now!"

"It's only a little over two weeks. He said Mr. Gray was out of the country until then."

"Wait, who were you speaking to?"

"He introduced himself as Mr. Gray's personal assistant. He asked me if I was from the same Hadley family that helped establish Rivers. I said I was. He said Mr. Gray was very interested in meeting me...well, us. You're coming too."

Ari continued scheduling the date in the calendar on her phone. "Six-thirty p.m., right?

"No, in the morning."

"Are you sure?" Ari raised an eyebrow.

"Yep, that's what he said. Actually he said, 'please be there precisely at six-thirty a.m." Dane mimicked what the personal assistant had said.

"Hmmm. That is *really* early."

Dane shrugged. "Maybe he's a morning person?"

Ari typed the address into her phone and brought up a map application. "Kendall Heights Drive is thirty-eight minutes from here," she said, showing Dane the phone. "It looks like it's up in the hills above Woodward. We'll have to be ready to leave around five-forty a.m. if we want to be there *precisely* at six-thirty."

"Will your parents be ok with that?" Dane looked worried.

"I'm sure they will be. I'll let them know where we're going. Looks

like it's a Monday."

Ari finished entering the information into her phone. A tiny part of her started to feel apprehensive about meeting Mr. Severin Gray, so very early on a summer morning.

chapter twenty-nine

"Where is this place you guys are going to?" Ari's mom wrinkled her nose. Ari was setting the picnic table in the backyard, Dane was tending the barbecue, and Ari's dad was smoking a pipe on the back deck. Riley was over, but none of the other friends could make it that night. It was the last day of July, and while Ari was excited that the next morning they'd be finally meeting Mr. Gray, a tiny bit of her was mourning the end of her favorite month.

"It's called Kendall Heights Drive," Ari said as she put cups down on the table. She next reached for a box of matches to light the candles that were hidden all over the garden. "It's about forty minutes from here. We'll have to leave early."

"*Really* early." Dane mused from the barbecue.

Riley followed Ari around the garden and they worked on illuminating all the tealights.

"Six-thirty in the morning seems like an, um, early appointment," Ari's dad mused.

"Maybe he has to be to work at a certain time?" Riley speculated. "Dane, do you know anything about him at all? How do you know this guy is on the level and not a murderer?"

Ari snorted but her dad nodded. "Riley's right. Ari, please make sure you call us when you guys leave there, alright? And," her dad put his pipe down next to the rocker, "Dane, would you step into my office for a moment?"

Ari froze. Riley looked at her with wide eyes. Ari felt her heartbeat start to race. Suddenly the atmosphere became unbearably uncomfortable, but Dane nodded silently and followed Mr. Cartwright into the house.

"Mom..?" Ari looked over at her mother, who was bringing a dish to the table. Her mom just shrugged.

"No clue," she shrugged.

*   *   *

Ari was quite sure she had never gotten out of bed on a summer morning before the sun had risen. Yet, here she was, hitting at the alarm on her phone in the darkness of an August morning. Unlike many summer mornings, this particular one had a slight chill. Overnight the temperature had dropped and silver-blue stars were just starting to fade as Ari chose what she was going to wear for the day.

She chose a pair of dark jeans, black ballet flats, and a white short-sleeve button down blouse. Usually she wore her long, straight brown hair down, but as she stood at her vanity mirror, she thought about parting it at the side and pulling the rest up into a tidy bun. She pulled a thin gold headband from her drawer and nodded. The ensemble looked classic, professional.

The house was quiet and dark as she descended the staircase. She grabbed a light cardigan and her bag and quietly opened the front door. She had told Dane that she'd be waiting on the front porch swing so nobody would be woken up at her house. Minutes later, Dane pulled up in his truck.

It was warm inside the cab as Ari got in. Dane was also dressed nicely, with a buttoned shirt, only he was wearing his beanie with a zip-up hoodie over that. Ari realized he *would* be headed to work after they'd returned from Mr. Gray's house, so it made sense for him to be dressed as he was.

"Good morning," Dane said with a smile. "How was getting up at five-something in the morning?"

Ari stifled a yawn but nodded. "It was fine. I didn't grab any coffee but I think I'm awake enough. You?"

She could see a small smile on his face, although his expression was somewhat obscured by both the hat and the hood he had pulled over his head. "I've been up for awhile," he said quietly. They had turned onto the highway and Dane methodically shifted through the gears. They headed toward the eastern sky, that was just beginning to take on the blush of dawn.

"When did you get up?" Ari wondered.

"I usually get up around five every morning. Doesn't matter if it's summer or not."

"Really? I didn't know you were a morning person."

Dane smirked. "It's not really by choice. I just wake up and I can't go back to sleep."

Ari remembered the night before. "Hey, can I ask…what did my dad want to talk to you about last night?"

She thought she detected a pause. "He just wanted to make sure I don't let you out of my sight while we're at Mr. Gray's house today."

Ari gave him a questioning look. For the first time that morning, Dane looked over at her and made eye contact. "We're going to some guy's house that we've never met before, Ari. And it's kinda weird to be going this early in the morning. Your dad just wanted to make sure you are safe."

"And…what did you say to my dad?"

Dane kept his eyes straight ahead on the road for a long second. "I said that I always feel responsible for you no matter where we are." He reached over and put his hand on hers. This time it was Ari who interlaced her fingers with his, feeling the warmth of his hand against the chill of the morning air. A flutter went through her heart, and she couldn't stop the smile that stayed on her lips.

The sky was quickly lightening to an azure hue. "Hey, can you tell me where the first turn will be?" Dane asked. They were still in the sparse landscape between Rivers and Woodward, but Ari pulled up the map on her phone with the address she'd saved.

"Ok, you'll be making a left turn on Hollis Gap Road in about three miles," Ari concluded. She watched the sparse landscape; only a house here and there had lights glowing behind curtained windows. She spotted a green road sign in the distance. "I think that's it up there," she said, and Dane began to slow down.

Turning north on Hollis Gap, Dane guided the truck along a narrow country road. It started straight at first, but after a minute began to climb and twist in areas. In the brightening morning light, Ari could see grassy meadows dotted with crooked oaks. Mailboxes on one side of the road indicated there were houses somewhere, although Ari couldn't see a single one. They all had gravel driveways that spurred off the paved road and twisted away out of sight.

"Alright, you're going to have a right turn in a half mile," Ari read. "It's called Sanders Road."

Dane followed along the perfectly straight road. They were now passing alongside farm fields that had been shorn short. In the distance, Ari pointed out the street sign. Dane braked quickly and turned onto the road, which straightened out and then hit a series of ninety-degree turns around the corners of the fields.

"Our next turn is Kendall Heights Drive. It veers left off of this road. So, instead of going straight, take the left-hand curve." Ari saw the split. "Right up there."

As she pointed at the curve, Ari's eyes traveled up the steep and densely forested hill that rose in front of them. A thick stand of evergreen trees covered a mountainous ridge that they had been skirting since turning onto Sanders Road. If it hadn't been for the white trim underneath the steeply-pitched eaves, Ari never would've spotted the giant mansion that was perched on the top of the ridge. It looked to be a brick house that sat on a landing in front of a backdrop of towering evergreens.

"Whoa, Dane...look at that house up there," Ari breathed, craning her neck up to see. "Can you imagine living in a place like that?" She smiled as she imagined being atop an entire ridgeline, blanketed in three directions by thick forest.

As soon as she'd seen the house, Dane made the last turn and they started up a small incline along Kendall Heights Drive. Ari noticed her phone showed they were nearly at the address. She started searching for a mailbox or any indication of the addresses along the road. They drove past a heavy iron gate suspended from two brick pillars. She did a double-take as the map on her phone showed they'd already gone past their destination.

"Wait, Dane…I think we need to turn around. We just passed the house."

"Where?" Dane slowed the truck until he found a place to turn around. Heading back, Ari checked the address that was on the gated driveway. A brass plaque on the side of one column declared it to have the numbers they were looking for.

"It's the gated driveway," Ari said quietly. Dane drove up to the iron gate. Ari looked at her watch. It was 6:28 a.m.

A call box was mounted to the side of the gate. Dane pushed the button and a small click could be heard. Dane looked over to Ari and raised an eyebrow. After a moment, a voice came over the speaker:

"Who is this, please?"

Dane cleared his throat. "Dane Hadley. I'm here to see Mr. Gray."

Silence. Ari started to get a nervous pit in her stomach for reasons she couldn't fathom.

"You may proceed," the voice finally returned. In front of them, the iron gate slid open smoothly. Dane passed between the brick pillars. Ari swiveled to look behind them; the gate was already sliding shut.

The gravel road they were on started a slow ascent. On one side, there were stands of oak trees; on the other, tidy rows of grapes curved along the hillside. The sun shone through bright green grape leaves as the morning light began to warm the hills and valley.

Suddenly the vineyard rows fell away and they entered into the evergreen stand that blanketed the hill. Nothing could be seen on either side of the truck except for dense forest. The road took gentle turns to the south and started to climb more rigorously.

"How far up here do you think his house is?" Ari wondered aloud.

"No clue. If I lived up here, I think I'd have myself a log cabin though," Dane smiled.

They continued following the road. Ari kept looking out her window, expecting to see a clearing or a break in the trees. They hadn't stopped climbing, and were still curving back to the east. No other buildings or houses or breaks in the trees could be seen. Under the cover of thick fir trees, sunlight was completely blocked.

They'd been driving for about four minutes when the road turned due east, turned to pavement, and leveled out. The conifers stopped succinctly at the edge of a manicured lawn, which opened up to reveal a mansion, streaked in light with sun coming through the tops of the trees. Ari gasped as Dane slowed the truck to a stop.

chapter thirty

"It's the house we saw from the road," Ari whispered. An enormous old brick manor, with steeply pitched rooflines, was at an angle to the clearing. Tall conifers stood behind it, towering at almost twice the height of the roofline. Ari counted seven steeply-pitched gables, all outlined in a crisp cream color. The estate had dozens of windows; most of the largest ones were arched and bordered with bricks. One enormous window was partially obscured by ivy that had proliferated on a corner of the house.

Dane inched the truck around a paved circular driveway that circled an enormous bowl-shaped fountain. He parked off to the side of the drive.

Getting out of the truck, Ari couldn't help but take her eyes off the house to admire the view: only the southern exposure was cleared of trees, and from where she was standing, she could see everything along the valley floor. Sunlight crossed the expanse of fields, rolling hills, and patches of evergreens and oak trees for as far as the eye could see. The air was still and quiet with the exception of the caw of a raven somewhere in the distance, and the lapping splash of water in the fountain.

"Are you ready?" Dane finally asked after a moment. He'd also been silently absorbing the view. Ari noticed he'd taken off his sweatshirt and beanie to reveal his more professional-looking business attire underneath. The morning was still chilly, but Dane didn't seem bothered by it.

They walked to the enormous front exterior entryway. It had a high and narrow arched entryway. Ari arched her neck and looked up: from the cross-vaulted ceiling hung a single iron-and-glass porch light. Dane rang the doorbell. They waited at the heavy mahogany front door, which mimicked the entryway arch in both shape and height.

Finally, footsteps could be heard approaching the door. An older man dressed in a black dress shirt and slacks answered the door.

Before Dane could introduce himself, the gentleman stepped aside and motioned for them to enter. "Mr. Gray will be seeing you in the library this morning."

As the man turned to have them follow, Ari looked at Dane. He only shrugged. If the man wasn't Mr. Gray, then Ari assumed he was the personal assistant that Dane had spoken with on the phone.

Ari and Dane stepped into the interior entryway. Under her feet was a diagonal checkerboard of black and cream marble tiles, dull with age, but beautiful still. The square entry was bordered by thin black lines of tiny square tiles. Just like outside, a beautiful cross-vaulted ceiling held a light, only this one was an extravagant chandelier of delicately-curled wrought iron and dimly glowing Edison bulbs. Windows on the left side of the entry allowed filtered, indirect light inside.

The man proceeded to walk ahead, straight down a short hall. He then took a turn to the right and Ari and Dane quickened their pace in order to keep up. They were heading east through the building, and the hall they had turned into was very similar to the entryway: more sections of vaulted ceilings, with one arched window and one hanging light in each section. As they walked, Ari noticed that the windows that lined the entire wall were actually doors that could be opened directly to the southern-facing outside lawn. Sunlight was beginning to make angled shadows on the ecru marble floor; the light was ethereal and glowed as it reflected off the floors and off-white walls.

The assistant stopped at the end of the hall. Two ten-foot tall doors were opened for them. He stood aside and motioned for them to enter.

"Mr. Gray will meet you momentarily. Please make yourself comfortable at the meeting table."

With that, he turned and left, his shoes making succinct clicks on the marble.

Ari and Dane stepped inside the library. Once again, Ari could hardly make sense of the enormity of the mansion they were in. Two full floors of books rose in front of them; the second floor was defined by a mezzanine level bordered by an iron railing, curled in much the same fashion as the entryway chandelier. Any wall space that didn't contain a bookshelf was a deeply carved square of dark mahogany paneling. The worn wooden floor was covered nearly entirely by Oriental rugs. Ari looked to the far end of the room and the jaw-dropping arched window that consumed one entire wall of the room.

The south-facing window was currently the only source of light; the green banker's lamps on the long, dark reading table were all turned off. A massive fireplace was on the eastern wall of the room, but it looked like no fire had been lit inside for many years. Framing the giant window were two iron spiral staircases that mirrored each other; they ended at the mezzanine level on the second floor.

"Dane, this is unbelievable," Ari whispered. Dane shadowed her as she approached the window. It had the same view as at the driveway; only this wing was closer to the edge of the property.

"Did you remember to bring the journal?" Ari whispered.

"I did, but I left it in the truck," Dane said quietly. Suddenly the sound of a turning doorknob echoed across the room. A gray-haired man, short and wrinkled, entered. He had a slight stoop to his back, but his walk was direct and purposeful.

Dane and Ari crossed the room to greet the man. Ari noticed he was wearing an argyle sweater with sleeves that were tattered at the cuffs. His wingtip shoes were scuffed and shabby. Before they reached him, Ari saw he'd looked Dane up and down with hard, tired, gray eyes. Wordlessly, the man extended a hand to Dane.

"I'm Severin Gray," the man said. His voice was gravelly, rough. "You may call me Mr. Gray. And you are...?"

Dane met Severin's grip. "Dane Hadley, sir." Mr. Gray sniffed, then looked at Ari.

"Who is this?" he asked. His expression regarded Ari with disdain. The butterflies in her stomach twisted. She could tell as well as anyone when her presence wasn't wanted, and that was certainly the case here. This short, stooped man, with a look of utter contempt, didn't seem to care one bit for Ari.

"I thought you would be alone, Mr. Hadley."

Ari sucked in her pride and extended her hand to Mr. Gray. "I'm Ari," she declared with the strongest voice she could muster.

"Ari Hadley?" Mr. Gray assumed. Ari's heart caught for a half-second at the sound of the name he'd just spoken. Dane stepped in, saving Ari from her own speechlessness. Her mind ran through the scenarios of how Mr. Gray thought the pair could be related.

"This is Aribelle Cartwright. She also lives on Hadley Hill with me. Our houses were the estate of Nadia and Grekov Hadley when they were living."

Severin eyed Ari, then refocused on Dane, never having shaken Ari's hand.

"Have a seat," Severin motioned at the table. Ari across from Dane, and Dane sat to the side of Mr. Gray, who was at the head of the long reading table. Ari opened her notebook and posed herself to begin writing.

Mr. Gray began speaking, looking only at Dane. "You say that you're the great-great-grandson of Nadia and Grekov?"

Ari cocked her head to the side. She hadn't remembered Dane telling him that detail, at least not in front of her.

"I am," Dane answered. "My father is William Marcus Hadley, and my grandfather was Alexander. His father was Sergei, Nadia's only son. Ari and I have spent the last year researching my family," he explained. "We're actually wondering if you know anything about one of Nadia's daugh—"

Severin cut him off. "You say your grandfather was Alexander? Do you remember what he was like?"

Ari watched Dane. She realized he had never talked with her about his grandparents at all. She leaned in and listened with interest.

Dane shrugged slightly. "I honestly don't remember much about him, Mr. Gray. By the time I came along, I get the sense that my family wasn't very close to any relatives, and many of them had moved out of the state anyway. Most of my dad's family was in California, including the grandparents on my Father's side. I know they visited a few times when I was younger, but—" Dane shook his head, "—my memories of them are fuzzy."

Ari thought Mr. Gray looked slightly disappointed. "You said you both live on Hadley Hill."

Dane nodded. "That's right. Ari lives in the main house and my mom and I live in Nadia's first house; the smaller one, which later became the servant's quarters after the main house was built."

Mr. Gray narrowed his eyes at Ari. "But she is not a Hadley?"

Ari thought she'd have an opportunity to speak, but Dane continued. "My uncle's wife divided the property after he passed. The main house went up for sale last year. As far as I know, it's the first time a non-family member has lived on the hill. From what my dad told me, his grandparents lived in the main house and my dad grew up in the house I'm in. Things changed as dad grew up and people started moving away."

Mr. Gray said nothing. Dane used the opportunity to ask about Ezra. "Ari and I actually have been researching the family that lived closest to the Hadleys—the Abshires. We were hoping to find out more about his life. Do you know anything about Ezra?"

Mr. Gray cleared his throat and smoothed the sleeve of his sweater, picking at a single stray thread. "Ezra Abshire came to Woodward as a young boy, desperate for work, with his family indebted. He began working long days at the mercantile in town, which you probably already know. He saved money for himself and also sent funds home to his family."

Ari was about to ask about Ezra's father but Dane glanced purposefully at her.

All it took was one single look—so subtle and deft it would be unnoticed by anyone but Ari—to warn her not to say anything. Ari caught herself and quickly looked down at the notebook. She realized that Dane had not revealed that he knew anything about Ezra, so Ari followed his lead.

Dane was sitting straight in his chair, shoulders back and chin up. She realized his posture was guarded. She'd seen this plenty enough to know when Dane was being cautious.

"Can you tell us about his family?" Dane asked.

"I do not know much," Severin said, and it seemed to Ari he was being honest. "Unfortunately the details of his family have been lost to time. All I know about Ezra is that he worked hard for two long years before he was able to afford his own place to stay. The owner of the mercantile joined with Ezra in a partnership to establish the hardware store, and that's when Ab's Hardware was built. It's essentially the same store today, with a few modern conveniences added."

At that, the door to the library opened and the personal assistant came in with a bistro cart.

"Coffee, sir?"

Mr. Gray twitched a single nod and the assistant handed Severin a cup. The assistant looked at Dane and Ari.

"Would either of you like coffee?"

"They're too young for coffee," Mr. Gray declared gruffly.

"Actually, I would love some," Ari said, her voice firm. She saw a small smile twitch up one side of Dane's mouth.

"I'll take some too, please," Dane said. The assistant promptly handed them both delicate cups. Ari took a sip and realized the coffee she was drinking was better than any cup of coffee she had ever had, period. She looked at Dane with a surprised look, and he nodded back. Mr. Gray continued speaking.

"Ab was a kind man, with a generous heart. Despite this, he had much difficulty gaining the acceptance of his wife's family. He lived in the ever-present shadow of his in-laws, or so it seemed. You see, Ezra and his wife spent their days living outside of Woodward in a modest home. Ezra never was rich, but he was good at what he did, and well-respected in his community. Nonetheless his wife's family worried their daughter was not well provided for."

"Who was his wife?" Ari asked.

"Katia Hadley."

Ari's heart jumped at the name, and she was grateful that Mr. Gray didn't look in her direction to see the excitement in her eyes.

Severin's stare had settled on Dane. Without expression, Dane stared back at Mr. Gray. Ari realized Dane could make a fabulous living as a poker player if he chose not to pursue a degree in history. Finally, Dane spoke.

"Did Katia and Ezra have children?"

Mr. Gray cleared his throat. "They had one child. Her name was Elise." At that, Mr. Gray abruptly got up from the conference table. Ari was startled by his quick motion; too quick for man his age. "If you'll excuse me, I will be going now. Mr. Wells will show you to the door."

Severin Gray turned around and walked out the room. Ari looked at Dane, blank-faced. The abruptness and curt persona of Mr. Gray was jarring. Mr. Wells, the assistant, stood at the door with the bistro cart until Ari and Dane realized that was their cue to leave as well. Ari gulped the last of her coffee and the pair followed the assistant down the windowed hall.

The sounds of their shoes on the marble floor echoed through the brightly-lit hallway. Sunlight was now fully streaming through the floor-to-ceiling doors that doubled as windows. Mr. Wells led them into the front entryway and escorted them out the front door.

They both got into the truck and Dane slowly drove around the driveway and back out onto the gravel road. Ari took one last look at the enormous mansion. "You didn't tell Mr. Gray about the journal. You didn't let tell him what we know about Ezra."

Dane shrugged. "Well, we took the journal from a house we weren't supposed to be in, in the first place. Besides, I want to know what he knows. *And* he was a total jerk to you. I don't trust anyone who would treat a complete stranger the way he treated you. Did you notice that? He completely ignored you." Dane's tone was turning edgy with anger.

"That guy was definitely odd," Ari said. "I did get the distinct impression that for whatever reason, I was *not* welcome there. But that *house…*" she trailed off, thinking of what it was like to stand in the grand library, with floor-to-ceiling books.

"Yeah, that was incredible," Dane agreed. "I could get used to living in a house like that."

"Really?" Ari said. "It didn't feel quite like a home to me. It seemed more like a museum."

Dane nodded. "I guess so. But can you imagine the parties you could have in that place?"

At that, Ari had to laugh. "You would throw parties?"

"Well, yeah. Pool parties."

"Did you see a pool there?" Ari smiled and rolled her eyes.

Dane scoffed. "I'm sure the pool was behind the house somewhere. I mean, come on. You don't have a house like that without having a pool."

Ari smiled, but then got serious. "Hey, if nothing else, we learned that Katia and Ezra got married. That's amazing, right? You know what that means, right?"

Dane looked at her, amused at her excitement.

"You might have family out there that you don't know about."

"Really distant family, yeah."

*   *   *

It was still early in the morning when Dane and Ari arrived back on Hadley Hill. Dane left for the museum, and Ari got her bike and rode to Eleanor's house. Ari had requested earlier times with each of her customers, to account for the ever-rising summer heat that often happened in the later part of summer.

Eleanor greeted her, as usual, at the front door of her Craftsman home. She motioned for Ari to come inside, and Ari stepped into the living room, which was nearly exactly the same temperature as it currently was outside.

"How are you today, dear?" This time, Eleanor had a tray with tea sitting on her coffee table. She poured a cup for Ari and motioned to the couch.

"Fine, thanks," Ari smiled.

"Last time you were here, we were chatting about Ab. Did you ever find anything out about him?"

Ari took a sip of her tea. "Funny you should mention that," Ari explained. "My friend and I just met with Mr. Severin Gray today, to ask about Ezra. We did find out who he was married to—turns out the daughter of my friend's great-great grandma ended up marrying Ezra, which was part of the puzzle we were trying to solve. Other than that, though, we didn't really learn anything new."

Eleanor had a blank look on her face. "Did you say you met with Severin Gray?"

"Yes, ma'am."

"Where did you meet him?"

"At his estate, at the top of Kendall Heights."

Eleanor was speechless for a moment. Ari raised her eyebrow.

"What is it, Eleanor?"

"That is quite unusual, Aribelle. For Severin Gray to allow visitors at his house is almost unheard of. Poor Mr. Gray," she shook her head in sympathy. "Everybody across the valley heard about the day he lost his family. Oh," Eleanor put a hand to her heart, "that was such a tragedy, dear."

Ari leaned forward. "What was, Eleanor?"

"Oh, I'm not surprised he didn't say anything. Severin had a wife and a daughter who were in a terrible car accident about twenty-six years ago. The wife died immediately, but the daughter survived, initially. Everyone had such high hopes that Willow would pull through…but she didn't. It was after that that Severin Gray was rarely seen about town. Few even knew if he still lived up at his estate." Eleanor paused, thinking back.

"Long ago, when Severin's mother and father lived in the house, grand parties were thrown and the gardens were decked out in grand splendor. I even got to attend a party there, when I was about thirteen. Oh, Aribelle, it was unbelievable. For that party," Eleanor's eyes sparkled, "my mother allowed me to buy a new pair of shoes. They were my first heels. Oh, I felt like all eyes were on me the moment I set foot on the shining marble floors of Gray Manor. I remember every door was open to the courtyard in front of the house. In the very middle of the house was an enormous ballroom. Tell me, Aribelle, did you get to see the ballroom while you were there?"

Ari shook her head. "We met Mr. Gray in the library."

Eleanor nodded. "I'm sure the library was just as grand. Severin and Roberta kept up the tradition of inviting friends to lavish parties. That all continued until Roberta and Willow died. Then there were no more parties; Gray Manor was no longer the hub of the social elite. Time passed and generations came and went, erasing memories of Mr. Gray and his estate."

Eleanor sighed. "Such sad stories. Sorry to darken your day, dear."

Ari waved her hands. "It's fine. I just learned more from you than from Mr. Gray himself. It's all helpful. Mr. Gray didn't seem happy to have visitors. He wasn't especially fond of me, I can tell you that."

Eleanor just waved her off. "Pay no mind to Mr. Gray," she encouraged.

Ari shrugged. "It didn't bother me, really. You can't please everyone." With that, Ari got up and excused herself to do the gardening.

The morning was already sweltering, and Ari figured the proximity to the wetlands didn't help things along. It was so humid that even the birds and frogs had gone silent for the day. Ari watered every plant in sight and mowed crisp lines in Eleanor's still-lush lawn. By the time she was finished working for Eleanor, Ari's clothes were soaked in sweat, and her hair no longer stayed in its bun; limp strands of hair stuck to her face and neck.

The ride home was nearly unbearable. The only consolation Ari had as she pushed her bike up the gravel road was the shade provided by the tall trees on either side.

She was thankful that her house was empty and quiet when she got home. Ari considered getting her laptop and trying to find more information on Severin Gray and his family, but her bones ached and fatigue threatened to overtake her. Without even taking a shower, Ari grabbed a book from her room and went to the backyard.

The back deck was far hotter than she had expected it to be. Even the gentle breeze from the porch fans didn't do much to alleviate the heat-seared air. She crossed the formal garden, went through the pasture, now knee-high with dry grass, and crossed through the stately stone pillars. The only place with any possibility of being cool, save the circular pool, would be the underground room.

Ari turned the key and popped the latch to the circle. She dropped into the blissfully cool room, book in hand. In minutes she had just enough candles lit to be able to see the pages, and nothing in the world felt better than leaning back into the softness of the beanbag chair. She hadn't read more than a page when drowsiness tugged at her eyes.

*　　　*　　　*

For a few disorienting seconds, Ari couldn't figure out where she was or *when* she was. Her eyes snapped open; something had pulled her out of a blissfully deep sleep into a state of full, confused awareness. The glittering glass tiles with flecks of gold gleamed in the candlelight, and Ari realized that she'd fallen asleep in the underground room. And sitting in front of her, with his back against the wall, was Dane.

Ari took the opportunity to watch him. He was nose-deep in the book she'd brought and he hadn't noticed yet that she was awake. He wasn't wearing his work clothes anymore; he'd changed into cargo shorts but was shirtless. His profile was perfectly backlit by a candle on the far wall; Ari loved his slightly-curved nose and rounded chin and strong jaw. She watched as his eyes traveled the page in front of him.

"Well, is it a good book?" Ari asked, visibly startling Dane. She started to laugh, and Dane nearly dropped the book in surprise.

"How long have you been awake?" he asked, scoffing at his own jumpiness.

"Long enough to see that you're really enjoying my book. How long have you been down here? What time is it?"

"I got down here about an hour ago. It's four-thirty."

"Holy cow, Dane. I've been asleep for hours. I went to Eleanor's today and it was so stinkin' hot…"

"Still is," Dane mused. "Lucky we have a nice cool room in the ground, huh?"

Suddenly Ari remembered her conversation with Eleanor. Ari sat up straight. "You won't believe what I learned at Eleanor's today! She asked if we'd gone to Woodward to find out about Ezra, and I told her about seeing Severin Gray this morning. She was floored that we were invited to his house, Dane. Sounds like he doesn't entertain many visitors since his wife and daughter—"

"—died?" Dane finished for her. Ari's expression froze.

"I did some research on Mr. Gray after work today. I was able to pull up some articles about his family's accident. Agnes saw what I was reading and told me that Severin's father built Gray Manor—at least, that's what it used to be called—and they were the height of the social elite in the entire area. To be invited to a party at Gray Manor was an instant connection with high society." Dane's voice lowered. "Told you it was a party house."

Dane smirked, but then got serious again. "That's sad about his wife and daughter. It sounds like he became a hermit after they passed."

"That's what Agnes said, too. She was actually surprised that he was still alive. What were the details of the accident?" Ari asked.

"His wife and daughter were coming back home from a friend's house. On the highway, a car crossed the line and Severin's wife and driver of the other car died instantly. The daughter was taken to the hospital in Woodward. Sounds like they thought she would pull through…but she didn't."

"How old was she?"

"Fourteen. There were pictures of the accident. It was pretty bad. And cars back then didn't have airbags and stuff, so…" his voice trailed off. There was a somber pause in conversation.

"You're lucky *you* made it out alive from your accident," Ari said quietly. She watched as Dane's hand subconsciously went to the scar he couldn't quite reach.

"The night after you told me about your accident, I went online and found the article about it," Ari confessed. Dane furrowed his brow and looked straight at her, waiting for her to explain. "The pictures of your own accident were horrible."

"I think the airbags saved my life," he said quietly. "Well, those and the guy who actually pulled me from the car, of course. What made you want to look that up, anyway?"

Ari shifted uncomfortably. For once, it would've been so much easier if Dane wasn't in such close proximity. "I don't know. I guess I wanted to understand better what you've been through…to better understand *you*." Her heart flip-flopped and despite the coolness of the room, she felt her cheeks burn hot at the confession.

A look of softness crossed Dane's face. He reached out and rested his hand on Ari's knee.

"I'm lucky to be here. *Right* here," he gestured at the room. "I've been thinking about everything that's happened in my life up to this very point, Ari. I could've been given up for adoption…but I wasn't. I could've gone to live with another relative, but I didn't. I could've died in that car accident, but I survived. I'm supposed to be here," he repeated again in a whisper. "I guess what I've been trying to figure out is, what comes next?"

Ari held her breath. Dane glanced over at her with a thoughtful look. Her heart increased a measure.

"Mom and I have been talking about colleges. In about a week, we're going to visit the state college in Cascade Grove. It's the closest one to home that has the degrees I'm interested in."

Ari smiled and swallowed hard at the same time. "That's awesome, Dane! I'm excited for you." It wasn't a lie, though Ari had never been so divided between feeling genuinely happy for someone while trying valiantly to hide the sadness that was starting to creep in.

"It only takes two hours to get there, but I think we're planning on staying for about a week. Maybe try and get a feel for what it would be like to live there. We'll be back just in time before school starts."

"Well," Ari said, succeeding at swallowing the lump in her throat, "if we're losing a whole week of what's left of summer, we'd better figure out all of Ezra's story sooner than later."

"Agreed. How about we go down to the Abshire house after dinner tonight?" Dane asked.

"What are we looking for?"

"Nothing. Let's just take a walk."

Ari smiled. "Sounds good to me."

"Meet me at seven in my backyard," Dane said as he helped Ari up out of the circle.

*   *   *

The sun was casting long shadows in the orange light of evening as it slipped just behind the tops of the highest trees. Ari had never traversed the downhill path in the evening, but the sun was beautiful as it wove through the foliage along the trail.

They reached the glasslike pond. Cattails and their darker mirror images lined the water's edge while clouds of flying bugs hovered just above the surface. Ari and Dane followed the trail that hugged the pond's perimeter. Before they knew it, they'd reached the side of the Abshire property.

Upon crossing the front yard, Ari immediately noticed something was different. Even in the dimmer light of the approaching sunset it wasn't hard to see the glittering halo of brown broken glass that surrounded the remains of a beer bottle. A freshly shattered front window had spewed outward a trail of gleaming clear glass. The *No Trespassing* sign had been ripped from the siding and lay shredded next to the open front door.

"Oh no..." Ari breathed. She jumped up to the porch and gently pushed the door all the way open. The house greeted her with a sad stench of old food and spilled beer. Red cups were scattered across the entire first floor; bags of potato chips and crushed beer cans and ashy cigarette butts had been ground into the wood planks.

She turned in a circle. Behind her, the kitchen walls had been spray painted; ugly unintelligible scrawls blackened the once-white surfaces.

"Oh man...someone really trashed this place," Dane whispered behind her.

Ari blinked back tears. She didn't understand why seeing the damage caused her such emotion. *It's just a house*, she thought. *An abandoned house. Just a house.* But then, swallowing the lump in her throat, Ari remembered the upstairs room. Rounding the newel cap, she sprinted upstairs. Ari breathed a sign of relief as she realized the vandals hadn't scarred the second floor. She walked to the room that overlooked Hadley Hill.

Ari put her hand on the doorframe that had the height marks etched in them. Her finger found each line, every initial, every date.

"Dane, throw me your pocket knife," she asked.

The house was so empty that he could've heard her even if she'd spoken in a whisper. She carefully leaned over the railing and Dane tossed his pocketknife up to her.

Ari opened the largest blade and slipped it between the doorframe and the wall. Slow creaks on the stairs announced that Dane was approaching.

"Ari, what are you doing...?"

She carefully ran the blade down the length of the frame, twisting it carefully. With a slight cracking sound, the thin strip separated from the wall.

"I'm taking this with me," she stated. "If people are going to destroy the house, they won't be able to wreck this history. It's important that this comes with us."

Dane wordlessly moved in behind her and stretched to help reach the top of the doorframe. Within seconds, Ari was holding the whole seven-foot strip of wood in her hands.

She went downstairs and out the front door, carefully navigating so as not to catch the frame on anything. She found a patch of sunlight; now every inscription could be seen on the wood: at the top were the initials "J.J.," with several notches becoming interspersed with initials of "E.A.," followed by the lowest height marks bearing the letters "A.A."

"Joseph Junior, Ezra Abshire, Aliza Abshire," Ari mused. "They're all here."

Dane looked up at the sky, which was already darkening. "Anything else you want to save from the house?"

Ari thought back to the ugly spray-painted walls and the trash that littered the home.

"No," she shook her head. "Let's get out of here. I don't want to get caught by either the sheriff or by more people coming to party here."

Dane nodded in agreement as he took one end of the doorframe and headed back to the trail, Ari close behind.

chapter thirty-one

Ari lay on her back porch after she'd returned home from work. It was Friday and the afternoon heat was dispersed only slightly by the ceiling fans above her. She had her eyes closed and she was hoping to take a nap, but the day's awful situations kept running through her head.

Ari's new customer for the day, Albert Winsor, had a deceptively simple yard: a postage-stamp sized lawn without a single plant or bush in sight. Ari had misjudged the plainness of the yard, and by extension, the man who loved its perfect simplicity.

Mr. Winsor had explained to Ari that a professional lawn care service usually tended to his lawn, 'with exacting precision,' he'd added. But due to a scheduling glitch, he'd been left without an appointment, so he decided to give Ari a try.

She'd seen the surprise on his face when he'd opened the door to the small, brown-haired girl. Mr. Winsor had carefully explained Ari's tasks for the day: edge the grass that grew up against the curb, use a trencher to cut a line along said curb, then finish by mowing the lawn.

Ari figured it would be easy, but because of the precise perfection of Mr. Winsor's lawn, every mistake Ari made showed with glaring volume.

She'd shorn part of his lawn too close. She'd cut an edge of his lawn away with the string trimmer. And figuring out exactly how to draw a perfect line along the curb with the trencher was a nightmare. By the end of the appointment, Ari feared what Mr. Winsor would say upon inspection of his once-perfect lawn. His reaction had been far worse than she could've imagined.

When Albert Winsor had seen the far-from-straight line along his curb, Ari noticed his face turn a slight shade of red. She was nearly holding her breath as they rounded the corner of his yard where the scalped patch of grass was. Sure enough, he spotted the mistake.

"Ari, do you know what will happen to this patch of grass now? Do you?" His tone was irritated, and his face was now a decent shade of purplish-red.

Ari just shook her head.

"This grass will die. It will die! Just like that. After that I'll have to reseed it. You're lucky it's on the side of the house and not the front."

She'd felt a lump in her throat, but was determined to swallow it. She wasn't going to let a cranky old man bring her to tears over blades of grass. Still, she knew she'd failed, and it wasn't a comfortable feeling.

Ari opened her eyes and watched the outdoor ceiling fan. She figured the only good thing about the day was that it was Friday, but even that wasn't as encouraging as it should've been. Dane would be leaving the next day with his mom and Lily on their one-week vacation that would include his college visit in Cascade Grove.

There was nothing more Ari wanted to do than go over to Dane's house and see if he was home from work yet, but she didn't want to bother him. Or worse, randomly start crying as she explained her awful day. So she just lay there on the cool porch, waiting for intermittent breezes to weave their way past.

She must've drifted off, because at some point an unusual noise brought her to full awareness. At first, Ari thought it was a train, but it was different than the rumble of a freight train. The noise was stopping and starting, with different pitches. They were engine noises coming from a vehicle, not a locomotive.

Whatever was making the noise, it had to be heavy: just like when a train passed by on the tracks at the base of Hadley Hill, there was a slight vibration that could be more felt than heard.

Ari stood up and walked off the porch, following the noise. It sounded like it was coming from the highway, or the base of their hill, or both.

She walked down her gravel driveway, past the mailboxes, and down the steeply-sloping shady portion of the road. When she reached the railroad tracks, Ari looked left and right. No trains were anywhere in sight, but now she could hear recognizable sounds: diesel engines and the distinctive clinks of heavy machinery treads on gravel.

The highway was devoid of cars. The sounds were coming from the west. Ari walked down the country highway until she reached the crooked mailbox at the Abshire place. That's when she saw it: a large backhoe was parked right in the front yard of the house. A dump truck was next to it. Two workers in hard hats and reflective vests were standing next to the vehicles, chatting over the din of the idling engines.

Ari started to jog along the gravel driveway toward them. One worker pointed at her and the other turned. When she saw them looking at her, she suddenly realized she had no idea what she was doing.

"Hey, you can't be here," one worker hollered.

"What are you guys doing with the machinery?" Ari shouted back, finding her voice.

"House is scheduled to be demolished on Monday. First thing in the morning," the taller worker yelled.

For a moment Ari just stood there, trying to catch her breath. Her stomach flopped and she felt the blood drain from her face. It seemed to startle the workers when she took off at a run through the marshy grasses onto the perimeter path that skirted the lake.

She ran up the trail until she was gasping for air; the path had turned upwards and she knew she was more than halfway to Dane's backyard. Ari could no longer run; she doubled over with a side ache but kept moving until she exited out into Dane's backyard.

Ari circled around to the front of the house. To her relief, Dane's truck was in the driveway. She pounded on the front door, but without waiting for a response, she let herself in.

"Dane?! Are you here?" she yelled up the stairs. Loud music was thumping from the upper floor. "Dane!"

A startled Dane poked his head out of his room. "Ari? What's wrong?"

She once again doubled over, grabbing at her side and wheezing from her uphill sprint.

"The Abshire place. They're tearing it down."

"What?" Dane stared at her, agape.

"Monday morning, the workers said. They start demolition Monday morning! Didn't you hear the machinery? It was shaking the whole hill." She then realized his music was far too loud for anything to be heard, let alone machinery a quarter-mile away. "What do we do?" she asked.

Dane came down and met her on the stairs.

"I don't think there is anything we *can* do, Ari. It's just a broken-down old house." He saw Ari's face fall. "I mean, it's a cool old house, but…" he just shrugged. "Hey, come up to my room. I gotta finish packing. Maybe we can think of something."

He put his arm around Ari's waist, meaning to lead her upstairs, but Ari wouldn't move. She bowed her head and leaned against his chest and closed her eyes. Dane gently put both of his arms around her.

For that brief moment, everything about the day fell away. Ari breathed in the soap-and-cologne smell of Dane's shirt, she listened to his heart beating against her ear, she felt him brush aside her hair as he rested his chin against her neck. It was right here that she realized she couldn't bear to think of him leaving; not for a week, not for college in a year. She suddenly pulled away as she felt her chin start to tremble.

"I've gotta go," she said, turning to head down the stairs. She could feel the pit in her stomach growing, gnawing at her. Dane caught her arm.

"Ari, what's wrong?"

She looked up at him. Words that she wanted to say were hopelessly stuck, jammed by the lump that had grown in her throat. Dane reached out and touched the hair at her temple, tucking it behind her ear.

"I know this is really important to you, Ari. I'll help you figure something out, ok?"

She wanted to smile at him, but his kindness threatened to make tears rush to her eyes. She turned and ran out the door, heading to the brass circle.

*   *   *

Space to think: that's what Ari needed. She didn't understand the sadness she felt about the destruction of some old house that she'd only known about for two months. As for Dane, he'd only be gone a week. They had a whole year ahead of them, and as Dane had said, anything was possible.

Ari picked at the trail that led to the underground room. Before she'd even reached the hatch, her phone vibrated in her pocket. She reached for it and saw a message from an unknown number: *"Check the state's historic site registry online. Find out if it's been approved as a historic home."*

The message startled her. Only Dane knew about the house. She texted back: *"Who is this?"*

Instead of stopping at the underground room, Ari changed her mind and jogged toward her house. She went to her room and opened her laptop. Using a search engine, she found the historic site registry without difficulty. A long form presented itself. She then realized she'd need the address of the Abshire house to access the site's records. Ari opened up a new page and, using an online map, found the address of the homestead. Toggling back to the historic registry, she entered the street address. A long form popped up on the screen.

Ari checked her phone again. There was still no response from the unknown number.

A holler came from downstairs. Mrs. Cartwright was calling for Ari's help. Without reading the form, Ari jogged downstairs.

"Hey!" Ari's mom greeted her. "I really need your help with unloading groceries. Do you have a minute?"

Although she wanted nothing more than to get back upstairs, she ran out to her mom's car and grabbed as many bags as possible.

"Is everything okay, honey?" her mom asked.

"Um, yeah. Well—not really. I just found out the Abshire place is being torn down on Monday. Right before you called me, I was trying to figure out if it's on the historic registry."

"Why?"

Mid-step, Ari stopped. She realized she didn't have a plan, and she didn't know who her mystery informant was who suggested she look up the property owner in the first place. "Uh, I don't know. Hold on, I gotta make a call."

With that, Ari started walking back upstairs and opened up her text messages. She clicked on the number that the message was from.

"Hello?" answered a familiar male voice.

"Dane?" Ari was incredulous. "You got a phone?"

She could hear a mock sigh on the other end. "Yes, I finally did. I figured if I'm going to be gone for a week, I'd better be able to keep up with what's going on." For the first time that day, Ari smiled wide. "Did you find the property on the historic registry?"

Ari had reached her laptop and switched to speakerphone. "Yeah, I have the form up on my screen right now. How will this help us?" Ari asked.

"Agnes once told me if a home is on the historic registry and it's received certain types of federal funding, it would be much more difficult to get permission to demolish it. It's a long shot, but…"

Ari scanned the page. "Let's see…" Ari scrolled down the form and started reading. "It says the home was built in 1900. Architectural style is farmhouse…oh, crap…"

"What?"

"The form says the home was denied for the historic registry because the architectural style 'lacked distinction.'"

"Shoot. Sorry, Ari. I thought it was a long shot, but…" his voice trailed.

"It's ok, Dane." There was a long pause as Ari clicked on another document. "I found the tax information for the property here. Lots of the same information, actually." She scanned through lines and lines of data that was unfamiliar and had no meaning to her. "I'm trying to figure out who the property owner is…"

Suddenly she stared at the screen in disbelief and gasped audibly. "Oh my gosh…" Ari sat down hard in her chair. "Dane, you have to come over here, *now!*"

chapter thirty-two

Ari hadn't taken her eyes off the screen, even as she heard footsteps pounding up the stairs. Dane came flying into her room. Ari pointed at a single line on the screen and shook her head in utter disbelief.

"Look," she whispered.

Dane leaned over her shoulder and read the line on the form. "Property owner, Severin H. Gray."

"What are the chances of that?" Ari was still numb with disbelief.

Dane turned to her and knelt beside the chair. "Why on earth would he be the owner of the Abshire house? This makes no sense...." His voice trailed off.

"You've got two days, Ari. You've gotta call him and figure out how he's the owner and why he's tearing down that house." Suddenly Dane's voice was urgent. "I'm so sorry I won't be here to help you."

Ari hadn't noticed Dane had been carrying something. He reached up and handed her Ezra's journal.

"Here," he said. "I want you to have this now."

He looked up at her. The light from her windows caught the glimmer in his eye. "I somehow know without a doubt that when I get back, that house will still be standing down there. You can do anything, Ari Cartwright."

Her heart started to pound as he rose from his kneeling position. In getting up, he deftly leaned in and kissed her once, ever so gently. She was left surprised and breathless as he turned and left.

*   *   *

It was midnight. Ari was still awake and lying in her window seat. All the lights in her room were off, save a small round porcelain nightlight that cast tiny stars on her wall. Out her window, brilliant stars wavered in the warmth of the summer night. For once, she wished she was sitting on the roof of the house across the treetops. She wondered if Dane was awake. Ari pulled out her phone and typed a message to his number: *Have a good trip. I miss you already.*

She paused before sending it. *What if he was asleep?* She hit send anyway and caught her breath as nervous tingles rushed through her.

Almost immediately, her screen lit up with a reply: *I miss you too, but that's normal whenever we're not together.* Ari exhaled and closed her eyes. She wished more than anything that he wasn't leaving.

*   *   *

The next morning, at ten o'clock on the dot, Ari found Severin Gray's number in her phone. She took a deep breath and dialed. She didn't know what she was going to say; all she was certain of was that she *had* to make that call to Mr. Gray. To her disappointment, a generic message instructed her to leave her name and number.

Ari cleared her throat. "Hello, Mr. Gray, this is Ari Cartwright. I was with Dane when we met at your house the other day." Her mind raced. Her eyes darted to Ezra's journal on her desk, and suddenly she knew exactly what to say: "I need you to know that we found a journal underneath the floorboards of Ezra Abshire's house here in Rivers. He wrote it before he moved to Woodward. I looked up the home on the historic registry, and I know you're the owner. We've heard it's being demolished on Monday. Can we please meet again as soon as possible?" Ari left her number and reluctantly hung up. She knew it was a long shot, but she'd done all she could do.

*   *   *

Saturday came and went without any calls from Mr. Gray. Ari sat at the table eating lunch on Sunday when her mom looked over at her.

"Ok, Ari, you gotta fill me in on what's going on with you. You look so sad. Can I help with something?"

Ari took another bite of sandwich and considered her mom's question. "The guy Dane and I went to see early that one morning happens to be the owner of the Abshire house. What are the chances of that?" Ari mused. She pushed around a piece of toast on her plate.

Ari's dad raised an eyebrow. "Really? That *is* quite the coincidence. Or—maybe not. This is a small area with many families who have been here for generations. If Mr. Gray purchased Ab's Hardware, he may have also bought property from him or his family."

"Good point," Mrs. Cartwright agreed. "Ezra may have thrown in the old house as part of a package deal."

Ari suddenly realized that her mom *would* have to help her.

"Mom," Ari looked straight at her mother from across the table. "We need to take a drive."

*   *   *

"Where exactly are we?" Mrs. Cartwright craned her neck to look at the high forested hill in front of them.

"Somewhere near Woodward. That house up there—," Ari pointed from the driver's seat, "—is where we're going...hopefully."

"That huge house?" her mom's eyes widened.

"That's Gray Manor," Ari explained.

Ari's nerves were causing her stomach to roll and her hands to sweat. She hadn't called Mr. Gray again; he had never returned her call, so going to his estate was her last resort.

The sun was still high in the sky at three o'clock that Sunday afternoon. Ari pulled up to the gate and pushed the call button. With each passing second, Ari's hopes started to fade.

Ari was about to put the car in reverse when the buzzer sounded.

"Yes?" The voice coming through the speaker sounded like the assistant, Mr. Wells.

"I'm Ari Cartwright. I'm here to see Mr.—"

"Come up, please." Before he'd even finished speaking, the gate started rolling open.

Ari started driving the car up the gravel road. Ari's mom hadn't said a word as she took in the scenery around them: the afternoon light cast long shadows along the rows of grapevines until they entered the dark, shadowy portion of the road that was bordered by stately conifers on both sides.

"Can you tell me again about Mr. Gray?" Ari's mom looked over at her. "He's the owner of the Abshire property, and owns a hardware store, right?"

Ari nodded. "Right. We wanted to talk with him the first time because we figured he might know something about Ezra Abshire, which he did. He knew that Ezra and Katia got married, but it sounds like Katia's parents, Nadia and Grekov, weren't pleased with the fact that their daughter married someone who wasn't wealthy. We know that Ezra and Katia had one daughter, Elise. At that point, Mr. Gray stopped talking with us. Mom, I have to warn you that Mr. Gray isn't very personable. He was rather gruff when we met with him."

Ari's mom raised an eyebrow. "Got it." By now, they had been climbing up into the timbers and the road was turning eastward. Sunlight could be seen reaching the tops of the fir trees, whose crowns were pointing to the sky like thin green arrows.

Gray Manor came into view. Ari heard her mom gasp, and Ari couldn't help but give a tiny smile. The southwestern sun was bathing the mansion in orange hues. The water in the fountain was like streaming gold as it caught the reflections of sunlight off the house's windows. The towering trees that formed the backdrop to the house caught the southern light.

Ari parked the car and took Ezra's leather-bound journal gently in her hands. They approached the front door and Ari rung the bell. Her mom looked up at the tall doors and arched ceiling, then down to the massive stone urns that held geraniums and trailing ivy that bordered the outdoor entryway. "This place is amazing, Ari. What does Mr. Gray do besides own a hardware store?"

At that, Ari could only shrug.

The front door opened and Mr. Wells stood inside. "This way, please, ladies."

Mrs. Cartwright and Ari followed the assistant through the entryway to the smaller hallway, and then turned, like before, into the light-filled hallway with tall ceilings and doors disguised as windows. But instead of leading them to the library, he stopped at one of the heavy mahogany doors that ran along the wall to the left.

"Mr. Gray is in his study today. Please follow me."

He opened the door and Ari and her mom stepped into what Ari could only imagine was the ballroom. There simply couldn't be any other use for the vast room with gleaming wood floors. The ceiling ran up to the second floor, with windows bordering a mezzanine level. Giant, flowing drapes framed each towering window. A half-dozen massive crystal chandeliers hung from the ceiling. The chandeliers weren't turned on, but sunlight from the south-facing windows were catching every facet of every crystal, sending an explosion of rainbow-hued circles all around the room. Ari thought quickly and silently snapped a photo with her phone. She smiled to herself as she realized she'd be able to send the photo to Dane.

Mr. Wells walked half the length of the ballroom and stopped at a wood door with a full-length frosted window. He knocked once, then opened the door and motioned for Ari and her mom to enter.

The ladies entered a much smaller room: there were no windows here; it was fairly dark except for a banker's lamp on Mr. Gray's desk, and a floor lamp behind him. Although the room was less decorated than the rest of the house, it still had an aura of grandeur.

Ari immediately recognized the scent that was permeating the small space: although he wasn't at the moment, Ari was certain that Mr. Gray smoked a pipe. The familiar scent of sweet, stale smoke had woven its way into the floors, the books, the walls.

Mr. Gray stood from behind his desk, but did not extend his hand to Ari or her mother. Ari noticed he was wearing the same shabby sweater as before, and it looked like he hadn't shaved in several days. He cleared his throat.

"Mr. Hadley could not join you today?" he asked, then sat back down in his high-backed leather chair.

Ari and her mom sat as well. "He's gone for a week. He and his mom are touring a college." Ari explained simply. Mr. Gray just looked at her, then glanced at Mrs. Cartwright.

"What is it you wish to discuss?" His manner was direct and edged with impatience.

Ari matched his directness. "The Abshire homestead is at the base of our hill, Mr. Gray. I know there are plans to demolish it on Monday. I looked on the historic registry and found that you are the property owner. I'm here to ask you to not destroy the house."

Severin Gray looked at Ari for a moment. He shifted his gaze to Ari's mom, then back to Ari.

"Why?"

Ari pulled out Ezra's journal and held it gently. The leather cover was worn to the point of disintegrating; some areas of the edges had already worn away.

"Because at the beginning of the summer, Dane and I found this journal under the floorboards of the Abshire home. It belonged to Ezra Abshire. It's a historic house, Mr. Gray. What if there are other artifacts in that house, just waiting to be discovered?" Ari's voice was strong, direct.

"Let me see that," Mr. Gray held out his hand. Ari didn't move. Ezra's journal was still clutched in her hands.

"Please don't demolish the Abshire house."

It suddenly dawned on Ari that she was holding a stranger's stolen journal as ransom; leverage for a worthless house owned by an eccentric millionaire, who could at any minute, have them thrown out of his estate. Her heartbeat increased a measure.

Severin narrowed his eyes. Ari held her breath at what was coming next.

"Fine. Agreed. Let me see the journal."

Ari could hardly believe what he had just said.

"Your word?" She held out her hand, waiting for a handshake while looking at him square in his steel-colored eyes. He cocked his head to the side, then extended his hand. Ari took it; it was larger than her own hand but she managed to grip it with firm intensity. A look of admiration suddenly crossed Mr. Gray's face.

"Miss Cartwright, I will make a call to the foreman and have him remove the demolition equipment. Now, the journal please?"

Ari handed him the book. They watched as his eyes scanned the pages. "Explain again where you found this?"

Ari cleared her throat. "Dane and I were looking for a carving that we'd found both at my house and along the trail from his house to the Abshire homestead. We were in the basement when I walked across the floor. My boot hit a hollow-sounding plank. Underneath was this journal. Ezra writes about his father, his family, and about Katia. The journal stops writing right before he moves to Woodward."

"You were looking for a carving?" He stopped skimming and looked at Ari over the top of his bifocals.

"Yes, Dane and I found a symbol carved into a tree and also at the base of one of the stone pillars in my backyard. It the carving was of two hearts with points touching, and a circle around those points."

Mr. Gray stared at Ari for an extended moment, expressionless. He then looked back down at the journal. Several minutes of silence passed as Mr. Gray continued to skim the pages. "May I keep this to read, Miss Cartwright?"

Ari nodded. "Yes, of course. Thank you for agreeing to save the house."

Mr. Gray raised an eyebrow. "And what do you propose that I do with the Abshire home?"

Ari smiled. "The house deserves to have a family in it again, Mr. Gray. It's lonely right now. Fix it up and sell it. Give it life again."

Severin was quiet for a moment. Then he nodded once. "Fine." He looked down at the journal before he could see Ari's wide smile. "Mr. Wells will show you ladies to the door," he said, adjusting his bifocals. "Oh, and Miss Cartwright, when Mr. Hadley returns, please tell him to meet with me. We have something to discuss."

This time it was Ari's turn to raise an eyebrow. "I'll tell him, Mr. Gray."

The two ladies were escorted through the ballroom and out the front door.

Once outside, Ari's mom nudged her and whispered excitedly, "You did it, Aribelle! You just convinced someone to save a house…way to go!"

As they walked to the car, Ari smiled and looked out at the expanse in front of her. The valley was bathed in warm light, highlighting every field and rolling hill, as far as the eye could see. Ari felt like she was on top of the world.

*   *   *

The stars were piercing the night sky as Ari sat in her window seat that night. She sent Dane the photo of the ballroom and a message to call her when he could. Not three minutes later, her phone rang.

"Where did you take that picture?" Dane asked, without even saying hello. She could hear the smile and excitement in his voice.

"Care to guess?" Ari said. She realized how much she'd simply missed talking with him over the past two days.

"I have no idea. I mean, I guess it looks like a ballroom or something—wait, is that Gray Manor?"

"You got it," Ari chuckled.

"You went to Gray Manor…alone?"

"Well, Mom was with me. I called Mr. Gray on Saturday but he never called back. So, Mom and I showed up at his gate this afternoon. I was actually surprised when he let us in. Mr. Gray was in his study this time, which was in a room off to the side of the ballroom. I've never seen anything like that ballroom before, Dane. It was incredible. I wished so badly that you could've been there with me."

"So what happened?" Dane asked impatiently.

"I told him I had a journal written by Ezra. He seemed quite interested in looking at it. He asked to see it, but…I wouldn't let him have it until he agreed to stop demolition on the Abshire house."

"You *what?*" Dane coughed. "Oh my gosh, Ari. You're crazy, in the best possible way." By now Dane was laughing on the other end, and Ari beamed.

"Well, I told him that if the journal was under the floorboards, there might be something else in that house that was important, you know? He seemed to understand. He even asked me what he should do with the house if he's not going to knock it down."

"Are you serious?" Dane had stopped laughing. "What did you say?"

"I told him to fix it up and sell it. Another family deserves to live there…and…he agreed."

"Aribelle Cartwright, you're amazing."

Ari suddenly felt shy. "Thanks, Dane. I just did what I thought was the right thing, you know? Oh…right before we left, Mr. Gray said he wants to see you when you get back."

"Did he say why?"

Ari shook her head. "No. I have a feeling he wouldn't have told me even if I asked…Hey, how has your trip been so far?"

She heard him sigh. "It's ok. We do the first campus tour tomorrow. This is all new territory for me, Ari. It's just different, and I guess I miss being home. I have a feeling this is going to be a long week."

You're telling me, Ari thought.

*   *   *

The next morning was strangely foggy when Ari rolled out of bed. Downstairs, the hustle of her mom and dad getting ready for work, combined with Lily gathering all her things for summer camp, made quite a commotion. The phone rang while Ari was pouring her cereal. She heard her mom answer it in the living room.

"Oh, yes, Mr. Bellamy, I can let her know, she's——"

Ari leapt into the other room and grabbed the phone before her mom could finish. "Mr. Bellamy, it's Ari," she said breathlessly. "What can I do for you?"

"Oh, hi, Ari," he said. She thought Mr. Bellamy didn't sound that old, which was surprising. "I just wanted to call and make an appointment for this week. Can you do Wednesday morning?"

Ari went in and checked the calendar they kept on the fridge. "That will work. Oh, Mr. Bellamy, will you be at the house this time? I have some questions about how you'd like things done."

"Sure, I will. I've actually been at the house while you've been working, but I'm renovating the interior and haven't been able to take a break to come outside. Since Dad died, I've been trying to fix the place up to sell."

Suddenly a thought dawned on Ari. "Was your dad's name Arthur as well?"

"Yeah, Arthur senior. I'm Arthur Bellamy Jr. Why?"

Ari chuckled. "Well, that clears something up. I was told that Arthur Bellamy had passed last year, so I was wondering who was making appointments."

The man on the phone laughed. "Oh, yeah, I guess that might be confusing. Sorry about that."

Ari shook her head and chuckled as she marked off Wednesday on the calendar.

*   *   *

Ari's hands were slick with sweat. Her anxiety started spinning into a million different scenarios. What if her hands literally slipped off the wheel while making a turn? Ari wiped her hands on her jeans one more time. Ari desperately wanted to pass her driver's test the first time, and she knew that hitting something with the car would mean automatic failure. *No hitting anything,* she repeated to herself over and over in her mind, the mantra on an unsettling loop.

The DMV employee was buckling himself into the passenger seat. He was an overweight middle-aged man who breathed noisily as he thumbed through the forms on his clipboard.

"Ah, alright, Miss…uhm, Cartwright, go ahead and let's get started. Back out of the parking spot and exit the lot. We'll take a left here onto the road once you exit." He took an oversized breath and sounded bored before Ari had even started.

She turned onto the road and headed toward downtown Rivers. The DMV employee led Ari through a series of instructions as he guided her around town. They'd made a fifteen-minute loop through Rivers, driven for five minutes on the highway toward Woodward, turned back, and then the instructor told Ari to return to the parking lot at the DMV. From the sound of his voice, she couldn't tell if she'd done well, or if she'd failed…or if he was just bored.

She turned off the ignition off and the instructor handed her a sheet of paper. A large "95" was written in red and circled at the top of the form.

"Congratulations. You passed," he grunted. "Inside, we'll get your picture and then make up your temporary license. Just remember to stop *before* the white line at stop signs. That was the only consistent error I noticed. Good job."

Ari's mom was waiting in the lobby and smiled when she saw Ari.

"You passed! I knew you would!" her mom beamed.

"Got a ninety-five. How did you know I passed?"

"I could see it on your face. It's kind of the same look you have whenever you're around Dane." Her mom winked, but Ari just blushed.

*   *   *

The rest of the week passed slower than just about any frame of time Ari had ever experienced. Although work was steady, with an appointment nearly every day, the moments she looked forward to the most was the time in the evening when Dane would call her each night. Sitting in her window seat, looking at the night sky, Ari would listen as Dane talked about his vacation and about the college he was visiting. In turn Ari would tell him about her work. On Wednesday night, she told him the story of the Bellamy house and how it had actually been Arthur Jr. making appointments, not the deceased Arthur Sr. Ari had finally met the younger Bellamy that day, and was thankful she would no longer have to wonder about the noises coming from inside the house. She'd loved the sound of Dane's laugh over the phone when Ari explained that it had indeed not been a ghost inside the large Italianate house.

Friday finally arrived. The evening sun was just beginning to hide behind the trees and Ari's parents were busy in the formal gardens setting up for an evening party they were hosting. They'd put up as many tables as could fit in the backyard; lit candles were on every surface. Ari had helped her mom string white lights around each tree and shrub that they could reach, and the garden glowed and twinkled when they were finished. The formal garden had an almost dreamy atmosphere and Ari wished more than anything Dane could be there.

Friends of Mr. and Mrs. Cartwright were starting to arrive on the hill; the driveway and road were clogged with the cars of guests. Ari stood on the front porch and directed people where to park and how to get to the backyard. It was the first party her parents had thrown at their house, and Ari loved the fact that people were filling the garden and appreciating its beauty.

After a half hour of guests arriving, there was a lull. Ari sat in the porch swing and leaned back, listening to the soothing chorus of crickets. Pipe smoke intermittently wove through the air and Ari smiled as she heard conversation and laughter coming from the backyard. A sound of footsteps crunching on the gravel road caused her to rise to her feet; she prepared herself to guide the next set of guests to the backyard.

The figure walking toward her was alone and coming from up the driveway. As he stepped into the light from the porch, he started jogging toward where Ari was standing. Ari held her breath as a smile crossed her face.

Dane leapt up to her, taking the steps three at a time, and scooped her up in the strongest hug she'd ever had. Her feet dangled as he lifted her completely off the ground and buried his chin against her neck. Ari smiled and hung on to him, feeling his breath on her neck and his hands holding her back. She'd forgotten how ridiculously strong he was as he held her and wouldn't let go. Not that she minded; she breathed in and filled her lungs with his scent memorized in her heart exactly how it felt at that moment to be securely in his arms.

Only after minutes passed did Dane back up enough to look at Ari. Neither of them had spoken a word. Dane took her face in his hand and looked at her at eye level.

"I missed you *so* much, Ari," he said quietly. "That was the longest week ever."

She smiled and agreed, taking his hand and pulling him to the porch swing. He put his arms around her and pulled her in next to him, resting his chin on her head. She put an arm behind his back and a hand on his chest; she could feel his heartbeat through his shirt.

"Did your parents throw me a party?" Dane whispered and Ari chuckled.

"You should see the backyard. Mom and Dad invited friends over for dessert, and we strung white lights everywhere; it's beautiful. Although…it's pretty nice right here, too," Ari said, and she snuggled in closer to him. After a week of feeling like something was missing, Ari realized that incomplete feeling was gone. Everything, at this moment, was perfect.

*   *   *

Ari had been deep in a dream when something pulled her from the visions that had been playing in her head. Someone was gently touching her face. She opened her eyes to see Dane, leaning down at eye-level to her. It was morning, and Ari's room was filled with sunlight.

Dane whispered something to her as she struggled to wake up. She thought he had said something about Mr. Gray wanting to meet them again. But in her half-asleep state, she hadn't quite understood what Dane had been talking about.

"What? What's happening?" Ari rubbed at her eyes.

"Mr. Gray wants to meet us tonight." Dane smiled at the sight of Ari's sleepy demeanor.

"What time?" Ari asked.

"Nine p.m."

"What time is it now?" Ari squinted at the clock next to her bed, which had been blinking 12:00 for days now.

"Ten a.m." Dane was kneeling next to her bed.

Ari sat up and rubbed her eyes again. Her hands automatically went to her hair, and she tried smoothing the wild, knotted strands that were sticking straight up. She saw a glint of amusement pass over Dane's face.

"You could've texted me?" she asked, arranging her hair.

"And not get to see Bedhead Ari? No way," he joked. Ari snorted in laughter.

"Now that I'm home, it goes back to the way it used to be. If I have something to tell you, I'll say it in person. Plus, as I came through the kitchen, your parents handed this to me." He held up a mug of steaming hot coffee. "I guess it was meant for you, but…" He took a sip.

"Hey!" Ari said, and Dane chuckled and handed her the mug.

Ari looked at him and his hazel-eyed gaze. The diffuse light in her room was showing every fleck of brown against the green in his eyes. She was so thankful he was back that for a moment she couldn't even think of words to say; she just took the opportunity to stare at him, which seemed to be ok with Dane. His hair looked like he'd just woken up, and the t-shirt he was wearing was slightly wrinkled.

"Nine p.m., you said? Are you sure? What's up with Mr. Gray and his crazy schedule? Can't he have meetings at normal times?"

"Something tells me he's not exactly a normal person," Dane said, and he perched himself on Ari's bed.

"Did he say what he wanted to see you about? Are you sure I'm supposed to come too?" Ari took a sip of coffee and cleared her throat of morning hoarseness.

"Yes, he specifically asked for you to come as well, but no, he didn't say what he wants to see us about. It's a mystery," Dane shrugged.

*   *   *

Dane's truck rounded the corner on Kendall Heights Drive. The large ridgeline that Gray Manor sat atop loomed in front of them in the darkness of night, and the only indication of a house above were some soft lights that illuminated a row of second-story windows.

Once stopped at the gate, Ari realized that the days were getting shorter, and darkness was coming earlier each day. The gate rolled open after being buzzed in, and Dane started up the gravel drive. Once they entered the corridor of tall trees, blackness surrounded them, and they could only see as far as the headlights allowed.

"This is kind of spooky," Ari said quietly.

A sudden flash of movement caused Ari to startle. Dane braked quickly and came to a complete stop. Two deer appeared directly in front of them, picking their way across the road. In the middle of the road, both animals paused. One flicked its ears and stared at the truck; the other stood stock-still like a statue.

"Look at that," Dane whispered.

They both watched as the deer both moved at the same time, collectively leaping up with delicate strides, until they'd disappeared up into the thicket of tree trunks.

Dane continued driving; Ari leaned forward and looked up as far as she could. Above the treetop silhouettes, the stars shone with a brightness that Ari had never seen before.

"Stop for a second." Ari put a hand on Dane's arm.

Dane stopped the truck.

"Look up," Ari said, and they both craned their necks forward. The stars were no longer individual pinpoints of light, but a vast textured band. Dane turned off the headlights and their eyes adjusted to the new level of darkness, and the intensity of the sky above.

"That's amazing," Dane said. "This is what the stars used to look like at the Lawton house. Every summer night, the band of the Milky Way stretched from the north to south, just like this."

Dane turned the headlights back on, and they made the final eastward turn that led them to the driveway. The conifers that surrounded them fell away and Gray Manor came into view.

Ari hadn't noticed the groups of aspen trees that were placed around the property. They were all illuminated at the base with warm-hued floodlights, their stark white trunks standing like sentinels in the night. The fountain was lit as well, both from underneath and within the pool of water at the base. The enormous porch light was on and the entire row of second-story windows had a soft light emanating from within.

As they approached the house, Ari craned her neck upward and looked at the towering fir trees that stood at twice the height of the house: they were pitch-black silhouettes against the azure blue night sky. Dane rang the doorbell and they both heard its melodious tone resonate from somewhere within the house. A slightly tired-looking Mr. Wells appeared at the door.

"Good evening. Mr. Gray will see you in his study. Please follow me."

His shoes clicked along the marble tiles as he led them to the hallway with the row of mahogany doors. Ari was excited that Dane would get to see the ballroom; however as Mr. Wells opened the door, even Ari was taken aback.

Every crystal chandelier was turned on to a soft glow and the floors reflected a golden hue. Ari stopped short and Dane couldn't help but trip into her. Although the ballroom was empty and silent, Ari could only imagine strains of music swelling through the air. The room echoed with parties of decades past, just like how Eleanor had described them. Ari wondered when the floor had last seen dancers; she could almost feel the music that resonated through the polished wood floors.

Dane had followed Mr. Wells and was now looking back at Ari, who was still standing in the doorway. Mr. Wells' knock on the frosted-glass door brought Ari out of her reverie, and she walked quickly to catch up.

Mr. Wells had opened the office door slightly, but nodded once and closed it.

"Mr. Gray is presently on the phone. You two may wait here until he's ready to see you," he said, adding, "Mr. Gray conducts most of his business internationally these days. It makes for some interesting hours." With that, he nodded at Dane and Ari and left through another door that exited to the windowed hallway.

As soon as his footsteps had disappeared somewhere into the house, Dane leaned over and whispered, "that would explain Mr. Gray's odd schedule."

Ari nodded, still looking up at the awe-inspiring ballroom. "It does make sense."

Dane followed her gaze to the massively large chandeliers, to the columns that lifted to the ceiling, and the ornate second floor railing that ran the length of the mezzanine level. They'd been waiting for about two minutes when Dane held out his hand to Ari.

"Care to dance?" he whispered.

Ari's eyes widened, but a bemused look crossed her face. "Now?"

"Why not?" Dane took her hand and she followed him to the center of the room. Being in the middle of such a space was incredible. Ari could hardly believe that Dane would dare do this, but as soon as he slipped his hand behind her back and started leading her around in an easy waltz, she fell into the rhythm of every step he made. It wasn't hard to remember the basic step they'd learned at the Last Dance, especially with Dane leading her. She wished with every fiber of her being that music could fill the magnificent room; as it was, only their footsteps were heard across the entire space. For a brief moment, Ari closed her eyes as Dane led her in a wide circle across the glowing floor.

The sound of someone clearing their throat caused them both to freeze. Mr. Gray was chewing on a pipe out the side of his mouth and standing in the doorway of his office. Ari sheepishly backed away from Dane; they both immediately walked over to Mr. Gray. Their footsteps echoed across the great room.

"Mr. Hadley," he addressed Dane, motioning to the chairs at his desk. Mr. Gray held out his hand to Dane, then looking at Ari, he held out his hand to her as well in a firm shake.

They all sat. Mr. Gray folded his hands in front of him. "Mr. Hadley, Aribelle informed me that you were away visiting a college, is this correct?," he stated. His voice was a bit hoarse and he cleared it, then took a puff on his pipe. Ari smiled slightly at the familiar smell; the only thing that was missing in his office was jazz, she concluded.

"Yes, Mr. Gray. I was in Cascade Grove checking out the state college there."

"What degree are you seeking?"

"I'm thinking about a degree in history, sir."

Mr. Gray nodded. "And what are you hoping to do with that degree, Mr. Hadley?"

"I would like to work at a museum and help others with research, I think. Right now I work at the Rivers Historic Museum, helping catalog the archives."

Severin Gray looked over his bifocals at Dane. "My alma mater is Apperson University in Idaho, Mr. Hadley. The knowledge I gained from attending that college started me on the journey to becoming the businessman I am today. If you chose to attend Apperson, I would be willing to pay your full tuition, Mr. Hadley."

Ari saw Dane's eyes widen. For a moment he was speechless.

"Thank you, Mr. Gray. I...I will definitely consider it. But...why would you do that for me? We just met a few weeks ago." Dane was clearly stunned; Ari could hear it in his voice. At the same time, Ari was just as stunned as Dane, but also the tiny pit in her stomach started to grow. *Idaho.* An entire state away, not just a mere two-hour drive.

Mr. Gray slowly turned in his chair and reached for a wooden box that was on the bookshelf behind him. Ari hadn't noticed it before; it had blended in perfectly with the books and heavy wooden panels and everything else that was old and wooden in the room.

As Mr. Gray lifted the lid to the box, Ari gasped and put her hand on Dane's arm. On the lid was a very familiar carving.

chapter thirty-three

"It's the same symbol we found," Ari whispered, and Dane's mouth dropped open. Mr. Gray saw their reaction.

"I take it you have seen this symbol before," he said. "This box belonged to my grandmother, God rest her soul." From the box Mr. Gray handed Dane a black-and-white photograph. In the picture, a man dressed in work clothes and suspenders stood next to a statuesque lady who was holding a baby. The lady had a striking, familiar mischievous grin that turned up at one side.

"Katia," Dane and Ari said at once. Mr. Gray nodded.

"Katia was your grandmother, and Ezra was your grandfather..." Ari suddenly realized the implications of this.

Dane sat up straight in his chair. An expression that Ari had never seen was frozen on Dane's face. "If Katia was your grandmother, that means Nadia was your great-grandmother, making us..." Dane was calculating what the correct connection would be, but Mr. Gray beat him to it:

"Family." Mr. Gray leaned forward in his desk chair, resting his elbows on the table. "Mr. Hadley, I have no family. My parents only had one child, and my wife and daughter are no longer on this earth. So, you see, if I offer you a chance at a full tuition, it is in the hopes that I can help along a younger generation of our family, even if the connection is distant.

"I have read all of Ezra's journal. I owe a debt of gratitude to you and Miss Cartwright for bringing the journal to me. Now I know better the early life of my grandparents. All I remember of Ezra and Katia were the years I spent as a young boy with them in their happy home outside of Woodward. Now I have their history—at least, some of it. I would love to know what happened those two years they were apart, but I have to be satisfied with what you have brought me."

Ari pointed at the box. "Do you know what the carving means? And why it would be in two places on our hill?"

Mr. Gray shook his head sadly. "All I know is that this was my grandmother's treasured box. She kept all her favorite photos and other small mementos. I had no knowledge of other carvings. It's as much a mystery to me as it is to you."

"Do you know if Ezra's dad survived his illness?" Dane chimed in. Again, Mr. Gray sadly shook his head.

"I don't remember my grandfather saying much about his own father. Again, another unknown."

Mr. Gray looked at his watch. "It's getting late," he said. "Mr. Hadley, please let me know if you wish for me to arrange a visit to Apperson."

Dane stood and shook Mr. Gray's hand once more. "I will."

They turned to exit through the ballroom. Ari couldn't help but stare at the exquisite room they were walking through. When they arrived at the front door, Ari turned to Mr. Wells.

"When was the last time the ballroom was used?" she asked the assistant.

"It has never been used since I have been employed here, miss. I have been here nearly twenty years."

Ari thanked him, and they headed out to Dane's truck. Before turning the key in the ignition, Dane sat and stared straight ahead, expressionless.

Ari put her hand on his shoulder. "Everything ok?" she asked.

Dane still looked straight ahead. "Yeah." He still hadn't started the truck, but looked ahead at the manor.

"It's just that I feel like I have some pretty big decisions coming up. This is all a little overwhelming, you know?"

The pit in Ari's stomach grew, twisted. She nodded.

"I know."

*　　*　　*

The days of summer ripened and hints of fall began working their way into the late days of August: shorter days brought quicker nights that no longer had the heady smell of sun-heated grasses. The crisp scents of fall began in the cooler mornings; Ari lamented that her treasured days of summer were coming to an end. To make matters worse, school was scheduled to start one week earlier than usual.

On the first day of school, Ari was missing the freedom of summer, although starting her days with Dane each morning wasn't such a bad thing.

"Are you ready for your junior year?" Dane asked as Ari got into his truck. She smiled, thinking this was much better than riding their bikes in the cool morning air.

"Are *you* ready for your senior year?" she fired back.

He shrugged with his usual nonchalance.

Ari noticed Dane was wearing new clothes; he'd decided on a black long-sleeved ribbed shirt with a warm gray field jacket, and his black beanie was pulled low over his brow.

"People aren't going to recognize you, Dane Hadley."

He grinned and looked over at her, his hazel eyes shaded by his hat. She took another mental photo of him just as he was, sitting there in the driver's seat, one hand on the shifter.

They reached the base of their hill. Heavy equipment was lumbering down the usually-empty highway. A roofing truck turned at the Abshire mailbox.

"Hey, I bet they're starting to fix up the place," Dane said, looking at Ari. "You did a good thing, Ari."

*   *   *

The first week of school passed by in a blur: Riley had once again ended up in a science class with Ari; this time it was chemistry. Amara and Rob were in history with Ari, and to her delight, Dane shared a Spanish class with her.

Ari continued to meet with Eleanor on Fridays after school, and on some Saturday mornings she worked for Mr. Bellamy. September's weather was usually beautiful, with misty cool mornings that turned to blazing heat by four p.m. As long as the rainy weather held off, there was yardwork to be done. Besides, Ari was starting to look forward to having tea with Eleanor and hearing her stories about Rivers before Ari started her work.

Agnes had requested that Dane continue to work at the museum two afternoons a week. Julia and the other summer employee had completed their internships, but Agnes took notice of Dane's interest in history. Dane had made such progress in cataloging the archived photos that Agnes had recommended to the board of directors that they keep him.

On days that Ari didn't have yard work and Dane didn't go to the museum, they would meet at Cinema Coffee with Riley and Jace to do homework. Sometimes Amara and Aaron would stop by; everyone would scoot over to make room as they squished into the old booths.

It was on one of those afternoons at the coffee shop when Aaron looked over the screen of his laptop and motioned to Jace.

"Hey, you like photographing old buildings, right?" he asked. Amara looked over his shoulder at the screen.

"Yeah," Jace said, glancing up from his textbook.

"Have you ever been to the old radio station on the way to Allendale?" Aaron swiveled the laptop around so Jace and Riley could see. Ari and Dane were on the far end of the booth; they leaned over everyone and strained to get a look at the photo on Aaron's screen.

"No, I've never even heard of it." Jace pulled the computer closer and scrolled through the image search. "Are you sure it still exists? All of these photos look pretty old."

Ari had to agree with Jace; every photo on the internet was in black and white and showed the radio station while it was still in use.

"Sure does. You have to know exactly where to look, though," Aaron said with a sly smile.

"Ever been inside?" Jace asked. Even Ari could hear the excitement in his voice.

Aaron shook his head. "Nah."

"But I bet it wouldn't hurt to try," Riley said, sounding almost as excited as Jace looked.

"I'm not doing anything Friday night," Jace said, raising an eyebrow. "Who's in?"

*   *   *

The sun hadn't quite yet set on the horizon as Jace's van sped down the highway to Allendale. The afternoon had been warm, but as the sun dropped closer to the horizon, the day's heat drained away and chill air swirled through Riley's open window.

Dane sidled next to Ari in the back row. He'd brought his backpack and water bottle, and he was wearing the same excited grin as when they'd gone to the Air Force station in Allendale. His jacket carried the faint smell of laundry detergent and cool-scented cologne that Ari had become so accustomed to. His hair, which had grown out a little, was slightly damp and perfectly mussed.

"Looking forward to this?" Ari whispered as she looked up at him.

"Well, yeah. You?"

Ari smiled. "It's been awhile since we've gone exploring somewhere new. I'm actually really excited to see this old radio station."

Dane's eyes reflected the waning light of the setting sun. "I miss summer," he quipped randomly as he looked out the van window. By now, fields were skimming by along the lonely stretch of highway. She turned toward him so she could better see his eyes, though he was looking away.

"What do you miss about it?"

Dane looked over at her and leaned in close.

"I miss the freedom," Dane said. So quiet that no one else could hear, he added, "it seems like we don't get to spend as much time together during the school year. It's just so much busier now." He shrugged, looking straight at Ari, and held her there with his gaze.

"What do you want to do to change that?" Ari said with a grin, nudging him.

Dane smiled back and was about to say something when Aaron's voice caught their attention.

"Over there," Aaron called as he pointed at a row of tall trees that ran perpendicular to the highway. "There's a road behind those trees, and the old radio station is at the very end."

Ari noticed an old white-and-red striped radio tower in the middle of a field, silhouetted against the evening sun. Guy-wires tethered the old tower on all sides.

"Best place to park?" Jace asked.

"I'm not sure," Aaron said. "I've never actually driven up to it," he admitted.

Jace reached the gravel driveway and turned onto the road. Ari figured the row of trees would help hide their vehicle; Jace must've figured the same thing as he pulled the van to the side of the building where it was almost completely concealed by a large tree.

Everyone piled out of the minivan. Ari stopped and backed up slightly so she could see the whole building. Though small, the radio station was impressively built, with subtle Art Deco details on its stucco walls. Chunks of stucco had fallen away, leaving the walls with a rough texture, interrupted by hairline cracks and areas of peeling paint. Barely-noticeable neon tubes above the front door spelled out *KOAC*. A short concrete staircase led the way to the single, glass-paned front door.

"Do you think we should try the front door?" Amara whispered.

"Can't hurt," Dane mused.

"Unless it's alarmed," Jace countered. "Guys, look for any signs of electricity or sensors," he directed.

Ari went to the front door and peeked through the window. Though the building was dark inside, she could make out panels of dials and buttons that ran the entire length of the front lobby area. An old schoolhouse clock was centered above the panels, frozen in time at 2:10. No lights appeared anywhere inside.

"I don't see anything in here," Ari said to Jace, who was looking in another front window that was far to the left side of the building.

"No lights in this little room either. Looks like an office or something," he said.

"Good to go, then?" Ari asked. Her hand rested on the old brass handle.

"Yeah, try and open it," Jace answered.

Ari tugged on the door. To her complete surprise, the heavy door opened. She heard Riley and Amara gasp behind her.

"That was easy," Riley remarked.

They all quietly filed into the building. The first room was an open space, much like a lobby; the control panel on the back wall gave it a very industrial feel. Old composite floor tiles were arranged in a subtle checkerboard pattern under their feet.

Shelves of items lined the other walls: old radio parts, microphones, clocks, and instruments that Ari had never seen and had no idea of their purpose. The room smelled like an old library; musty with a slight scent of dirt. Ari walked around the room with her phone flashlight on; she could see wires that were wrapped in haphazard coils; glass tubes were lined up in a box, even a stately old phonograph rested in one corner of the room.

"I bet nothing has been touched in here for decades," Riley whispered. "It's like we've stepped back in time."

"It's kind of beautiful, isn't it?" Ari mused to nobody in particular. She ran her finger along a vintage microphone that was sitting atop a filing cabinet.

"I'm shocked this stuff hasn't been stolen," Dane said. "Especially with the front door being unlocked like it was. How has this place escaped vandalism?"

Jace had made his way around the room, snapping photos of every single item he could find. He was rushing to get every aspect of the building recorded before evening light turned to night; the sun had dipped below the horizon and only a dusky orange glow lit the inside of the building.

"To be honest, it makes me a little nervous," Jace admitted.

"What does?" Aaron asked.

"That the door was open but everything is untouched. It kind of makes me wonder if the door was unlocked recently."

"Hey! Guys! Look at this!" Riley called from inside a room to the right of the lobby. Everyone gathered in the doorway.

"It's an...apartment, maybe?" Riley pointed at an old, fifties-style fridge in what looked to be a kitchen area. A sink, tiny countertop, and two cabinets were crammed into the corner of a much larger room. On the other half of the space, between two small side windows, stood an old bed frame.

"Did someone live here when it was a radio station?" Ari asked.

"Probably," Jace figured. "I'm sure they had a person on site at all times…maybe. Dane, have you ever seen anything at the museum about this place?"

Dane thought for a minute. "To be honest, I don't think so. I'll keep an eye out from now on, though," he promised. "If you came in after school, I could always help you start a search."

Jace nodded and started to say something, but instead of talking, he cocked his head to the side, listening.

"What?" Riley whispered, and Jace held up a finger to his lips.

"Did you hear something?" Jace hissed and pointed toward the back of the building. The group followed him as he crossed the main lobby and headed into a short hallway. From a landing at the end of the hall, they could see a staircase that doubled back under the lobby. It ended in a closed door on what Ari figured must be the basement level.

Suddenly Ari heard noises behind that door: male voices, then a tremendous thud. Everyone in Ari's group froze in place. Her eyes went wide and she looked at Dane; his head was tilted, listening.

"Let's go!" Amara started moving toward the front door, but Dane held out his hand.

"Wait," he hissed.

Jace raised an eyebrow. Dane quietly walked across the lobby and into the office, where he was able to glance out a window that overlooked the back of the building and the tall antenna that stood alone in the field.

"Down there," Dane pointed. Ari sidled up beside him to see what he was looking at. Exiting out of a basement door, three guys could be seen hauling items to a truck. Ari could tell the group was doing their best to be as stealthy as possible but were failing miserably at it. One guy dropped an old-fashioned speaker on the ground and it broke into brittle pieces.

Even through the window, the group could hear their conversation: one of the guys swore at the one who dropped the speaker.

"I told you to be careful with this stuff, you idiot! No pawn shop is going to buy broken speakers!"

"I *said* I was sorry."

The yelling guy turned around and Ari gasped. She recognized the face instantly.

"It's Pat McCleary," she groaned. "Are they stealing stuff from the basement?"

She felt Jace huff next to her. "They can't do that," he growled. Dane nodded in agreement and he and Jace started moving for the front door.

"What are you guys doing?" Ari had to quickly move aside so she wouldn't get trampled by the boys as they strode for the door.

"Jace, where are you going?" Riley jogged after them and the rest of the group followed, exiting the building. Jace and Dane had already reached Pat and his friends by the time the rest of the group had caught up.

The look on Pat's face was one of surprise and annoyance. His two friends momentarily stopped loading audio equipment into the back of Pat's truck.

"Are you guys stealing that stuff?" Jace asked, incredulous.

"It ain't stealin' if nobody don't want it no more, now is it, Jacey?"

Even in the dark, Ari could see Dane bristle. "You can't just take stuff from here, McCleary," Dane said. "These speakers, that microphone—they're part of the history of this place. It doesn't matter if nobody wants them. They belong here."

"Naw, Hadley, you just want 'em for your museum. Lock 'em up where nobody can use them, just look at 'em from behind glass. No, sir, we're gonna get some cash for these bad boys."

Ari could see Pat was finished with the conversation as he turned back to the stack of speakers and equipment they'd piled next to the truck.

"No, McCleary, put the stuff back," Dane raised his voice a tick. Decade-old wounds inflicted by Pat McCleary were boiling just under the surface.

"Or what?" Pat snorted. Ari saw Dane's arms tension and flex with every word that Pat spoke. "By the way, we didn't see you two at that old house at the base of your hill when we threw a party there awhile ago. I've heard you and your girl like to go there—" Dane took a step toward Pat, but it was Ari who cut Pat off.

"It was you guys who wrecked the Abshire house?" Ari could barely speak. She stood there, her mouth agape.

"Yeah, what of it? It's just a broken down ol' house that was perfect for having a kegger," Pat shrugged, then loaded another speaker into the bed of the truck.

Dane swore at Pat, and Pat stopped what he was doing.

"What's your deal, Hadley? Mad that I trashed your makeout spot?"

Dane tensed, and Ari immediately thought he was going to hit Pat. Instead, he held out his hand to Ari.

"Give me your phone."

Ari tilted her head to the side, wondering what he was doing.

"Uh, ok ..." she handed Dane her phone, and she noticed he took it without even glancing at her.

"What are ya doin'?" Pat hissed.

"Calling the cops. You guys can't take this stuff."

348

"And you're all trespassing! You'll get in just as much trouble, idiot!" one of Pat's friends hollered from the bed of the truck.

Ari was standing to the left of Dane. She studied Dane's face: his jaw was set hard and his eyes were fire; he was staring Pat down with such intensity the air was almost hot between them. She watched Dane's chest rise and fall with every hard breath; she could nearly see his heart beating in the veins in his neck. Without saying a word, he looked down at the phone and began dialing.

With a swift swat, Pat hit Dane's hand and Ari's phone went flying into the grass. As if in slow motion, Ari saw Dane's hand ball into a fist, and his muscled arm swung hard at Pat's head. Ari heard Riley yelp from somewhere behind; Pat immediately dodged and returned the punch. Ari saw Pat's fist connect with Dane's face. Dane stumbled backwards, caught off-balance. A white-hot flash of fury ripped through Ari; before she could stop herself, Ari lunged at them both, lodging herself between the fighting boys.

Suddenly Ari felt a sharp pain on the side of her face; Dane's fist had connected with her head as she'd jumped between him and Pat. With stunning force she was propelled to the grassy ground. Her hands went to her face, trying to cover the pain in her cheek. As Ari lay on the ground, all she could hear over the buzzing in her ears was Pat's surprised gasp and Dane's panicked voice, calling her name.

chapter thirty-four

"Ari? Oh my gosh...oh, Ari..." Dane dropped to the ground next to her.

She hadn't been knocked out, but Ari's vision was fuzzy and the pain in her cheek seared through her skull. She kept a hand over the painful spot. Tears welled in her eyes and she held her breath to hold off crying.

"Is she ok?" Riley's voice broke through the scuffle around Ari.

"She's gonna some need ice," Aaron looked down on Ari, who was still laying crumpled on the ground.

"Way to go, Dane," one of Pat's friends smirked.

Dane's hands went to Ari's head; he was holding the side of her face that hadn't gotten punched.

"Ari? Can you stand up? Let's get you back to the van." Ari's hearing was still buzzy in one ear but she could still recognize the panic rising in Dane's voice.

Still holding her head, Dane supported Ari as she tried to stand. The pain in her face intensified and she felt warm tears stream down her face. She tried wiping at them with her free hand, but it was too late. Dane had seen the tears fall; he shook his head and a look crossed his face that Ari couldn't categorize. *Fear?*

The pain in her face started to lessen after Dane helped her into the van; she lay down across the seat and closed her eyes.

"Ari, I am *so* sorry. That was so stupid of me to start fighting with Pat...again. I am so, *so* sorry," he repeated. "Are you ok? Please say something?" Dane got in and Ari rested her head on his lap.

The van started and Jace headed back toward Rivers. Dane put his hand on the top of Ari's head; she closed her eyes and tried to focus on anything but the pain. He gently ran his hand along her hair, smoothing it slowly, being careful to not touch the side where he'd hit her.

Ari opened her eyes. Dane was looking out the window, his hand on his forehead. His face was a mixture of concern and fear, and as she looked at his eyes, she noticed thin lines of water rimming the edges.

"Hey, I'm fine," she said quietly, and Dane looked down at her. Ari reached up and touched his face, her thumb brushing at the edge of his eye. He closed his eyes and exhaled, then wiped at his eyes with the heel of his hand.

"I can't believe I did that, Ari. It's already starting to bruise." Dane said.

Ari sat up and noticed they were halfway to Rivers. Riley, riding shotgun, looked back in the rearview mirror.

"Are you ok, hon?"

"Yeah, I will be," Ari assured her.

Motioning to Jace, Riley pointed at a convenience store in the distance. "Stop up there; let's get some ice for Ari."

Jace pulled into the parking lot, and Dane got out of the car with Riley. They returned a few minutes later; Dane had a half-gallon of ice cream in his hand.

"Um, here…" Dane handed her cold carton as he sat next to her; she put it on the side of her face. "Sorry about the ice cream. It was really the only thing they had that would work," he said.

Ari shrugged. "I'm really ok, Dane. But you have a strong right hook, that's for sure," Ari tried to joke, but Dane couldn't laugh. In fact, the closer they got to Rivers, the more agitated he seemed.

Finally, Ari removed the carton from her head and took Dane's hand with her own, ice-cold hand.

"Hey, what's wrong? It was an *accident*, Dane. It's not like you meant to hit me. I got in the way."

Dane leaned in and shook his head. "It doesn't matter, Ari. I hurt you. What are you going to tell your parents? They're never going to let you do anything with me if this is what happens…"

Ari shrugged. "I'll just say I bumped into something during our exploring."

"Don't lie to them for me."

"Dane, you're usually the one telling me not to worry. This time—" Ari took the carton and placed it on the side of Dane's head; the spot where Pat had punched him was also turning shades of blue and purple "—I'm telling *you* not to worry."

Dane placed his hand over Ari's as she held ice cream to his face. The pain in her own head was lessening; the buzz in her ears had finally stopped.

"Ari, I'm gonna drop you two off first, ok?" Jace called back from the driver's seat. Instead of heading into downtown Rivers, as Jace usually did to drop Riley off, he headed out the old west highway and up Hadley Hill.

Dane got out with Ari at her house. He held his hand out for her to take as she climbed out of the van. Riley and Amara called goodbye.

"Hey!" Riley called from the passenger seat. "Don't forget this." Riley tossed Ari her phone. "I grabbed it before we left."

"Good thinking, Riley. Thank you."

The chill air bit at Ari's skin; she rubbed her arms for warmth and Dane put his arm around her shoulders. They waved at the van as it pulled away; the sound of crunching tires on gravel disappeared into the night.

The porch light was off at Ari's house; the stars above were crisp and clear in the cold night. Dane turned to Ari and squinted as he tried to see the bruise on the side of her face. Even in the darkness that obscured his features, Ari could sense Dane was nervous. He kept glancing at her darkened house, then back at her bruise.

Ari remembered something he'd said in the van.

"Hey, do you want to do something tomorrow? Just…hang out? You said earlier you felt like we haven't been able to spend as much time together as during the summer…you know…but, I mean, we don't have to…" Ari stammered. She could see Dane didn't look any less uncomfortable as he started to shake his head.

"Do you really think your parents will allow you to still hang out with me, Ari? After they find out what happened?" Dane shook his head, almost sounding angry—or fearful. "Your dad has only had one request of me, ever: keep you safe. I failed him—and you—miserably tonight. If I could've kept my temper in check, this wouldn't have happened…" Dane growled as he started to walk up the driveway. "I'm just like my dad," Ari heard him mutter under his breath.

A cold shiver ran from Ari's heart to her stomach. She wanted to yell at Dane to stop, but she also knew him well enough by now that she understood he needed to cool off. Ari climbed the dark front steps and stopped, looking up the driveway. Dane had stopped and was looking back at her as well. A half-second passed and he turned back and disappeared around the bend, his crunching footsteps fading into the darkness.

*   *   *

The clock's red numbers switched from 12:54 a.m. to 12:55 am. Ari flopped over in her bed. She'd been trying to fall asleep since eleven-thirty. Her mind couldn't stop replaying what Dane had said before walking away. Ari finally gave up trying to sleep and got out of bed to find her bathrobe.

When she'd arrived home that night, Ari's parents hadn't noticed the purplish, crescent-shape hue that had spread across her cheekbone…but Ari had also carefully parted her hair so it covered that side of her face quite completely.

Moonlight was filtering in through the arched window in her bedroom. She climbed into the window seat and looked out across her backyard, over the top of the vein-like oak branches, and her gaze settled on Dane's house. No lights were on.

Ari looked at the nightstand where her phone was. She was tempted to text Dane, but she hesitated.

The window seat was cold and Ari pulled her bathrobe around her tightly. An ache in Ari's heart propelled her from her seat to her phone. She grabbed it and her slippers, then pulled a coat over her bathrobe. In an uncharacteristic venture, Ari quietly padded down the stairs and exited her house out the back door, then found her way through the pasture. She thought she'd need the flashlight on her phone, but the moon was high and bright enough that everything was bathed in its flat, blue-hued light.

Ari paused at the square columns that stood at the edge of the oak grove. She placed a hand on one of the brass bees, feeling the chill against her palm. The oak grove looked absolutely terrifying in the odd, depthless light of the moon, with clawing branches leaning low, but Ari took a breath and stepped into the wooded passage.

She hurried as quickly as she could to the brass circle. To her complete surprise, the hatch was slightly open and dim light escaped from inside.

Ari quietly lifted the lid and poked her head down before descending. Dane's familiar silhouette was leaning against the far wall, facing away from her. One arm was up on the wall; his head was buried in his elbow. His thin sleeveless shirt was hanging loosely from his broad, stooped shoulders; Ari noticed he was wearing plaid pajama pants. She smiled to herself, realizing she'd never seen him in his pj's.

Dane startled and whirled around when Ari reached the bottom of the steps.

"Hey," she said. In an instant, she realized that perhaps Dane was down there just to be alone; to have space. "I, um, can leave if you. I just couldn't sleep and I thought I'd come here for awhile. Actually…I wanted to text you but I didn't know what to say——"

Dane turned around and waved her off. "Ari, it's ok. Don't leave…I couldn't sleep either," he said quietly. "Does your face still hurt? And…what did your parents say when they saw your bruise?" His voice was almost a whisper.

"Actually, my face feels alright; the skin is just a little sore. And, my parents didn't even see the bruise. My hair covers most of it. Tomorrow I'll just put some makeup over it. Please stop worrying about what happened." Ari crossed the room and leaned against the wall next to Dane.

"I couldn't sleep because I was worried about you," Ari confessed.

"Worried about *me?*" Dane looked at her with questioning eyes.

She hesitated, examining the gold-flecked glass tiles that glinted in the candlelight. His eyes captured hers. She got caught in his gaze; only brief slivers of jade green were visible in his pupils. She took another mental photograph of him at this exact moment: the candlelit shadows on his face, his slightly-curled eyelashes, the depths of the color in his eyes. How the striations of muscle in his crossed arms twisted with every slight movement he made. How his hair was swept slightly to the side and roughed up from turning on his pillow.

"Yeah," she finally admitted. "When you left tonight you were so upset. I couldn't stop thinking about what you said, about you being like your dad…"

"Well, it's true."

Ari stared at him hard. "I don't want you to change. If you're like your dad, then so be it."

Dane looked at her, unbelieving.

"But you're terrified of him," he concluded.

"I like who *you* are, Dane. That means that I like the Pat McCleary-punching guy who has a bit of a temper, who gets mad about injustices and who stands up for what he believes in and who is haunted by his past but is working through it anyway," Ari said all in one breath. She was nose-to-nose with him now, staring him down. She backed up a little, realizing she'd invaded his personal space with her confrontation.

Dane didn't say anything. If anything, his expression was a bit shocked.

"Accept who you are," Ari said. "I have."

She didn't mean to sound so forthright, but she couldn't take it back now, nor did she want to. She pulled her coat tightly around her and backed up to the steps. Dane was still leaning against the wall, arms crossed, with a stunned expression.

Ari climbed up the steps. She paused at the top and looked over her shoulder.

"I wish you could see yourself the way I see you," Ari confessed. "Goodnight, Dane," she said quietly as she lifted herself out the hatch.

The night air was stunningly cold as she closed the lid and started on the path back to her house, crunching through the dry detritus layer under her feet. The stone columns were in sight when footfalls could be heard behind her.

Ari whirled around to see Dane jogging up to her. Without saying a word, he caught her in his arms and held her there, his warmth contrasting starkly with the frigid air. Ari turned in his grasp until her face was buried in his chest. He held her like he couldn't let go; for a moment Ari could hear his heart galloping in his chest.

His mouth was next to her ear. "I'll walk you home," he stated, his voice just above a whisper.

She nodded and reluctantly eased out of his arms, though he kept one arm around her shoulder until they reached her back deck.

"Let's do something tomorrow, just you and me." His eyes glinted in the stark moonlight.

Ari smiled. "It's a date."

*　　*　　*

"When you said you wanted to do something today, I thought it would be something more adventurous than homework," Ari joked, turning to look at Dane. She was laying on her stomach on the ornate Oriental rug in Dane's study. Textbooks were open around her; Dane laid on his stomach next to her, as close as he could be, his own textbook open next to hers.

"I had something planned, actually," Dane mused, not taking his eyes from his chemistry book. "But the weather decided to not cooperate."

Although it was ten in the morning, it could've been evening outside. Dark gray clouds had blanketed the sky and rivulets of water streamed down the windows of the study. The room looked downright bright compared to the clouds outside; amber-glassed floor lamps cast warm pools of light on the rug. Thunder rumbled somewhere in the distance, and an occasional gust of wind would whip a smattering of rain against the thin panes of glass.

"I like this just fine," Ari said quietly. "Besides, this chemistry homework isn't going to do itself."

She could feel Dane looking at her. Finally she returned his stare.

"What?"

"I'm just looking at your bruise. It's barely noticeable. Did your parent say anything about it this morning?"

"Nope." Ari smiled and looked back at her chemistry book. "I used a little bit of concealer to cover it up. They'll never even see it."

"You think I'm in the clear?"

"Yes. Now stop worrying about it. It was an *accident.*" Her tone indicated she wouldn't speak of it again; Dane went back to his book and she felt him scoot close enough that their shoulders touched. After five minutes of trying to read a single paragraph, Ari realized she had re-read the same sentence four times over. She couldn't concentrate with Dane so close.

Suddenly a white-blue flash filled the room, followed nearly instantly by a deafening, crackling crash. Thunder followed, growling directly above them and shaking the house. Ari yelped and Dane instinctively covered her head with his arm.

"*Whoa!* That was *really* close!" Dane leaped up and looked out the south-facing window. "Ari, look out there!"

Ari scrambled to the window and saw that a large oak tree on the edge of the grove had been hit by lightning and cleanly split in two: fresh exposed inner wood lay splintered and bark had been blown off the trunk. Wisps of steam rose up in a haze above the shattered tree.

"Oh my gosh…"

"C'mon, let's go downstairs and watch the storm from there."

Ari followed Dane down the narrow stairs, and upon entering the living room, she saw Molly had buried herself under a fort of couch cushions. Mrs. Hadley was trying to coax her out.

"That really scared her. This is quite the sudden storm," Dane's mom remarked.

"Did you see that it hit a tree on the edge of our yard? Look out back," Dane whispered so Molly wouldn't hear. Another flash of lightning flattened everything in the room in a wash of white light. Ari gasped as another core-shaking peal of thunder surrounded the air.

Ari's phone vibrated in her pocket; her mom was trying to reach her.

"Ari, are you ok? Are you still at Dane's?"

"I'm fine. The storm is right overhead, though. A tree got hit."

"Stay there, ok? Do not try and come home."

"Wasn't planning on it—" Another flash, followed by thunder, this time not as close. It was still loud and long and rolling, but not directly overhead. Ari relaxed a bit.

"Alright. Just stay safe," her mom pleaded.

Dane took Ari's arm and guided her over to the window. Sheets of rain were pouring from the sky so heavily that the oak trees that surrounded Dane's backyard could barely be seen. Water was pooling in the yard, rising to the top of the grass. A jagged vein of nearly-purple lightning snapped through the sky.

"I don't think I've ever seen it rain this hard here," Ari said, gazing out at the back deck. Water was gushing off the roof and bypassing the gutters completely; a small waterfall was pouring out over the deck.

"Me neither," Dane said. He put his arms around Ari, holding her in front of him, as he rested his chin on her head and watched the storm.

Ari felt her cheeks burn, acutely aware that this was the first time Dane had ever held her, or even touched her, in the presence of his family. He seemed perfectly at ease holding her there, so she relaxed into his arms and watched as the storm turned from a petulant downpour to a gentle, quiet rain.

chapter thirty-five

The warm smell of coffee permeated Ari's senses. Spanish books were open in front of Ari and Dane, but Ari was staring at the foggy grayness that had settled over the little town. The earlier rains that had pelted the area had held off long enough to be replaced by low-lying mist.

Dane had been quizzing her on the latest lesson at the coffee shop, but they were interrupted when Dane's phone rang. His eyebrows went up in surprise to see the number belonged to Severin Gray.

"Hold on, gotta take this," he said. He rose from the booth and walked to an empty corner of the coffee shop. Ari couldn't overhear the conversation, but it didn't last for more than a minute. When Dane returned to the booth, he started collecting his books.

"We gotta go," he said, his voice carrying a hint of excitement. "Mr. Gray is at the Abshire house. He wants us to come by as soon as possible."

"Oh! What's going on?" Ari stood and stuffed her books into her backpack.

"As usual, he didn't say, but for Mr. Gray, he sounded excited." Dane put on his jacket and beanie. Ari smiled, noticing how strong Dane looked, both physically and in the way he carried himself.

During the short drive to the Abshire place, Ari wondered why they'd been summoned by Mr. Gray himself. When they turned at the crooked mailbox, her face lit up upon seeing the house: its siding was refinished; not replaced, but repaired and with a fresh coat of paint. The house wasn't entirely level still, but it looked like it had been shored up and sections of foundation had been repaired. A new roof replaced the moss-covered shingles that had once covered the house; windows were no longer shattered and gaping but replaced with panes that were new but historically correct. The two chimneys had new bricks and the porch railing was repaired.

Mr. Gray was standing near the front porch, with Mr. Wells standing at his side holding a clipboard. Workers were streaming in and out of the front door like bees around a hive; Mr. Gray had to step aside as two hardhat-clad men carried a load of insulation inside. Mr. Gray waved Ari and Dane over after Dane had parked the truck.

Dane extended a hand and Ari shook Mr. Gray's hand as well. Mr. Gray was dressed in a new-looking camel trench coat and hat, and for the first time ever, Ari thought he looked happy—possibly.

"Thank you for coming over on such short notice. I hope, Miss Cartwright, you are pleased with what we have done so far."

Ari beamed. "It's beautiful, Mr. Gray. Just...perfect."

"Won't you come see the inside?" Mr. Gray motioned to the door.

The front door was the original one, right down to the doorknob, but it had been restored to its original condition.

"I had all the pieces and parts of the house taken out. Everything that could be salvaged, was. I sought restoration experts for the doors and windows, even for the floors and walls."

Ari's mouth dropped open as they entered the house. The living room looked like it was ready to be moved into: all the windows that had been covered with tangles of blackberry vines were cleared of brush and diffuse light came through. The floors were the same, though sanded clean and finished with a matte sealant. The walls were clean and freshly painted. Whatever damage Pat McCleary and his friends had inflicted during their party had been completely repaired.

Ari walked to the staircase. The giant wooden newel cap was unchanged, just cleaned. The stairs were polished but the original paint remained, as did the indentations where generations of feet had worn them down. Ari knelt down and touched the smooth impressions.

"I decided to keep some things as they were," Mr. Gray explained quietly. "My intention was not to erase the character of the house, but make it livable, as you requested," Mr. Gray looked at Ari. Ari beamed back. She then went up the stairs to the room overlooking Hadley Hill.

The molding around the door, where Ari had taken the height chart, had not been repaired.

"Mr. Gray," she said, "I have this piece. After the house was vandalized this summer, I removed the molding here." She ran her hand along the frameless jamb. "It was a height chart for your grandfather and his brother and sister. It has their heights and initials carved into it. If you'd like, I can return it."

Mr. Gray looked pleased. "I would like that. We can put it back where it rightfully belongs."

Ari nodded. "I'll get it to you, then."

Mr. Gray then nodded to Mr. Wells, who had been following him with the clipboard. Mr. Wells made a note.

"What about the piano that was downstairs?" Dane asked.

"Ah, the piano. I had that moved into my study," Mr. Gray said. "It's not in the best shape, but I intend to try and have it restored."

Suddenly some muffled hollering came from somewhere in the house. Everyone went down the stairs and to the door that led to the basement.

Yellow construction lamps had been set up all across the floor of the cellar, which was now missing its floor planks. The removed planks were all stacked against a wall; Ari could see places where the foundation was being patched. A worker motioned to Mr. Gray.

"You might want to see this, sir." Ari thought it was amusing that the husky, bearded construction worker addressed Mr. Gray with such politeness. Her attention was then drawn to what the worker was holding.

A thick stack of yellowed envelopes were bundled together with twine. "We found these between the floor joists," the worker said, handing them to Mr. Gray. "They're yours now." The worker turned and resumed pulling up planks.

Ari and Dane moved to look over Mr. Gray's shoulder. The top envelope was addressed to Katia Hadley, 3311 Hadley Lane. The return address simply said E. Abshire, 412 Laurel Street, Woodward.

"Letters to Katia," Dane whispered. Ari gasped. Mr. Gray's hands shook slightly as he untied the twine, which crumbled to dust in his fingers. Just like in the journal, the paper felt heavy and soft and kept its shape as Mr. Gray unfolded the first letter.

He read silently; it was written in the same elegant cursive as in the journal. After a moment, he pulled a white hankerchief from his breast pocket and dabbed at his eyes.

"If you two will excuse me, I must be going now," he said quietly, and Ari and Dane looked at one another. As he was ascending the stairs, he suddenly turned to Ari.

"Miss Cartwright, you were correct. Thank you for insisting that this house be preserved." With that, he disappeared onto the first floor.

Ari looked around at the house being built up around her. She suddenly realized that she was a small element of something much larger happening right in front of her.

*   *   *

Friday afternoon was another foggy one. It had been two weeks since Ari and Dane had been at the newly restored Abshire place, and Dane had sent a rare text message to Ari: *meet at the circle after work*. While she had long since ended her yard care appointments, Dane was still working till close at the museum, so Ari took her dinner down to the underground room as she waited for Dane to arrive. She carefully lit all the candles and put each one in the recesses around the wall. Despite the chill fog outside, the little room glowed with warm light.

Minutes later, the hatch opened and frigid air swirled downward. Dane hopped down into the room. Ari was happy to see an excited spark in his eyes.

"Guess what," Dane said, and without even waiting for her reply, "Mr. Gray called me this afternoon and we met at the Abshire house again. In that stack of letters was two years' worth of correspondence from Ezra to Katia, and vice versa. Mr. Gray was able to answer some of our questions, Ari."

"Did Ezra's dad survive?" Ari stated.

A smile crept over Dane's face. "Against all odds, he did. Three months after Ezra moved to Woodward, Katia wrote to Ezra and told him that his dad was well enough that Aliza was able to move back home. A few months after that, his dad was strong enough to start working on the farm again. Get this," Dane sounded especially excited, "remember how in the beginning of the journal Ezra talked about the ryegrass crop they had planted?"

Ari nodded.

Dane handed her a photocopy of an internet article. "The agricultural school at the university in Cascade Grove wrote an article about the founding ryegrass farmers in our valley. Look at the photo."

Ari squinted and read the caption to a photo of a man dressed in overalls, leaning on his pitchfork. "Joseph Abshire was among the first of the valley farmers to adopt ryegrass as an annual crop. Today, about two-thirds of the nation's crops are grown in the valley."

"Wow…not only did his dad survive, but their gamble on ryegrass paid off. Amazing," Ari smiled.

"One more thing." Dane handed her a photocopied letter.

Ari squinted in the dim light. Elegant handwriting belonging to Katia filled the page. Near her signature was the carved symbol they had seen: two hearts with their points encircled.

"All my love, your Katia," Ari read, tracing the hearts with her finger. "Katia was the one who made the carvings?" Ari asked in astonishment.

"It would seem so," Dane answered.

Ari beamed. "Your great-great aunt was such a rebel," she chuckled.

Dane continued, "Mr. Gray wanted me to thank you again for insisting that he save the house. He told me that it will go up for sale within the week."

"Did Mr. Gray say anything else?"

Dane paused. It wouldn't have been noticed by anyone else, but his demeanor shifted.

"What?" Ari leaned in closer to where Dane was sitting. For a moment, Dane looked at her silently.

"Mr. Gray said he would be going to Apperson University next week, from Thursday to Sunday. He has business to do there; he's on the board of directors for the college. He invited me and Mom to go with him—he's even paying for our airfare."

Ari's heart started to race. Ari ignored its fluttering and smiled for Dane.

"That's awesome, Dane. I am so, *so* happy for you that Mr. Gray is willing to help you out."

The look on Dane's face was unsure at best.

"It's in Idaho, Ari. I'm not sure I want to be that far away from everyone."

Ari couldn't believe what she said next. "Maybe it won't be the right fit, or maybe you'll fall in love with it. You'll never know until you go, Dane."

She wanted to take back everything she had just said and tell him that she wasn't sure she could fathom any more days without him being around, but Ari knew that wouldn't be helpful or fair to him at all.

"You're right." Dane looked up at the ceiling, sighed, then looked right at Ari. The dim light didn't allow her to see any of the depth in his hazel eyes. He pulled her head to his and closed his eyes, their foreheads touching. At that moment she could feel tension rolling off him like ocean waves. She put her hands on either side of his face, feeling day-old stubble against her skin and the warmth of his cheeks. Ari's heart was pounding with both fear and anticipation; everything was so tenuous at the moment that she felt her hands start to shake.

Without moving away, Dane spoke in a whisper.

"Ari."

She opened her eyes and backed away, keeping her hands on his neck. Before he could say anything more, Ari leaned forward and kissed him. She could tell that her touch had stunned him; he was frozen in place as she backed away. He wouldn't take his eyes from hers.

Suddenly Dane's phone rang, startling them both. He looked down at the screen to see his mom was calling. "I gotta go. Dinnertime," he sighed. He held out a hand to help Ari out of the circle, but she shook her head.

"I'm going to stay here for awhile."

Dane stopped halfway up the steps. "Thank you for encouraging me, Ari." He ran his hand through his short hair. He cleared his throat and shook his head. "I just wish I had a better idea of what I need to do."

*　　　*　　　*

Riley had declared Saturday to be a girls' night: Amara, Ari, and Riley all met at Cinema Coffee to watch *My Fair Lady*. Rain had poured down on the town all day long, and the lights from the theater reflected on the wet pavement as the girls got in line at the ticket booth. Ari was thankful once they all were inside the warm theater; the scent of buttery popcorn mingled with coffee as they purchased their tickets.

Amara grabbed a giant tub of popcorn while Ari balanced three coffees. Riley saved their seats in the auditorium. Once they all were settled, Ari was glad to finally have something to take her mind off the fact that Dane would once again be leaving for almost a week.

After the movie, Mrs. Cartwright picked up the three girls and brought them back to Ari's house. Once they had packed all the pillows, sleeping bags, and backpacks up to Ari's room, each girl staked out her spot to sleep. Instead of choosing her bed, however, Ari claimed the window seat as her spot.

"You don't want your bed?" Riley asked, incredulous. Ari shook her head and Riley shrugged as she rolled out her sleeping bag on Ari's bed.

"Some nights I just fall asleep here," Ari said. "A lot of nights, lately," she confessed.

Amara brushed soft curls away from her face as she got ready to sleep. "Ari, is everything ok? Riley and I have noticed this last week that you seem a little more down than usual," she said in her gentle way.

Ari just shrugged. "Dane is leaving on Thursday to visit another college. This one is in Idaho."

Riley's eyes got big. "He's going out of state? For a history degree?"

"Remember Mr. Gray? The owner of the Abshire house?" Ari had told the girls all about Mr. Gray's eccentric personality and his fabulous estate, and even that he was a distant relative of Dane's. But she hadn't filled them in on Mr. Gray's college offer.

"He's on the board of directors at the college he graduated from. He asked Dane what his future plans were, and after Dane told him, Mr. Gray offered to pay all of Dane's tuition if he went to Apperson University."

Riley's jaw dropped and Amara's eyes got big.

Ari looked at Riley squarely. "Are you concerned about what's going to happen with you and Jace once he graduates this year?"

Riley shook her head. "I take things a day at a time, hon."

Ari sighed, her shoulders drooping. She looked out the window from her seat and saw the roofline of Dane's house. "Why can't I just do that with Dane? Take things a day at a time? When I think about him, all I can do is think about the future."

Amara smiled. "Why don't you tell him that, Ari? Are you afraid he doesn't feel the same way?"

"I don't know, Amara. Right now he's trying so hard to sort out what he wants to do. This new offer from Mr. Gray has complicated things, I think. Dane is trying really hard to plan out his next four years, and I'm not going to get in the way of that, Amara. I can't ask him to turn down an amazing, once-in-a-lifetime offer just because I hate being away from him."

Riley and Amara shook their heads in understanding. Ari hugged her pillow and looked out the window at the dark night: past the unlit garden below, past the crooked vein-like oaks that separated her house from his. She put her hand on the cold windowpane and realized that one year from now, Dane would no longer just be a house away.

chapter thirty-six

On Thursday morning, Ari rode her bike to school for the
first time since Dane had gotten his truck. Even on days that Dane had to
work after school, he still would wait in her driveway and, once she came
out, he'd help lift her bike into the bed of his truck. She missed starting
her day with Dane; the sound of his voice in the morning was one of her
favorite things about the school year thus far.

This morning, there was no conversation on the way to school.
Nothing but the sound of Ari's bike tires crunching down the hill.

Fat raindrops were falling from the bare branches of the trees above.
Ari pulled her hood tighter. The entire ride to school was unpleasant;
water fanned up from the road soaked her jeans from the knees down,
and rain pelted her shoulders. By the time she arrived at school, Ari was
drenched.

Ari was thankful her friends were in a few classes; however, when it
came to Spanish class, the empty desk next to her reminded her of
Dane's absence. After school, the ride home was equally as miserable.
The temperature had dropped significantly, and Ari could see her breath
form a cloud in front of her as she pushed her bike up the hill.

Friday was much of the same, only ice had formed overnight and
the ride to school had proved difficult at times. Ari had dressed in layers;
over a long sleeve shirt she'd worn her heaviest wool peacoat, a scarf, and
a hat. She was thankful she'd remembered gloves; even so, her hands
were nearly frozen by the time she arrived at school. By the time the
school day was done, the temperature had risen to a point where the ice
had melted and a thick fog had settled over the entire town of Rivers.

After school, Ari arrived to an empty house. It would be hours
before anyone would arrive home. She decided a walk might serve as a
distraction so she'd stop thinking of the next two days without Dane. A
light rain was falling, but Ari dismissed it and continued on.

Ari headed down her driveway and found herself turning west
toward the Abshire homestead. She immediately noticed that the

crooked mailbox had been straightened and the old rusty box had been replaced with an oversized, shiny white mailbox. A tall For Sale sign hung proudly next to it.

She walked down the driveway, which had a thick layer of new gravel. It was almost difficult to walk through; not enough cars had driven down the road to pack it down.

The yard had been landscaped nicely: the massive rhododendrons that had overtaken the property had been trimmed back and shaped. The blackberry bushes were completely gone and all sides of the house could be clearly seen. The windows gleamed and Ari admired the alcove bump-out that was now the most prominent feature upon first glance.

Ari then rounded the front of the house: a new porch light was illuminating the porch, and a red berry wreath had been hung on the front door. It contrasted beautifully with the bright white of the house's new paint.

She cupped her hands around the front window to look inside. A few pieces of furniture had been moved into the house; Ari figured it was staged for photographs. Even though the furnishings were sparse, it looked more beautiful than she could have ever imagined the once-broken down house could ever be.

Its character had remained intact and now it stood proud and ready for another family.

Ari slowly headed back toward her house by way of the highway; there were still no cars in the driveway when she arrived. She then went around the side of the house, through the formal gardens, and headed into the oak grove.

The trees were skeletal, dressed only in bright green moss that seemed to glow. The light rain had ceased and the clouds were breaking to the west, causing the entire sky to lighten. Drops of water still fell from moss-covered tree branches, making audible plops all round Ari. She'd reached the brass circle and looked around.

The air was thick with woodsmoke and it swirled around Ari as she stood in awe of the early evening. A breeze pulled at her hair as she stepped atop the brass circle. A gust of wind then sent forth a flutter of rust-colored oak leaves which swirled around and through the shedding oaks.

Ari closed her eyes and tried to numb the ache that had settled in her heart since Dane had left, and her hand went to the honeybee necklace that she always wore. *This is ridiculous*, she thought. *He's just gone for two more days. Take it one day at a time, Ari.* Then she remembered that next year, this is what it would be like: Dane would be gone, possibly moved to another state...Ari hung her head and slowly turned and faced the direction of her own house.

Ari was about to head home when a crunching sound directly behind her caused her to stop. She didn't turn around; she wanted to believe it could be Dane, just like on the first day they'd met at the circle. She shook her head and started to step off the brass lid.

Another sound, closer. Ari couldn't help but turn around.

Dane appeared from behind, standing feet from her.

Ari's mouth dropped open slightly, but there were no words. She felt her heart stutter.

"You're back!" She grinned broadly, more than a little surprised to see him. But the look on his face seemed hesitant, maybe apprehensive. Missing was his confidence and bravado.

"I decided to come back early," Dane said, stepping to the edge of the brass circle. "Two days was enough time to figure out everything I needed to know."

Ari tilted her head with a questioning glance. "What did you decide?"

"I told Mr. Gray that as much as I appreciated his offer, I've decided that I wanted to stay and work at the museum for a year after I graduate."

371

Ari's eyes widened in excitement. "How did Mr. Gray respond?"

"He said he understood, and that his offer still stands if I choose to go to Apperson any time in the future."

"That's awesome, Dane." Ari relaxed as a sigh of relief escaped from her lungs.

"What I didn't tell him," Dane's voice lowered, "was that I had to get home as soon as possible."

Ari furrowed her brow.

"Why?"

Dane paused, looking straight at her.

"Because I love you, Ari."

A shock of disbelief rippled through Ari and she caught her breath. She wanted to respond, but the look in his eyes caught her off-guard. Ari was stunned, immobile, although heat ran through her heart and she could feel her hands start to shake at her sides.

His expression was no longer hesitant. She didn't have a moment to respond; Dane took her face in his hand and quickly brought his lips to hers, kissing her with an intensity and immediacy that surprised her. There was no hesitation he ran his hand through her hair to the back of her neck. The warmth of his kiss and his closeness nearly overwhelmed her. Then he backed away only enough to speak.

His voice was low, as if he didn't want the low-bending branches of the oaks to hear what he needed to say. "This whole year I've been terrified of telling you how I feel because I've never felt something so strongly in my entire life. I didn't know what to do with the feelings I have for you, Ari."

He took a deep breath and backed up a little more, staring at her; right through her. "When I was gone, I couldn't think about anything but you. Everything we've done together since you moved here has changed me. Moving away to study history—or anything, for that matter—wouldn't be the same without you. You are everything to me." Dane kept one hand on her cheek and the other around her waist. His voice was nervous; his breath jagged.

Ari exhaled a single breath and smiled, unbelieving. The air around them swirled and Ari was caught speechless. She realized, in her silence, that Dane was starting to look apprehensive. Ari reached for Dane, bringing his face to hers, and with her hands around his neck, kissed him slowly.

She then backed away, caught her breath, and put her hand to his chest.

"I love you more than anything, Dane Hadley."

Dane reached around Ari's waist and nearly picked her up off the brass circle. The breeze swirled around them, lifting leaves into the air. A light rain started falling. Dane held onto Ari like he'd never let her go, standing there in the middle of the oak grove.

A NOTE ON ELEANOR ABSHIRE

The namesake for the Abshire family stemmed from research I've been doing on and off for the past seven years. Albany is home to Oregon's only national laboratory, which was a part of the Bureau of Mines before that. Our site (then called the Northwest Electro-Development Laboratory) was the home of several key discoveries regarding rare earth metals, especially during the late 1940's and early 1950's.

During that time, and employee named Eleanor Abshire served as both the head security officer (a rare position for a woman at the time), and established the Bureau's technical library. Eleanor was also a published author, having written two technical compilations, *The Bibliography of Zirconium*, and *The Bibliography of Hafnium*. After her retirement from the Bureau, there were plans to name the future technical library in her honor. Unfortunately, that never came to pass. With the advent of the digital age, Eleanor's library was dismantled.

I chose the Abshire name in her honor; a small gesture in remembrance of the hard work of a single lady who was at the forefront of the birth of the rare metals industry.

Made in the USA
Middletown, DE
18 April 2022

64130236R00215